CHARLIE BONE
AND THE TIME
TWISTER

CHARLIE BONE
AND THE TIME
TWISTER

CHILDREN OF THE RED KING

BOOK 2

JENNY NIMMO

ORCHARD BOOKS
AN IMPRINT OF SCHOLASTIC INC.
NEW YORK

For Ianto,

who likes to travel,

with love.

—J. N.

Text copyright © 2003 by Jenny Nimmo
First published in 2003 in Great Britain by Egmont Books Ltd.

Library of Congress Cataloging-in-Publication Data available.
0-439-49687-X

10   07

Printed in the U.S.A.   23
First Scholastic edition, September 2003

Cover illustration © 2003 by Chris Sheban
The text type was set in 11-pt. Diotima Roman.
The display type was set in Latino-Rumba.
Book design by Marijka Kostiw

CONTENTS

THE ENDOWED   ix

A GAME OF MARBLES   1

GRANDMA SLAMS A DOOR   19

A TREE FALLS   34

HIDING HENRY   52

OLIVIA MAKES A MESS   72

INTO THE FREEZER   92

THE BLACK GLOVE   116

"YOU CAN'T GO BACK!"   137

THE THUNDER HOUSE   159

SKARPO THE SORCERER   184

THE PETS' CAFÉ   202

"TAKE HIM TO THE DUNGEONS!"   223

EZEKIEL'S VISITORS   245

RUN OVER!   269

THE TOLLROC   288

THE WAND   303

TANCRED AND THE TREE   317

AMBUSHED!   338

THE TIME TWISTER   363

A JOURNEY TO THE SEA   382

PATON HAS A PARTY   395

THE ENDOWED

These characters are all descended from the ten children of the Red King, a magician-king who left Africa in the twelfth century, accompanied by three leopards.

The Red King had already lived for several centuries and he made a marvelous glass sphere, putting into it all the memories of his travels through the world. He used the sphere to twist through time, visiting the past and the future.

In any other hands, the Time Twister is dangerous and unpredictable.

THE CHILDREN OF THE RED KING, CALLED THE ENDOWED

MANFRED BLOOR Head boy of Bloor's Academy. A hypnotizer.

CHARLIE BONE Descended from the Yewbeams, a family with many magical endowments, Charlie can hear the voices of people in photographs and paintings.

ZELDA DOBINSKI Descended from a long line of Polish magicians, Zelda is telekinetic. She can move objects with her mind.

ASA PIKE Descended from a tribe who lived in the Northern forests and had an affinity with strange beasts, Asa can become a beast at dusk.

BILLY RAVEN Descended from a man who conversed with ravens that sat on a gibbet where dead men hung. For this talent he was banished from his village. Billy can talk to, and understand, animals.

LYSANDER SAGE	Descended from a line of African wise men, he can call up his spirit ancestors.
GABRIEL SILK	Descended from a family of psychics, Gabriel can feel scenes and emotions through the clothes of others.
BETH STRONG	Descended from a family of circus performers — strong men and acrobats. She is also telekinetic.
EMMA TOLLY	Descended from the Spanish swordsman who accompanied the Red King on his journeys, Emma can become a bird.
TANCRED TORSSON	Descended from a Scandinavian storm-bringer named after the thunder god, Thor, Tancred can bring wind, rain, thunder, and lightning.
BINDI AND DORCAS	Endowed. But their gifts are, as yet, undeveloped.

A GAME OF MARBLES

It was January 1916 — the coldest winter in living memory.

The dark rooms in Bloor's Academy were almost as cold as the streets outside. Henry Yewbeam, hurrying down one of the icy passages, began to hum to himself. The humming cheered him up. It warmed his spirits as well as his feet.

On either side of the passage the eerie blue flames of gaslights flickered and hissed in their iron brackets. The smell was horrible. Henry wouldn't have been surprised to find something dead in one of the dark corners.

At home, in a sunny house by the sea, his sister, Daphne, was very ill with diphtheria. To avoid infection Henry and his brother, James, had been sent to stay with their mother's brother, Sir Gideon Bloor.

Sir Gideon wasn't the sort of person you would choose to spend your holidays with. There was nothing remotely fatherly about him. He was the head-master of an ancient school and he never let anyone forget it.

Bloor's Academy had been in Sir Gideon's family for hundreds of years. It was a school for children gifted in music, drama, and art. Bloor's also took children who were endowed in other, very strange, ways. Just thinking about them made Henry shudder.

He had reached his cousin Zeke's room. Zeke was Sir Gideon's only child and a more unpleasant cousin Henry couldn't imagine. Zeke was one of the endowed children, but Henry guessed that Zeke's gift was probably nasty.

Henry opened the door and peeped inside. A row of glass jars stood on the windowsill. Inside the jars strange things writhed gently in a clear liquid. Henry was sure it couldn't be water. The things were pale and shapeless. One was blue.

"What do you think you are doing?"

Aunt Gudrun came marching down the passage, her long black skirt drowning her footfalls with a sinister hiss. She was a very tall woman with a great amount of yellow hair piled into a bun on the back of her head. A real Viking of a person (she was, in fact, Norwegian), with an enormous chest and lungs to match.

Henry said, "Erm . . ."

"'Erm' is not good enough, Henry Yewbeam. You were spying in my Zeke's room, were you not?"

"No, not at all," said Henry.

"You shouldn't be lurking in passages, boy. Come down to the living room." Lady Bloor beckoned with her little finger, and Henry had no choice but to follow her.

His aunt led him back past the mysterious locked doors that, only a few moments ago, Henry had been vainly trying to open. He was an inquisitive boy and easily bored. A huge sigh escaped him as he trundled down a creaking staircase to the first floor.

The Bloor family lived in the west wing of the academy, but they only occupied the rooms above the ground floor, which was almost entirely taken up by a drafty grand hall, a chapel, and several assembly halls and classrooms. Henry had already explored some of these rooms and found them very disappointing. All they contained were rows of battered desks and chairs, and shelves of dusty-looking books.

"Here we are!" Lady Bloor opened a door and thrust Henry into the room beyond.

A small boy, who had been kneeling in the window seat, leaped down and rushed across to Henry. "Where've you been?" he cried.

"Just exploring," said Henry.

"I thought you'd gone home."

"Home is miles and miles away, Jamie." Henry plunked himself in a deep leather chair beside the fire. The logs in the big iron grate smoldered with strange images. When Henry half-closed his eyes he could almost see the cozy living room at home. He sighed again.

Aunt Gudrun frowned at Henry and said, "Behave yourselves, boys." She went out, closing the door behind her.

When she had gone, James came and sat on the arm of Henry's chair. "Zeke's been doing funny things," he whispered.

Henry hadn't noticed Zeke, but now he became aware of his strange cousin, enclosed in a gloomy silence at the other end of the room. He was sitting at a table, absorbed in something laid out before him. His pale, bony face was frozen in an attitude of intense concentration. Not a muscle twitched, not a breath escaped him.

"I was scared," James said quietly.

"Why? What did he do?" Henry asked in a hushed voice.

"Well, he was doing a puzzle. There were pieces all over the table. Then Zeke stared at them and they all crawled together. Well, most of them. They made a picture. He showed it to me. It was a ship, but some of the pieces wouldn't fit."

"It's rude to whisper," said Zeke, without taking his eyes off the puzzle.

Henry pulled himself out of the chair and strolled

over to his cousin. He glanced at the twelve pieces lying beside the puzzle and then at the picture of the ship. It took less than a minute for him to see exactly where each piece fit.

"Hm," said Henry, and without another word he picked up the single pieces, one by one, and deftly placed them into the picture; two in the sky, three in the ship's hull, two in the rigging, and four in the sea.

For a moment Zeke watched Henry's hands in fascination. It was only when Henry was putting the last piece in place, that Zeke suddenly leaped up, crying, "Who asked you? I could have done it. I could!"

"Sorry," said Henry, stepping back. "I thought you wanted some help."

"Henry's good at puzzles," said James.

"Well I'm good at other things," snarled Zeke.

James was too small to see the danger signs. The angry glitter in Zeke's black eyes went straight over his head. "Magic doesn't always work," the little boy said blithely. "Henry's cleverer than you are, Zeke."

With that remark poor James Yewbeam sealed his brother's fate and, of course, his own.

"Get out!" cried Zeke. "Both of you. Hateful Yewbeams. Go, now. I can't stand the sight of you!"

Henry and James ran for the door. There was a violent gleam in their cousin's pale face, and they didn't want to wait around for him to do something nasty.

"Where are we going?" panted James as he tore down the passages after his brother.

"We'll go to the big hall, Jamie. We can play marbles there." Henry pulled a small leather bag out of his pocket and waved it at his brother.

It wasn't to be. Before they could go any further, there was a shout from Aunt Gudrun.

"James, bedtime." James pretended not to hear her. "Now, this minute."

"Better go," said Henry gently. "She'll punish you if you don't."

"But I want to play marbles," said James.

Henry shook his head. "Sorry, Jamie. Not now. Tomorrow. But I'll come and read to you later."

"Promise? Will you finish the story of the Wally-pug?"

"James, come here," shouted Aunt Gudrun.

"I promise," said Henry, and he meant to keep his promise. But Zeke had other plans for him.

Hanging his head, James trailed back toward the tall figure at the end of the passage.

"And you, Henry!" called Aunt Gudrun. "You keep out of trouble."

"Yes, Aunt," said Henry.

He was about to descend the rather grand staircase down to the hall when he had an idea. It was already so chilly he could see his own breath, billowing away from him in little gray clouds. The great hall would be even colder. He might freeze to death.

Henry retraced his steps until he found the door to a room he had already investigated. It was a huge storeroom, full of clothes left behind by past students of the academy. There were rows of colored capes: blue, green, and purple; shelves of hats and suits, and boxes of ancient leather boots.

Henry selected a warm blue cape and put it on. It reached well over his knees, a perfect length for a drafty hall. He would be able to kneel on it without feeling the cold stone floor.

Henry descended into the hall. His collection of marbles was the envy of all his friends. Henry's father traveled extensively and never came home without at least one precious new marble for his son's collection. Henry's leather bag held onyx stones, polished agate, glass, limestone, quartz, and even spheres of painted china.

There were no lights in the hall but an early moon sparkled through the long, frosted windows, giving the gray stones a soft pearly glow.

Henry decided to play Ring Taw, his favorite game. Deprived of an opponent, he would try to improve his skill by playing alone. With a piece of chalk, kept handy in his pocket, Henry drew a large ring in the center of the hall. He then chalked a smaller ring inside the first. Selecting thirteen marbles from his bag, he placed them in a cross inside the smaller circle.

Now Henry had to kneel on the icy floor, just outside the large ring. Already his hands were blue with cold and he could hardly stop his teeth from rattling. Tucking the blue cape under his knees he took out his favorite marble; it was a clear blue with a silvery glint inside it, like starlight. This was always his taw, or shooter.

Placing the knuckles of his right hand, palm outward, on the floor, Henry put the blue taw on the tip of his first finger and flicked it with his thumb toward the marble cross. With a sharp clink it hit an orange marble right out of the two circles.

"Bravo!" Henry shouted.

There was a light creak from behind him. Henry squinted into the deep shadows on the oak-paneled walls. Was he imagining it, or did a long tapestry shiver slightly? On the other side of the tapestry a small door led into the west wing. Henry preferred the main staircase, for the passage behind the door was dark and creepy.

A cold draft swept past his knees and the tapestry

billowed again. A flurry of hailstones clattered against the windows, and the wind gave a sudden moan as it rushed around the snowy courtyard.

"Wind." Henry shivered and drew his cape closer. For good measure he even pulled the hood over his head.

In the passage behind the tapestry, Ezekiel Bloor stood with a lantern in one hand, and in the other — a glowing glass sphere. Dazzling colors swirled out of the glass; a rainbow laced with gold and silver. Sunshine and moonlight, one after the other. Zeke knew he mustn't look at them. He held one of the oldest marbles in the world.

On her deathbed, Zeke's Great-aunt Beatrice, a witch if ever there was one, had pressed the marble into his hand. "The Time Twister," she said in her cracked, dying voice. "For journeys through time. Do not look on it, Ezekiel, unless you want to travel."

Ezekiel didn't want to travel. He thrived in the great gloomy building that was his home and could seldom be persuaded to leave it. However, he longed to know what would happen if someone did look into the Time Twister. No one, in Zeke's opinion, was more deserving of a shove through time than his wretched cousin Henry Yewbeam.

Henry had by now knocked another three marbles out of the small chalked ring. He hadn't missed once, in spite of his freezing fingers. He was just stepping back to his place outside the circle when a glass ball came rolling toward him. It was slightly larger than Henry's blue taw, and tiny points of colored light danced and shimmered all around it.

"Oh my," breathed Henry. He stood where he was while the strange marble rolled on until it reached his foot.

Henry picked it up. He gazed into the bright depths within the glass. He saw domes of gold, cities in sunlight, cloudless skies, and much, much more. But even as he watched the scenes taking place before his eyes, Henry became aware that a change was taking place within his body, and he knew that he shouldn't have looked upon those unbelievable and breathtaking scenes.

The oak-paneled walls were breaking up. The frosted moonlight was fading. Henry's head whirled and his feet began to float. Far, far away a cat began to meow. And then another cat, and another.

Henry thought of his small brother. Would there be time to reach him before he faded away completely? And if he did, and James saw a brother disappearing before his eyes, might he not be so frightened he would have nightmares forever? Henry decided to leave a message.

While he still had the strength, he took the chalk from his pocket and with his left hand (the right was still clamped around the Time Twister) he wrote on the stone floor, "SORRY, JAMES. THE MARBLES . . ."

It was all Henry had time for. The next moment he had left the year of his eleventh birthday and was traveling forward, very fast, to a year when most of the people he knew would be dead.

• • •

In a small, chilly room at the top of the west wing, James waited for his brother. He was so cold he had put his coat on over his flannel nightshirt. On the table beside him the flame from his candle quivered in a draft from the door. Where was Henry? Why was he taking so long?

James rubbed his eyes. He was very tired but too cold to sleep. He drew the bedcovers up to his chin and listened to the patter of freezing sleet against the windowpane. And then his candle went out.

James sat rigid in his bed, too frightened to call out. Aunt Gudrun would be cross and Cousin Zeke would tease him for being a baby. Only Henry would understand.

"Henry! Henry, where are you?" James closed his eyes and sobbed into his pillow.

Before he had completely run out of tears, James stopped shivering. The room was getting warmer. He opened his eyes and found that he could see his pillow, his hand, the window. A soft glow had spread across the ceiling. When James looked to see where it was coming from, he was amazed to find that three cats were silently pacing around his bed. One was orange, another yellow, and the third a bright coppery color.

As soon as the cats knew they had been observed, they jumped up and rubbed their heads against the boy's cold hands, his neck, and his cheek. Their gleaming fur was as warm as sunlight, and as James stroked them, his fear began to leave him. He decided to go and look for Henry. Hardly had this thought entered his head than the cats leaped off the bed and ran to the door. They waited, meowing anxiously, as James pulled on his socks and his small leather boots.

With light sparkling on their silver whiskers and bright fur tips, the cats led the way down the dark passages and narrow steps, while James hurried after them. At last he came to the wide staircase leading down into the hall. Here the cats' worried meowing became loud and urgent, and James hesitated before he descended into the vast moonlit room.

Henry was not there. His marbles lay scattered on the stone floor, winking in the bright frosted light from the windows. As James moved slowly down the stairs, the cats ran before him, wailing and growling.

James reached the bottom step and walked to the chalked circle. He could see that Henry had been playing Ring Taw, his favorite game.

"Henry!" James called. "Henry, where have you gone?"

Never had a place appeared so vast and empty to small James Yewbeam. Never had his brother's absence seemed so utterly complete. He wouldn't try to call again. It was quite clear that Henry was gone. And he hadn't even said good-bye.

Before the tears could fall again, the three cats pounced into the white circle, drawing the boy's attention to four words chalked on the floor. A message? If only James could read. Henry had been patiently trying to teach him for weeks, but, so far, James hadn't managed a single word.

Perhaps he hadn't really tried. Now, when it was a serious matter . . .

"S . . . s . . . s . . . ," murmured James as the cats paced along the row of letters.

Next came an "o" and then two "r"s, and further on his own name. And all at once James found he could understand the words his brother had left for him.

"SORRY, JAMES," he read, "THE MARBLES . . ." There the message ended.

Obviously Henry wanted his brother to keep the marbles safe for him. James picked up the leather bag but before he could reach the blue taw, the orange cat tapped it playfully and it sped across the hall. The yellow cat raced after it while the copper cat swept another three marbles out of the ring.

Now the great hall was alive with the sound of clinking glass and joyful purring. James was surrounded by dancing, glistening spheres of color. The cats were playing a game and, as he watched them, a big smile broke over the boy's face.

"Stay with me," James begged the cats.

The cats would stay. For as long as he was in that cold, dreary building, they would keep James Yewbeam as warm and safe as any small boy had a right to expect.

GRANDMA SLAMS A DOOR

Winter held the city in an iron fist. Roofs, trees, chimneys, and even things that moved were covered in a thick crust of frozen snow.

Charlie Bone had been looking forward to an extra day of Christmas vacation. The new term surely couldn't start in this weather. But Grandma Bone had dashed his hopes.

"No shirking for you," she said in her usual sneering way. "Bloor's Academy opens come rain, wind, or snow. The snowplows have cleared the main road, and the school bus will stop at the top of Filbert Street on Monday morning at eight o'clock sharp." Her lips made a nasty backfiring noise as she said the last word.

Charlie was a weekly boarder at Bloor's Academy and on Sunday nights he had to pack a bag for five days away from home. On this particular Sunday

Charlie was paying more attention to the snowflakes brushing his window than to his packing.

"Pajamas, toothbrush, pants," Charlie muttered to himself, "socks, clean shirts. . . ." He scratched his head. He was supposed to wear a blue cape to school but he hated putting it on before he got to the academy. The other children on Filbert Street snickered at him. Bloor's was a rather unusual school. Only children who were talented in music, art, or drama could get in. Charlie had none of these talents. He was one of the twelve endowed children who were there because of unique other gifts. In his case it was a gift he often thought he would rather be without. He could hear photographs, or rather the people in them. As soon as Grandma Bone and her three nasty sisters found out, they had packed him off to Bloor's. Theirs was a family of clairvoyants, hypnotizers, werewolves, witches, and worse. They were descended from a mysterious Red King, a magician of amazing powers and, like all endowed children, Charlie must be watched, his talent nurtured.

The doorbell rang and Charlie ran downstairs, eager to escape the dreary packing. As soon as he opened the door his friend Benjamin's dog, Runner Bean, pushed past Charlie and began to shake wet snow off his back. His feathery tail sent sprays of water flying across the hall, straight into the path of Charlie's other grandma, Maisie Jones.

"You'd better dry that dog in here," said Maisie cheerfully as she stepped back into the kitchen. "I'll fetch his towel." She kept a special towel for Runner Bean, who was a frequent visitor.

The big yellow dog bounded after her while Charlie took Benjamin's coat and hung it on the hall stand.

"Are you on for building a snowman tomorrow?" Benjamin asked Charlie. "Our school definitely won't open."

"Mine will," said Charlie gloomily. "Sorry, Ben."

"Aw!" Benjamin's face fell. He was a small straw-haired boy with a permanently anxious expression. "Couldn't you pretend to be sick or something?"

"No chance," said Charlie. "You know what Grandma and the aunts are like."

Benjamin knew only too well. Charlie's aunt Eustacia had once been Benjamin's sitter. It was the worst two days of his life: disgusting food, early bedtimes, and no dogs in bedrooms. Benjamin shuddered at the memory. "OK," he said sadly. "I guess I can make a snowman on my own."

A door opened on the landing above them and a voice called out, "Is that you, Benjamin Brown? I can smell dog."

"Yes, it's me, Mrs. Bone," said Benjamin with a sigh.

Grandma Bone appeared at the top of the stairs. Dressed all in black and with her white hair piled high on her head, she looked more like the wicked queen from a legend than someone's grandmother.

"I hope you don't intend to stay more than ten minutes," said Grandma Bone. "Charlie has to have an early night. It's school tomorrow."

"Mom says I can have another hour," Charlie shouted up to his grandmother.

"Oh? Oh, well, if that's the case, why should I bother to take an interest in your welfare. I'm clearly wasting my time." Grandma Bone swept back into her room, slamming the door behind her.

Whether it was this door-slamming or a minor earth tremor, Charlie would never know, but something caused a small picture to fall from its hook in the hall.

Charlie had never studied the faded old photographs that adorned the walls of the dark hallway. In fact, since he had discovered his unwelcome talent, he had positively avoided them; he didn't want to hear what a group of crusty-looking forebears had to say.

"Well!" exclaimed Benjamin. "How did that happen?"

Charlie realized this was a photograph he wouldn't be able to avoid. As he picked it up and turned it over, he felt a strange fluttering in his stomach.

"Let's see!" said Benjamin.

Charlie held out the black-framed picture. It was one of those faded sepia-colored photographs. The glass was cracked but hadn't fallen out, and through the cracks the boys could make out a family of five, grouped together in a garden. Behind them, the yellowed wall of a cottage could be glimpsed, and on the other side of the photo, beyond a stone wall, a small sailing boat sat on a velvety sea.

"Are you OK?" Benjamin glanced at Charlie.

"No," muttered Charlie. "You know why. Oops, here we go." Already a thin buzz of voices was coming through to him.

It was the mother who spoke first. *Henry, stand still. You'll spoil the picture.* She was a pretty woman in a lacy dress with a high collar. A brooch, like a star, was pinned just beneath her chin. A boy of about four sat on her lap, and a girl of perhaps six or seven leaned against her knee.

Beside the woman stood a man in a soldier's uniform. He had such a merry face Charlie couldn't imagine him with the fierce and solemn look a soldier was supposed to have. But it was the boy, standing in front of the soldier, who held Charlie's gaze.

I can't breathe, muttered the boy.

"Hey, Charlie, he looks a bit like you!" Benjamin pointed a grubby finger at the older boy.

"Mm!" Charlie agreed. "Same age as me, too."

A stiff white collar seemed to be giving the boy called Henry some trouble. It was clamped around his neck above a tightly buttoned jacket, and almost brushed his chin. He wore knee-length pants, long, black socks, and shiny, black boots.

Ouch! muttered Henry.

His mother sighed. *Is it too much to ask you to stand still?*

I think there's a fly under my collar, said Henry.

At this the soldier burst out laughing, and Henry's brother and sister dissolved into helpless giggles.

Really, said the serious mother. *I'm sure our poor photographer doesn't find it amusing. Are you all right, Mr. Caldicott?*

There was a mumbled, *Yes, thank you, madam,* and then something fell over. Charlie couldn't be sure if it was Mr. Caldicott or the camera. The figures in the photograph swung all over the place, making Charlie feel quite dizzy.

"You look green," Benjamin remarked. He led the rather shaken Charlie into the kitchen, where Maisie was rubbing Runner Bean with a towel.

"Oh dear," said Maisie, taking in the situation at a glance. "Have you had one of your thingies, Charlie?"

"He has," said Benjamin.

There was a loud sizzle as Charlie's mother, Amy, dropped an exotic-looking vegetable into a frying pan. "What was it this time, love?" she asked.

Charlie put the photograph on the kitchen table. "This fell off the wall when Grandma Bone slammed her door."

"It's a wonder there are any doors left hanging in this house, the way that woman slams them," said Maisie, emptying the cracked glass into a newspaper. "What with the slamming and your Uncle Paton's lightbulbs, and your mom's rotten vegetables, I sometimes think I'd be better off in a home for the elderly."

Everyone ignored this remark. They'd all heard it so often. Maisie wasn't old enough to be in a home, and she'd been told a hundred times that her family couldn't live without her.

"So do you know who these people are?" Charlie pointed to the family in the black frame. Without the cracked glass, the soldier and his family could be seen more clearly.

Charlie's mother came and looked over his shoulder. "They must be Yewbeams," she said, "Grandma Bone's relations. You'd better ask her."

"No way," said Charlie. "I'll ask Uncle Paton before I go to bed. Come on, Ben."

Tucking the black frame under his arm, Charlie led Benjamin and Runner Bean up to his room. An hour playing computer games passed very quickly, and then Grandma Bone was hammering on Charlie's door and telling him, "Get that dog off your bed." How did she guess? But then a lot of the Yewbeams had powers.

The boys trailed downstairs with Runner Bean behind them, and Charlie let Benjamin and his dog out of the front door.

He stood in the hall a moment, staring at the rectangle of pale wallpaper where the framed photograph had hung. What had caused that photo to fall? Could it really have been a door being slammed? In this house the force at work was bound to be more mysterious.

"Perhaps Uncle Paton will know," Charlie murmured. He ran upstairs.

Uncle Paton was Grandma Bone's brother, but he was twenty years younger, and had a good sense of humor. He also had a talent for exploding lightbulbs when he got near them, so he spent most of the day in his room and only went out after dark. Even in the daytime, lights were on in shop windows. At night he was not so easily seen.

Charlie retrieved the photograph from his room, and knocked on his uncle's door, ignoring the permanent DO NOT DISTURB sign.

There was no response to his first knock, but his second drew an irritated, "What is it?"

"It's about a photo, Uncle Paton."

"Are you hearing voices again?"

"'Fraid so."

"Come in, then." This was said in a weary tone.

An extremely tall man with a great amount of untidy black hair looked up from a desk by the window. As he moved, his elbow sent a stack of books toppling to the floor.

"Bother," said the tall man, "and other more rude things."

Paton was writing a history of his family, the Yewbeams, and he needed a great many books to help him do it.

"Where's the photo, then? Come on, show, show!" Paton clicked his fingers impatiently.

Charlie laid the photo in front of his uncle. "Who are they?"

Paton squinted at the family group. "Ah, that's my father." He pointed to the small boy sitting on his mother's knee. "And that," putting an ink-stained finger beside the girl, "that's poor Daphne who died of diphtheria. The soldier is my grandfather, Colonel

29

Manley Yewbeam — a very merry man. He was on leave from the army. There was a war on, you know. And that's my grandmother Grace. She was an artist — a very good one."

"And the other boy?"

"That's . . . good lord, Charlie, he looks rather like you. I never realized that before."

"His hair is different. But I suppose he could have had it squashed down with something." No amount of squashing would keep Charlie's thick, wiry hair flat.

"Hmm. Poor Henry," muttered Paton. "He disappeared."

"How?" Charlie was amazed.

"They were staying at Bloor's, Henry and James, while their sister, Daphne, was dying. It was the coldest winter for a century, my father has never forgotten it. One day, in the middle of a game of marbles, Henry just vanished." Paton stroked his chin. "My poor father. Suddenly, he was an only child. He idolized his brother."

"Vanished," murmured Charlie. "And now he's talking to me."

"My father always suspected his cousin Ezekiel had something to do with it. He was jealous of Henry. Ezekiel was a magician, but Henry was just naturally clever."

"Is that the Ezekiel who's . . . ?"

"Yes. Dr. Bloor's grandfather. He's still there, festering away somewhere in the academy, surrounded by gas lamps and bad magic."

"Wow! So he's about a hundred years old."

"At least," said Paton. He leaned forward. "Tell me, Charlie, these voices you hear, do they ever say anything that isn't directly connected to that moment in time when they are being photographed?"

"Erm, no," said Charlie. "Not yet. I don't like looking at them for too long."

"Mm, pity," said Paton. "Could be interesting. Here you are, then." He held out the photograph.

"No, thanks," said Charlie. "You keep it."

Paton looked disappointed. "My father would be so happy to know a little more."

"Is he still alive, then?" Charlie was surprised. He'd never seen his great-grandfather. In fact, he'd never heard anyone speak of him.

"He's a grand old fellow," said Paton. "He's in his nineties now, but he still lives in that very same cottage by the sea." He tapped the photograph. "I visit him every month. If I start at midnight, I can be there before sunup."

"What about Grandma and the aunts? They're his daughters, aren't they?"

Uncle Paton made one of his here-comes-a-bit-of-scandal expressions. His thin lips compressed and his long black eyebrows arched up toward his hairline. "There was a rift, Charlie. A terrible quarrel. Long, long ago. I can hardly remember what caused it. For them our father doesn't exist."

"That's awful!" But somehow Charlie wasn't surprised. After all, Grandma Bone wouldn't even speak of Lyell, her only son and Charlie's father, when he disappeared. She had simply sliced him out of her heart.

Charlie said good night to his uncle and went to bed. But as he lay awake, trying to imagine his first day back at Bloor's, Henry Yewbeam's mischievous face kept breaking into his thoughts. How had he disappeared? And where did he go?

A TREE FALLS

The temperature dropped several degrees during the night. On Monday morning an icy wind sent clouds of sleet whipping down Filbert Street, blinding anyone brave enough to venture out.

"I can't believe I've got to go to school in this," Charlie muttered as he struggled through the wind.

"You'd better believe it, Charlie, there's the bus! Good luck!" Amy Bone blew Charlie a kiss then turned onto a side street and made her way toward the greengrocer's. Charlie ran up to the top of Filbert Street where a blue bus was waiting to collect music students for Bloor's Academy.

Charlie'd been put in the music department only because his father had been in it. His friend Fidelio, on the other hand, was brilliant. Fidelio had saved a seat for Charlie on the bus, and as soon as Charlie saw his friend's bright mop of hair and beaming face, he felt better.

"This semester's going to seem very boring," sighed Fidelio, "after all that excitement."

"I don't think I mind a bit of boringness," said Charlie. "I'm certainly not going in the ruined castle again."

The bus parked at one end of a cobbled square with a fountain of stone swans in the center. As the children left the bus, they noticed that icicles hung from the swans' beaks and their wings were laced with frost. They appeared to be swimming on a frozen pool.

"Look at that," Charlie exclaimed as he passed the fountain.

"The dormitory's going to be like a fridge," Fidelio said grimly.

Charlie wished he'd packed a hot-water bottle.

Another bus had pulled up in the square. This one was purple and a crowd of children in purple capes came leaping down the steps.

"Here she comes!" said Fidelio as a girl with indigo-colored hair came flying toward them.

"Hi, Olivia!" called Charlie.

Olivia Vertigo clutched Charlie's arm. "Charlie, good to see you alive. You, too, Fido!"

"It's good to be alive," said Fidelio. "What's with the Fido?"

"I decided to change your name," said Olivia. "Fidelio's such a mouthful and Fido's really cool. Don't you like it?"

"It's a dog's name," said Fidelio. "But I'll think about it."

Children in green capes had now joined the crowd. The art pupils were not as noisy as the drama students, and not so flamboyant and yet when their green capes flew open, a glimpse of a sequined scarf, or gold threaded into a black sweater, made one suspect that more serious rules would be broken by these quiet children than by those wearing blue or purple.

The tall gray walls of Bloor's Academy now loomed before them. On either side of the imposing arched entrance, there was a tower with a pointed roof and, as Charlie approached the wide steps up to the arch, he found his gaze drawn to the window at the top of one of the towers. His mother said she had felt someone watching her from that window, and now Charlie had the same sensation. He shivered slightly and hurried to catch up with his friends.

They had crossed a paved courtyard and were now climbing another flight of steps. At the top, two massive bronze-studded doors stood open to receive the throng of children.

Charlie's stomach gave a lurch as he passed through the doors. He had enemies in Bloor's Academy and, as yet, he wasn't quite sure why. Why were they trying to get rid of him? Permanently.

A door beneath two crossed trumpets led to the music department. Olivia waved and disappeared through a door under two masks, while the children in green made their way to the end of the hall where a pencil crossed with a paintbrush indicated the art department.

Charlie and Fidelio went first to the blue coatroom and then on to the assembly room.

As one of the smallest boys Charlie had to stand in the front row, beside the smallest of all, a white-haired albino called Billy Raven. Charlie asked him if he had enjoyed Christmas but Billy ignored him. He was an orphan and Charlie hoped he hadn't had to spend his holiday at Bloor's. A fate worse than death in Charlie's opinion. He noticed that Billy was wearing a pair of fur-lined boots. A Christmas present, no doubt.

They were only halfway through the first hymn when there was a shout from the stage.

"Stop!"

The orchestra ground to a halt. The singing died.

Dr. Saltweather, head of the music department, paced across the stage, arms folded across his chest. He was a big man with a lot of white, wiry hair. The row of music teachers standing behind him looked apprehensive. Dr. Saltweather was just as likely to shout at them as the children.

"Do you call that singing?" roared Dr. Saltweather. "It's a horrible moan. It's a disgraceful whine. You're musicians, for goodness sake. Sing in tune, give it some life! Now — back to the beginning, please!" He nodded to the small orchestra at the side of the stage and raised his baton.

Charlie cleared his throat. He couldn't sing at the best of times, but today the assembly room was so cold he couldn't stop his jaw from shaking. The temperature had affected the other children as well, even the best singers were hunched and shivering under their blue capes.

They started up again, and this time Dr. Saltweather couldn't complain. The old paneled walls vibrated with sound. Even the teachers were doing their best. Merry Mr. O'Connor threw back his head and sang heartily, Miss Chrystal and Mrs. Dance smiled and swayed, while old Mr. Paltry frowned with concentration. The piano teacher, Mr. Pilgrim, however, did not even open his mouth.

Charlie realized that Mr. Pilgrim was not standing up. He was next to Mrs. Dance, who was extremely small, and being very tall himself, it was not immediately apparent that he was still sitting down. What was wrong with him? He never looked you in the eye, never spoke, never walked in the grounds like other teachers. He seemed to be completely unaware of his surroundings, and his pale face never showed the slightest flicker of emotion.

Until now.

Mr. Pilgrim was staring at Charlie and Charlie had the oddest sensation that the teacher knew him, not as a student, but someone else. It was as if the dark, silent man was trying to recognize him.

There was a sudden, violent crack from beyond the window. It was so loud they could hear it above their boisterous singing. Even Dr. Saltweather paused in his conducting. Another crack resounded over the snow outside, and then a tremendous thump shook the walls and windows.

Dr. Saltweather put down his baton and strode to one of the long windows. When some of the children followed he didn't bother to stop them.

"Good grief!" exclaimed Dr. Saltweather. "Look at the old cedar!"

The huge tree now lay halfway across the garden; its branches broken and its tangled roots pulled clear off the ground. There was another crack as a long branch supporting the crown of the tree finally broke, and with a horrible groan the trunk sank into the snow.

So many games had been played under its sweeping branches, so many whispered secrets kept safe by its wide shadow. It was every child's favorite tree, and now it was gone, and in its place there was only a wide expanse of snow and an unbroken view to the ramparts of the ruined castle. Snow encrusted the top of the walls and clung to the uneven surfaces, but the blood red of the great stones stood out ominously in the white landscape.

As Charlie stared at the castle walls, something happened. It could have been a trick of the light, but he was sure another tree, smaller than the cedar, appeared in the arched entrance to the castle. Its leaves were red and gold and yet other trees had lost their autumn colors.

"Did you see that?" Charlie whispered to Fidelio.

"What?"

"A tree moved," said Charlie. "Look, now it's standing by the castle wall. Can't you see it?"

Fidelio frowned and shook his head.

Charlie tried to blink the tree away. But when he looked again it was still there. No one else appeared to have seen it. Charlie had a familiar fluttery feeling in his stomach. It always happened when he heard the voices, but this time there had been no voices.

A bang from the stage made him look back. Mr. Pilgrim had gotten to his feet very suddenly, knocking over his chair. He gazed over the heads of the children into the garden beyond the window. He could have been looking at the fallen tree, but Charlie was sure he was staring past to the red walls of the castle. Had he seen the strange, moving tree?

Dr. Saltweather swung away from the window.

"Next hymn, children," he said as he marched back to the stage. "You'll never get to your classes at this rate."

After assembly, Charlie had his lesson with Mr. Paltry—Wind. Mr. Paltry was an impatient, elderly flautist. Teaching Charlie Bone to play the recorder was like trying to fill a bucket with a hole in it, he complained. The old man sighed frequently, polished his glasses, and wasn't above whacking the recorder while Charlie was in midblow. Charlie reckoned that if Mr. Paltry continued attacking him in this way he would eventually lose his teeth and then perhaps he would be released from his horrible music lessons.

"Go, Bone, go!" Mr. Paltry grunted after forty minutes of mutual torture.

Charlie went very happily. Next it was on with the boots and out into the snowy garden. In cold weather the children were allowed to wear their capes outside; in summer, capes had to be left in the coatroom.

Fidelio was late arriving from his violin lesson, so when the two boys finally ran outside, the snow had already been trampled by three hundred children.

Snowmen were being built, snowball fights were in progress, and Mr. Weedon, the gardener, was trying to shoo children away from the fallen tree.

"I want to see something by the castle," Charlie told Fidelio.

"You said you didn't want to go near it," his friend reminded him.

"No, but . . . it's like I said, I saw something. I want to know if there are any footprints."

"OK." Fidelio gave a good-natured shrug.

As they ran past the fallen cedar, Billy Raven called out, "Where are you going, you two?"

Almost without thinking, Charlie shouted, "None of your business."

The albino scowled and shrank against the dark branches of the tree. His ruby-colored eyes flashed behind the thick lenses of his glasses.

"Why did you say that?" Fidelio asked as they hurried on.

"I couldn't help it," said Charlie. "There's something wrong with Billy Raven. I don't trust him."

They had reached the entrance to the ruined castle. The snow beneath the huge arch was clear and smooth. No one had been in or out of the ruin.

Charlie frowned. "I saw it," he murmured.

"Let's go in," said Fidelio.

Charlie hesitated.

"It doesn't look so bad in daylight," said Fidelio, peering through the arch. He bounded in and Charlie followed. They tramped across a courtyard and took one of the five passages that led deeper into the ruin.

After several minutes of shuffling through the dark, they emerged into another courtyard. That's where they saw the blood. Or something like it. A few deep red flecks lay in the snow beside a patch of red-gold leaves.

"The beast!" cried Charlie. "Let's get out."

It was only when they were standing safely outside the walls again that Fidelio said, "It might not have been the beast."

"There was blood," said Charlie. "And it was the beast. It's killed something. Or wounded it."

"But there were no other marks, Charlie. No sign of a fight, or footprints . . . or . . ."

Charlie didn't wait to hear the rest of his friend's very reasonable doubts. He raced away from the ruin as if he were reliving the long night when a yellow-eyed beast had chased him through the endless passages and cold, echoing chambers. When he reached the fallen tree he waited for Fidelio to catch up with him.

"Clear off, you!" said a deep voice behind him.

Already nervous, Charlie jumped and swung around. Mr. Weedon's red face appeared through the mesh of broken branches; he was wearing a shiny black helmet and Charlie caught the glint of a saw, held in the big man's black gauntlet.

"This tree's dangerous," said Mr. Weedon. "I've told you kids not to play here."

"I wasn't playing," said Charlie. Fidelio had caught up with him and he felt a little more confident.

"Oh, no. Not you, Charlie Bone. You never play, do ya? A very serious boy, aren't cha?"

"You don't know anything about me," Charlie said angrily. "You can't . . ."

There was a loud roar followed by a grinding noise as Mr. Weedon made his way through the tangle of branches toward Charlie. Twigs flew in all directions as the saw bit through wood and foliage.

"Come on!" Fidelio pulled at Charlie's cape. "Let's get out of here."

"That man's dangerous," Charlie muttered as they ran away from the tree. "How does he know who I am?"

"You're famous," said Fidelio breathlessly. They were now far enough from Mr. Weedon to take a rest. "Getting lost in that old ruin last term was quite an event. Everyone knows who you are."

Charlie wished it wasn't so.

The sound of a hunting horn rang out across the grounds, a signal for the end of break.

The temperature was still falling. After supper the twelve endowed children went, as usual, to the King's room, to do their homework. It was there that a very nasty argument broke out between two great friends: Tancred Torsson and Lysander.

Lysander was feeling the cold more than most, but being a good-humored person his complaints were made in a friendly, almost jokey, way. What he actually said to Tancred, was, "Tanc, what have you done to the weather?"

"Not you, too!" Tancred jumped up and stamped his foot. "I thought that you, of all people, would know better."

Before Lysander could reply, Manfred Bloor spoke up. "Come on, Tancred! Spare a thought for our friend, here. You're freezing him to death."

"I'm not!" screeched Tancred, tearing at his crackling hair.

"He's only joking, Tanc," said Lysander with a smile.

By this time some of the children were beginning to feel uncomfortable. Charlie was particularly concerned. Lysander and Tancred had saved him from the ruin. Together they were a powerful force against the darker powers that lurked in Bloor's Academy. He couldn't bear to see them quarreling.

"Are you on his side now?" Tancred demanded, glaring at his old ally.

"Everyone's on my side," sniggered Manfred.

Lysander silently shook his head, but unfortunately Zelda Dobinski chose that moment to show off her particularly nasty gift for moving things. She was staring at a huge reference book on the shelves behind Tancred. The book launched itself across the room and caught Tancred in the back just as he whirled toward the door.

"Owww!" roared Tancred.

Six children burst into wild laughter, while five looked on in horror.

Tancred didn't notice the sympathetic faces. He was only aware of the mocking laughter. Wind rushed furiously around the room as the stormy boy swept through the door, leaving it banging violently against the wall.

Charlie couldn't stop himself. "Wait!" he cried, leaping after Tancred.

"And where do you think you're going, Bone?" said Manfred.

"I've left my pens in the coatroom," lied Charlie.

A scrawny, red-haired boy looked up and sneered, "Always forgetting things, aren't you, Bone?"

"Not always, Asa." Charlie was scared of Asa Pike. He was Manfred's sidekick and had a very nasty talent for changing his shape.

"Close the door," said Asa, as Charlie stepped outside.

Charlie pulled the door shut behind him. The passage outside was deserted. Charlie decided to try the hall.

As he descended the wide staircase a blast of arctic air almost rocked him off his feet. He stepped down into the stone-slated hall and stood very still. Something was happening to his eyes. He was seeing things that should not be there. A cloud of sparkling particles swirled in the very center of the long room. Was it an ice storm?

Gradually the pale fragments grew more vivid. Now they were forming a blurred shape, blue with a touch of black beneath it. Before Charlie's astonished gaze, a figure in a blue hooded cape was materializing.

Charlie had no doubt that he was seeing a ghost. But when the figure turned to face him, he found, to his horror, that he was looking at . . . himself.

HIDING HENRY

It was the other Charlie who spoke first.

"What a joke," said the boy. "I haven't traveled very far at all."

He had such a normal sort of voice Charlie was reassured. This wasn't a ghost. But if not a ghost, what was it? Clearing his throat, he asked, "Where have you come from, exactly?"

"Here," said the boy. "Just now I was here, but," he shaded his eyes with his hand and gazed up at the row of electric lights illuminating the hall. "It wasn't like this. How did it get so bright?"

"Electricity," said Charlie. He was beginning to recognize the boy. "Are you . . . ?" he began. "I mean have you . . . well, the thing is, I've seen you in a photo. Are you Henry Yewbeam?"

"That's me," said Henry, beaming. "I think I've seen you, too. Somewhere. Who are you?"

"I'm your . . . erm . . . sort of cousin, Charlie Bone."

"No! This is very good news. A cousin, well, well." Henry marched over and shook Charlie's hand. "Very glad to meet you, Charlie Bone."

"The news isn't that good," said Charlie. "What was the date when you . . . just now?"

"January 12, 1916," said Henry. "I always know the date."

"I'm afraid it isn't that now."

"No?" Henry's smile began to fade. "So . . . ?"

"You're almost ninety years ahead of where you were," said Charlie.

Henry's mouth opened but no words came out. Instead there was a sharp ping as something dropped out of his hand and hit the floor.

Charlie saw a large glass marble rolling across the hall. "Wow!" he exclaimed, but before he could pick it up, Henry shouted, "Careful, Charlie. Don't look at it."

"Why?"

"It's what brought me here."

Charlie stood back from the shining glass marble. "You mean it brought you through time?"

Henry nodded. "It's a Time Twister. My mom told me about it, but I'd never seen it until just now. I should have guessed what it was. I knew Zeke would try and punish me."

"Zeke?"

"My cousin, Ezekiel Bloor." Henry suddenly grinned. "I say, he's probably dead by now." And then a sad and solemn expression crossed his face. "They're probably all dead: Mother, Father, even my brother, James. There's no one left."

"There's me," said Charlie, "and I think your brother is . . ."

At that moment a dreadful howl came from the stairs above them. The boys looked up to see a squat, ugly-looking dog standing at the top of the stairs. It howled again, raising its long nose toward the roof, while folds of almost hairless skin shook beneath its whiskery chin.

"What an ugly beast," Henry whispered.

"It's Cook's dog, Blessed." Charlie didn't wait for the dog to howl again. "Quick," he said, grabbing

Henry's arm. "You've got to hide. This isn't a good place for you to be right now. There are people here who might — do something nasty, if they find out who you are."

"Why?" asked Henry, his eyes widening.

"Just a feeling," said Charlie. "Come on." He dragged Henry toward the door into the west wing.

"Where are we going?" said Henry, scooping up the Time Twister and slipping it into his pocket.

For a moment Charlie had no idea why he was taking Henry into the west wing. He turned the heavy brass ring in the door and pushed his new friend into the dark passage beyond.

"I know this place," whispered Henry. "I never liked it."

"Nor me," said Charlie. "But we have to go this way to find somewhere safe." He closed the door behind him just as Blessed gave another mournful howl.

The two boys made their way along the passage until they reached an empty, circular room. A dim light hanging from the ceiling showed an ancient wooden door and, opposite the door, a flight of stone steps.

"The tower?" Henry looked at the steps and made a face.

It was then that Charlie realized why he had brought Henry to this place. "You'll be safe at the top," he said.

"Will I?" Henry looked doubtful.

"Trust me," said Charlie.

As Henry began to mount the steps, Charlie noticed his peculiar tweed pants. They reached only to the knee, where a button held them in place over loose gray socks.

Henry's boots looked distinctly feminine: black and shiny, they were neatly laced just above the ankle.

"We'd better find you some new clothes," Charlie muttered as they reached a second circular room. A door led off this room into the west wing, but Charlie urged Henry up a second flight of steps. "The Bloors live through there," he said.

"Interesting," said Henry. "Some things haven't changed, then."

They kept climbing upward but long before they reached the top of the tower, the sound of a piano could be heard, echoing down the narrow stairwell.

Henry stopped. "There's someone up there."

"It's the piano teacher, Mr. Pilgrim," said Charlie. "No one else comes up here, and Mr. Pilgrim doesn't really notice things. He won't be a problem, promise!"

Another two sets of stairs brought them to the small room at the top of the tower. Sheets of music lay scattered on the floor and the shelves that ran from floor to ceiling were crammed with huge leather-bound albums, and thick dog-eared scores.

"It'll be warm here," said Charlie, moving several piles away from the bookcase. "You see, if we put some paper on the floor like this," he spread several sheets of music between the bookcase and a wall of piled scores. "It'll make a sort of bed, and you can hide here till morning."

"And then what?" asked Henry.

"Well . . ." Charlie scratched his head. "Then I'll find a way to get you some breakfast, and maybe some new clothes."

"What's wrong with my clothes?" Henry gave an anxious frown.

"They're just different. We don't wear that kind of stuff now."

Henry glanced at Charlie's long gray trousers and thick-soled shoes. "No. So I see," he said.

"I'd better be getting back," said Charlie. "The head boy, Manfred Bloor, will be after me, and I don't want to get on the wrong side of him. He hypnotizes."

"Oh. One of those." Henry had heard about the hypnotizers in his family. "Are you one of them?" he asked Charlie. "The endowed?"

"'Fraid so," said Charlie. "That's how I knew you."

"What about him?" Henry pointed to the door behind which the rich piano music flowed on.

"He won't bother you," said Charlie. "'Bye, now." He

gave a wave and backed out of the small room, feeling inexplicably guilty.

In the King's room a boy with a long, sad face glanced anxiously at Charlie's empty seat. The boy's name was Gabriel Silk, and he worried about Charlie. He should have gone after Tancred, not let Charlie go. Charlie was younger and likely to land in some sort of trouble. He was the kind of boy unfortunate things happened to.

And then the howling began. At first they all tried to ignore it, but in the end Manfred flung down his pen and exclaimed, "Bloody dog! Billy, go and shut it up."

"I'll go," Gabriel offered.

"I said Billy." Manfred gave Gabriel one of his horrible stares and then turned his piercing black gaze on Billy. "Go on," he said. "You can talk to the wretched thing. Ask it if it's got a bellyache."

"Yes, Manfred." Billy scurried to the door.

As he ran down the chilly stairwells and dark corridors he talked to himself. He hated it when everyone else was shut away doing homework. He was afraid of meeting the ghosts. He knew they were there — gliding about in the dark. Billy never went home. He had no home to go to. Sometimes, he stayed with an aunt. But not often.

He had reached the wide landing where a grand staircase led down into the hall. Blessed was sitting at the top of the stairs, still howling.

Billy sat beside the dog and put one hand on its plump back. "What's the matter, Blessed?" The words came out in a series of little grunts and sniffs. A language that Blessed could understand.

The old dog stopped howling. "Boy came," he said. "Bad thing. Wrong."

"What boy? Why was it wrong?" asked Billy.

Blessed considered this question. He seemed to be having some difficulty with his reply. At last he grunted, "Boy came from nowhere. With ball, very small. Shiny. Blessed not like this ball. It bad magic."

Billy was perplexed. "Was it Tancred?" he asked. "Boy with lots of yellow hair?"

"No. Boy was like that one." Blessed stared down the hall.

Following the dog's gaze, Billy was surprised to see Charlie Bone quietly closing the door into the west wing.

"Where've you been?" Billy called.

Charlie looked up, startled. "Nowhere," he said. "Just looking for Tancred."

"Blessed said another boy was here; a boy like you."

"Blessed's got a vivid imagination." Charlie began to cross the hall.

"He says there was a ball. It was small and shiny and he didn't like it."

"I think Blessed was dreaming," said Charlie, climbing the stairs toward Billy.

Billy looked at the old dog. "Blessed doesn't lie," he said. "Dogs can't."

"They can dream, can't they? Come on, Billy. We'd

better get back to our homework or we'll get detention."

"Go back to Cook," Billy told the dog. "Go on, Blessed. No more howling."

Blessed gave a sullen grunt and began to flop down the stairs, while Billy and Charlie ran back to the King's room.

When homework was over, Charlie had half a mind to go and visit Henry. He didn't like leaving him alone in the tower, nearly a hundred years from where he was supposed to be. Of course, he wasn't quite alone, but Mr. Pilgrim hardly counted. Charlie badly needed to confide in someone.

When he reached the dormitory, he found Fidelio filling his closet with the clothes from his bag. There were two boys from the drama department in the room and Charlie couldn't risk being overheard. "I want to ask you something," he whispered to his friend. "Can we go somewhere else?"

"The art room," Fidelio said softly.

As they came out of the dormitory they walked straight into Billy Raven.

"Be careful what you say," Fidelio whispered as they sped down the corridor. "I used to feel sorry for Billy, but I don't like the way he watches people."

"Someone's got to him," said Charlie. "I don't know who it is, but they're making him spy for them. I don't think Billy can help it."

They had reached the art room.

"Light's still on," Charlie commented. "But no one's here."

"Mr. Boldova might come back," warned Fidelio. "We'd better hide over there."

A large painting of trees had been propped against two easels near the wall, and the boys managed to squeeze behind it and squat on the floor. In a hushed voice, Charlie began to tell his friend about the sudden appearance of Henry, the boy with the Time Twister, who vanished nearly a hundred years ago. However, as soon as he mentioned the voices in the photograph, Fidelio clutched his arm.

"Hold on," he said. "D'you mean you can hear what's going on in photos?"

Charlie nodded. He had never told Fidelio about his peculiar talent. "I don't like people to know," he muttered.

"I don't think I would, either," said Fidelio. "Don't worry. I won't tell a soul. Go on about Henry. Where is he now?"

"I took him up to the top of the music tower. I couldn't think of anywhere else."

"What about Mr. Pilgrim?"

"He won't even notice Henry, and if he does . . ." Charlie hesitated. "I don't think he'll harm him."

"Hmm. I wonder! You can't tell with Mr. Pilgrim," murmured Fidelio. "So, what are you going to do with this long-lost great-great-uncle?"

"I thought I'd try and smuggle him home at the weekend. But first I've got to get some food to him."

"Lunch break would be best," said Fidelio. "He can have my meat — if it's not mince; and you can sneak up to the tower, while I . . ." He broke off, suddenly, as a face appeared at the top of the tree painting.

"What are you doing?" asked Emma Tolly.

Charlie was tempted to tell her; she was, after all, a friend, as well as endowed, but something held him back. "We're just talking," he said. "Can't get any peace in the dorm."

"I know," Emma sighed. "I came to finish a drawing."

"We were just going," said Fidelio.

The two boys wriggled out from behind the painting.

Just as they were leaving the art room, Charlie caught sight of a large sketch book, lying open on a table. He stared at it, and moved closer.

"It's mine," said Emma. "Just sketches, nothing special."

But they were special. Both pages of the open book were covered with pictures of birds: birds in flight; swooping, hovering, soaring, and diving. They were so real Charlie felt that if he touched them he would feel real feathers.

"They're brilliant," he murmured.

"Brilliant," Fidelio repeated.

"Thank you!" Emma gave one of her shy smiles.

All at once, the door behind them opened, and a voice said, "What's going on in here?"

Mr. Boldova appeared. You could tell he was an art teacher, because his clothes were covered in splashes of paint. Even his green cape, which he often forgot to wear, had little flecks of color on the sleeves. Mr. Boldova always looked as if he had just been on vacation. He had bright hazel eyes, a very healthy complexion, and long brown hair tied in a ponytail.

"I was showing my work to Charlie and Fidelio," Emma said confidently. "We were just going."

"That's all right, Emma." The art teacher beamed at them all.

It was impossible to be afraid of Mr. Boldova. He never gave detention, never punished pupils for untidiness, forgetfulness, or even being late. The only thing that made him angry was bad art. He gave Charlie a searching look and said, "Ah, Charlie Bone."

"Yes, sir," said Charlie. "Good night, sir."

The three children slipped past him and ran for their dormitories. It was already five minutes to lights out. Matron would be on the warpath, and Matron was not an understanding person. She was, in fact, Charlie's great aunt, Lucretia Yewbeam.

As they dashed into their dormitory, the boys heard Miss Yewbeam shouting at some poor girl who had lost her slippers.

"We'll just make it before she gets here," said Fidelio, rushing to the bathroom.

Billy Raven was sitting up in bed. "Where've you been?" he asked Charlie.

"Had some extra work to do," said Charlie. He pulled on his pajamas and jumped into bed, just as Matron poked her long face around the door.

"Lights out!" she barked, flicking the light switch.

Out went the bare bulb hanging in the center of the room.

"That was a close one," murmured Gabriel Silk from the bed next to Charlie.

Just before Charlie finally drifted off, he thought

of the boy in the tower; cold, hungry, and probably frightened. What was to be done with Henry Yewbeam?

Unable to sleep, Henry Yewbeam was staring out across the city. There was a small, round window in the wall between the bookcases and Henry, anxious to know if the world had changed in ninety years, had climbed onto a stool to find out.

The world had, indeed, changed. The sky above the horizon seemed to be on fire. It had a terrifying orange glow. Could it be the rows of streetlights leading into the distance? Pinpricks of radiance shone out from the dark blocks of houses and below the tower pairs of shining lights, some red, some white, swept across Henry's field of vision, like earthly shooting stars.

"Motor cars," murmured Henry, as one came closer. "So many."

"So many," said a voice, like an echo.

Henry became aware that a man was standing in the darkness beside him. The piano music coming from the room next door had stopped. Henry was relieved; he didn't have much of an ear for music.

"Are you Mr. Pilgrim?" Henry asked.

There was no reply to his question. In the soft light coming through the window, Henry could make out a pale face and very black hair. The man's expression was solemn and faraway.

"I'm Henry Yewbeam," said Henry.

Still no reply.

It was like talking to someone who wasn't really there. Perhaps it wouldn't matter if Henry told him the truth.

"I'm very old," he said. "Or at least I should be."

In the distance a clock began to strike. The deep chimes of the cathedral pealed out across the city. Mr. Pilgrim turned to Henry. His eyes held a strange glitter.

Henry had just counted the twelfth stroke when Mr. Pilgrim said, "Are you cold?"

"Yes," said Henry.

The piano teacher took off his blue cape and wrapped it around the boy's shoulders.

"Thank you," said Henry, stepping off the stool.

Mr. Pilgrim smiled. He stretched up to a high shelf and pulled a tin from a row of books. Lifting the lid he offered the tin to Henry. "Oatcakes," he said. "You see I live up here, practically. And one gets hungry."

"One does," Henry agreed, politely taking only one oatcake.

Mr. Pilgrim didn't offer him any more. He put the tin on the stool and said, "Help yourself." The faraway look had come back into his eyes. He seemed to be trying to remember something. Frowning, he murmured, "Good night."

And then he was gone, slipping away down some stone steps with hardly a sound.

Henry would have liked the strange man to stay. He was grateful for the extra cape but, to tell the truth, it was not as cold as it had been. In fact the temperature was rising rapidly. The icicles hanging outside the window were beginning to melt.

All around the tower there was a steady drip, drip, drip of ice turning to water. It was a sound that filled Henry with foreboding. He had just worked out that his sudden twist through time must have had something to do with the cold. He had arrived in Bloor's when the temperature had reached exactly the same degree as when he had left, in 1916. A change in the weather could make a difference in time travel.

"I won't be able to get home," Henry said to himself. "I'll never see my family again." And suddenly his situation seemed almost too grim to bear. "But I must!" he murmured.

OLIVIA MAKES A MESS

Billy Raven lay wide awake. For two weeks he had slept alone in the long dormitory. Now he must get used to the grunts and snores, the heavy breathing and tiny whimpers of other boys. It wasn't easy. Billy had always been a light sleeper.

Tonight he was feeling excited. He had something to tell old Ezekiel Bloor. Perhaps he would be rewarded. When he was quite sure the other boys were asleep, Billy swung his feet into his slippers and pulled on his bathrobe. The floorboards gave only the slightest creak as he crossed the room and slipped out of the dormitory.

Manfred Bloor had given Billy a present for Christmas; a long black flashlight with a very powerful beam. Billy hadn't expected a gift from the head boy of all people, but when Manfred bent down and whispered, "We must keep our spies happy," Billy had understood.

He switched on the flashlight and a brilliant shaft of light swept right to the end of the passage. Billy began his long journey to the upper regions of the west wing. He usually waited for Blessed to lead him. But tonight he couldn't wait.

As Billy made his way closer to the old man's room, he had to navigate a gloomy realm that never changed. It was one of the few places where Ezekiel's flawed magic had worked as he wished. So Billy's slippered feet made no prints in the thick dust, and the cobwebs he walked through wove themselves together as soon as he had passed. If it were not for the occasional hiss from a gaslight, you would have thought the creaking steps and shadowy passages had been deserted for a hundred years.

Billy had reached a black door, the paint scarred by years of dog scratchings. He knocked twice and a voice croaked, "Who is there?"

"Billy Raven," said Billy.

"Enter, Billy Raven," said the voice.

Billy walked in.

Ezekiel Bloor sat in his wheelchair beside a blazing fire. A sheepskin blanket was draped around his shoulders, and his ancient skull-like face poked from beneath a black woolly hat. A pile of faded velvet cushions were propped behind his back, and he wore a black velvet jacket studded with gold buttons. For all his finery, though, Billy couldn't help thinking the old man looked a bit like a dead sheep.

Without being invited, the small boy sat down heavily in the chair opposite Ezekiel. The sudden change in atmosphere made him feel dizzy.

"Where's the dog?" asked the old man.

"I don't know. I couldn't wait for him. I wanted to tell you something." Billy's glasses had misted up in the steamy atmosphere. He took them off and rubbed the lenses with his thumb.

"Ah good. Something about Charlie?" The old man leaned forward eagerly.

"Sort of," said Billy.

"Come on, then. Tell, tell."

"Well, it was Blessed really. He saw it."

"It?" wheezed the old man. "It? What 'it' was this? And the dog's name is Percy. How many times do I have to tell you!"

"Sorry. But he thinks he's Blessed."

"Yes, yes. Never mind. Go on!" Ezekiel waved his hand impatiently.

Billy put his glasses back on, and then wished he hadn't. The old man's wizened face loomed unpleasantly close. Billy could see every wart and bristle in vivid detail.

"The dog was howling and Manfred sent me to find out what was wrong, knowing I could understand dog talk, and all that."

"Wish I could understand the wretched dog." Ezekiel shook his head. "So what did he say?"

"Said he'd seen a boy, come from nowhere. And this boy had a ball, very small and shiny. He said it was bad . . ."

"WHAT?" The old man clapped a hand over his mouth. "What? A boy and . . . and was it glass, this ball?"

"Could be," said Billy, amazed by the excitement his news had caused.

"No, no, it can't be." Ezekiel stood up, but his useless legs let him down, and he sank back into his cocoon of sheep's wool and velvet.

"And then I noticed Charlie Bone in the hall, and Blessed said he looked like the appearing boy." Billy smiled and waited for the effect these words would have. He wasn't disappointed.

"Charlie Bone," breathed Ezekiel. "Yes, yes, of course. He was a bit like Charlie Bone. No wonder I can't stand the boy. Find him, Billy. Bring him here."

"Who? Charlie?"

"No, you fool. The other one. My cousin Henry."

"Your cousin?" said Billy, confused. "How? I don't know where he is."

"You've just told me he's in the building. It can't be that difficult."

"You mean he's your . . . ?"

"My cousin, yes. I sent him packing years ago.

Never thought I'd see the wretch again." The old man's voice dropped to a low mumble. "Must be the weather — coordinating temperatures. Mm, hmm . . . Time Twister works that way . . . Ho hum." He drummed his fingers on the arm of his wheelchair.

Billy was intrigued. "What's a Time Twister?"

Ezekiel looked up. His small black eyes seemed to be staring right through Billy. "It's a marvelous thing," he murmured. "A crystal ball, hardly bigger than a marble. It can twist you through the years. No wonder the dog didn't like it. Never look at it, unless you want to travel, that's what my aunt told me. Ask the dog where that boy is. Percy knows everything. Now get out and close the door."

Billy was very disappointed. He'd expected to be rewarded with a cup of hot cocoa at the very least. "Er . . . you know what you said about my parents . . . ," he began.

"Parents? You haven't got any," said Ezekiel. Clearly his mind was on other things.

"No, but you said someone wanted to adopt me," Billy said hopefully.

"Did I? Can't remember. We'll see about them when you've found the boy. And don't forget the Twister." Ezekiel dismissed Billy with a wave of his bony hand.

Billy slipped out of his chair and made for the door. Then he turned to the old man and said, "Thanks for the boots. My chilblains are much better."

Ezekiel grunted. He wasn't listening to the boy. When Billy had gone the old man stared into the flames and uttered a stream of strange words and sounds. Now and again the name "Henry" bubbled to the surface, and then "Time Twister." Other recognizable words were "Never!" "How?" "No, no!" "Why?" "Impossible!" These were spat so hard into the flames they began to sizzle. The fire might have gone out altogether if the old man hadn't reached into a silver box beside him and tossed a handful of sparkling sticks into the grate. But these small magic sticks caused such a violent explosion, clouds of black smoke billowed out into the room, and the old man was overcome by a violent fit of coughing.

"Idiots!" he croaked at the innocent silver box.

Charlie was awake, he couldn't think why. Something must have woken him. What was it?

The distant chimes of the cathedral clock began to ring out across the city. It was midnight and the back of Charlie's neck began to tingle. He felt as he always did when he heard the clock strike twelve. Afraid and elated at the same time.

A bed creaked at the end of the room and he wondered if Billy had been out and about. Even if he had he wouldn't be punished for it. Last semester Billy had won the ruin game, and he was now the proud possessor of a bronze medal, a medal that would give him extra privileges and a whole year free of detention.

"Billy, is that you?" Charlie whispered.

No answer, but there was another long creak, and Charlie was sure that it came from Billy's bed.

"Where've you been?" he asked.

"None of your business," came the reply.

It was definitely Billy's voice. Charlie burrowed under the covers. *If Billy wants to be secretive, let him,* Charlie thought. He had other things to worry about: rescuing Henry, for one thing. The whole enterprise needed very careful planning. First of all, he would have to get some food to Henry. Before he could decide how to do this, Charlie had fallen asleep.

Fidelio's dreams had been more productive. He had devised a way for Charlie to sneak up the music tower after lunch. But they would need help.

Over breakfast next morning, Fidelio outlined his plan to Charlie. "Olivia will do it," he murmured in Charlie's ear. Although there was a great deal of noise all around them, Fidelio didn't want their plans to be overheard.

"Olivia? How can she help?" Charlie said softly. He tried to keep his lips as rigid as possible because Billy Raven, sitting opposite, was watching him intently.

Fidelio was also aware of Billy's intense stare. He

turned his head away from the table and whispered harshly, "She can create a diversion. We need someone to stop Manfred and Asa Pike reaching the hall, when you go through the door to the tower. They both use the drama cafeteria; if Olivia can hold those two up for a few minutes, you stand a chance. No one else would bother to watch us."

"What are you whispering about?"

Charlie and Fidelio looked up to see Manfred Bloor leaning over Billy's chair. He was studying them closely. It was almost as if the younger boy had called him over.

"Well, come on, share your secret, Charlie Bone!" Manfred's black eyes glittered dangerously.

Charlie immediately lowered his head. He knew he could fight Manfred's hypnotizing stare, but he didn't want to get into trouble with the head boy before Henry had been rescued.

Fidelio said quickly, "We were just discussing Olivia Vertigo's hair."

"Oh?" Manfred raised a thin black eyebrow.

"Yes, we thought blue looked very nice on her," said Charlie, "but we didn't like to say it out loud, in case she heard us."

"As if," said Manfred scathingly. "It's not exactly quiet in here, is it? Personally, I think Olivia Vertigo's hair looks ghastly."

He shouted this last remark and, hearing her name mentioned, Olivia looked over from the table behind him. When she saw Charlie's serious face, she grimaced and returned to her attack on the lumpy oatmeal.

Manfred drifted away and began to shout at a small girl who was wearing her cape inside out.

"Phew!" muttered Charlie. "Let's talk at break."

"Good idea," agreed Fidelio.

By the time the two boys had managed to call Olivia away from her friends, break was almost over. Olivia came bouncing across the snowy ground in bright pink lace-up boots studded with sequins.

"The snow's taking all the paint off," she complained, holding out her left foot. The toe of her boot was a nasty gray color.

"Olivia, we need a favor," said Charlie, coming straight to the point.

"Oh?" Olivia put her foot back into the snow. "What sort of favor?"

Charlie knew it was no good trying to get Olivia to do something without a proper explanation. She would have to know all about Henry Yewbeam before she agreed to help. So, as quickly as he could, Charlie told her everything.

Olivia's mouth dropped open and her large gray eyes grew even wider.

"D'you mean that he got himself, sort of, whizzed out of the past to here and now?"

"Yes." Charlie looked over his shoulder. He thought he saw Billy Raven hovering behind a group of music students. "But we want to keep it a secret until we know how to help him. I've got to get him some food."

"And we thought Charlie could sneak my sausages up the tower at lunch break," said Fidelio, "if you could keep Manfred and Asa in your cafeteria for a few extra minutes."

"No problem," said Olivia. "Leave it to me."

A long blast from the hunting horn sent children racing in from the field, and Olivia ran off to join her friends.

"We'll just have to trust her," said Charlie. "She's usually reliable."

Each department had its own cafeteria, and the drama cafeteria was always the noisiest and most undisciplined. Manfred had done his best to stop them from wearing fancy shoes and long skirts but the drama teachers were very lax with the rules. They seldom complained about their pupils' choice of clothing, in fact they rather encouraged hats with ears, unusual footwear, and colored facepaint. Mrs. Marlowe, head of the drama department, considered clothes a means of self-expression, the more unusual the better. All this infuriated Manfred, but there was little he could do about it, so he took it out on the children in the music and art departments.

Today the drama cafeteria was a mess. Someone's jacket was molting and white fur lay all over the floor. Someone else's hat was shedding feathers and these had floated into the gravy boat. Glitter had stuck to some of the chairs, and the tables were littered with paint flakes, tinsel, and bits of false hair.

"It's disgusting," grumbled Manfred, staring at a sequin in his custard. "Why can't people be more conventional?" For himself, he favored plain black with occasionally a purple shirt to match his cape. Even the ribbon on his ponytail was black.

Asa Pike gave a nervous snigger. The mustache he was fond of wearing had just dropped onto his plate. "Oops," he said. "Forgot I was wearing it."

Manfred shot his companion a look of contempt. "There are times, Asa, when I would enjoy giving you a good kick."

Asa's yellow eyes took on a nasty gleam. Manfred began to regret his words. He and Asa were not true friends, they stuck together because everyone else disliked them. Asa might fawn on Manfred but Manfred knew quite well that Asa could be as dangerous as he was. Manfred could hypnotize, but when night fell, Asa could become something wild and deadly, a creature beyond Manfred's power.

So the two boys sat at their table, with tight lips and brooding eyes, until a sudden commotion by the door broke their disagreeable silence.

"It's Olivia Vertigo again," said Asa, looking toward the disturbance.

Manfred stood up. "Not her." He strode over to the door.

Olivia had managed to tip the entire contents of a tray right in front of the door. Most of the glass and dishes had broken and now lay in jagged pieces caked with gravy and custard.

"Sorry, sorry, sorry," said Olivia. "I slipped."

"Sorry's not good enough," said Manfred. "Go and get a mop."

"Yes, Manfred." Olivia walked briskly across the

cafeteria and into the kitchen. "I'll give them five minutes," she muttered, looking at her watch.

No one paid any attention to Olivia until Cook came through a door at the back of the kitchen. She marched up to Olivia and said, "You're on the wrong side of the door, dear!"

"I came for a piece of bread," lied Olivia.

"Didn't you have enough to eat?" asked Cook.

"I was late," said Olivia, glancing at her watch.

"Tch! Tch! I'll see what I can do." Cook was about to turn away when the door behind Olivia was suddenly flung open.

Manfred stood glaring at Olivia. "Where's the mop, you idiot? We can't get out until that mess is cleared up."

"I er . . . ," Olivia began.

"Hold your horses, Manfred Bloor," said Cook sharply. "Everything comes to those who wait."

"Ha!" grunted Manfred.

Cook ambled across the kitchen and took a mop, a bucket, and a pair of rubber gloves from under the sink. Manfred shouted, "For goodness' sake, hurry up, woman."

Cook froze. She dropped the bucket and stared at Manfred with her hands on her hips. "Don't you speak to me like that. Don't you dare. Don't you ever, ever use that tone with me again."

"Yeah, yeah!" said Manfred nervously.

"Apologize," said Cook.

"Sorry," mumbled Manfred, pretending to examine his fingernails.

Olivia could hardly believe it. In a few words Cook had reduced the head boy to a jittering junior.

Cook picked up the bucket and handed it to Manfred. "If you want a mess cleared up, do it yourself."

"But I didn't make the mess!" cried Manfred, turning scarlet.

Cook shrugged and walked away.

Manfred gave Olivia a vicious shove through the door and, as soon as they were on the other side, handed her the bucket.

At that very moment, Charlie and Fidelio were crossing the hall. Now that the children from drama were all trapped in their cafeteria, there were fewer people about, and Charlie managed to sneak through the door into the west wing without being seen. Fidelio stood guard. When Charlie had completed his mission, he would give two taps on the door, and if the coast was clear, Fidelio would tap back.

Charlie raced up the deep spiraling steps that led to the top of the tower. By the time he reached the music room he was out of breath and had a stitch in his side.

Henry had gone. A large blue cape lay over the back of a chair, and there was an empty tin on a stool. Some of the books were covered in crumbs and two candy wrappers had been dropped by the window.

Mr. Pilgrim was playing very softly today. He kept repeating the same notes over and over again, as if he couldn't remember where the music was going.

Without knocking, Charlie opened the door and looked in. Mr. Pilgrim was alone. He wasn't wearing his cape, and Charlie remembered that he'd been without it at assembly; but then, Mr. Pilgrim often forgot things.

The music teacher looked over the piano and frowned at Charlie.

"Excuse me, sir," said Charlie. "Have you seen a boy? A boy a bit like me?"

Very much to his surprise, Mr. Pilgrim answered quite clearly. "Yes. There was a boy."

"And do you know where he is now, sir?"

"He shouldn't have been up here alone," said Mr. Pilgrim. "Not at night. It's too cold."

"Yes but — where did he go?"

"He was hungry." Mr. Pilgrim must have suddenly recalled the notes he'd been searching for, because he played two loud chords and then launched himself into a very complicated piece of music.

Charlie realized that it would be useless to ask the teacher any more questions. Besides, if he didn't get back soon, Manfred and Asa would be prowling around the hall.

"Thank you, sir." Charlie left the room and, closing the door behind him, ran all the way down to the bottom of the tower. He descended the winding stairs so quickly, by the time he reached the ground floor he felt very wobbly on his feet.

Before he went into the dark passage that led to the hall, he stopped to listen. He could hear nothing. It was safe to enter the passage. All the same he tiptoed over the stone floor. He had only gone a few meters when he walked straight into something; a small, thin figure that was hardly a person at all. It whimpered slightly and scurried away, but when Charlie turned to look back at it, the person or thing turned back, too. Its eyes glittered behind a thin black veil, and it whispered, "Boy," then it was gone.

INTO THE FREEZER

Charlie tore to the end of the passage and whizzed through the door at the end, almost knocking Fidelio off his feet.

"You forgot to tap," said Fidelio fiercely. "Someone's watching."

"Who?" Charlie saw Billy Raven disappear into the coatroom. "Oh no," he groaned. "Not him."

At that moment, Manfred and Asa appeared at the far end of the hall. Manfred looked furious. As soon as he saw the two boys, he shouted, "Out! Out! Why aren't you two outside?"

"It's — er — wet," said Charlie.

"Wet? Of course it's wet, you idiot. Not afraid of a bit of snow are you?"

"We couldn't find our boots," said Fidelio quickly.

"Then, go out in your shoes!" barked Manfred.

"But . . . ," began Charlie.

"So you'll have wet shoes. So what? That'll teach

you to lose your boots." Manfred had worked himself into a fine temper. His normally pale face was quite pink.

Charlie and Fidelio scuttled out into the garden without another word.

"Phew. I bet that was all due to Olivia," said Fidelio.

"I hope she hasn't got detention," said Charlie. "Henry wasn't there, by the way. Now I don't know what to do."

"We'll find him," said Fidelio confidently. "But we'd better get to him before Manfred. What scared you in the tower? You looked as if you'd seen a ghost."

"I think I did," said Charlie. "It was horrible. All black and wispy."

"The dark lady," said Fidelio. "Gabriel told me about her. She hangs around the music tower. I think she likes Mr. Pilgrim's piano playing."

A few minutes later, Olivia joined them in the garden. "Hi, folks, did it work?" she asked.

"It was brilliant," said Charlie. "You must have held them up for at least ten minutes."

"How did you do it?" asked Fidelio.

Olivia told them about her accident with the tray. "But now I've got detention," she said, "so I won't be going home till Saturday night."

Charlie's face fell. "I'm sorry. I should have known that would happen."

"Oh, I don't mind," said Olivia. "I can do a bit of exploring. As long as someone else gets detention with me. I don't like being on my own."

"Oh." Charlie felt even worse. "Well, if you don't mind, I think I'm going to be busy."

"Of course. Cousin Henry," Olivia said cheerfully. "I understand. And I know Fido will be doing some musical thing or other."

"Well, now that you mention it . . . ," said Fidelio.

"It's OK. Don't look so guilty, both of you. I'll try Emma Tolly." Olivia bounced off in her pink boots, and headed toward Emma, who was walking around with her nose in a book.

The two boys spent the rest of break walking up and down on the stones outside the garden door. It was several degrees warmer and the snow was turning into a watery slush. Charlie's left shoe was leaking.

Just before the horn went for the end of break, Olivia came up to them looking very fed up. "Guess what?" she said. "Emma Tolly doesn't like to leave her aunt alone at weekends. I ask you! I helped to rescue her from those awful foster parents and now she won't even spend a few hours with me."

"In that case I'll try and get detention," said Charlie. "Henry can wait a bit longer."

"No, he can't," said Olivia. "You get him out of here as soon as you can. It's OK. Bindi's going to stay with me." She shook her head. "I don't know what's gotten into Emma. She's so prissy these days."

"She's never had a real home before," said Charlie. "I suppose she just wants to be in it as much as she can."

"Hm." Olivia sauntered off.

As the two boys walked to their history lesson, Fidelio said quietly, "Charlie, I think you're going to have to carry out your rescue mission tonight. You won't get another chance today."

Charlie agreed. But he had no idea where to start looking for Henry.

"Try the kitchens," Fidelio suggested. "He must be starving by now."

That night, as Charlie lay in bed, he tried to remember all the stairs and passages that eventually led to the kitchens. He knew there were three kitchens, one behind each of the three cafeterias. They were connected by swinging doors, so he would be able to creep through all three, once he had found his way to the first one.

"D'you think Cook will still be in the kitchen?" Charlie whispered to Fidelio.

"Not after midnight," Fidelio said softly.

"Shut up, all of you!" said Damian Smerk.

"Shut up, yourself." Fidelio threw a damp shoe in Damian's direction. It was a good shot and grazed Damian's cheek.

"I'll get you, Fidelio Gunn, you wait!" screeched Damian.

"You're on," said Fidelio. "See you by the garden door, straight after breakfast."

Damian sniveled and pulled the covers over his head. He was terrified of violence, but he often made silly remarks about getting people, and then pretended he had hurt his arm or his leg, so he could excuse himself from a fight.

Charlie was just about to speak, when the door opened and the light came on.

"Who was talking?" Matron stood on the threshold.

No one answered.

"Own up!" she said.

"We were," said Charlie.

His great aunt swung her long nose in his direction. "Oh? Is that a confession?"

"We all confess," said Fidelio.

Matron stared around the room unpleasantly. "If I have to come in again, you'll all be put on detention," she said.

"Except me," said Billy.

Ignoring Billy, Lucretia Yewbeam walked out and slammed the door.

"That was close," Fidelio whispered so softly no one but Charlie could hear him. "Do you want me to come with you tonight?"

"No," Charlie whispered back. "It's better if just one of us goes. Thanks anyway."

"Good luck!" Fidelio turned over and was soon asleep.

For a few moments Charlie lay with eyes wide open, fighting sleep. In desperation, he threw off the covers. Now he was so cold, sleep was impossible.

He waited until he heard the cathedral clock strike twelve, and then, with a mixture of fear and excitement, he quickly pulled on his bathrobe and slippers and crept out of the dormitory.

"Right, then left, then down the stairs," Charlie murmured to himself. The beam of light from his flashlight was so feeble he couldn't see much beyond his feet. By the time he'd managed to find his way down two staircases, he realized he was lost, or certainly in a place he didn't recognize. Everything looked so different in the dark.

Taking a chance, Charlie continued for several meters until he came to another set of steps. He descended two when something bumped into his knees and sent him crashing to the floor.

"Ow! Ooo! Ouch!" Charlie muttered under his breath. No bones were broken but he felt bruised and shaken. "Can't go back now," he muttered.

Picking himself up he turned a corner and found himself on the landing above the hall. The lights here were left burning all night and, with a soft whoop of relief, Charlie ran down the stairs and on into the long passage that led to the cafeterias.

Stumbling against chairs and tables, Charlie made his way through the blue cafeteria and into the kitchen. Here, counters covered in saucepans blocked his way. Machines jutted out at odd angles, mops and buckets were hidden beside cupboards. A heavy pan crashed to the floor as Charlie felt his way along a shelf. He froze for a second, and then became aware of a low light coming from the frosted glass at the top of a door beside him. Very slowly, Charlie opened the door.

He looked into a small room with walls of tall white fridges and freezers. Henry Yewbeam stood in front of the tallest.

"Henry," breathed Charlie. "What are you doing?"

"Hello, Charlie," said Henry. "It's good to see you."

"It's freezing in here," said Charlie whose teeth had begun to chatter.

"I know," Henry smiled mysteriously. "It's just what I want."

"What are you talking about? Please come out of there. I think we could die of cold."

"I don't want to die," said Henry. "But I think I will if I don't get home." He stepped out of the freezing room and closed the door.

Charlie relaxed. It was warm in the kitchen and he found it easier to think. He perched himself on a counter and Henry jumped up beside him.

"I looked for you at lunch break," Charlie said. "I sneaked some food up to the music room, where were you?"

"There was a lady, very small, all in black. She took me to her room. I was a bit frightened of her, but she gave me a cup of tea and some sweets." Henry held out a candy wrapped in silver paper. "Have one! She gave me a handful."

Charlie took the sweet. It was chocolate with a strawberry center. One of his favorites. "Yummy," he said. "I bumped into that woman. I thought she was a ghost."

Henry shook his head. "Not quite a ghost. She used to play the violin, but now her left hand doesn't work and that makes her very, very sad. You could say she was in mourning for her fingers."

Henry had an odd way of putting things. Charlie was intrigued. "Who is she?"

"I didn't like to ask. Mama said it was rude to pry. The lady told me to go to the kitchens at night. So here I am. But, Charlie," Henry's face lit up. "I have found a wonderful thing."

"What?"

"In there," Henry pointed to the cold room, "a closet that's full of ice."

"A freezer," said Charlie.

"A freezer?" Henry repeated. "Well, I never. It hums in a very comforting way. Charlie, I think it will take me home."

"What d'you mean?" said Charlie anxiously.

"I have come to the conclusion that I arrived in this new century because the weather was right. When I left 1916, it was the coldest day for many, many years. And when I got here, it was exactly the same. But now it's getting warmer and if I use the Time Twister, I could end up anywhere."

"You'd be crazy to use it," Charlie agreed.

"Not if I go into the freezer," said Henry earnestly.

"What? You'd freeze to death."

"You could help me, Charlie. Just open the freezer door, now and again, to make sure I'm breathing.

Once I hit the right temperature, I'll be gone." Henry leaned forward. "Please help me. I want to go home so much. I want to get back to 1916 and see my family. I'll never survive in this new world. I don't belong."

Charlie had only known his new relation for a day, but already he had begun to like him a lot. He would miss him, he realized. "It's a bit chancy," he said evasively. "I mean you could end up back in the Ice Age, with mammoths and things."

"I've considered that, but I want to take a chance. If I think hard about Mama and Papa, and my brother and sister, I'm sure I'll get back." He grinned encouragingly at Charlie, "What do you say?"

"OK," said Charlie reluctantly. "Let's give it a go. But if you turn blue, I'm pulling you out of there."

"Thank you, Charlie."

The two boys swung themselves off the counter and went into the cold room. For a moment Henry stood looking at the tall, white freezer and then he took the Time Twister out of his pocket. Charlie caught a glimpse of sparkling light in Henry's hand and he looked away quickly. But the light was reflected on the low ceiling, and through a mist of swirling colors Charlie could make out a city of dazzling golden domes, and then a range of snow-clad mountains. The snow became a forest, and the trees turned into the crashing green waves of a mighty sea. And then a river of glass swept beneath the bluest sky Charlie had ever seen.

Mesmerized by the amazing world above him, Charlie felt himself being drawn toward it. When his feet began to slide out from under him, he tore his gaze away from the ceiling, but he was too late to see his cousin step into the freezer. Henry had already disappeared.

Charlie stared at the tall white door. How long should he wait? He didn't want to ruin Henry's chances, but what if he should freeze to death before the Time Twister did its work. He closed his eyes and slowly counted to ten. Then, seizing the freezer door, he pulled.

The door wouldn't open. Charlie pulled again. He put both hands on the handle, braced himself, and tugged with all his might. The freezer door was stuck fast. Either it was ice, or some tremendous force inside the freezer was holding the door shut.

Charlie tried again. He banged on the freezer, he twisted, pulled, had a short rest, and then tried again. "Henry! Henry!" he called, pummeling the door.

"And what d'you think you're doing, Charlie Bone?"

Charlie whirled around to see Cook standing in the doorway.

"I . . . I . . . ," Charlie began. "Cook, there's a boy in the freezer. I don't know if he's dead or . . . or gone. You see he might've, but I've got to know . . ."

"Lord save us," cried Cook, almost knocking Charlie off his feet as she charged at the freezer.

With one mighty heave, she pulled open the door.

Henry was crouched at the bottom, under a huge frozen carcass. His face was blue and his hair and cape were covered in frost.

"Heaven's above!" exclaimed Cook as she pulled Henry out of the freezer.

He was cold and stiff, but Charlie was relieved to hear him give a small groan as Cook gathered him into her arms.

"Follow me, Charlie Bone," she commanded. "You'd better tell me what all this is about."

Cook crashed her way through the door, across the kitchen, and into what started out as a broom closet, but ended up being a long, softly lit corridor. Even though she was carrying Henry, Cook walked so fast, Charlie found it hard to keep up with her.

At the end of the corridor, several steps led down to another small closet and this opened into one of the coziest places Charlie had ever seen. Bright pictures hung all around the room, from just beneath the very low ceiling, almost to the floor. The chairs looked old and soft, and a gleaming ancient dresser had been filled with gold patterned cups and plates. In a deep alcove there was a large black stove; a kettle boiled on the top, while bright coals flickered in a window at the bottom. They filled the room with a warm, glowing light.

Cook laid Henry in a large armchair beside the stove and began to rub his hands. As she did this, Henry's stiff fingers relaxed and the Time Twister dropped to the floor.

"What's that?" said Cook.

"It's er . . . um . . . a Time Twister," said Charlie.

"Huh!" grunted Cook, not at all surprised. "I might have known. It always causes trouble. Put it in that red mug on the dresser. But don't look at it."

"I won't," said Charlie. He picked up the shining marble and dropped it into the mug. Vivid colors spun and twisted inside the mug, and Charlie was tempted to wait and see what sort of picture they would make.

"Don't look, Charlie!" Cook warned again.

"No, no. I won't." Charlie stepped away from the dresser.

Cook continued to rub Henry's fingers, but he didn't stir or make a sound. She looked back at

Charlie and said, "You stupid boy. You of all people, Charlie Bone. What were you thinking of?"

"I was trying to help," whispered Charlie.

"Help? Help? Murder more like," Cook said coldly.

"No, no, I didn't . . ."

"Who is this boy?"

It took Charlie a few seconds to remember his exact relationship to Henry. Very slowly he said, "He's my great-great uncle Henry, I think. But I just call him cousin. He came from 1916."

"And the Time Twister's responsible, I presume."

"Yes, poor Henry's come a long way. I mean he's come from a long time away."

"I'll say," said Cook. "Get my bathrobe." She nodded at a large red garment lying over a chair.

Charlie brought it to her.

"Now, take off this poor boy's cape."

Cook gently lifted Henry out of the chair, while Charlie took off the frost-covered cape. On Cook's instructions he wrapped his cousin in the big red bathrobe, but still Henry showed no sign of life.

Cook felt the frozen boy's pulse, shook her head, and then put her ear to his heart. "Something," she murmured. "Something there."

Charlie felt terrible. He sank into a chair and covered his face with his hands.

"All's not lost," said Cook. "They're here."

Charlie heard a faint meowing above his head. He looked up to see a skylight of small green glass panes. Peering through the glass were three cats with glowing yellow eyes.

"The flames," breathed Charlie.

"Yes, the flames. Look out, Charlie."

Charlie jumped out of the chair as Cook came toward him. She climbed on the chair and opened the skylight. A blast of cold air and a shower of snow brought one of the cats sliding down onto the back of the chair. He was a handsome creature with deep copper-colored fur.

"Aries!" said Charlie.

The cat gave a long, welcoming meow.

"You know these creatures, then?" said Cook, as an

orange cat, and then a yellow, followed Aries. They landed either side of him and greeted Charlie with loud purring voices.

"Leo and Sagittarius," said Charlie. "Yes, I know the flames. And I think I know what they're going to do."

The three cats leaped down from the chair and ran over to Henry. Charlie could hear the crackle of tiny flames as the cats rubbed their heads against the red bathrobe. They began to circle the chair where Henry's blue-tinged face rested on a faded cushion. Cook closed the skylight and stepped off the chair.

"They saved my friend's dog," Charlie told Cook. "And I think they've saved a lot of people. But I can't understand how they know when they're needed."

"Sixth sense," said Cook. "Now, hush. Let them do their work."

Charlie sank into a chair opposite Henry. Already he could feel the heat from the cats as they ran around the frozen boy. Soon all Charlie could see was a bright golden red streak circling Henry's chair.

Charlie yawned. His head drooped and his eyes closed. In a few minutes he had drifted off to sleep.

When he woke up, Henry, still wearing the red bathrobe, was sitting up and smiling at him. He held a mug of something steamy and sweet smelling.

"Hello again, Charlie!" said Henry.

Charlie blinked and rubbed his eyes. "I'm sorry, Henry," he said. "It didn't work, did it? I tried to get you out but something, I don't know what, it seemed to be fighting me."

Henry nodded. "I'm going to stay here with Cook," he said. "No one knows about this room, so I'll be safe until we can decide what to do next."

Cook was bustling around the stove. She took a tray of small cakes out of the oven and shook them onto a plate. "Take one of these," she said, offering the cakes to Charlie, "and then I think you'd better creep off back to bed."

"Thanks!" Charlie took a cake and bit into it. It was delicious. "Very good," he said quietly.

"It wasn't your fault, Charlie," said Cook, guessing Charlie's thoughts. "I shouldn't have been so quick to blame you. You of all people."

"Why d'you keep saying that?" asked Charlie. "Me of all people. What d'you mean?"

"I'll tell you another time."

Charlie looked up at Cook. For a moment he glimpsed another face behind Cook's lined, worn features; a face that was young and beautiful. He would have liked to hold the moment for a long time. He had never felt as warm and safe as he did now, sitting in Cook's wide shadow, with the glowing room behind her, the humming of the stove, and the deep contented purring of the three cats, as they sipped a bowl of milk before the fire.

"Who are you?" he asked Cook.

"Me?" She smiled. "I'm the lodestone of the house. I keep you all from flying off into the dark."

"But your name?"

"Another time."

"Can I come back tomorrow?" asked Charlie. He wanted to know so much.

"Better not," said Cook. "Wait a while. Certain persons will be watching you. And not just persons." She nodded at a fat form that had appeared in the shadows at the back of the room.

Blessed waddled into the light. It was obvious that he wanted to sit in front of the stove, but the three cats gave warning growls and the old dog retreated.

"I've seen him before," exclaimed Henry. "He's very old, isn't he?"

"He's a spy," said Cook. "So if you've seen him, he's already told someone about you. Charlie Bone, you'd better go back now. Someone might have noticed your bed's empty."

Charlie swallowed the last of his cake and said good night to his cousin. Then he followed Cook through the labyrinth of closets and passages that led to the hall. Here, Cook took a small flashlight from her pocket and gave it to Charlie.

"It has a good light," she said. "Off you go now. And don't tell anyone about tonight. And I mean 'anyone.'"

"My best friend already knows about Henry."

Cook shook her head. "Can't be helped, I suppose. But the fewer people know about Henry, the better."

"OK. I promise I won't tell anyone where he is."

Cook watched Charlie cross the hall and begin to mount the stairs. She gave him a quick wave and walked speedily back to her room.

She was pleased to see that Henry Yewbeam had fallen into a deep untroubled sleep. Taking the empty mug out of his warm hand, she replaced it on the dresser. The three cats had finished their milk and were looking at her expectantly, so she stepped onto the chair beneath the skylight and opened it once more.

The flames ran to the chair, jumped up onto the back, and from there leaped out through the skylight.

"Thank you, my dears," called Cook. She fastened the skylight and stepped off the chair.

"Now for you," she said to the fat dog that had moved into his favorite place before the stove.

"I know what you are," Cook said to Blessed, "but you've been a good boy up to now and kept my room secret even from your friend Billy Raven."

Blessed looked at Cook and whined softly.

"Now, listen. Don't you dare tell that friend of yours about this boy." She pointed to Henry asleep in the big armchair.

Blessed stared at Cook with sad brown eyes. Although he didn't speak his language, he knew her well enough to understand exactly what she was saying.

"If you give the game away, there'll be no more of Cook's chops. No more bed by the stove, or walks in the park. You'll be out on your ear, for you're of no use to me, you lazy lump of lard. I've mothered you only out of the goodness of my heart." She wagged a finger at him. "Are we clear about this?"

Blessed grunted and heaved himself into his basket. He knew when he was well off.

THE BLACK GLOVE

Cook's flashlight was unusual. Although the beam wasn't very bright, it lit the way ahead in such a way that Charlie could see details that he'd never noticed before. In fact some of the things he passed were definitely different.

For instance, there was a row of paintings along the entire length of a wall beside one of the staircases. There was a pair of man-sized boots outside a door, and a pair of satin shoes outside another. On one of the landings, a tall plant grew in a blue china pot, and ivy trailed out of a large brass urn.

"That wasn't there," muttered Charlie.

In spite of these small changes it was easy for Charlie to find his way back. However, he had only taken a few paces down the passage to his dormitory, when a narrow beam of brilliant light almost blinded him. Instinctively, he turned off Cook's flashlight and waited, hardly daring to breathe.

The blinding light went out. Whoever stood at the other end of the passage was waiting to see what Charlie would do. Charlie cautiously felt his way along the wall. He knew his door was the second on his left. He passed the first door and stopped, listening intently for footsteps. Hearing nothing, he made a rush for his door and ran straight into a body.

Charlie gasped. At the same time the body squeaked, "Ouch! You're standing on my foot."

"Is that you, Billy?" whispered Charlie.

"What if it is?"

"Don't be silly. It was just a question." Charlie turned on his flashlight.

Billy Raven blinked up at him. He had a large blob of chocolate on his chin. "Where've you been?" he asked Charlie.

"Where've you been?" said Charlie, lowering Cook's flashlight.

Billy didn't answer.

"I just popped out to the toilet," said Charlie. "I can

see you've been to see someone who had a bit of chocolate to spare."

"It's cocoa, actually," said Billy. "And the toilet isn't down there, it's the other way."

"I just missed it in the dark," said Charlie.

Billy stared at him suspiciously, then he pushed past Charlie and went into the dormitory. Charlie followed and crept over to his bed. He heard a soft rustling as Billy burrowed under the covers and then there was silence.

Charlie wondered who had been giving Billy cocoa in the middle of the night. Was it a reward for spying? Blessed had seen Henry in Cook's room, and Billy could understand the old dog's language. So before long the person who was supplying Billy with cocoa would know about Henry. Charlie was too tired to wrestle with the problem anymore. Somehow he would have to find a way to warn Cook.

• • •

The next morning, something extraordinary happened, and Charlie's worries about Henry were temporarily forgotten.

Breakfast was almost over when a violent gust of wind came howling down the passage to the dining hall. The doors flew open and the wind roared into the room, sending cups and plates, spoons and knives, spinning off the tables. There were shrieks of terror as sharp pieces of cutlery came zooming through the air. Most of the children pulled their hoods over their heads and ducked under the tables.

Charlie and Fidelio met Olivia crawling behind one of the benches.

"What's going on?" cried Charlie.

"I reckon it's one of Tancred's storms," shouted Olivia. "I heard he had a terrible argument with Lysander last night."

"Tancred? I'd better try and get to him," said Charlie.

"Why? What can you do? It's happened before, you

know." Fidelio tugged Charlie's sleeve. "Just leave him to calm down."

"No. I must see him." Charlie couldn't explain why he suddenly had an overpowering need to reach Tancred. Tancred had helped to save him when he was trapped in the ruin and Charlie felt he must at least try to calm him down.

Holding his hood firmly over his head, Charlie crawled to the open door, and then out into the windy passage. The force of Tancred's anger was amazing. Charlie guessed a ninety mile an hour gale was blowing toward him. His nose and mouth were soon full of dust, and the portraits that had been hanging on the walls kept flying off and whirling into his path. Occasionally the sharp corner of a frame whacked his head, or caught the hand that was shielding his face.

Charlie gritted his teeth and kept going. He saw two figures crawling in front of him. Their capes billowed above them like angry purple clouds.

Manfred and Asa, thought Charlie.

The race to reach Tancred was now even more

critical. He was likely to be hypnotized if Manfred got to him first, and not just for a few minutes. Tancred might be taken by surprise. Before he knew it, he would be lost — put to sleep, like Emma Tolly had been. Her sleep had lasted for eight years.

As Charlie emerged into the hall he could see Manfred and Asa clinging to pieces of furniture. The handle of an oak chest suddenly came off in Asa's hand, and he slid across the floor with a howl of surprise. Manfred had been more successful. His arms were wrapped around the newel post at the bottom of the stairs.

Charlie didn't know how he could stop himself from being blown into the wall. Tancred's furious energy filled every space in the hall. Chairs were tumbling about like matchsticks. As he raised his head, he saw Tancred standing in front of the huge doors leading to the outside world. His blond hair was standing up like a stiff, sparkling brush. A few meters behind him, Dr. Bloor, bent double, was shouting into the wind.

"Tancred Torsson, calm down. Come away from those doors. Immediately!"

Tancred took not the slightest notice. Indeed, Dr. Bloor's voice was almost drowned by the noise.

All at once, Manfred let go of the newel post and began to crawl across the floor toward Tancred.

Charlie knew it was no use shouting a warning. Tancred would never have heard him.

Manfred had almost reached the stormy boy, when Tancred wheeled around and, seeing Manfred, let loose such a fierce bolt of electricity, the head boy was sent sprawling away from him. At the same time, the massive doors cracked down the middle and, with a loud splintering sound, they flew open.

Tancred turned and marched out, taking his stormy power with him.

Dr. Bloor rushed to close the doors, but they were so badly cracked it was impossible to lock them. The big key Dr. Bloor always carried with him clicked uselessly in the lock.

"Bring the chest," he ordered, waving at Manfred and Asa.

As the two boys pushed the heavy chest across the hall, Charlie got to his feet. The floor was littered with debris. It was incredible how much hidden garbage Tancred's storm had drawn out of the shadowy corners in the hall.

Lying at Charlie's feet was a black leather glove and, almost without thinking, he picked it up and put it in his pocket.

Manfred and Asa gave the big chest a final shove, and it came to rest in front of the doors.

"That'll do for now," said Dr. Bloor. "I'll have to get Weedon to fix it. We don't want anyone else escaping."

It makes this place sound like a prison, thought Charlie.

Some of the other children were peering cautiously into the hall, but it was Charlie whom Manfred saw first.

"Charlie Bone, what are you doing here?" shouted the head boy.

"I'm trying to get to assembly," said Charlie.

Manfred could hardly quarrel with that. "Get moving then," he said irritably.

Fidelio rushed across the hall and caught up with Charlie just as he was going into the blue coatroom.

"What about that?" whispered Fidelio. "It was practically a hurricane."

In all the excitement many of the children behind them had forgotten the rule of silence.

They were immediately given detention and then dispatched to the kitchen to fetch brooms and dustpans.

"Olivia won't be lonely on Saturday," said Fidelio. "I heard at least six people get detention."

Charlie sat on one of the benches and began to pick off the bits of dust and garbage that clung to his cloak. A great weariness stole over him, and he slumped back against the wall.

"What's up, Charlie?" said Fidelio. "You look done in."

"I wish Tancred hadn't gone," Charlie murmured. "We've got to get him back."

"Why?"

"I can't explain. He helped me once, and now he's gone. Suppose he's expelled?"

"He won't be," said Fidelio confidently. "The endowed are never expelled. Sooner or later he'll calm down and come back."

"I hope it's sooner," muttered Charlie. He wasn't mistaken. Without Tancred there was something definitely amiss.

That night Charlie was the first to reach the King's room with his homework. Gabriel came in a few seconds later. He looked ill at ease. Carefully placing his books beside Charlie's, he said, "Something's wrong."

"It's Tancred, isn't it?" said Charlie. "I feel sort of unbalanced."

"Me, too," said Gabriel. "We've got to get him back. Will you come with me over the weekend, Charlie?"

"To Tancred's house?"

Gabriel nodded. "It's not far from where I live. But it's a pretty stormy place. They call it Thunder House."

"Does anyone else in his family have an — er — weather talent?" asked Charlie.

"I'll say. His dad's really turbulent."

"Oh." Charlie wasn't sure if he was looking forward to this mission.

"Where on earth is everyone else?" muttered Gabriel. "They're ten minutes late. Manfred's nearly always here first."

Lysander walked into the King's room clutching a pile of sketches. His usually cheerful face looked troubled and confused. "I thought I was late," he said. "Where's everyone else?"

Charlie shrugged. "They've all disappeared — like Tancred." He immediately regretted his words because Lysander looked even more depressed.

"What went on between you two?" Gabriel asked Lysander.

"It was a misunderstanding," muttered Lysander. "Manfred's fault. He asked if Tancred had made it warmer just for me. Tancred shouted that it was nothing to do with him, and I said, 'Don't get upset, Tanc, I'm really grateful.'"

"But Tancred doesn't do temperature, right?" said Gabriel.

"Too right." Lysander slumped in his chair. "And he's so touchy about things like that, he hit the roof. I forgot, you see. He's my best friend and I forgot. You know I think Manfred made me forget. He didn't exactly hypnotize me, but he was staring at me in a funny way. I was sort of disabled."

"We're going up to the Thunder House on Saturday," said Gabriel. "Come with us. He's more likely to listen to you."

"Don't know about that," said Lysander glumly. "But sure, I'll come."

The three boys sat in gloomy silence for a while, and then, because there didn't seem anything better to do, Charlie brought the black glove out of his pocket. He laid it on the table saying, "I found this in the hall, when Tancred had gone."

"It's not Tanc's," said Lysander. "Probably some old thing that's been lying under a closet for years."

The glove was made of very soft leather. The fingers were long and narrow, and there was an opening at the wrist, with four small leather buttons on one side, and four neat holes on the other.

Gabriel frowned at the glove. He stretched out his hand. Charlie found himself crying, "Don't, Gabriel!"

But it was too late. Gabriel had pulled the glove on to his left hand. His face suddenly creased with pain and he let out a terrible moan.

Charlie reached out to pull off the glove, but Gabriel fell forward, his head crashing onto the table.

"He's fainted," cried Lysander. "What's going on?"

"It's the glove. You know Gabriel's gift. He can feel what happened to the people who wore things before him."

"The owner of that glove must've been hurt pretty badly," said Lysander. He touched Gabriel's head. "He's gone cold."

"Gabriel! Gabriel, wake up!" cried Charlie. He tried

to pull the glove off Gabriel's hand but it was stuck fast.

Gabriel turned his head. "My hand! Oooo, my hand," he groaned.

"It's the glove," Charlie told him. "I can't get it off you."

"Oooow!" Gabriel sat up and began to tear at the glove with his right hand. "My fingers are broken. Help! Help, someone!"

Charlie tugged the fingers of the glove while Lysander tried to peel it away from Gabriel's wrist. It was no use. Gabriel was now panting heavily. Between small grunts of pain, he said, "She put her fingers on the door and he slammed it."

"Who?" asked Charlie. "Who slammed it?"

"A woman, I think. Yes, a woman. She was trying to get out, and she was shaking her head like she wouldn't do what they wanted." Gabriel gave another moan. "But the boy, I think it was Manfred, he slammed the door and pushed and pushed until he crushed her fingers. Oooow. Oooh! Manfred it is but he's smaller. Ooow!" Gabriel's head fell forward again.

At that moment there was a tap on the door and Olivia looked in. "There you are," she said. "Fidelio sent me to look for you. He couldn't get away because he's in the front row."

"Front row?" said Charlie.

"Don't tell me you all forgot," said Olivia. "There's a concert in the theater tonight. What's wrong with Gabriel?"

"He's not well," said Lysander.

"I can see that, but you'd better get him to the theater quickly if you don't want detention."

"Gabriel, can you walk?" Lysander asked gently.

Gabriel moaned. "If I have to."

"Come on, then. Charlie, help me!"

Lysander pulled the stricken boy upright, and putting Gabriel's arm around his shoulders, clutched him by the waist. Charlie did the same. He got the arm with the glove on it, and it worried him to see how limp and crushed Gabriel's left hand looked.

"I'd better go ahead and make sure there are three seats in the back for you." Olivia rushed off.

By the time the three boys had staggered into the dark theater, the concert had begun.

"You'll have to manage on your own for a bit," Lysander whispered to Gabriel.

"Uh!" Gabriel grunted.

Olivia had been as good as her word and there were three empty seats waiting for them at the back of the auditorium. Charlie pulled the sleeve of Gabriel's cape over the black glove, and helped Lysander maneuver him into a seat.

Unfortunately, Dr. Saltweather saw the boys come in late. He frowned at them and shook his head, then turned his attention back to the stage. Dr. Bloor was making a speech about music, and it soon became clear that he was describing the life and work of the other man on the stage: Mr. Albert Tuccini.

Behind Dr. Bloor a man with a deep tan sat at a grand piano. He had brown curly hair and a rather morose expression. His arms were folded across his chest and he occasionally glanced at the red velvet curtains at the back of the stage.

Dr. Bloor came to the end of his speech. The audience clapped enthusiastically. Albert Tuccini swiveled around to face the piano and his long fingers pounced on the keys.

Gabriel was a pianist himself, and he listened intently to the complicated chords that Albert Tuccini rung out of the piano. Gradually, his hard breathing eased, he forgot the pain in his fingers and managed to enjoy the music.

The pianist's second piece seemed familiar to Charlie. But he couldn't remember where he had heard it before. A memory was buried at the back of his mind. Far, far back. Could it have been the music his father played? He began to nod off. And then he was asleep and dreaming. He dreamed of a room Grandma Bone had described to him. A white room, with pale curtains at the long windows. A room empty of everything except Lyell, his father, and a grand piano. But he couldn't see his father's face. He didn't even know what he looked like. Grandma Bone had hidden or destroyed every photo of her only son.

"Charlie, wake up!" Gabriel was nudging his arm.

Charlie opened his eyes. The lights were on in the auditorium and children were moving up the aisles toward the exit doors. The stage was empty.

"How long have you been asleep?" asked Gabriel.

"Don't know," Charlie murmured. "Most of the time, I think." He dragged himself out of his seat.

Lysander left the theater with them, but then he had to get to his own dormitory. "Are you going to be OK?" he asked Gabriel before he parted from them on the landing.

"I'll live," said Gabriel, grinning.

"We'll have another try at getting that glove off," said Charlie, who was feeling more awake.

In the dormitory, Charlie told Fidelio what had happened and they spent several minutes trying to tug the glove off Gabriel's hand. It was impossible. Gabriel went to the bathroom and tried soap and water but the glove clung even tighter. He came back and sat on the edge of his bed. "Poor woman," he murmured. "She must have broken all her fingers."

"Do you know who she was?" asked Charlie.

"Is," said Gabriel. "She's still here. I've seen her. It's the dark lady from the tower. I used to think she was a ghost, but she isn't. She's just sort of useless and alone."

Billy Raven had crept up behind them. He stared at the black glove on Gabriel's hand. "What's that?" he asked.

"What does it look like?" said Fidelio.

"A glove. Why are you wearing one glove, Gabriel?"

Gabriel sighed. "Because I can't get it off, that's why."

Billy frowned. He didn't ask any more questions, but wandered back to his bed with a thoughtful expression.

Charlie and Fidelio made one more attempt to pry the glove off Gabriel's hand, but the water had made it cling like a second skin.

"It's no use, guys," sighed Gabriel. "I'll just have to sleep with it on. Maybe it'll come off when it's dried out." He yawned. "I'm so tired, nothing will keep me awake tonight."

Gabriel was right. He fell asleep almost as soon as he got into bed. But while he slept his dreams became nightmares, and he moaned with pain as he tossed and turned in his bed.

Gabriel made so much noise Charlie couldn't sleep a wink. The other boys woke up, too. Damian Smerk threw his pillow at the moaning boy, but it didn't wake him. He was buried deep in his troubled sleep.

The next night, Charlie and Fidelio tried, once again, to pull off the clinging black glove, but now it had shrunk. It wouldn't even peel away at the wrist. Gabriel's hand hung uselessly at his side. He couldn't even feel his fingers, he said.

They didn't know what to do. Telling Matron was out of the question. Charlie had an idea. After lights out he leaned close to Gabriel's bed and whispered, "I know someone who can help."

"Who?"

"Someone who lives behind the kitchens. We'll have to wait till after midnight, though."

"Wake me up when it's time to go," said Gabriel.

"OK."

Charlie had promised Cook that he wouldn't tell anyone where Henry was hiding. But that wasn't quite the same as taking someone to her secret room. Besides, this was an emergency.

"YOU CAN'T GO BACK!"

At five minutes past midnight, Billy Raven left the dormitory. Charlie wondered if he could get Gabriel down to Cook's room and back before Billy returned.

"Gabriel," he whispered, shaking Gabriel's shoulder. "Wake up! It's time to go!"

Gabriel dragged himself out of bed and fumbled with his pajamas. "Ready!" he murmured.

Charlie grabbed his arm and led him out of the dormitory. Only then did he turn on Cook's flashlight. Its soft light illuminated every tiny detail of the long corridor.

"Wow," said Gabriel. "That's impressive."

"Follow me," Charlie whispered.

He began to jog, as quietly as he could, while behind him Gabriel floundered and tripped in his badly fitting slippers.

By the time Charlie had found his way to Cook's closet entrance, Gabriel looked exhausted. The fingers on his left hand had begun to throb again, and the pain made him ache all over.

Charlie didn't like to burst in on Cook unannounced, so he knocked politely on the closet door.

There was a shuffling noise behind the door and then it was opened, just a crack.

"Shoot me," said Cook, peering out at Charlie. "What are you doing here?"

"I'm sorry, Cook," said Charlie. "But . . ."

Behind him, Gabriel gave a low moan.

Cook opened the door a little wider. She was wearing her red bathrobe. "Shivering cats," she said. "Who on earth is this?"

"Gabriel Silk," Charlie told her. "He's had a sort of accident with a glove."

"Tch! Tch! You'd better come in."

Charlie led his friend through the closet and Gabriel looked around Cook's secret room in amazement. "What a lovely place," he said.

Cook made him sit down and examined his gloved hand, while Charlie told her how he'd found the glove, and how poor Gabriel had an unfortunate talent for experiencing other people's feelings, when he wore their clothes.

"Hm," muttered Cook. "That's Dorothy's glove."

"Dorothy's?" said Charlie.

"It's the dark lady's," said Gabriel. "She haunts the music tower. I've seen her. She had her fingers broken in a door."

Cook nodded. "That's what you call her, do you? The dark lady. Well, I'll have you know that the dark lady is Mrs. Bloor."

"What? Manfred's mother?" said Charlie. "I thought she was — well, dead."

"So do most people," said Cook. "Poor thing. She lives a terrible half-life. When Manfred crushed her fingers, she gave up. Faded away, so to speak. She comes down to my little room, now and again, and we talk. But she's a sad, sad creature."

"Too right she is," said Gabriel. "This glove makes me feel so miserable I could do myself in."

"Now then, we'll have none of that talk," Cook said

sternly. "We'll have that glove off you in no time. Mind you, the only person who can do it is the owner of the glove."

"Why's that?" asked Charlie.

"It's just the way it is. Musician's hands are very special. There's a lot of feeling in that glove, and I can see that it's really made itself at home on your skin, Gabriel."

"I'd rather not lose any skin, if you don't mind," said Gabriel. "I'm a bit squeamish."

"Endowed children were a lot more stoical in my day," Cook remarked as she ambled across the room. "I'll fetch Dorothy." She opened the door of a small corner closet and the boys caught sight of a narrow stairway before Cook squeezed herself into the closet and closed the door.

They heard the soft tap of footsteps behind the wall, and then over their heads. For a plump person Cook was surprisingly light-footed.

"What a place," Gabriel murmured, gazing around at the bright pictures and gleaming antique furniture.

"You'd never guess that all this was right under that gloomy old building."

"Never," agreed Charlie. "Mind you, I think part of it must be under the city. You can see the sky through that window." He nodded at the small window in the ceiling.

Gabriel turned to look at the skylight. "So what's up there?" he said.

Charlie shrugged. "Who knows? Someone's garden. A road." He was wondering what had happened to Henry. Had Cook sent him back through time? Had he run away?

Soft footfalls overhead told them that Cook was returning with someone who walked with a peculiar shuffling sound.

A few moments later, the door to the closet opened, and Cook came in, followed by a small woman in a long, shapeless, black dress. A dark shawl covered her head so her face could hardly be seen; she walked with her head bent as though she were searching the ground.

"Now, Dorothy, you sit here, dear!" Cook pushed a chair close to Gabriel's. "This is Gabriel, and he seems to have gotten himself stuck into your glove."

Dorothy looked at Gabriel's limp hand, and then she stared at Charlie. Her shawl fell to her shoulders, revealing long gray hair and a pale face with two gray eyes in deep dark sockets. "And who is this?" she asked in a tiny voice.

"I'm Charlie Bone," said Charlie. "Pleased to meet you, Mrs. Bloor."

"Oh?" said the faint little voice. "So you're Charlie. I know . . . I knew . . ."

Mrs. Bloor appeared to have forgotten what she knew, or had known, for she turned her attention back to Gabriel and said, "Poor boy. You play the piano, don't you? I like to listen. I'll do my best for you, but I can only use one of my hands. The other has been cursed, you see."

The boys gasped in horror.

"Who cursed you?" breathed Charlie.

Mrs. Bloor just shook her head. With her right

hand she began to peel the leather glove away from Gabriel's wrist. It took a long time, and after a while, in a light trembling voice, Mrs. Bloor began to tell them her story.

Dorothy de Vere had been a very talented violinist. Soon after she inherited a large fortune from her aunt, Dr. Harold Bloor had courted her. They were married within a year and Dorothy gave him half her fortune. And then her troubles began. Her son, Manfred, hated all forms of music. He screamed when she picked up her violin. She only dared play in a room where no one could hear her. Old Ezekiel Bloor demanded that she hand over the rest of her fortune. She refused. On her father's advice she had put it in a secret bank account in Switzerland. Nothing would make her hand it over. She was deeply unhappy in the gloomy academy and planned to leave it.

"They did terrible things to people," she murmured, "and I couldn't stand it. One day, one wild, stormy day . . ." Her voice grew so faint they couldn't hear it, and then she stopped altogether, and it was

Cook who told them what had happened. There was a violent thunderstorm and hoping the noise would cover the sound of her departure, Dorothy had packed her bag.

"She had been about to leave her room, when Manfred looked in. 'You can't go,' he had snarled. 'We won't let you. Not until you've signed over the money.'

"Once again, Dorothy had refused. Manfred said he'd lock her in her room. Dorothy put her hand on the doorframe to stop him, and he slammed the door — crack — on her fingers."

Mrs. Bloor's head drooped. She shuddered. "Tell them, tell them," she murmured. "Tell Charlie Bone."

"She fainted, poor thing," Cook went on. "When she came to, she was on her bed. Old Ezekiel was sitting beside her. He'd soaked her injured fingers in one of his vile potions. He told her she'd never play her violin again. Never leave here. As far as they were concerned, she didn't exist, so she might as well give them the money."

"But I didn't," whispered Dorothy. "I never will." She had peeled the glove back, so that Gabriel's fingers could now be seen. With a light tug, she pulled it right off.

"Phew!" said Gabriel, shaking his hand. "It feels OK. It really does. Thanks!"

"I'm glad, so glad," murmured Mrs. Bloor.

Charlie was relieved but anxious to get back to the dormitory before Billy. "I think we'd better go now," he said. "But, Cook, where's — you know who?"

"Fast asleep," said Cook.

Charlie looked around the room. There was no sign of a bed.

Cook laughed. "I have other rooms," she said, "and I've got a very nice bathroom and toilet, but I'm not showing you around tonight. Off you go, both of you."

"But I'll be going home tomorrow," said Charlie. "How am I going to get Henry out?"

"I'm afraid there won't be a chance," said Cook. "And perhaps it's better that those Yewbeam sisters don't see him. We'll have to have a good long think about Henry's future."

She seemed to know a lot about Charlie's family.

Charlie and Gabriel said good night to the two women and, before they left, Gabriel did something rather surprising. He seized Mrs. Bloor's injured hand and kissed it. Mrs. Bloor smiled for the first time that night. It changed her face completely.

Charlie turned away in embarrassment. Gabriel really was a most peculiar person. "By the way," he said to Cook, "the flashlight you gave me — it's magic or something, isn't it? It showed me things I've never seen before."

"That was you, Charlie, as well as the flashlight. And there'll be more."

As the boys made their way back to the dormitory, Gabriel asked, "Who is this mysterious Henry?"

In a deep whisper, Charlie told the amazed Gabriel about Henry and the Time Twister. He knew he could trust him.

They reached the dormitory without any mishaps

and, luckily, just a few minutes before Billy Raven came back from his midnight ramble.

In the morning Gabriel handed Charlie a slip of paper. "It's my address," he said. "Don't forget we're going to the Thunder House to see Tancred."

Charlie showed the paper to Fidelio. "D'you want to come?" he asked.

"Hail Road, The Heights," said Fidelio, reading the address. "How are we going to get there?"

"I'll think of something," said Charlie.

He spent the rest of the day trying to get a message to his cousin before the weekend. Twice Manfred found him hovering outside the cafeterias. The second time he threatened Charlie with detention, and though Charlie was tempted to chance it, he knew Tancred's problem was more urgent. The stormy boy's absence was having a strange effect, especially in the King's room. In the King's room the empty seat next to Lysander was like a cold, airless hole. It stole their energy and made some of the endowed children shiver. They lost their appetites and couldn't think straight. This happened to Charlie, Lysander, and Gabriel. Even Emma complained that she felt ill.

Manfred, Asa, and Zelda, and even Billy Raven, sailed through their homework and bounced their way to meals and lessons with energy and enthusiasm.

Something had to be done.

At the end of the day as everyone trooped out through the main doors, Charlie caught sight of Olivia and Bindi on the stairs. He gave them a guilty wave, but Olivia was looking very excited. He hoped she wouldn't do anything too dangerous.

The blue bus dropped Charlie off at the top of Filbert Street and, as he made his way to number nine, Benjamin and Runner Bean came rushing up to greet him.

"It's been such a boring week," sighed Benjamin. "What did you do?"

As they walked home together, Charlie told Benjamin everything that had happened.

"You lead a very interesting life, Charlie," Benjamin commented, "but I think I'd rather be me."

"I don't have a choice," said Charlie. "I've just got to do the best I can to survive it all."

The front door opened before he'd had time to ring the bell, and Maisie pulled him inside with a violent tug. "Tea's ready," she said, dragging him toward the kitchen, "all your favorites. Yours, too, Benjamin. Come along. And I've got a nice bone for Runner Bean."

The boys had just sat down to enjoy Maisie's wonderful spread when Grandma Bone walked in. You could tell right away that she was going to spoil Charlie's appetite.

"What's this?" she said, slamming the photo of Henry beside Charlie's plate.

"An old photo," said Charlie. Grandma Bone had evidently been snooping in Uncle Paton's room.

"And what happened to it?" she demanded.

"It fell off the wall when you slammed the door."

That was the wrong thing to have said to his grandmother.

"I slammed the door? Me? You broke the glass, Charlie Bone, and you didn't confess."

"He brought it straight in here," said Maisie hotly. "And it wasn't his fault."

"It was my frame, my glass," said Grandma Bone. "I should have been told. But let that pass. It's this boy I'm interested in." She planted a bony finger on Henry's face. "You've seen him, haven't you?"

"Of course I haven't," said Charlie. "That photo's ancient. He must be a hundred years old."

Benjamin was digging into a plate of ham sandwiches. He kept his head well down, not daring to look at Charlie.

"I have it on good authority that Henry Yewbeam is about again," Grandma Bone said in a chilly voice, "and that you have seen him."

So the dog has told Billy, thought Charlie. And Billy has passed on the news, to Grandma's sister, Matron Yewbeam, or to Manfred.

"You're being silly, Grizelda," said Maisie. "Charlie's been locked away in that horrible old academy all week. How could he have seen the fellow, unless he was a ghost, of course."

"Keep your nose out of this!" barked Grandma Bone.

"And you keep your nose out of Charlie's tea," Maisie shouted, rolling up her sleeves.

Arguments at number nine nearly always started this way. The pattern was familiar to Charlie. He just wished it hadn't happened quite so soon after he'd come home. He followed Benjamin's example and grabbed a sandwich. Benjamin grinned at Charlie across the table, and Charlie grimaced back. They managed to get quite a lot of food inside themselves while the grandmas insulted each other over their heads. Runner Bean added to the noise with long anxious howls. He hated arguments.

When the shouting match was over, Grandma Bone, shaking with fury, said, "Don't think I'm going to let this matter rest." She marched out of the kitchen, slamming the door behind her.

"Well," said Maisie. "That was fun, wasn't it?"

"I wouldn't say it was fun exactly," said Charlie. "I've had a rather tiring week."

"Grandma Bone is going crazy," grumbled Maisie. "As if you'd seen a boy who must be a hundred years old."

"Not quite a hundred," Charlie said without thinking.

"Oh?" The truth dawned on Maisie. "I see. You've had peculiar things happening to you, have you?"

"It happened to Henry, not me," said Charlie, reaching for a slice of cake.

"This is a great meal, Mrs. Jones," Benjamin said quickly.

"It's all right," said Maisie. "My lips are sealed, certainly where your other grandma is concerned."

The two boys managed to finish their tea in peace, and then went up to Charlie's room. Runner Bean came bounding after them. Grandma Bone had been so angry, she'd forgotten to remind Charlie that dogs weren't allowed in bedrooms.

When Benjamin had helped Charlie unpack his bag, the boys sat on the bed while Runner squeezed in behind them. Charlie told Benjamin of the plan to visit the Thunder House. He wondered if Benjamin's mom would take them up there.

Benjamin shook his head. "Mom's working on an important case at the moment. A really gruesome murder. She'll be out till late on Saturday. So will Dad."

Benjamin's parents were private detectives. They worked very odd hours and Benjamin often had to cook his own meals.

"I thought your mom promised to stay home a bit more often," said Charlie.

"She has," said Benjamin. "She's been at home all week, but then yesterday this case came up and it was so interesting, she just couldn't refuse it."

"Hm. I'll have to think of someone else then," said Charlie. "There's always Uncle Paton."

"But he wouldn't take us till it was dark, would he?" said Benjamin. "I don't like going up to the

Heights in the dark. Especially to a place where you might get struck by lightning or something."

Charlie had to agree. Still it was worth a chance. When Benjamin had gone home, Charlie knocked on his uncle's door.

There was no answer. Charlie wondered if his uncle had gone out. It was now very dark. At that moment, his mother came in and Charlie ran down to greet her. She'd brought a bag of moldy eggplants home with her.

Maisie was very pleased. "They're only half moldy," she said, spreading the eggplants across the kitchen table. "We'll make a nice ratathingy."

Charlie hoped she didn't mean anything with rats in it. With Maisie anything was possible. He decided he'd rather not know. "Have you seen Uncle Paton lately?" he asked.

"Very little," said his mom. "Poor Uncle Paton. He was getting very fond of Julia Ingledew, and now she has no time for him at all. She spends the whole week preparing for Emma to come home, and then devotes her entire weekend to the girl. They visit museums and castles and talk a great deal about books, apparently. She's shut poor Paton out altogether."

"That's tough," said Charlie. "So he's in right now."

Charlie went upstairs and tapped on his uncle's door again.

"What?" said an angry voice.

Charlie opened the door and looked in. The mess in his uncle's room was even worse than usual. There was also a very bad smell. Perhaps Paton had hidden a few unfinished meals under his bed.

"Can I talk to you?" asked Charlie meekly.

"If you must," murmured Paton. He was studying a book and didn't look up.

When he'd managed to reach Paton's desk without knocking anything over, Charlie said, "I've met that boy. The one in the photo. Your dad's brother."

"What?" Paton's head shot up. "Tell me more."

Charlie told him about the Time Twister and Henry's strange arrival. When he began to describe his part in the freezer experiment, however, Paton roared, "You did what?"

"He wanted to go back," said Charlie, "and I had to help him."

"You stupid, stupid boy," thundered his uncle. "People can't go back. You can't change history. Think about it! When my father was five years old, he lost his brother. It changed his life. He became an only child, grew up as an only child. All his memories are of being an only one. You can't change that now, can you?"

"No," Charlie said quickly. "I'm sorry."

His uncle hadn't finished. "Henry's parents mourned him, just as they mourned poor little Daphne. James was their only child and, as a result, he was probably spoiled. His father died and his mother left everything to him, including her lovely cottage by the sea. You can't change that, can you?"

Charlie sighed. "No," he said. And then he had an idea. "Would your father like to see Henry again?"

Paton's angry expression gradually changed. Charlie could almost see thoughts chasing each other across his uncle's face.

"Now there's a thought," said Paton as if he'd suddenly found the right one.

"So what d'you think?" asked Charlie.

"I don't think anything yet," said Paton. "You'll have to leave me to ponder."

Charlie judged that now would be the right time to ask his uncle a favor. But when he mentioned going up to the Heights to visit the Thunder House, he didn't get the answer he'd hoped for.

"Ha!" said Paton. "I'm not going anywhere near those storm people. It's useless to meddle with them when they're in a mood. I strongly advise you not to try."

Charlie began to explain how urgent it was to get Tancred back to the academy, but his uncle wouldn't listen. It was obviously going to take Paton a long time to become the brave and helpful uncle that he had once been.

"We've got to get there somehow," Charlie said desperately.

"I don't go out in daylight," snapped Paton. "You'll have to find someone else."

THE THUNDER HOUSE

Henry Yewbeam was bored. Cook's underground rooms were cozy and interesting, but Henry had explored every inch of them. He wished Charlie would come and talk to him. But Cook said Charlie had gone home for the weekend.

Cook seemed to be very busy, even on a Saturday. She had found a pair of old pajamas for Henry, and some modern-looking clothes: long trousers, black shoes, and gray socks. And she had persuaded him to exchange his warm jacket for a blue sweater. Henry found this wasn't as warm as his jacket, but at least he still had the blue cape he was wearing when he came twisting through time.

Cook had hidden the Time Twister. "I don't want you trying anything silly again," she said, wagging her finger at Henry. "You're here for good now. Thing is, what to do with you?"

Henry hadn't given up hope. There had to be a way

back to 1916, otherwise what would become of him? He didn't want to return to Bloor's, of course. But if he could just get to the right year, he would eventually reach his happy home beside the sea.

"But I'll have to go through that other world first," he said to himself. "The world in the Time Twister."

When Henry had traveled through time he'd briefly glimpsed the world of the Red King. His mother, who was a Bloor, had told him once that he was descended from this mysterious Red King.

"Some of the king's descendants have inherited a part of his magic," Grace Bloor had said. "But as far as I can tell, none of us have." And she had looked around at her family and laughed in her playful comforting way, and added, "Thank goodness!" Henry wished he could hear her laughter again.

"Charlie's got some of that magic," he said to himself.

Perhaps he could live with Charlie? That wouldn't be so bad. Charlie could teach him to use all the newfangled things, Cook had told him about: televisions, videos, computers, and other amazing things.

He'd been told that Cook would be back to give him his lunch at half-past twelve. But, according to the little clock beside Henry's bed, it was still only ten o'clock.

"More than two hours of nothing," sighed Henry.

He had an idea. Now that he was dressed like all the other boys at Bloor's, surely he could do some exploring. He had always wanted to go into the ruin, but Sir Gideon had forbidden it. Now was Henry's chance.

He tiptoed out of Cook's room, carefully closing the closet door behind him. After several more closets he found himself outside the cafeteria and running toward a loud noise that was coming from the hall. He looked in and saw a big man with a shaven head, hammering something into the main door.

Without stopping his work, the big man said, "Who might you be?"

"I'm — er — Henry," said Henry nervously.

"Henry what?"

"Er — er — Bone." Henry didn't know why he'd said Bone. He just thought it might be a bad idea to say Yewbeam.

"Don't seem very sure, do ya?" The man continued hammering.

"I'm quite sure, thank you," said Henry.

"We've got another Bone here. A real terror of a Bone."

"He's my cousin."

"I s'pose you're one of them endowed kids. Trouble-makers, all of them." The man delivered a really savage blow to the door. "Broke the door, that's what the stormy one's done, blast him!"

"Oh!" Henry continued on his way to the garden.

"Taking the dog for a walk, are ya?" said the man.

"What?" Henry increased his stride.

"The dog. Miserable beast."

Henry looked down to find Blessed panting at his

feet. "Oh, yes. Come along," he said and walked briskly to the garden door.

Once outside, Henry stopped to catch his breath. Blessed looked as nervous as he did.

"What's the matter?" said Henry. He bent down and patted the old dog's head. Blessed was very ugly, there was something so sad about his solemn, wrinkled face, Henry couldn't help feeling sorry for him.

There were four boys playing soccer in the snowy slush just ahead of them. They paid no attention to Henry and Blessed as they walked past. A huge tree had been sawn into logs in the center of the field and Henry was tempted to climb up on them, but time was precious and he had to see the ruin.

When they reached the great red walls, Henry felt very excited. The place smelled of age and danger. He imagined knights in armor scrambling over the walls, battle horses charging through the entrance, and arrows whizzing overhead. He was about to walk through the huge arched entrance, when a voice said, "You boy, come here!"

Henry turned to see two older boys marching toward him. They both wore purple capes and had grim, unfriendly faces.

"Who are you?" shouted the taller boy.

Henry plunged into the ruin. He found himself in a square courtyard with five passages leading out of it. Henry took the middle one.

He could hear the other boys murmuring behind him. Henry ran as fast as he could. The passage opened into another open courtyard. Henry ran across it and stumbled down a flight of steep stone steps. He was now in a grassy glade, ringed with headless statues. In the center of the glade, two girls in purple capes sat on a large stone tomb. One was very small and very dark, with a long black pigtail and gold-rimmed glasses. The other had a bright, healthy-looking face and amazing blue hair.

"Hello," said Henry breathlessly. "I'm er . . ."

"You're Henry, aren't you?" said the girl with blue

hair. "Charlie told me about you. They're looking for you, you know. The place was in a turmoil this morning. Manfred threw loads of music books out of the tower; he was in such a fury. I'm Olivia and this is Bindi."

"I'm very glad to meet you." Henry went to shake their hands. "How do you do?"

"You are polite," said Olivia. "I expect that comes of being old."

"Old? I suppose people would consider me to be old. But actually I only feel about eleven years."

"Me, too," said Olivia. "But then I am. We wouldn't normally be here on Saturday, but we've got detention."

There was a shout from the courtyard above them and Blessed came stumbling down the steps.

"They must have followed the dog," muttered Henry. "Two boys chased me in here. One was very tall and wore his hair like a girl."

"A ponytail," said Olivia. "That's Manfred Bloor, the head boy."

"We can't let him find you," said Bindi. "Quick, get in here."

With surprising speed, the two girls leaped off the tomb and slid back the top. Henry stared into the dark gap. The inside of the tomb smelled of mildew and decomposing things.

"Go on," said Olivia. "You can breathe in there. We've tried it."

Another shout from above made Henry climb into the tomb. The girls pushed back the lid, leaving a tiny gap for air. They swung themselves back onto the top just as Manfred and Asa came rushing down the steps.

"Have you see a strange boy?" said Manfred.

"We've seen Daniel Robottom," said Olivia, choosing a boy about the same size as Henry, who also wore a blue cloak. "He went that way!" She pointed to an arched entrance in one of the walls.

"Daniel Robottom? Are you sure?" Asa's yellow eyes narrowed suspiciously.

"Of course we're sure," said Bindi. "He was humming. Daniel always hums."

Manfred and Asa rushed through the arch.

There was a tap from inside the tomb.

"Shh!" hissed Olivia. "You can't come out. It's not safe yet."

She was right. A few minutes later, Manfred and Asa came running back.

"Are you positive he went that way?" said Manfred.

"Cross my heart and hope to die," Olivia said blithely. "But he went back up those steps about five minutes ago. You must have missed him."

"What's he done?" asked Bindi.

"None of your business," said Manfred.

"We're looking for someone else," added Asa.

Manfred shot him a look that said, "Keep quiet!"

"What's my great-grandfather's dog doing in here?" asked Manfred.

"We thought we'd take him for a walk," Bindi told him.

The two boys turned away, but as they mounted the steps, Asa looked back and said, "Why are you two here, anyway?"

"We came for a bit of peace." Olivia sighed. "The boys are so rough."

"I wouldn't stay in the ruin too long," Asa gave her a peculiar smile and followed Manfred up the steps.

"He gives me the creeps," muttered Bindi.

They waited another five minutes before deciding it was safe enough to let Henry out. He scrambled over the side of the tomb and dropped onto the grass. His cloak and trousers were covered in green dust and bits of cobweb clung to his hair.

"There's a huge toad in there," he said. "I'm not very fond of toads."

The girls brushed him down and then all three sat on the tomb and shared a roll that Bindi had managed to sneak out of the cafeteria.

Henry told the girls about his home beside the sea, and how he had come upon the Time Twister. Olivia recounted some of her famous mother's adventures while filming in the jungle. And then Bindi described how she had traveled to India to visit her amazing grandparents.

When the horn called them in for lunch, Olivia said, "Come with us, Henry. Stay calm. Don't look nervous, and when we reach the cafeteria you can slip through into the kitchen."

Henry had only told the girls he was hiding in the kitchen. Although he trusted the girls, he felt it would be safer if no one knew exactly where he was.

Unfortunately, when he reached the cafeteria he walked straight into a lunch lady.

"What are you doing in here?" she asked.

"M . . . m . . . message for Cook," stuttered Henry.

"She's in the cold room." The dinner lady smiled. She was young and cheerful-looking.

Henry made his way through the kitchen. Cook wasn't in the cold room. He tried to find the closet he'd come out of, but he kept blundering into broom closets and cupboards full of pots and pans. Cook's secret entrance seemed to have disappeared.

Henry was fumbling behind a row of plastic aprons when a firm hand came down on his shoulder. Henry froze.

A voice in his ear hissed, "Henry Yewbeam, where have you been?"

Henry turned to see Cook's angry red face.

"I just went for a little walk," he explained.

"Didn't I tell you not to leave here," she whispered harshly. "Didn't I? Never do that again. It's dangerous out there."

"I'm sorry," said Henry contritely.

"Took you long enough to find the right place, didn't it?" Cook turned a handle beside the row of aprons and a door swung inward. Without a word she pushed Henry through the door into a stack of mops and brooms. "You'll have to find your own way now," she said. "If you're lucky, you'll get lunch in half an hour." She swiftly closed the door.

Henry made his way back to Cook's rooms. He sat beside the stove, feeling rather sorry for himself. Was he to spend the rest of his life like this? Hiding from people who wished him harm? Why was it dangerous "out there"? He recalled something Manfred Bloor had said to the girls. "What's my great-grandfather's dog doing in here?"

Who was Manfred's great-grandfather? Was it possible . . . ? No, it couldn't be. Could it? Cousin Ezekiel would be over a hundred years old.

It is possible, thought Henry. He shuddered. Cousin Ezekiel is still alive, and he still wants to get rid of me, one way or another.

Henry wished the Time Twister had taken him somewhere else — Charlie Bone's house, for instance.

At that moment, Charlie would rather not have been in his house. He and Benjamin were sitting in the kitchen at number nine, wondering what to do. Frantic phone calls had been made between Charlie, Fidelio, and Gabriel. But no parent could be found, or persuaded to give them a lift up to the Heights.

"We could get a taxi," Benjamin suggested. "I've got some money."

Charlie didn't think they had enough. His mother

was out at work and Maisie was shopping. He didn't think his uncle would have any money, and he certainly couldn't ask Grandma Bone.

"We're stuck." Charlie stared glumly out of the kitchen window.

He had hardly spoken when a luxurious car drove into view. It pulled up right in front of number nine, and Lysander jumped out of the passenger seat. He waved at the kitchen window.

Charlie scribbled a note to his mother, checked the door key in his pocket, and ran to the front door. He opened it just as Lysander was about to ring the bell.

"Hi there, Charlie!" said Lysander. "My dad's going to give us a ride up to Gabriel's place."

Benjamin and Runner Bean appeared behind Charlie.

"Can my friend and his dog come?" asked Charlie.

"Of course. More is merrier," said Lysander. "Come."

Benjamin, Charlie, and Runner Bean followed

Lysander down the steps to the car. Lysander got in the front, while the others climbed in the back. They found Fidelio already tucked into the deep leather seat.

"How do you do, boys," said the very handsome black man sitting in the driver's seat.

"My dad," said Lysander quickly. "He's a judge, but don't let that scare you."

"How do you do, Judge," said Benjamin and Charlie, slightly daunted by this imposing man.

The car purred away from the curb, sailed down Filbert Street, around the park, and then up through the city. Up and up and up. None of them noticed the yellow taxi that was following them. The car was now climbing the steep road up to the Heights. They passed several grand houses and then they were beyond the fashionable area and skirting the borders of a wild-looking wood. The judge pulled up outside a rather dilapidated building with a very muddy yard. Hens scratched in the dirt and a goat with large horns was chewing a bush.

"This is as far as I go, boys," said the judge.

"Couldn't you take us up to the top, Dad?" asked Lysander.

"I'm not driving my new car up there," said his father. "Too much turbulence."

As they got out, they could hear thunder rumbling in the distance.

"Good luck, young fellows!" The judge backed into the muddy yard, turned his car, and drove down the hill.

"Will he come and get us?" asked Benjamin, anxiously.

"Might," said Lysander. "Might be Mom, though."

A little further down the hill, and out of sight of the boys, the yellow taxi had pulled up. An odd-looking creature got out; an old man in a long, dirty raincoat. He had a white mustache but tufts of ginger hair stuck out from under his filthy tweed cap. He paid the driver and then began to run up the hill, not moving like an old man at all, but more like a schoolboy.

Charlie had never been so high above the city. The view was magnificent, but there was something unsettling about such a high and windy place. The trees behind them sighed ominously, and the thunder became more persistent.

They were about to walk into the yard when Gabriel came out of the dilapidated house. He was wearing long, muddy boots and splashed deliberately through the deepest puddles. His jeans were so dirty the mud hardly made a difference.

"Hi!" Gabriel raised his left hand. "Look! Good as new."

"Glad to hear it," said Lysander. "Are we all ready, then?"

"Ready for anything," said Fidelio.

They set off, Lysander and Gabriel leading the way. After a while the road became rough and narrow, and then it petered out altogether. They found themselves at a gate. A wooden sign, marked THUNDER HOUSE, had been nailed to the top bar. Beneath this a smaller sign read, BEWARE OF THE WEATHER!

"What does that mean?" said Benjamin.

"We'll soon find out," said Fidelio.

Beyond the gate a narrow lane led between rows of dark evergreens. The tops of the trees thrashed violently in the wind that swirled overhead and twigs, stones, and dead grass came bowling down the lane.

"Here goes," said Lysander, opening the gate. "I've been here before, but it's never been this windy."

The others followed him through. They were immediately struck by flying debris.

"This isn't going to be easy," muttered Charlie.

Leaning into the wind, the two leaders set off up the lane. Behind them Fidelio, Charlie, and Benjamin walked in a huddle, with Runner Bean anxiously winding around their legs.

With every step they took, the wind grew fiercer, and now sharp little bolts of hail peppered their faces. Charlie took a peek around Lysander and saw an awesome gray stone building. The roof was divided into three very steep triangles, the middle section resembling a tower. The windows were long and narrow, and the porch roof echoed the sharp angle of the center gable. A weather vane in the shape of a hammer whirled madly at the very top of the building. Every now and again the whole building shook violently.

As they drew near to the house, the porch door opened and out came a man with frizzy blond hair and a beard to match. He must have been nearly seven feet tall because he banged his head on the top of the door frame when he stepped through it.

"It's no use," the big man roared, as the boys battled their way toward the house. "I've tried to calm him down, but we've got to let this storm blow itself out."

"We need him, Mr. Torsson!" Lysander shouted through the wind.

"I know! I know, but Tancred's got this weather thing worse than I have. I can't manage him at all."

The determined gang had now reached the shelter of the house. Not that it gave them much protection. The wind came at them from every direction, tearing their hair and making their eyes stream with tears.

Mr. Torsson stood with his arms across his chest, braced against the hail that battered his broad back. "I've tried to reason with him." He coughed and a deep rumble echoed somewhere in his chest. "He's locked himself in his room. Furniture's probably in smithereens by now. My wife . . ." He gave another cough, this one coinciding with a bolt of lightning that came sizzling down a nearby tree.

They all watched the tree crash to the ground, its feathery branches alight with flames. These were soon put out, however, by the deluge that suddenly poured from the sky. In a brief moment of quiet before the next clap of thunder, Mr. Torsson said sadly, "My poor wife's got a terrible headache."

"Can we just come in and talk to Tancred?" begged Lysander.

"Not a chance," said Mr. Torsson, planting himself firmly inside the porch. "It's too dangerous. You'll just have to come back another time. Be careful on the way back. There's something out there."

"What . . . ?" Gabriel began.

His next words were drowned by a furious crack of thunder, and they all found themselves ducking. Something hit the ground with a heavy thud right behind them.

Runner Bean howled hysterically and Benjamin shouted, "W . . . w . . . what was that?"

"A hammer," said Mr. Torsson. He disappeared into the house and they heard the rattle of locks and bolts behind the door.

"Well, that's that, I guess," sighed Lysander. "Let's go back through the woods. There'll be more shelter under the trees."

They raced to the woods but Runner Bean, barking with excitement, began to dig at the ground.

"What's the matter with him?" said Charlie.

"He's found the hammer," said Benjamin breathlessly. "Runner, here, boy. Leave it. Now! It's not a bone!"

The woods were full of thorny bushes and brambles that scratched their faces and tore their clothes. And there was something else: a feeling of being watched.

"I don't like this," muttered Lysander. "Let's try and get back to the lane."

The lane couldn't be found. They fanned out, calling to one another as they searched. "Not this way!" "Can't see it." "Help, we're lost!" "Must be this way." "Not here."

All at once, Charlie found himself alone. It had become very dark. Thunder still grumbled in the distance, but the trees were eerily still. And then he saw the terrible eyes: twin pools of light, moving closer through the undergrowth. With a yell of terror, Charlie turned and threw himself at a tangle of bushes.

"Help!" he shouted. "Help! Where are you all?"

He could hear barking, but it was difficult to tell where it came from. "Runner!" he shouted. "Runner Bean, here, boy!"

There was a deep snarl behind him and Charlie hurled himself away from it. He tore through the woods, banging into trees, tripping, falling, scrambling on his knees, until he saw a pale strip of road. He crawled onto it and looked up to see four boys staring at him in horror.

"Charlie! You look a real mess," Fidelio exclaimed.

"You don't look so good yourself," said Charlie. "How did you find the road?"

"We'd still be in the woods if it wasn't for Runner," said Gabriel. "What happened to you, Charlie? We called and called."

"Didn't hear," said Charlie. He got to his feet and shook the twigs out of his hair. "There was something in there. An animal."

"I know, we heard it," said Lysander grimly. "Whatever it was, it didn't want us in those woods. Let's get away from here."

They staggered back to Gabriel's house and found the inside of the ramshackle building surprisingly warm and comfortable. When the boys had cleaned themselves at the kitchen sink, they fell into their chairs and gazed at mounds of roast beef, mashed potatoes, and vegetables, not knowing where to start.

"Charlie, your mom was on the telephone," said Mrs. Silk. "I told her you'd gone for a walk with your friends, and would be coming back here for your tea."

"Thanks, Mrs. Silk!" Charlie wondered if his mother had gotten his note. He wouldn't put it past Grandma Bone to have hidden it.

Gabriel had three sisters who squeezed themselves in between the boys and kept up an endless stream of chatter. The boys were too exhausted to join in. Lysander hardly said a word throughout the meal.

"Not a very promising start to the new term, is it?" said Mrs. Silk. "What with Gabriel's glove and all." She was a neat, pretty woman with round blue eyes and brown curly hair; not a bit like Gabriel.

It wasn't easy having an endowed child in the family, but Mrs. Silk did her best. She had no idea where Gabriel's strange talent (if you could call it that) came from. She and her husband were always arguing about which side of the family was responsible for it. She had a strong suspicion that it came from the Silks, some of whom were peculiar to say the least. Gabriel could never wear secondhand clothes, and as they were not a rich family Mrs. Silk often had to buy secondhand things for the girls. They found this very unfair.

After tea Gabriel took his friends to see his famous gerbils, and then as it began to get late, Mrs. Silk drove everyone to their own front doors in a battered Land Rover. "Hope your mom wasn't worried," she called as Charlie climbed the steps of number nine.

Maisie met him in the hall.

"The Yewbeams are here," she muttered. "I'm off to watch my TV. Good luck, Charlie!"

SKARPO THE SORCERER

Grandma Bone's three sisters were usually enter-
tained in the tidy room across the hall, but today, here
they were, sitting around the table and swamping the
normally cozy room with their dreadful dark clothes
and sour faces.

They had draped their black coats across the chairs
and dumped their large black bags on the dresser. There
was a half-eaten cake, oozing cream, on the table and
the room smelled of stale pastries and old lavender.

Charlie tried to make the best of things. "Hello,
aunties," he said cheerfully. "What a surprise!"

"I'm surprised your mother lets you stay out so
late," said Aunt Lucretia. "Where've you been?"

"Where's Mom?" said Charlie, looking around.

"Where's Mom? Where's my mommy?" said Aunt
Eustacia in a silly voice.

Charlie looked at the cake. No one offered him a
slice.

"Your mother is out," said Grandma Bone.

"Where?"

"Dearie me, we are in a state about our mommy, aren't we?" cooed Venetia, the youngest and most deadly of the sisters.

"I'm not in a state," said Charlie indignantly. "It's just that I'm surprised she's not here."

"She's gone to the theater," said Grandma Bone. "She had two free tickets to see *Divine Drums*. Naturally, she wanted to take you, but you weren't here, were you?"

"She didn't say anything about tickets to me," said Charlie. "Where did they come from?"

"We don't know everything about your mom, do we?" said Aunt Eustacia. "She probably got them from her boyfriend."

"She hasn't got a boyfriend," said Charlie.

"How do you know?" said Aunt Venetia, patting her hair, which was coiled above her head like a black serpent. "She's still a young woman."

"She doesn't need a boyfriend," said Charlie, "because my dad's still alive."

Icy silence descended on the kitchen. The four sisters stiffened. Their mouths tightened into grim dark lines.

Grandma Bone said, "Why do you persist in this nonsense, boy? Your father died. We had a funeral."

"But there was no body," said Charlie. He turned to leave but all four sisters shouted, "STOP!"

Taken by surprise, Charlie did stop.

"You haven't told us about Henry," said Grandma Bone.

"There's nothing to tell," said Charlie.

"You're a very stupid boy," said Matron Lucretia. "Do you think we don't know about the Time Twister? Do you think we haven't heard how Ezekiel Bloor sent his little cousin Henry spinning away through time. And now he has ended up at the academy, a few years too late for his own good."

"Ha! Ha! Ha!" cackled Aunt Eustacia nastily.

"It's not a joke," said Charlie angrily. "How would you like it?"

"Got you!" snapped Grandma Bone. "Admit you've seen him!"

Charlie stamped his foot. "I won't admit nothing."

"Anything," screamed Aunt Lucretia. "Grammar, boy! You won't admit anything!"

"Oh, yes, he will!" Grandma Bone leaped to her feet. "Where is he?" she screeched. "We'll find him eventually, you know. But if he doesn't come out soon, old Ezekiel's going to be in such a mood he'll send him back to the Ice Age."

"He can't," said Charlie. "Not without the Time Twister."

"You have no idea what Ezekiel can do," said Aunt Venetia in her dangerous, silky tone. "Some of it's too horrible for words. Why won't you tell us where this wretched Henry is hiding? He doesn't deserve your loyalty. He's just a nuisance. Why can't you be a good boy, for a change? I would hate for Ezekiel to hurt you, my pet."

Charlie had no idea what to say to this. Aunt Venetia

always managed to catch him off-guard by being nice. Luckily, the door opened and Uncle Paton looked in.

"What was all that noise?" said Paton. "I can't hear myself think."

"Thoughts are supposed to be silent," said Eustacia with a giggle.

"Don't be silly," said Paton. "Be so good as to turn down the volume. My work has reached a very critical stage. I can't have my concentration ruined by a gaggle of screeching geese."

"Screeching?" screeched Aunt Lucretia.

In a more reasonable tone, Grandma Bone said, "We're interrogating Charlie about something of vital importance."

"Well, I need him for something more important," said Paton. "Come along, Charlie!"

Charlie sprang gratefully toward his uncle, but Grandma Bone hadn't finished.

"The boy stays here," she said, "until we've got the truth out of him."

Uncle Paton sighed. He directed his gaze toward the lamp hanging over the table.

"Paton!" said Grandma Bone sharply. "You wouldn't dare."

"I would," said Paton.

The next moment there was a small explosion. The four sisters leaped away from the table as a shower of broken glass fell from the lamp and settled on the cake.

"Come on, Charlie," said Paton.

Charlie quickly followed his uncle out of the kitchen, while Grandma Bone and the aunts, twittering like birds, jumped about, looking for dishcloths, picking glass off the cake, and dusting down their clothes.

"Thanks for getting me out of there, Uncle Paton," said Charlie, as he closed Paton's door behind him.

"Not at all, not at all. I really do need you, Charlie." Paton seemed very excited about something. "I've been experimenting. Look!"

He took a book from his desk, opened it, and began to read. Still reading, he walked to the switch by the door and turned on the light that hung in the center of the room.

Expecting the light to shatter, Charlie ducked. But nothing happened.

"I thought that you took all the lightbulbs out of your room," said Charlie.

"So I did, so I did," Paton murmured, still intent on his reading, "but I've put one back."

"So what's going on?" said Charlie.

"Turn the light off, dear boy," said Paton. "I can't talk and concentrate on my book at the same time."

Mystified, Charlie turned off the light. His uncle's room was once again bathed in the soft glow from the oil lamp on his desk.

"So, Charlie, are you surprised the lightbulb didn't break?" asked Paton.

"Well, yes," said Charlie, "but then you don't always break them, do you? Not if you're, kind of, relaxed."

"Exactly." Paton gave a sigh of satisfaction. "When my mind's switched off," he laughed, "if you'll excuse the pun. When my thoughts are elsewhere, as it were, I'm less prone to accidents of the electrical kind. So — I decided if I read a very engrossing book while in the presence of an electrified lightbulb, the bulb might not shatter."

"I see," Charlie said slowly. "That's very interesting, Uncle Paton."

"More than interesting, dear boy. It worked. It's a darn miracle." Paton beamed with triumph. "I can go out in daylight if I'm reading a book. I can walk past lighted shop windows. I can walk near traffic lights without breaking them. Perhaps, I can even enter a coffee shop — if I'm reading."

Charlie could see drawbacks in his uncle's plan. It would be dangerous for Paton to wander through the city streets, not seeing where he was going. "It could be a bit chancy," he said. "You might get run over."

"That's where you come in, Charlie. If you were

with me, you could see the pitfalls. I thought tomorrow, we might take a walk in the direction of the cathedral, just to test my theory."

"I take it that you mean in the direction of Ingledew's Books," said Charlie.

His uncle went pink, especially around the ears. He gave a small cough and said, "I can't deny it. Miss Ingledew has been much in my thoughts. I feel that were she to see me, walking about in daylight, she wouldn't think me such a freak."

"She doesn't think you're a freak, Uncle. It's just that trying to be a mom to Emma is using up all her energy."

Paton gave a huge sigh and shook his head. "No, Charlie. She's wary of me, and who could blame her."

"OK. Tomorrow, we'll take a walk to Ingledew's," said Charlie, a little reluctant to be drawn away from the things on his mind.

"Thank you, Charlie!"

The telephone in the hall began to ring.

"I wonder if that's for me," muttered Charlie.

"Better find out," said Paton. "You can bet that my sisters won't pass on any messages."

Charlie went out to the landing and looked down into the hall. He was just in time to see Grandma Bone pick up the receiver, and shout, "He's not here!" and bang it down again.

"Was that for me?" asked Charlie.

Grandma Bone glared up at him. "Of course not," she said. "Who do you think you are?"

"I live here," said Charlie, "and it's just possible my friends might want to talk to me."

"Ha!" snorted Grandma Bone.

The Yewbeam aunts emerged from the kitchen. They were still brushing down their coats and patting their heads.

"There's a bit," cried Venetia, grabbing a lock of Eustacia's gray hair.

Eustacia yelled, "Get it out! Get it out!"

Unfortunately, Aunt Lucretia looked up and saw Charlie smiling. "You can wipe that grin off your face," she said. "We haven't finished with you, yet."

The three sisters trooped out through the front door and then stood on the step, whispering to Grandma Bone.

The telephone rang again and this time Charlie swooped down the stairs and picked up the receiver before Grandma Bone could get to it.

"Hi. Is that you, Charlie?" It was Gabriel.

"Yes," said Charlie cautiously.

"A nasty voice told me you weren't there, but I didn't believe her."

"My grandma," said Charlie.

Grandma Bone closed the front door and stood watching Charlie.

"Is she there?" asked Gabriel.

"Yes," said Charlie, turning his back on Grandma Bone.

"Look, Charlie. I found something in the lane outside our house. Several things actually. I think you ought to see them."

"Where shall we meet?" asked Charlie.

"Mom's delivering some stuff to the Pets' Café tomorrow afternoon," said Gabriel. "Meet me there."

Charlie had never heard of the Pets' Café. "Where's that?"

"Frog Street," said Gabriel. "Between Mud Lane and Water Street. Just behind the cathedral."

This was good news. "I'm going there with my uncle," said Charlie. "Can I bring him?"

"Sure. Is it your glass-breaking uncle? He's brilliant."

"It is."

"Great. Got to go now. See you tomorrow, about three o'clock. Ouch! Gerbil bit me. Bye!"

There was a loud clunk. It sounded as if Gabriel had dropped the phone.

When Charlie looked around, Grandma Bone had gone. He peeped into the kitchen. She wasn't there so Charlie made himself a quick snack and sat down. The table had been cleared of broken glass but something lay where the cake had been — a small picture, placed face down. Charlie guessed that it had been left there on purpose and, knowing his aunts, he was sure that it was a trick. But what sort of trick? He concentrated on his food, refusing to look at the picture.

And then he began to wonder if it really was a trick. Gradually, Charlie's gaze was drawn to the dark panel at the back of the picture. It looked very old; the wood was cracked and covered with tiny worm holes, the screws were rusty, and the string had broken.

Charlie took a breath and flipped the frame over. He saw a small painting of a room. But what kind of room? He couldn't resist taking in the details.

On the right of the painting, a tall man in a black robe was looking at a skull that lay at his feet. The man's dark beard was threaded with silver and he wore a round black skullcap on his silver hair. A table covered in red cloth stood in an alcove behind the man. The table was piled with books, bowls, feathers, bundles of herbs, animal horns, and gleaming weapons. The bare stone walls had been covered in strange symbols and the man was in the act of drawing another: a star with five points.

Charlie found himself staring at the skull. He tried to look away from it, but he couldn't. He began to hear sounds; a low chanting in a strange language, the scraping of chalk on stone, the rustle of heavy robes. And then, suddenly, the man turned his head and looked at Charlie, looked right into his eyes.

Charlie gasped and quickly whipped the painting over. Out in the street a car door slammed and he heard his mother's voice. A man spoke and his mother laughed. She rarely laughed. What had the man said, and who was he?

When Mrs. Bone walked into the kitchen, Charlie could still see the yellow eyes of the man in the black robe, fixing him with a glare of triumph.

"Charlie, are you all right?" said Amy Bone. "You look very pale."

"I, er . . ." Charlie touched the back of the painting. He found that he couldn't explain what had happened to him, so he asked, "Where were you?" There was a nasty whine in his voice that he couldn't help.

"I've been to see *Divine Drums*. I wanted you to come with us, but you weren't here. Charlie?"

"Us?" said Charlie, sounding even more sulky. "Who's us?"

"Bob Davies and myself." Mrs. Bone smiled encouragingly. "He got three tickets and you were supposed to have come. I couldn't disappoint him when I found you weren't here, could I?"

"Who's this Bob Davies?" asked Charlie, hating the whine in his voice.

"Charlie, what's come over you?" Mrs. Bone pulled out a chair and sat beside him. "Bob's just a friend, a very nice man who wanted to take us to the theater. Why are you so grumpy?"

Charlie was ashamed. He said, "I'm sorry, Mom. I . . . something happened to me, just now. The aunts left that." He nodded at the painting, not wanting even to touch it.

Mrs. Bone picked up the painting. "The Sorcerer," she said, reading the painted scrawl at the bottom of the picture.

Charlie hadn't even noticed that the painting had a title. "I think it was a trick," he murmured.

"What sort of trick, Charlie?"

"I don't know yet." He carefully turned the painting over again.

"Tell you what," said Mrs. Bone, patting Charlie's shoulder. "I'll just run upstairs and change my clothes, and then we'll have a nice cup of tea before you go to bed, shall we?"

"Yes," said Charlie, wondering how a cup of tea could take away the memory of the sorcerer's eyes.

He noted the sparkle of sequins on his mother's dress as she began to unbutton her coat. "Mom, Dad might not be . . ."

Mrs. Bone swung around. "Might not be what?"

"Might not be dead," Charlie said quietly.

"Oh, Charlie, bless you. Of course, he is." She gave Charlie a peck on the cheek and hastened out. She didn't seem as sad as she usually did at the thought of his father. This worried Charlie.

Mrs. Bone had only been gone a few seconds

when Uncle Paton poked his head around the door. He was holding a lighted candle. "I feel hungry," he said. "Mind if I turn the light out, Charlie?"

Charlie shook his head. The lamp above the table went out and Uncle Paton walked to the fridge. He brought out a plate of cold ham and tomatoes. He set the plate and a candle on the table. He was about to speak when he saw the back of the painting.

"I hope that isn't what I think it is," said Paton.

"What do you think it is?" asked Charlie, alarmed by his uncle's grim expression.

"I'm very much afraid that it might be . . ." He turned the painting face up and sighed. "Yes, I thought so. I suppose my sisters left it here."

"Is it someone in the family?" asked Charlie.

"Indeed, yes. His name was Skarpo," said Paton, "and he was a very powerful sorcerer."

"Uncle Paton, my . . . my endowment," Charlie spoke hesitantly. "I thought it only worked with photos."

Paton stared at Charlie. "Do you mean that you

have heard . . . ?" He pointed at the sorcerer. "Did this man speak to you?"

"Not exactly," said Charlie, "I just heard . . ."

"Charlie!" Paton slammed the painting face down on the table. "You didn't go in, did you?"

"Go in?" said Charlie wildly. "What do you mean 'go in'? I was just looking at it when he . . . when he turned his head and stared at me."

Paton regarded Charlie with a mixture of fear and concern. "Then he has seen you," he said gravely.

And as his uncle spoke, Charlie heard the moan of a chill wind. He heard the rattle of chains, a terrible cry and the shrill, dry chanting of Skarpo the sorcerer.

THE PETS' CAFÉ

For a few seconds, Charlie and his great-uncle looked at each other in complete silence. And then Paton sat at the table and said, "I wish I'd known about this before, but to tell the truth, Charlie, I've only just learned what your endowment could lead to."

"I don't understand," said Charlie. At the back of his mind he could still hear the dreadful chanting voice.

"It's like this," said Paton. "As you know, I've been working on a history of the Yewbeams and their ancestor, the Red King. This has entailed a great deal of research, in the course of which I have come across several characters whose talents are very similar to yours and those of your friends. One of them, a certain Charles Pennybuck, began by hearing portraits speak — he lived long before photos had arrived on the scene — this eventually led to his entering the portraits and conversing directly with the — how shall we say — the persons depicted in the paintings."

"You mean, they could see him, too?"

"Oh, yes," said Paton. "Unfortunately, poor Pennybuck came to a very sticky end. Got caught in the portrait of a really nasty character, the Count of Corbeau, if I remember rightly. Went quite mad."

"Who?" asked Charlie. "Pennybuck or the count?"

"Pennybuck, of course," said Paton. "Oh dear, I probably shouldn't have told you that, Charlie. Now, you mustn't worry. I'm sure it won't happen to you."

"But what about Skarpo?" said Charlie anxiously. "I mean if he's seen me . . ."

"Ah, Skarpo!" Paton went to the fridge and took out a bottle of cider. "Hm." He took two glasses from a cupboard and brought them to the table.

"Skarpo," Charlie prompted. "You were saying?"

"Skarpo lived about five hundred years ago. This portrait is very old." Paton tapped the back of the picture. "He was the kind of sorcerer that Ezekiel Bloor would like to have been, but old Ezekiel could never manage anything like Skarpo."

"Such as what?" asked Charlie.

"Better for you not to know." Paton held up the bottle. "Want some cider, dear boy? I'm sure you could do with some." He poured a glass for himself.

"No, thanks," said Charlie impatiently. "Uncle Paton, I think you might tell me a bit more about Skarpo. I mean what's going to happen to me now that he's seen me?"

"I've no idea," said Paton. "Perhaps nothing will happen. And then again, perhaps you can actually make use of his power. There was a lot of it, according to my books. Just be on your guard, Charlie. If you find yourself acting strangely, then come and tell me, and we'll try and figure something out."

This wasn't very reassuring, but Charlie realized it was the best he could hope for. He decided to take a sip of Paton's cider and then another.

"Feasting in the dark," said Mrs. Bone, turning on the light.

"Woops!" said Paton, averting his eyes from the lamp. "Watch out, Amy. I've already had one accident today."

"Sorry, Paton, I forgot." Mrs. Bone turned off the light and proceeded to make a pot of tea by candlelight.

Charlie took his mug of tea up to bed. When he left the kitchen Paton was listening, enraptured, as Mrs. Bone described every scene in *Divine Drums*. Because of his light-exploding problem he hadn't been able to visit a theater since he was a child, and he loved to listen to Amy Bone's animated accounts. She could be a very good storyteller, when she did something out of the ordinary.

The following afternoon, Charlie and his uncle set off for the Pets' Café. At the end of Filbert Street, they met Benjamin and Runner Bean.

"Why is your uncle reading a book?" asked Benjamin, as if Paton were not there.

Charlie's uncle was hardly aware of Benjamin, he was concentrating fiercely on the large book that he held only a few inches from his nose.

Charlie explained that it was an experiment.

"Ah," said Benjamin with a knowing smile. "Can me and Runner come, too? You might need extra help."

The two boys walked on either side of Paton, while Runner Bean loped ahead. It was a chilly, gray Sunday and luckily there weren't many people about. Charlie felt slightly embarrassed, walking beside a man with his nose in a large book.

There was a tricky moment when they reached the traffic lights. Paton was about to walk across a red light, when the boys shouted, "NO!" Paton glanced up startled, and Charlie whispered urgently, "Don't look at the lights, Uncle Paton!"

"Ahem," murmured Paton, stepping back onto the curb.

"Whew!" breathed Benjamin. "That was close."

They resumed their journey, avoiding traffic lights where they could, and guiding Paton across the busiest roads. At last they found Water Street and, a little further on, a narrow alley with the sign of a frog high on the wall.

"Doesn't look like a proper sign," Benjamin commented.

"It must be Frog Street," said Charlie, "because it's

next to Water Street." He didn't dare to ask his uncle for advice because there was a lighted window just below the frog sign.

Runner Bean settled the question. He ran down the alley barking excitedly and the boys had no option but to follow him. It seemed a very unlikely place for a café, but as they walked further from the main road they began to hear the barks, grunts, and screechings of many creatures.

"Sounds like a zoo," said Benjamin.

Runner Bean had disappeared around a bend at the end of the alley, and was now barking deliriously. Charlie put a hand on his uncle's arm and steered him around the corner.

And there was the Pets' Café. It appeared to have been built into an ancient wall and filled the entire end of the alley. On one side a small green door stood open to the street, and on the other a group of dogs stood barking at Runner Bean through a huge latticed window. Above the window there was a sign filled with paintings of animals. The words THE PETS' CAFÉ could just be made out between twirling tails, paws, whiskers, wings, and claws.

"This is it," said Charlie, guiding Paton to the door.

Benjamin grabbed Runner Bean's collar and they all went in.

The crescendo of animal noises was so loud Charlie could hardly hear his own voice. "I can see a counter right at the back," he shouted to Benjamin.

Before they could get there, a large man with curly black hair stepped in front of them. He was wearing a long white shirt decorated with elephant heads.

"Animals?" he said.

"No," said Charlie. "We're human."

"I know that," the man said impatiently. "Where are your companions? No one's allowed in without an animal, bird, or reptile."

"Oh." Charlie's face fell.

"We've got a dog," Benjamin piped up. "He's over there, talking to a labrador."

"One animal each," said the man. "Otherwise, out!" He pointed to the door.

Paton was finding it difficult to concentrate on his book. He held it even closer to his face in his efforts to avoid looking at the lights twinkling in the low ceiling. "Ahem," he muttered. And then, in a low voice, "Smells awful. Let's go."

Charlie was just wondering what to do next when Gabriel appeared, holding a large wooden box. He took two gerbils from the box, handed one to Charlie and popped another in Paton's top pocket.

"Er — no," Paton objected, touching a gerbil nose. But it was too late.

The large man said, "That's better," and ushered them up to the counter. Here they were faced with a difficult choice. All along the counter among plates of ordinary cookies there were bowls of sausages, cakes that smelled of fish, round pellets that could have been chocolate (or might not have been), and seeds of various sizes.

"I recommend the sausages," said Gabriel. "They're delicious."

"They look as if they could be for dogs," said Charlie.

"Probably are," said Gabriel. "They're still delicious. The gerbils love them."

"Cookies and three waters, please," said Charlie playing safe.

The man behind the counter said, "If it isn't Charlie Bone."

Charlie blinked. At last he recognized Mr. Onimous, the mouse-catcher. It was his pointy-toothed smile that gave him away. He looked very different in his chef's white hat and apron. The last time Charlie had seen him he'd been wearing a fake-fur coat and a velvet waistcoat.

"What are you doing here, Mr. Onimous?" Charlie asked.

"Giving my wife a helping hand," said Mr. Onimous. "It's her café, you know. Her idea entirely. Good, isn't it?"

"Brilliant," said Charlie. "But do the flame cats mind all these other visitors? I mean, they live with you, don't they?"

"The flames?" Mr. Onimous raised his whiskery eyebrows. "They're not often here, bless 'em. Far too busy with their own particular duties. They pop in around midnight for a quick bite and a snooze, and then they're off again. Unless they need me, of course. In which case I have to follow them."

"I see." Charlie paid for the food. It was very cheap.

"Good to see you, Charlie," said Mr. Onimous. "You take care, now!"

"You, too, Mr. Onimous."

The line behind Charlie was growing, so he took his tray to the table where his friends were sitting. He had to push his way through a crowd of dogs before he could reach the table. Gabriel had chosen a place right beside the window and they were able to watch the strange assortment of customers approaching the café.

At the table beside them a tarantula crawled around a red straw hat. The woman wearing the hat seemed quite happy about the situation. Now and again she passed tidbits up to the tarantula. Fearing the tidbits were alive, Charlie looked away.

"What have you got to show us, then?" he asked Gabriel.

Gabriel pulled a plastic bag from under the table. "Look!" He reached into the bag and drew out an old tweed coat and a battered cap.

"Asa's disguise!" said Charlie.

"Exactly. I even found the mustache." Gabriel held up a strip of white whiskers. "They were lying in the lane outside our yard. I reckon the wind from the Thunder House blew them there. Asa probably hid them in the woods."

Charlie shuddered. "You mean it was Asa in the woods. Asa as a . . . whatever he can turn into when it's getting dark?"

"Does he have to take all his clothes off," asked Benjamin, "before he turns into a beast?"

Gabriel frowned at him. "This is serious, Benjamin."

"Sorry. I just wondered."

"Why would Asa go all the way up to the Heights?" murmured Charlie. "Does he live there?"

"I don't know where he lives," said Gabriel. "But I think he was warning us off. He was trying to make sure we wouldn't go back to the Thunder House."

"But why?" asked Charlie.

Gabriel shrugged. "Perhaps it's got something to do with your cousin Henry. That evil old man who sent him through time knows he's come back. He's probably furious."

"Of course," said Charlie. "Ezekiel has ordered Manfred and Asa to find Henry. But they know that we'll protect him — you, me, Lysander, and Tancred. So they're trying to split us up, weaken us. Have you told Lysander about the clothes?"

"Couldn't contact him," said Gabriel. "I'll see him tomorrow."

At that moment a body flung itself at the window. Charlie looked up to see Asa Pike glaring at them through the small glass panes. His lips were drawn back in a horrible snarl, and his yellow eyes darted around the table until he saw the bag of clothes.

"Mine," he rasped. "Give them here, you wretches!"

His sudden appearance caused an uproar in the café. Terrified birds fluttered, screeching, to the ceiling; dogs threw back their heads and howled; cats hissed and spat; rabbits rushed under tables, and everything else hid behind the large potted plants standing around the room.

"He's not very popular, is he?" Benjamin said in a shaky voice.

"Keep reading, Uncle Paton," Charlie warned.

The café was already in turmoil without his uncle breaking glass. Food was flying everywhere, plates had been smashed, drinks had been spilled, and anxious customers were tripping over frightened animals.

"Look out," said Gabriel. "Here he comes!"

Asa crashed through the door and walked straight into the man in the elephant shirt.

"Animal?" said the man, who was evidently a sort of bouncer.

For a moment Charlie thought Asa was going to say he was an animal, but he just snarled into the man's face.

"That's it!" said the bouncer. "Out!"

He grabbed Asa by the scruff of his scrawny neck and thrust him out onto the pavement. Asa whipped around and was about to burst in again, when several large dogs rushed through the open door and set upon him.

Asa gave a high-pitched yell and ran off around the corner, followed by the pack of baying dogs. If Benjamin hadn't leaped up and grabbed Runner Bean's collar, he would have joined the chase. The big dog was very disappointed to miss the fun and whined monotonously until Mr. Onimous gave him a rainbow-colored bone to chew.

The Pets' Café was emptying rapidly. Several customers had gone racing after their dogs, and the others, having caught and calmed their pets, had decided to leave before things got worse.

Charlie and his friends stayed to help Mr. Onimous and the bouncer, Norton Cross, clear up the mess.

"That tall fellow is a bit of a lazy layabout," Norton remarked, glancing at Paton, who was still reading his book.

"He can have — accidents," said Charlie awkwardly. "So it's best that he doesn't help."

"He's special," said Mr. Onimous, winking at Charlie.

"Oh, no. Not one of them is he? We've got more than our fair share of oddballs in this city," grumbled Norton. "That one the dogs chased — you could tell he was peculiar. Animals always know when something ain't right."

Mrs. Silk, who had finished her deliveries, came through a door at the back of the counter. She was followed by an extremely tall woman with pale wispy hair and a very long nose. Surprisingly, this turned out to be Mrs. Onoria Onimous. She was a gentle, friendly person and seemed to like children almost as much as animals.

When, at last, the café was restored to order, Mrs. Silk offered the boys a lift back to Filbert Street. "And your father, too," she said, glancing at Paton. "If that is your father."

"No, I haven't got a . . . no, that's not my father," said Charlie. "And we've got to go somewhere else, thanks all the same."

"OK, then. 'Bye, boys. Come along, Gabriel." Mrs. Silk made for the door.

Gabriel reached over and rescued his gerbil from Paton's pocket, who didn't seem to notice. He pulled his other gerbil out of Charlie's pocket. Luckily, it had gone to sleep and had only eaten a peppermint stuck to the bottom of the pocket. "See you tomorrow," said Gabriel. "It should be interesting. I wonder if Asa's been bitten."

He staggered after his mother with the bag of old clothes under one arm, and his box of gerbils hugged to his chest with the other.

Charlie tapped his uncle's shoulder and said, "We can go now, Uncle Paton."

Paton stood up, his eyes still glued to the page he was reading. Charlie steered him outside where they found Benjamin clipping a leash to Runner Bean's collar. "Just in case he gets the urge to chase something," Benjamin explained.

Their walk to Ingledew's bookshop was relatively easy. No traffic lights had to be navigated, no roads crossed. As they walked around the huge cathedral they could hear the deep toned notes of the organ, and Charlie thought of his father. Lyell Bone had been one of the cathedral organists until one foggy night, eight years ago, he had gotten into his car and driven over the edge of a quarry. He had never been seen again.

"I know what you're thinking, dear boy," Paton murmured. Lyell was his nephew and had been one of his best friends.

There was a CLOSED sign on Ingledew's door, but a soft light in the window illuminated the piles of ancient-looking books.

Charlie rang the doorbell. There was no answer. He pressed the bell again. They could hear it ringing in the back of the shop, but no one came to the door.

"Didn't you say they went out at weekends?" said Benjamin. "They could be at a museum, or the movies, or something."

"Of course," said Charlie. "I forgot."

Paton snapped his book shut and stared despondently at the window.

"I wouldn't do that if I were you, Uncle P —" Charlie began.

But Paton's distress was too great. With a small pop the light in the window went out, and a shower of glass settled on the antique books.

"Darn!" muttered Paton. "She'll know it was me."

"No, she won't," said Charlie. "Miss Ingledew probably often has lights failing."

"Failing, yes," moaned Paton, "but not bursting. She knows it's what I do."

"Come on, Uncle."

"Oh dear. Oh, darn. I'll never be able to face her again," sighed Paton.

"Of course you will. Let's go home. You won't have to read anymore because it's dark."

"That's true!" Paton turned away from the shop and strode toward the nearest alley.

Charlie and Benjamin had to run to keep up with him, while Runner Bean dashed ahead, hoping for a game.

They were moving rapidly down Filbert Street when Paton said, "I don't want my sisters to hear about this little setback."

"Why are your sisters so mean?" asked Benjamin.

"It goes back a long way," said Paton.

"They always do whatever Ezekiel Bloor wants," said Charlie. "It's like they're afraid of him."

"They are," said Paton. "He's a cousin and at the moment he holds the power. They admire that."

"I'm glad I haven't got any aunts," Benjamin muttered. "I'm off now. Mom and Dad are home. Bye!"

Charlie and Paton climbed the steps to number

nine, but once inside, Paton marched grimly up to his room. Charlie went into the kitchen to give Maisie and his mother a progress report.

"How did it go?" asked Mrs. Bone. "Any mishaps?"

"It went perfectly," lied Charlie.

"I'll go with him next time," said Maisie happily. "It'll make such a difference to poor Paton if he can go out in the daytime."

Charlie noticed that Skarpo the sorcerer had disappeared. "Where's the painting?" he asked.

"Search me," said his mother. "Grandma Bone must have taken it to her room."

Grandma Bone had done no such thing. When Charlie went to bed he found Skarpo on his pillow.

"OK," he said grimly. "If they want me to go in, I will, but not until I'm ready, and not until I've decided how you can help me."

Before he shut the painting in a drawer with his socks, he took a quick look at the sorcerer. The man in black tilted his head toward Charlie and said, "Welcome, child of the Red King!"

Charlie closed the drawer quickly. He wondered how dangerous it would be to "go in" as his uncle put it, and ask for Skarpo's help. If Henry Yewbeam was to be rescued before old Ezekiel found him, then a bit of sorcery could come in handy.

"TAKE HIM TO THE DUNGEONS!"

Henry Yewbeam spent the rest of the weekend in Cook's secret rooms.

"If you leave here you'll get snatched," she warned Henry. "And then where will we be? Someone in this place wants you gotten rid of, you know!"

"I bet it's Zeke," murmured Henry. "He's never forgiven me for finishing his puzzle."

"It's Ezekiel, all right," said Cook. "There he is, a feeble old man at the end of his life, while the cousin he thought he'd banished forever has come back as a boy with his whole life in front of him."

Henry couldn't help grinning. "He must be in a rage," he said.

"Yes. And we don't want him to put a stop to the nice long life that lies ahead of you, do we?"

"No." And yet Henry found it hard to imagine what kind of life it might be.

Cook set about preparing a meal. Mrs. Bloor

would be joining them later and Henry helped to lay three places on a small round table in the corner.

As Cook worked she began to tell Henry her story. And Henry found himself curling up in the armchair by the stove, and listening to one of the strangest tales he'd ever heard.

Cook and her younger sister, Pearl, had once lived with their parents on an island in the north. Their father, Gregor, was a fisherman. When the girls were five and six it became apparent that they were like lucky charms. Whenever they watched their father set off in his little boat, he always caught more fish than he could carry. Soon people flocked to the island to buy Gregor's fish. He became very rich and was able to purchase the whole island. He built a grand house with breathtaking views of the ocean, and the sea around his island was always calm. This was because his daughters were endowed with luck and tranquillity, so it was said.

One day a young man came to the island. "He was handsome enough," said Cook, "but there was something about him that gave Pearl and me the creeps. It turned out that he'd come to marry one of us. It didn't matter which. We were fifteen and sixteen at the time, and my father said, 'Be off with you, Grimwald' — that was his name — 'Be off with you. My daughters are too young to marry. They want to see the world before they settle down.' Grimwald was persistent. 'I need one of your daughters now,' he said, 'while she's still young. I want her for her pure fresh beauty, for her sweetness and tranquillity, and for the luck she will bring me.' The young man's attitude annoyed my father. Again he refused him. And then Grimwald began to threaten us." Cook tasted the stew she'd been cooking. "More salt," she murmured.

"Go on," said Henry eagerly.

Cook continued, "My father ordered Grimwald to leave the island, and eventually he went, but not before he'd turned his fury on us. 'You think you control the oceans, don't you, you little minxes,' he said. 'Well, you don't. Very soon you'll find out that my power is far greater than yours. And then you'll come running to me, both of you, mark my words.' If only we had believed him," Cook said sadly.

"A year later, Pearl and I left our island. We traveled all over the world. We dined and danced and met our sweethearts — both sailors as it happened. We came home to tell our parents and found . . ." At this point Cook gave a terrible sigh and several tears dropped into the sauce she was stirring.

"Found what?" asked Henry.

"Found nothing," said Cook. "All gone: island, house, parents — all perished. Drowned by the biggest tidal wave in history. We suspected, but we couldn't be sure, and then when our sweethearts were drowned at sea we knew. It was Grimwald!"

Henry gasped. "You mean he could . . . ?"

"Oh, yes. He could do anything with water. My sister and I parted. It was safer to travel alone. We were less recognizable. We went underground, took work in secret, shadowy places where he couldn't find us. Wherever we went we tried to improve things, keep children safe. One day I learned that Bloor's Academy needed a cook. I'd heard it was where the Red King once held court, and I thought I could help some of the children who came here. I guessed that, just like Pearl and me, if they were endowed they wouldn't have an easy time of it." Cook licked the spoon she'd used for stirring, grunted approvingly, and put a lid on the saucepan.

Henry would have liked her to continue but, at that moment, Mrs. Bloor came through the little door in the corner, and Cook declared their supper was ready.

After supper Mrs. Bloor helped Cook to wash the dishes and then crept away to her lonely room in the west wing.

"Mrs. Bloor is a very sad lady," Henry remarked as he carefully placed Cook's china plates on the dresser.

"Sad indeed," sighed Cook. "If only she could go back to the way she was before her hand was crushed."

"Perhaps the Time Twister could help?" Henry suggested.

Cook darted a wary look at him. "People can't go back, you know that, Henry."

"Yes, but in her case it would only be five years. And she hasn't had a real life here. Who would notice?"

"Hm!" was all Cook said.

Later, as Henry lay in bed his thoughts kept returning to the Time Twister. Cook had no right to hide it from him. The glowing glass fixed itself in his mind so firmly, Henry couldn't sleep. He got up, threw his blue cape over his pajamas, and tiptoed out of the tiny room where he slept.

Moonlight, striking through the skylight, lent a pearly glow to the objects in the room beneath. The china on the dresser glimmered softly and Henry, looking up to the top shelf, saw a row of china mugs. They were decorated with hands of gold and silver leaves; two of them were placed closer together than the others, as though someone had moved one of them in haste.

Henry pulled a chair close to the dresser and climbed onto it. He still couldn't reach the top shelf, so he stepped onto the dresser itself. Now he could touch the row of mugs. The first one he picked up was empty. He replaced it and drew the second mug toward him. As he lifted it off the shelf, something rolled out and dropped to the floor.

Henry looked down to see the Time Twister glowing beneath him. He smiled with satisfaction but before he could climb off the dresser a shadowy form ran toward the glass ball.

"No, Blessed," said Henry, recognizing the dog's dumpy shape.

Blessed took no notice. He scooped up the Time Twister in his mouth and trotted to the door in the corner.

"NO!" Henry said. "This isn't the time for a game, Blessed."

Blessed nosed open the door and disappeared. Henry leaped from the dresser, knocking over the chair, but by the time he had reached the staircase behind the door, all that could be seen of the dog was his wagging bald tail. Henry tried to grab it and slipped off the first step. Getting to his feet, he leaped up the steps again.

At the top of the staircase Henry found himself in a dark passage. He could hear the tap of Blessed's claws echoing somewhere beyond him and ran toward the sound.

The passage curved in seemingly endless circles until it eventually led to a low door. The door was locked. Blessed had vanished. How could he have walked through a locked door? Henry stared at the empty passage behind him. He noticed a thin beam of light coming from a wooden panel at the bottom of the wall. Gently he pushed the panel with his foot. It opened like a cat flap. Or a dog flap? If fat Blessed could get through it, so could Henry.

He knelt down and crawled through the flap. On the other side was a corridor with highly polished floorboards. Gold-framed paintings hung on the walls and a lamp with a colored glass shade stood on a small round table.

A little further on Henry could see a dark closet. He guessed that it hid the door Mrs. Bloor used to visit Cook. As Henry tiptoed down the corridor he could hear a voice. "Tell me!" it said. "Speak to me, dog!"

Henry sidled to the end of the corridor and found that it led to the landing above the hall. On the other side of the landing, a small boy in a blue bathrobe was talking to Blessed. He stopped talking and began to grunt and whine like a dog. The boy had white hair and the glasses he wore made his eyes look like round red lamps.

Henry pressed himself against the wall and watched. The boy was having no success with his grunting dog language, so he began to use words again.

"Tell me, you stupid dog! Speak! Why won't you tell me where he is? Where's the boy from nowhere?"

Blessed gazed mournfully up at the boy, but he refused to speak.

"What have you got in your mouth?" asked the boy. "It's that thing, isn't it? The magic marble. Give it to me and I'll take it to Mr. Ezekiel."

At these words Henry froze. So the boy was working for Ezekiel. He was about to creep away down the corridor when something happened.

"Give it to me, dog!" The white-haired boy suddenly lifted his foot and kicked the old dog in the ribs. Again and again. Blessed groaned and sank to his knees.

As the boy lifted his foot again, Henry cried, "Don't!"

The boy looked up and smiled.

"You're him, aren't you? The one from nowhere."

"Leave the dog alone," said Henry. "He's old. You're hurting him."

"He's got the time thing, hasn't he?"

"Maybe," said Henry. "Who are you?"

"I'm Billy Raven," said the boy. "I talk to dogs. They usually answer me. I don't know what's wrong with silly old Blessed today."

At that moment Blessed dropped the Time Twister. It lay between the boys, glowing softly.

"Don't look at it!" Henry warned. He didn't like Billy,

but the white-haired boy was very small, and Henry didn't want him to be twisted into another century.

"It's beautiful" said Billy. He bent to pick it up but Henry kicked the marble away. It rolled across the landing and dropped through the bannisters. There was a light ping as it hit the stones below.

Billy Raven glared at Henry. "You shouldn't have done that," he said.

Henry was tempted to run down and find the marble, but the other boy was giving him such an odd sly look, he hesitated.

All at once Blessed gave a low rumbling howl.

The warning came too late.

A hand came down on Henry's shoulder and a husky voice said, "Well, look what the dog dragged in!"

Henry tried to twist away but the hand was strong and held him like a vice. He turned his head and looked into the long mean face of Manfred Bloor.

"Let me go," said Henry.

"You're joking," said Manfred. "Someone wants to see you very much." He pushed Henry along the landing. "Well done, Billy. A little present will be coming your way very soon."

"Thanks, Manfred!" called Billy.

Manfred shoved Henry into a passage leading off the landing, but Henry continued to struggle. They reached a staircase and, at this point, Henry almost got away, but Manfred shrieked, "Zelda, where are you?" and a thin, long-nosed girl leaped toward them. She grabbed Henry's arm, almost wrenching it out of its socket.

Henry let out a blood-curdling yell.

"Shut up!" said Manfred. "Zelda, hold him still."

Zelda twisted Henry's arms behind his back, and Manfred tied his wrists together with a length of sticky tape.

"We'll need the flashlight," said Manfred. "Where is it?"

"It's all right," said Zelda. "I haven't forgotten it."

Grunting and struggling, Henry was led up the stairs, along dark passages, down ancient spiraling steps and then up again and into a part of the building he almost recognized; the place where he and James had spent their last miserable Christmas together.

"We're not there yet!" hissed Manfred.

Up they went again. Up and up, into a shadowy world lit by a jet of gas, whispering from the wall in their rusty iron brackets. Henry remembered the gaslights, but the walls that had once been covered in richly patterned paper were now stained with damp and hung with gray cobwebs.

They reached a door, its black paint scratched and peeling. Manfred knocked.

Henry's mouth felt dry with fear and he could hear his own heart, thumping in his chest.

"Who's there?" The voice was old and slightly hoarse.

"It's Manfred, Grandpa. And guess who else? I've got a lovely surprise for you!" Manfred grinned at Henry.

"What?" There was a delighted shriek from within the room. "Bring it in! Bring in my lovely surprise!"

Manfred opened the door and shoved Henry into the room.

Henry found himself looking at the oldest man he

had ever seen. It was difficult to believe that the wizened creature in a wheelchair had once been his cousin Zeke. And yet there was something familiar about the spiteful, hooded eyes and thin cruel mouth.

The air in the room was stifling. Behind the old man, logs burned in a huge fireplace. The floor was padded with many worn carpets and the windows covered by thick velvet curtains.

"Well," said the old man. "Well, I never. If it isn't cousin Henry?"

Henry tried to swallow, but there was a lump in his throat. He couldn't think of anything to say.

"Come closer," said Ezekiel.

Manfred and Zelda gave Henry another push. He staggered forward feeling faint. The old man was draped in blankets. How could he stand the heat?

"My, my! You are young, aren't you?" Ezekiel said resentfully.

Henry tried to clear his throat. "I'm eleven," he croaked. "At least I was last week."

Ezekiel scowled. "Last week. You mean ninety years ago, don't you?"

"Not quite," said Henry, feeling bolder. "Not by my reckoning."

"Ooo! 'Not by my reckoning,'" the old man mimicked. "Always were the clever one, weren't you? Well you're not so clever now. Got yourself caught, haven't you?"

Henry nodded.

"So where have you been hiding?"

Desperately, Henry tried to think of an answer. He knew he mustn't give Cook away. "In a closet."

"In a closet? Where?"

"In the kitchen," said Henry. "No one saw me. I came out at night for food."

The old man sniggered. "This time you came out too far, didn't you?"

"Yes," said Henry meekly.

"What are you going to do with him, Grandpa?" asked Manfred.

"Put him in the attic," Zelda suggested. "With the rats and bats." She cackled gleefully.

The old man stroked his stubbly white chin. "Hm. Where's the Time Twister?" he demanded.

"I don't know. The dog had it."

"Did he now? He's a good doggie — bringing his old master another present. He was very scared of that Twister, you know." Ezekiel's smile was worse than his scowl. He had very few teeth and those that remained were chipped and black.

Henry figured that Blessed had just wanted a game but he decided to let Ezekiel think what he wanted.

"So, where's my doggie, now?" asked the old man.

"Had a bit of trouble there," said Manfred. "Billy Raven kicked the dog and he dropped the marble."

"Kicked?" shouted Ezekiel. "Kicked my dog? The wretch. So why didn't you get the Twister, you nincompoop?"

Manfred sucked his teeth and answered curtly,

"You wanted the boy, so we brought the boy. Billy will find the marble."

"Bah!" the old man spat into the grate. "He'd better bring it soon."

"So, is it to be the attic for this one, sir?" asked Zelda. "Until you can send him off again."

"No! There's too much going on up there. Take him to the dungeons." Ezekiel swung his chair away, turning his back on Henry.

Henry shuddered. "Couldn't I stay here? I wouldn't be any trouble. I could live with Charlie Bone. He . . ."

"Stay?" screeched Ezekiel. "Never in a thousand years. Get him away from me. Now! I can't stand the sight of him, all young and hopeful. Get him OUT!"

Henry was tugged away. "Please!" he cried. "Don't do this."

Manfred and Zelda pulled him out into the passage and slammed the door. While Zelda held him still, Manfred covered his mouth with a thick piece of sticky tape, and then Henry was dragged and bundled down to the hall and out into the freezing night. The cold hit him with such force he gave up struggling and allowed his two captors to lead him across the frozen ground.

The icy stars above them gave the world a strange, pale glow, but the moon had disappeared. Zelda's flashlight threw a narrow path of light across the patches of snow, and although Henry could hardly see a thing in front of him, he knew where they must be heading. It was still a shock, though, when the great walls of the ruined castle loomed before him.

He was pushed through the archway and then into one of the passages leading out of the courtyard. Unlike the passage he had entered yesterday, this one seemed to be leading downward. The ground was wet with mildew, and every now and again Henry found himself skidding into Zelda, who led the way.

"Stop that," she snarled, "or I'll drag you there on your bottom."

Where was there? Henry wondered.

Deeper they went. Deeper and deeper. The air was

so thick and musty Henry began to choke. The tape over his mouth made it difficult to breathe. Just when he thought he might die of suffocation they emerged onto a grassy bank. Tall trees reached into the night sky, rustling softly.

"Go on!" said Manfred, giving Henry a shove.

Henry tumbled down the bank while the others ran after him, giggling spitefully.

They hauled him upright and marched him over to a black rock, half-hidden in the undergrowth.

"OK, Zelda. Get to work," said Manfred.

Zelda gave a crooked smile. She stared at the rock. In the dim light, Henry saw her smile become a terrible grimace as, very slowly, the rock began to move. Zelda was obviously one of the endowed. No ordinary person could have done that. With a rough, grating sound the rock slid back, revealing a round black pit.

Before Henry knew what had happened, Manfred had pushed him to the edge.

"Go on," said Manfred. "Down!"

"Mm mm!" Henry shook his head.

"Oh, yes you will." Manfred gave him a thump on the back, and Henry tottered forward onto a narrow stone step.

"DOWN!" ordered Manfred, this time pushing Henry's head.

Henry bumped and slithered down a flight of steps, desperately trying to free his hands. Painfully he ripped one free of the tape and groped for something to stop his fall. At last he touched an iron ring driven into the side of the pit, and clung to it. But even as he started to climb back up the steps, the huge rock crunched across the top of the pit. Henry was plunged into a darkness so deep and dreadful he felt he must be dead.

Roused from sleep by a noise from the next room, Cook had found the empty mug and the upturned chair. She guessed what had happened. The flame cats were already scratching at her skylight. As soon as she let them in, they sped across the room and up the hidden staircase. They knew when a child was in trouble. But by the time the cats reached the landing, Henry Yewbeam had gone and they found Billy Raven peering over the railings. As soon as he saw them he ran back to bed.

The cats found Blessed, lying on his side and breathing heavily. Gently, they nudged the old dog to his feet, and then, with soft, encouraging voices they eased his pain and kept up his spirits until he reached the place he called home. Now he lay at Cook's feet, wrapped in a blanket and half-asleep.

"Poor dog, you paid dearly for keeping my secret, didn't you," Cook murmured. "Thanks to you, he'll live," she told the cats. "But somewhere in this godforsaken place, there's a poor boy who may not last the night." She buried her face in her hands. "Oh, Henry, you foolish boy, where are you?"

Aries couldn't bear the sound of weeping. With a gentle meow he stood up and patted Cook's knee.

Cook wiped her eyes. "You're right. This won't help will it? You'd better go and look for him, my dears."

She opened the skylight and the three flames leaped out into the dark. It did her heart good to see their bright forms streak into the night.

"What's become of the Twister, I'd like to know," Cook said to herself. "Has that wretched Billy Raven found it?" As she closed the skylight she heard the distant chimes of the cathedral clock strike midnight.

Billy Raven was fast asleep in bed. Down in the hall, the Time Twister still glimmered in a corner. The door to the west wing stood slightly open, and now a figure emerged. Keeping to the shadows, the dark form slowly circled the hall until it reached the marble. The glowing glass sphere was lifted out of its corner and slipped into a deep pocket.

EZEKIEL'S VISITORS

On Monday morning Olivia Vertigo's famous film star mother had to be at work very early; so Olivia was dropped off at the academy long before her friends. She was surprised to find the hall full of people. Cleaners with mops and brooms were sweeping in corners; Dr. Saltweather and some of the stronger teachers were moving furniture away from the walls; others were peering under the long tapestries and heavy curtains.

"Don't just stand there, girl, do something!" Dr. Bloor shouted from his seat in the middle of the hall.

Olivia wasn't sure what she should do. "Are you looking for something, sir?" she asked.

"Of course we are. A marble. A most particular marble. Get on with it."

"Yes, sir." Olivia dumped her bag by the door and wandered around the hall. She kept her eyes trained on the ground but there was hardly a speck of dust to be seen.

After an hour of fruitless searching, Dr. Bloor ordered the furniture moved back and the hall cleared. "It's not here," he muttered. "So who's got it?"

Olivia heard voices in the courtyard behind her and, picking up her bag, ran out to see if she could catch Charlie before he went into assembly. She found him coming up the steps with Fidelio. They were talking about a pets' café.

"Hi, you two!" said Olivia. "I've got news."

"Look out, vegetable," said Damian Smerk, almost knocking her off the steps. Damian was a bit of a bully, particularly where girls were concerned.

Olivia wasn't afraid of him. "I'd rather have green hair than a face like yours," she retorted, patting her freshly dyed spinach-colored hair.

"Weirdo!" grunted Damian, marching off.

Fidelio made a face at Damian's back. "What's the news, then?" he asked.

Olivia told them about the search for the marble.

"It must be that thing that brought your cousin here," she said to Charlie. "You know, the Time Twister."

While the boys stared at her, she took a breath and went on, "I met him by the way."

"You met Henry?" said Charlie.

"Yes, in the ruin. Manfred and Asa were looking for him. He said he'd been hiding in the kitchen, so Bindi and I took him back there before those two could catch him."

"Well done," said Charlie.

At that moment, Emma Tolly came up the steps and Olivia turned to follow her.

"Emma, stop," called Olivia. "I want to . . ."

But Emma had already gone into the hall where talking was forbidden.

"I don't know what's the matter with her," sighed Olivia. "She doesn't seem to want to be friends any more."

"Maybe you're too weird for her," joked Charlie.

"Look who's talking!" Olivia grinned and bounced up the steps into the hall.

Charlie and Fidelio made their way to the blue coatroom where they found Gabriel sitting on a bench. He was holding the bag of Asa's old clothes and he looked worried.

"What's up?" asked Fidelio. "Has Asa been after you?"

"I reckon he has," muttered Gabriel. "Something attacked our goats last night."

Charlie sat beside Gabriel. "None of them were killed, were they?" he asked gently.

"No, they were just scared, and they wouldn't be milked this morning." Gabriel sighed. "I think I ought to give this stuff back, but I don't know how to. Asa might get nasty."

"Give it to Olivia," Fidelio suggested. "She can slip it into the drama coatroom during break."

"OK." Gabriel pushed the bag under the bench and followed the other two into assembly.

After assembly, Charlie dragged himself off to his music lesson with Mr. Paltry—Winds. The old music teacher had decided to let him try the trumpet instead of the recorder, and Charlie liked this much better. His lesson was almost enjoyable.

At break he found Gabriel and Fidelio wandering around the field. Gabriel still looked worried. He told Charlie he'd given Asa's clothes to Olivia and, as far as he knew, she had managed to hang the bag on Asa's peg.

"So, everything's OK," said Charlie.

"Not exactly. When I went for my piano lesson, Mr. Pilgrim wasn't there."

Fidelio reminded Gabriel that Mr. Pilgrim had a terrible memory. He was always forgetting things.

"Not lessons," murmured Gabriel.

Olivia strode up, wearing a big smile. "Done," she declared. "I put the bag on Asa's peg, but guess what?"

"What?" asked the boys.

"Asa came in just a second after I'd done it and he looked a real mess. He's got bandages on his hands and he was limping."

This didn't surprise the boys. Charlie told Olivia about the Pets' Café, and Asa being chased by a pack of dogs. Olivia found this so funny she had a fit of giggles that turned into hiccups.

When Fidelio and Charlie went to English, Olivia, still hiccuping, went to recitation. Gabriel was supposed to have mathematics but he was feeling rather odd. He wasn't wearing any secondhand clothes so he didn't understand why he had butterflies in his stomach and a tingle creeping up the back of his head. Before he knew it he was in the west wing and climbing the stairs to the top of the tower. The sound of a piano began to echo down the stairwell. Mr. Pilgrim was evidently back in his room. When Gabriel reached the top of the tower he knocked on Mr. Pilgrim's door. There was no answer. The piano music swelled and bass chords thundered out a finale. In the silence that followed, Gabriel opened the door. Mr. Pilgrim stared at him over the gleaming black piano.

"Excuse me, sir," said Gabriel. "But you weren't here

before, so I . . . um . . . I missed my lesson, and I wondered if I could have it now?"

"Now?" said Mr. Pilgrim, looking puzzled.

"Yes. Please, sir."

"Now. Yes." Mr. Pilgrim moved up the piano stool to make way for Gabriel.

"Thank you, sir." Gabriel sat next to the piano teacher and, without waiting for instructions, launched himself into his scales.

When the scales were finished, Mr. Pilgrim made no comment. He sat patiently listening to Gabriel as he played two complicated Bach figures.

Toward the end of the second piece Gabriel felt a strange tension in the room. He came to the end of the piece and rested his hands on his knees, waiting for Mr. Pilgrim's remarks. Sometimes, the teacher said nothing at all.

From outside came the chimes of the cathedral clock as it began to strike twelve.

"I'd better go, sir," said Gabriel.

"You played very well today," said Mr. Pilgrim.

"Thank you, sir."

Gabriel was about to get up when Mr. Pilgrim said, "Gabriel, they have the boy!"

"What boy, sir?"

"The one that was here."

Gabriel suddenly realized who Mr. Pilgrim was talking about. "Do you mean Henry, sir? Charlie Bone's cousin?"

Mr. Pilgrim frowned. "Henry? They took him, Gabriel. He needs help."

"Yes, sir." Gabriel stood up. As he turned away Mr. Pilgrim caught his arm.

"Wait." The music teacher took something out of his pocket and pressed it into Gabriel's hand.

Gabriel could feel it was a large glass marble. It held a strange glow that cast reflections through his closed fingers.

"Take it," said Mr. Pilgrim. "You can go now."

"Yes, sir." Gabriel left the room. When he was half-way down the stairs, he sat on a step. He wasn't sure what to do. If Mr. Pilgrim was right, then Henry had been caught. The Bloors were searching for this marble — the Time Twister. Did they mean to send Henry back to a time where he couldn't survive?

Gabriel slowly opened his fist. He glanced at the swirling shapes and colors, and then closed his fingers over the glimmering ball. "Better not look," he murmured, remembering what had happened to Henry.

A movement caught his eye and he looked down into the shadowy stairwell. Mrs. Bloor's pale face came into view. She smiled up at him. "You played beautifully today," she said.

"Thanks." Gabriel stood clutching the Time Twister behind his back.

Mrs. Bloor walked toward him, a curious look on her face. "What do you have there, Gabriel?"

Gabriel slowly held out his hand, revealing the dazzling colors of the Time Twister.

"You're not supposed to look at it," warned Gabriel.

"Quite right," said Mrs. Bloor as she reached for the marble. "You shouldn't have this. It's too dangerous."

Her fingers wrapped around the marble and it disappeared into her pocket.

"It's a Time Twister," Gabriel said quietly. "It can take you back to how you were before."

"I know." She lowered her voice. "Cook told me. I thank you, Gabriel, from the bottom of my heart."

Her slight black figure whisked away so quickly, Gabriel hardly saw where she went. He felt a lot better and ran lightly down to the bottom of the tower.

"You're late," said Fidelio, as Gabriel put his plate of chips on the cafeteria table.

Gabriel looked over his shoulder. The noise in the cafeteria was loud enough to drown his voice, but he had to be sure no one was listening. He sat between Charlie and Fidelio and, leaning forward, said, "They've got Henry!"

"What!" cried Charlie.

"Shhh!" Gabriel looked around the room. No one was paying them any attention. "Mr. Pilgrim told me. I don't know how he knew."

"He's so peculiar he could say anything," said Fidelio.

"He seemed very sure," said Gabriel.

"Cook will know." Charlie stood up. "I'll take my plate into the kitchen and see if I can find her."

"Better go now," advised Fidelio. "There's a crowd around the counter, so no one will notice you."

Charlie walked toward the counter, and then quickly sneaked through the kitchen door.

It was very steamy in the kitchen and he kept walking into busy lunch ladies carrying pans of hot food and piles of plates. "You shouldn't be in here," one of them said sharply.

Charlie scurried to the back of the room where he found Cook. She was sitting with a bowl on her lap, peeling carrots. Her eyes were red and she looked very unhappy. When she saw Charlie she shook her head.

"Is it true?" Charlie whispered. "Have they caught Henry?"

"It's true, Charlie," said Cook. "They've got him. How did you find out?"

"Mr. Pilgrim told Gabriel."

"Mr. Pilgrim?" Cook looked puzzled. "That's strange. But who knows these days."

"Do you know where they took him?" asked Charlie.

"I can't be sure. But sometime after midnight I saw Zelda and Manfred come through the garden door."

"That means he's in the castle."

"I wouldn't be surprised." Cook shook her head again. "There's some nasty dungeons in that place, but the ruin is so big I wouldn't know where to start looking. Mind you, the cats probably know where he is. They'll take care of him."

"What can they do if Henry's locked up?" said Charlie. "I've got to get him out, Cook."

"Someone must, that's for sure. You'd better get back now, Charlie. We'll think of something. We mustn't give up hope."

Charlie had no intention of giving up hope. He sneaked back into the cafeteria, took a cookie from the counter, and joined his friends at their table.

"It's true," Charlie told them. "Cook thinks he's in

the dungeons."

"Then we'll get him out," said Fidelio confidently.

"We've got to find him first," Gabriel reminded them.

"Come on, let's start now," said Fidelio. "We've got half an hour before the next lesson."

They stacked their plates and went out into the garden. The snow had melted and the sun shone down from a bright blue sky. It all looked very promising — until they reached the ruin.

When they went through the great arch, they found Mr. Weedon in the courtyard. He was nailing several thick planks across the entrance to one of the five passages.

"Buzz off, Charlie Bone," said the gardener. "I'm busy."

"We won't get in your way," said Charlie.

"I said buzz off," shouted Mr. Weedon. "The place is getting dangerous. Why do you think I'm doing this?"

They had a very good idea why Mr. Weedon was blocking an entrance into the ruin. They left the courtyard quickly.

"That's obviously the way to the dungeons," said Gabriel. "Now what are we going to do?"

The three friends walked around the field in gloomy silence. Olivia came running up and asked why they looked so miserable. When she heard about Henry she was stunned.

"That's awful. How are we going to rescue him?"

"We don't know yet," said Gabriel.

Charlie found it difficult to concentrate on any of his lessons. Teachers shouted at him and badgered him. Twice he went to the wrong classroom. If Fidelio hadn't kept an eye on him, he would have been sent to the head boy, and that was something he definitely wanted to avoid.

There was a very bad atmosphere in the King's room that night. Lysander stared gloomily at his books, Bindi had a terrible cold, Emma worked away, silent and studious, and Asa grunted and fussed whenever he had to turn a page with his bandaged hand.

Tancred's empty chair seemed to hold a huge emptiness that kept drawing attention to itself, almost as if a ghost were sitting there.

The only happy person in the room was Zelda, who kept whisking everyone's books across the table. When she stared at Tancred's chair it whizzed around in circles, until even Manfred lost his temper.

"Stop doing that," he snarled at Zelda. "It's not clever. It's just stupid."

"It's called telekinesis!" Zelda retorted. "If you don't mind, darling!"

"I don't care what it is," barked Manfred. "It's getting on my nerves. So shove it."

Zelda made a face and went back to her homework.

Charlie would have found this funny if he hadn't been so worried. The minutes ticked by so slowly, he was sure someone had tampered with the clocks. He looked at the painting of the Red King, hanging above Tancred's chair. *What would you have done?* thought

Charlie.

The mysterious dark eyes gazed out at him. The circlet on the king's head glittered as if it were real gold. Shadows moved in the folds of the deep red cloak. Then unbelievably, the tall figure began to change shape and color, until Charlie became convinced he was looking at a red and gold tree. *Why can't I hear him?* he wondered. He closed his eyes. When he opened them again, the tree had gone. *My mind's playing tricks,* he thought.

By the time eight o'clock came around, Charlie could hardly contain himself. He rushed out of the King's room with Gabriel loping behind him.

"Have you thought of something?" Gabriel whispered as they hurried up to the dormitory.

"I haven't got a real plan," Charlie admitted, "but I'm going to the ruin tonight, whatever happens."

"I'll come with you."

"No," said Charlie. "It's best if only one of us goes. You can keep an eye on things in the dormitory."

"I don't like it," said Gabriel. "Anything could happen out there."

"Asa's injured. He won't be so dangerous." Charlie sounded a lot more confident than he felt.

When Fidelio heard Charlie's plan, naturally he wanted to go with him.

"No," said Charlie. "Two of us will attract attention. I think I should go on my own. Henry's my relation."

Billy Raven came into the dormitory and watched the three boys sitting on Charlie's bed.

"You look as if you're plotting something," said Billy.

"We're plotting your downfall," Fidelio told him.

Billy scowled. "You think you're so clever, Fidelio Gunn."

The dormitory began to fill up with boys getting ready for bed and the three friends said no more to one another.

When the cathedral clock struck eleven, Charlie put his blue cape over his bathrobe, and slipped on his socks and shoes. Tiptoeing in heavy shoes wasn't easy, but Charlie managed to creep out of the dormitory without making too much noise. He was beginning to feel rather excited about the adventure ahead. He was certain that he would eventually find Henry. And then he turned a corner and walked straight into Lucretia Yewbeam.

"Where are you going?" the matron demanded.

"I think I was sleepwalking," said Charlie.

"Rubbish. What's that you've got?"

"Nothing." Charlie held Cook's flashlight behind his back.

"Give it to me. Now!"

Charlie reluctantly handed over the flashlight.

"Hm, interesting," Lucretia turned the flashlight over in her hand. "Where did you get it?"

"I found it at home."

"Did you now? Well, it's confiscated. Go back to bed."

"But I can't see without my flashlight."

"Then, sleepwalk. Go on!"

Charlie turned back and felt his way along the dark passages. He had almost reached his dormitory door when he fell over something and crashed onto the floorboards. Picking himself up, Charlie groped in the darkness until he found what had tripped him up. A body lay sprawled across the passage.

Whoever it was, lying so still, had a mop of hair and seemed to be a bit taller than Charlie.

"Fidelio," breathed Charlie. "Fidelio, wake up!"

Charlie tapped his friend's cold forehead and shook his arm, gently at first and then desperately. "Wake up! Wake up!"

The body didn't stir.

Charlie ran into the dormitory and found Gabriel's bed.

"Gabriel," he whispered harshly. "Gabriel, help me!"

Gabriel grunted and sat up. "What's going on?"

"Fidelio's lying in the passage," said Charlie. "I can't wake him up."

Gabriel grabbed his flashlight, swung his feet to the floor, and followed Charlie into the passage. Between them they managed to lift Fidelio and carry him back to his bed. Fidelio slept on. He was limp and cold and barely breathing. Gabriel shone his flashlight on Fidelio's face. His eyes were wide open but they stared out with a blank, fixed expression.

"He's been hypnotized," gasped Charlie. "We can't leave him like this till morning, he may never wake up."

Gabriel went to the bathroom and came back with a mug of cold water. "Sorry about this," he said under his breath. He poured the water over Fidelio's head.

With a shiver and a moan, Fidelio opened his eyes even wider and looked up at Charlie. "What happened?" he said.

"You tell us," said Charlie. "I found you in the passage."

"I tried to follow you," mumbled Fidelio. "Manfred caught me. He held a flashlight up to his face. And made me look at him. His eyes were horrible — like coal, black and shiny."

"You were hypnotized," said Charlie. "Do you feel OK now?"

"Sleepy. Got to get some sleep."

"Me, too," said Gabriel. "Night, you two."

Charlie got into bed. He took a long time drifting off to sleep. He was worried. Now even his friends were being watched. Someone was determined to stop him from rescuing Henry.

At the other end of the dormitory, Billy Raven lay wide awake. When he was quite sure that everyone else was asleep, he got out of bed. It was time to see Mr. Ezekiel. He knew it was no use waiting for Blessed. The old dog was an enemy now and Billy was a little sorry about this. "Couldn't be helped," he muttered, wrapping himself in his new blue bathrobe.

The powerful beam from his new flashlight helped him to find his way quickly through the building, but once he was in the gaslit passages of the west wing, Billy turned off his flashlight. Almost as soon as he did this, he tripped over an empty jam jar. Something else lived in Ezekiel's shadowy regions, and occasionally it threw jam jars down the rickety steps that led to the attic. Billy wasn't sure if it was a ghost, or something worse. He ran toward Ezekiel's room, but as he approached it, he heard several angry shouts. Billy put his ear to the door.

"Someone's hiding it!" screeched Ezekiel. "One of those wretched children."

"The children were all at home," said a voice, "except for Billy, of course."

Billy stiffened. He recognized the voice of Miss Yewbeam, the matron.

"I want it," growled the old man. "I must have it."

"Calm down, Ezekiel. There are other ways of getting rid of the boy."

"Has Charlie got the painting?"

"Oh, yes," said the matron. "We made sure of that."

"You think he'll be tempted to go in?" Ezekiel's voice had turned sly and eager.

"I'm sure of it. But who knows if he'll fetch the dagger."

"Of course he will," said Ezekiel. "Any boy would choose a dagger; all sharp and shiny."

"We had a bit of trouble with Paton," said Lucretia. "I think he knows more than he should."

"You'll have to do something about that brother of yours. He reads too much."

The matron gave a nasty laugh. "Oh, yes, he reads," she sniggered. "And that will be his downfall. Leave it to us."

Miss Yewbeam's laugh was infectious and soon they were both swept into a bout of unrestrained giggling.

Billy chose this moment to knock.

"Who is it?" said Ezekiel, still chuckling.

"Billy Raven, sir," said Billy.

"Ah, I want a word with you," said Ezekiel.

Billy entered the room. He was feeling hopeful. Surely he was due for a reward. He was in for a nasty shock.

When the old man saw Billy, he screamed, "You wretch. You kicked my doggie."

"But I helped to catch the boy from nowhere," said Billy, taken aback.

Ezekiel ignored this. "Why did you kick my Percy?"

"He wouldn't talk to me." Billy was beginning to

lose hope. "When am I going to get new parents, sir?"

"You don't hurt my doggie. No parents for you. You'll have to do better. Now, get out!"

As Billy turned to go he saw a look of scorn cross Matron Yewbeam's face. It was quite obvious that she didn't like children one bit.

RUN OVER!

Charlie couldn't remember when he'd had such a horrible week.

It took Fidelio several days to recover from being hypnotized. He wandered along beside Charlie, hardly talking. Sometimes he forgot Charlie's name, and sometimes even his own.

During the day it was impossible to get into the ruin because Mr. Weedon was always there.

"Clear out!" the gardener would shout. "Go on. Buzz off!"

At night, whenever Charlie tried to leave the dormitory, Lucretia Yewbeam was always lurking around a corner, ready to pounce on him. In the end he just gave up. But Henry was on his mind all the time. Where was he? Was he being starved to death?

It suddenly dawned on Charlie that Henry had no parents to come looking for him. No one would miss him because he shouldn't really exist. There was

Cook, of course, and Mrs. Bloor. But what could they do, and who would believe poor Mrs. Bloor?

"It's up to me," Charlie murmured.

"What's up to you?" asked Fidelio.

It was Friday afternoon and they were packing their bags, ready to go home.

Charlie looked up. "Fidelio, that's the first sensible thing you've said all week. Are you feeling better?"

Fidelio nodded, "It's wearing off. But I've still got a headache. I'd like to give Manfred a taste of his own medicine."

"One day we'll get our own back," muttered Gabriel.

Billy Raven came in and Fidelio whispered, "It's all his fault. He's a spy."

But Charlie felt almost sorry for Billy, he looked so lonely and fed up.

"Don't be deceived," Fidelio muttered. "He's still dangerous."

The three boys ran down to the hall and out through the great oak doors.

"Another weekend of freedom!" cried Gabriel. "Gerbils, here I come!"

They leaped on the blue school bus and were soon on the move. Filbert Street was one of the last stops and Charlie could hardly wait to get home. He wanted to ask his uncle what to do about Henry.

As soon as Charlie got off the bus he saw Benjamin and Runner Bean racing toward him. From the look on Benjamin's face, Charlie knew that something was wrong.

"What's happened?" he asked when Benjamin stood panting beside him.

"Oh, Charlie, it's awful. Your uncle was run over!"

"What?" Charlie dropped his bag. "When? How? Is he . . . ?"

"No, he's not dead." Benjamin paused to get his breath back. "He's in the hospital. It was up near the cathedral," Benjamin panted. "Someone saw your uncle step into the road while he was reading a book. A car came around the corner and went straight into him. It didn't stop, it just sped off."

271

"No," Charlie moaned. "I was afraid this would happen."

When they reached number nine, Benjamin didn't come in with Charlie. "You'll want to be alone with your family," he said. "I expect they'll be going to the hospital."

Maisie opened the door and squeezed Charlie with a violent hug. "Oh, Charlie," she cried. "What a catastrophe. Did Benjamin tell you?"

"Yes." Charlie twisted himself out of Maisie's arms. "Is Uncle Paton . . . ? Is he OK? I mean, is he talking?"

"He wasn't yesterday," said Maisie. "His head was all wrapped up and so were his ribs. Poor Paton. He looked awful."

"Do they know who did it?"

"Hit and run," said Maisie grimly. "There were a couple of witnesses, but they didn't get the number. The car just raced away."

Maisie led Charlie into the kitchen where his mother was laying three places at the table.

"We're going to see your uncle later," she said, pecking Charlie's cheek. "Do you want to come, Charlie?"

"You bet," said Charlie.

After tea they took a taxi up to the hospital. It was a large building and they spent a long time looking for the right ward. As they walked down the long aisle between the rows of beds, they recognized two people sitting beside one of the patients: Emma and Miss Ingledew.

"I'd like to give that woman a piece of my mind," Maisie muttered. "It's all her fault. She's been horrible to Paton."

When it came to it, Maisie couldn't say a word, because as soon as she saw them, Miss Ingledew jumped up and said in a tearful voice, "I'm so, so sorry for what's happened. I blame myself entirely. Paton was coming to see me, and I . . . Oh, he shouldn't have put himself at risk like that. I feel so guilty." She blew her nose very loudly.

"It's not your fault, Julia," said Amy Bone, putting an arm around her shoulders. "Paton was just trying out a little experiment. One of us should have been with him, but he just slipped out without our knowing."

All that could be seen of Paton was his white face. He had a black mask over his eyes and a bandage around his head.

"Is he conscious?" Charlie asked in a whisper.

"Yes," said a thin voice that was still unmistakably Paton's.

Charlie bent closer to his uncle. "How do you feel, Uncle Paton?" he asked. "You are going to get better, aren't you?"

"Of course." His voice dropped to a whisper. "It was one of them, Charlie."

"One of who?"

"My sisters. She was wearing a wig. I can't tell them apart without seeing the hair, but I know."

Charlie was so shocked he sat down heavily on

the side of the bed.

Miss Ingledew got up to leave, but before she went she handed Charlie a small, battered-looking book. "I found it in the gutter after your uncle's accident," she said. "He asked me to give it to you. That's right, isn't it, Paton?"

"Yes," he said weakly.

"Good-bye, Paton dear. I'll be back tomorrow."

As Miss Ingledew turned away Paton gave a very slight smile.

Emma came around to Charlie's side of the bed and said, "I'm sorry, Charlie. I haven't been very nice just lately. But I want to help."

"OK," said Charlie awkwardly.

"I mean, I will help."

"Thanks," he said. "See you on Monday."

Emma could fly, and that could be useful.

Miss Ingledew and her niece walked away and Maisie began to tell Paton all the news she could re-member, both public and personal. While she talked, Charlie looked at the small brown book. The name

Geiriadur was printed in faded gold on the cover. Inside there were columns of words in a strange language.

After a while Paton gave a huge yawn and murmured, "I'm wearing the mask because of the lights. I told them they hurt my eyes. It could've been nasty."

"It certainly could," said Mrs. Bone, gazing up at the rows of fluorescent lights.

"Good night, everyone," said Paton with another yawn.

Taking the hint, Mrs. Bone and Maisie got up to leave, but leaning closer to his uncle, Charlie said, "Uncle Paton, the book's in a foreign language."

"Welsh," muttered Paton. "You'll need it for Skarpo."

"Why?"

Paton didn't answer. He merely said, "Keep it safe."

Charlie wanted to ask his uncle's advice about Henry but he didn't see how he could while Paton was so ill.

A nurse appeared with a cart full of pills and, promising to return next day, the three visitors said good night to Paton and left the hospital.

At number nine they found Grandma Bone in the kitchen eating cake.

"You haven't been to see Paton," Maisie said accusingly.

"I've been busy," grunted Grandma Bone.

"Grizelda! Your own brother!" Maisie turned away in disgust. "You've got a heart of stone."

Grandma Bone ignored her. She took a large bite of cream cake and then noticed the book Charlie was holding.

"What's that you've got?" She stared at Charlie's hand.

"A book," said Charlie.

"I can see that," she said irritably. "What sort of book? Give it here."

"No. It's private."

Charlie ran upstairs. He didn't trust Grandma Bone. She was bound to come snooping in his room as soon as she got the chance. He found that the book just fit into his pants pocket. He would keep it with him wherever he went. Tomorrow they would pay another visit to the hospital and he could have a private chat with his uncle.

It was not to be. Next day, when Charlie asked to visit the hospital, Maisie looked glum. "Grandma Bone and the Yewbeams are going today," she said. "And I'm not traveling up there in Eustacia's car. She drives like a maniac."

"What about Mom?" asked Charlie.

"She can't get away from work until after visiting hours."

Charlie didn't know what to do. At length he decided he must see his uncle, so at three o'clock when Eustacia's black car pulled up outside number nine, Charlie got in the back with Grandma Bone. Aunt Venetia was in the passenger seat.

"What a treat," exclaimed Aunt Venetia. "We're going to have little Charlie with us."

"Not little, if you don't mind," muttered Charlie.

"Sensitive about our size, are we?" Venetia giggled.

Charlie didn't think there was any point in replying.

As soon as they reached Paton's ward, Charlie

realized that any conversation with his uncle would be impossible. When Paton heard his sisters' voices his face took on a blank, shuttered look, and he refused to speak.

"He doesn't appear to be conscious," said Grandma Bone. She raised her voice, "Paton, it's US. Your SIS-TERS. Aren't you going to talk to us?"

Paton's face remained blank.

"We've bought grapes," said Eustacia, plonking a bag on the bedside table.

"And Charlie's here," added Venetia.

Paton gave no sign that he'd heard them. Charlie didn't blame him. The three sisters sat around the bed discussing the weather and the national news as if their brother were not there.

After half an hour they stood up, and Charlie took his chance. Leaning over his uncle, he whispered. "See you next weekend, Uncle P."

"You're on," murmured Paton.

"He spoke!" cried Venetia. "Charlie, what did he say?"

"Nothing," said Charlie. "He was just breathing."

They frowned at him suspiciously. On the drive back to Filbert Street, the three sisters ignored Charlie and chattered away to one another. He had never known Grandma Bone to be in such a good mood, but then poor Henry had been caught and was probably locked up in some dark, secret place. No wonder the Yewbeams were happy.

By the time he got home, Charlie was desperate to discuss Henry with someone. He decided to have a talk with his mother.

When Mrs. Bone got home, Charlie followed her to her small room at the back of the house.

"I've got a problem, Mom," he said. "Can we talk?"

"Charlie, of course."

Mrs. Bone took a bundle of clothes out of the armchair and made Charlie snuggle into it. Then she swung another chair around so that she could sit close to him.

Charlie's mom was a very good listener. She never

interrupted or exclaimed, but when she heard the extraordinary story of Henry Yewbeam, her eyes widened and her expression changed from curiosity to amazement and then horror.

"That poor boy," she said when Charlie had told her everything. "What can we do? And Paton — his own sisters! But I suppose that shouldn't surprise me."

"Why, Mom?" asked Charlie.

"Because of your father. I know they had something to do with his accident. And Grandma Bone, removing all his photos. As if he didn't exist."

"One day he will exist, Mom," said Charlie.

She shook her head and smiled sadly. "I'm afraid not, Charlie. But I've had an idea. Miss Ingledew knows something about the little book. She found it, and she was talking to Paton before we got to the hospital. Why don't you go and see her?"

Charlie thought this was a very good idea. "I'll take Benjamin," he said. "And Runner Bean." He didn't like to admit it to his mother, but he always felt nervous in the narrow streets around the cathedral.

Benjamin was, as always, very happy to join Charlie on an expedition. So was Runner Bean. On Sunday afternoon, all three set off for Ingledew's bookshop while Grandma Bone was taking a nap.

Dark clouds hung over the city and there was still a hint of snow in the air. By the time they reached the bookshop, the boys were ready for a hot drink and a bite to eat.

"I hope they're in," Benjamin muttered as Charlie rang the bell.

They were in luck. Emma answered the door.

"Come in," she said with a bright smile. "But excuse the mess."

She led them into the cozy room behind the shop. A large sketchbook lay on Miss Ingledew's desk. Emma had apparently been working there. The drawing of a huge bird covered both pages of the open book. It looked like a golden eagle and yet there was something far more menacing and powerful about it.

Apart from Miss Ingledew's piles of books the room seemed to be full of feathers. Black, white, blue, and gray, they covered the floor and lay on every table and chair in the room.

"I've been copying them," said Emma, sweeping a pile of feathers off the sofa. "Watch where you sit."

The boys perched on the sofa where there were less feathers than anywhere else. Runner Bean was confused. He started hunting for the birds that must surely be hiding somewhere in the room.

"What's that?" asked Charlie, nodding at Emma's drawing.

"A tollroc," she said.

"Never heard of it," said Charlie.

"No, you wouldn't have. I invented it." Emma held up the book. "It's supposed to be like the 'roc in "Sinbad the Sailor." You know, the giant bird whose egg was fifty paces around."

"Wow! Some egg!" said Benjamin.

"Some bird!" added Charlie.

"It has to be strong," said Emma. "Very strong. And fierce. See its talons! Each one will be the size of my hand."

"Nasty," said Benjamin.

It dawned on Charlie that this bird wasn't just a drawing made for fun. It had a very special purpose. "Emma," he said, "is that how you . . . ? I mean do you have to be a bird before you can — fly?"

"Yes. But I have to think of the bird first. I see it in my mind, and then — it happens."

The boys stared at her in awe.

"Wow. That must be awesome," Benjamin said at last.

"It's a bit scary, actually," Emma admitted. "I've only done it three times in my life. When I came to live with Auntie Julia, she didn't even want to talk about it, but now she's gotten used to it. There are times when I shall just have to fly."

"Hello, boys!" Miss Ingledew looked into the room. "How about some hot muffins? It's such a cold day."

"Yes, please," said the boys, both rubbing their stomachs.

Miss Ingledew popped out to the kitchen and came back with a tray of muffins and hot chocolate. Charlie told her about his visit to the hospital.

"I wanted to ask Uncle Paton about the book, but my awful aunts were there and he wouldn't talk." He handed Miss Ingledew the little brown book. "He said I would need it for . . . ," Charlie hesitated, "for visiting someone."

Miss Ingledew darted him a quizzical look. "I see." She opened the book and scanned the pages. "This is a Welsh dictionary, Charlie. Welsh and English, that is. Your uncle has marked some of the words, see!" She showed them the small stars that were scattered throughout the book.

"Why those words?" said Charlie.

"I've noticed that they're all verbs," said Miss Ingledew, "or commands. 'Move,' 'fly,' 'talk,' 'push,' 'listen,' 'look,' 'catch,' 'run,' et cetera. And look, he's written the pronunciations at the front of the book."

"But why?" asked Charlie. "What can it mean?"

"Welsh is an unusual language. It doesn't always

sound the way it looks. I can only think that your uncle wanted you to learn the Welsh for these words. But I've no idea why."

"When the time comes, you'll know," said Emma.

Miss Ingledew smiled at her niece. "What strange children you are," she said fondly. "I'm not sure that I would like to be endowed."

"Me, neither," said Benjamin.

A chilly dusk had begun to steal through the streets as Charlie and Benjamin left the bookshop. Runner Bean made sure they kept up a brisk pace.

As they approached number nine, Benjamin slowed down. "Who is this person you might be visiting?" he asked Charlie.

Charlie told him about the painting of Skarpo.

"You mean you can go in, right in, to the painting? And then what?" Benjamin looked alarmed.

"He's a magician, Ben. A sorcerer. And a bit of magic could help me to rescue Henry."

"Which bit?" said Benjamin gravely. "And how?"

"I don't know, do I — until I get in!"

"Suppose you can't get out?"

"Don't be crazy, Ben. It's not as if I'll go right into another time, like Henry. It'll be like when I hear voices. I don't go right into the photos. It's just my mind."

"Hm," muttered Benjamin. "Be careful." He turned away and crossed the road with Runner Bean bounding beside him.

Charlie ran up the steps to number nine. He wished he hadn't snapped at Benjamin. To tell the truth he was a little afraid of what might happen when he went into the sorcerer's room.

Mrs. Bone had laid clean clothes on the bed, ready for school. Charlie began to pack his bag. He left the painting until last. Without looking at it he began to wrap it in a shirt. But as he turned the painting over he caught sight of the sorcerer's dark figure. Once again, the face turned toward him.

"Soon!" said the sorcerer.

THE TOLLROC

Olivia had made a decision. If it was impossible for Charlie to find Henry, then she would. She wouldn't tell anyone about it. She would just do it.

During the first break on Monday, Olivia wandered around the field by herself. Bindi was still at home with the flu and Olivia didn't feel like joining the other girls. They were discussing the new play and Olivia hadn't been given a very good part. Mrs. Marlowe, head of the drama department, had told her that she must let others have a chance to shine. After all, she'd had a starring role in the Christmas play.

"What's up, Olivia?" called Charlie.

"What? Brown hair?" said Fidelio.

The two boys strolled over to her.

"I've been too busy for hair," said Olivia. "Anyway, I needed a change. Any news of Henry?"

Charlie shook his head. "I know he's in the ruin, but I can't get in. I'm still being watched. Look!" He glanced across the field at Zelda Dobinski and her friend, Beth Strong. They were both staring at him. On the other side of the field, Manfred and Asa were pacing beside the wood. Manfred looked over his shoulder, saw Charlie, and looked away.

"Asa's bandages are off, then," Olivia remarked.

"That means he's back in business," said Fidelio grimly.

This was bad news. Olivia gave a nervous shrug. She noticed Lucretia Yewbeam standing beside the garden door. The matron was watching Charlie.

"Your aunt's still on the warpath," said Olivia.

Charlie told her about Paton's accident. "He said they did it; his own sisters tried to run him over."

"But why?" asked Olivia.

"I'm not sure, but I think it's got something to do with a picture they gave me. It's a painting of a sorcerer called Skarpo. He might be able to help me rescue Henry."

"How?" asked Fidelio. "He can't come out of the painting, can he?"

"No, but I can go in."

Fidelio and Olivia looked dumbstruck.

"But you've got to find Henry first," Olivia murmured.

"I know." Charlie sighed. "And I haven't a clue how I'm going to do that."

Olivia looked up at the slate gray clouds and gave a mysterious smile. "Not long now," she said.

Before Charlie could work out what she meant, the horn sounded for the end of break and Olivia rushed off to her mime lesson.

That evening, when the juniors were getting ready for bed, Olivia prepared herself for the night ahead. She set the alarm on her watch for midnight, kept her tights on under her pajamas, and placed her outdoor shoes close to the head of her bed.

She needn't have bothered with the alarm. At midnight she was still wide awake. She was both anxious and excited at the prospect of going into the ruin alone at night.

Quickly slipping out of bed, Olivia put on her

shoes and swung her purple cape around her shoulders. She tiptoed across the dormitory and was about to open the door, when a voice whispered, "Is that you, Olivia?"

"What if it is?"

"Where are you going?" asked Emma Tolly in a hushed voice.

"Shh! To the bathroom."

"You're not. You're going out, aren't you?" There was a creak and, all at once, Emma was standing beside Olivia. "Let me come with you."

"No. It's got nothing to do with you. Go back to bed or we'll be caught." Olivia opened the door and leaped into the passage.

"I want to help," said Emma as Olivia closed the door.

Why's Emma being friendly? Olivia wondered as she hurried along the chilly passages. *Suspicious, that's what it is.*

She became more cautious as she passed the senior girls' dormitories. She didn't want Zelda Dobinski or Beth Strong to leap out and grab her. The assistant matrons always looked so tired they were bound to be asleep. That left only Matron Yewbeam, and she was probably lurking near Charlie's dormitory.

A cold wind had blown the clouds away and a full moon beamed through the windows that Olivia occasionally passed. There was just enough light in the long passages for her to see her way to the staircase.

The hall looked vast when it was empty, and here Olivia kept close to the paneled walls. As she skirted the great slate-stoned room she kept an anxious eye on the staircase, but no one appeared. She reached the garden door, drew back the bolts, and slipped out into the night.

The moon was so bright that every stone and plant, every bush and blade of grass was silvered with light. Olivia gave in to a sudden urge. She spread her cape out like wings, and rushed across the frozen ground in joyful, leaping strides.

The dark walls of the ruin brought her back to earth. This was the part she'd been dreading. She wrapped her cape tightly around her body and slipped through the entrance.

For a moment, Olivia thought she must be dreaming. A cat sat in the center of the paved courtyard. It was a bright coppery red, and every whisker, every hair was glowing.

The cat purred softly, and Olivia realized that she had seen it before, at Miss Ingledew's Christmas party. In the bookshop it had looked unusual, but here, in the dark, it was magical.

"You're Aries, aren't you?" breathed Olivia.

The cat purred, then he turned and ran to one of the dark tunnels that led into the ruin. It was boarded with thick wooden planks, but the cat stepped neatly through a gap at the bottom.

If he can do it, so can I, thought Olivia. Kneeling on the ground, she squeezed under the planks, just as the cat had done; arms first and then her legs. As soon as she was in the tunnel Olivia stood up and followed the glowing cat.

The tunnel had a dangerous slope; the ground

was slimy and black water dripped from the rocky walls. Olivia kept her eyes on the cat. He was leading her somewhere and she had to trust him.

They emerged at last onto a wooded bank and before Olivia had time to get her bearings the cat was off again, weaving his way down through the trees to a shadowy glade. In the center of the glade, an orange cat and a yellow cat stood on a large black rock. Their eyes glittered green and gold in the moonlight.

Using the trees to steady herself, Olivia walked down the steep bank. She crossed the glade and reached the black rock. The three cats, standing so close together, shone like a bonfire.

Olivia looked down to see her heavy black shoes turned to gold by the flames. And then she noticed a thin gap beside her feet. The rock seemed to be covering a pit. Could it possibly be a dungeon? She knelt in the grass and called, "Henry! Henry! Are you there?"

A thin voice came floating up to her. "Hello. I think it's me, but I'm not sure anymore."

"Well, I'm sure," said Olivia. "You're Henry, all right. Have they been starving you? I forgot to bring food."

"Zelda and Manfred push bread through the gap, and bottles of water."

Olivia heard a scuffling noise and all at once, two eyes were peering up at her through the gap.

"Hello, Olivia," said Henry. "I'm so glad to see you."

"It's good to see you, too, Henry. But not in that pit. How did they catch you?"

"A boy with white hair tricked me."

"Billy Raven," muttered Olivia. "I didn't think he'd sink that low."

"Manfred brought me out here, and a girl called Zelda. They put sticky tape on my mouth and arms! It hurt like anything when I pulled it off."

"Ouch!" said Olivia.

"Olivia, I've seen my cousin Zeke," said Henry. "He's so old and horrible. He still hates me after all this time. He made them bring me out here. Zelda moved that rock just by looking at it. I can't get out. I've tried and tried. But I can't budge the rock an inch."

"I'll try," said Olivia.

She threw her whole weight at the rock, but it didn't move. For the next few minutes Olivia tried pushing and pulling, kicking and hitting the rock, but it was useless.

"I'm sorry, Henry, we'll have to try something else." she said. "I'll tell Charlie where you are and we'll work something out, I promise."

"They're going to move me on Sunday," Henry said desperately. "I don't know where I'll be going. I don't think I'll see any of you again — ever."

"We'll get here on Saturday," Olivia said firmly. "Charlie's uncle will help. Will you be all right till then? Is it cold down there?"

"It was at first, but the cats keep me warm. They keep my spirits up. Their light is so cheerful. And then, there's the tree."

"What tree?"

"It must be very close," said Henry. "Whenever I feel really gloomy I can hear the leaves singing, and it makes me feel better."

Olivia was mystified. It was winter and the trees were bare. She looked around and was just in time to see two figures in plaid bathrobes rush down the bank. The cats yowled a warning and leaped at the strangers. There were two shrieks as Zelda and Beth tripped over the cats and tumbled to the ground.

Olivia jumped up and ran for the tunnel, but Zelda was on her feet again. She made a grab for Olivia and caught her arm. Olivia swung around and punched Zelda in the stomach.

"Help!" screeched Olivia, although there was no one else around.

The cats were having quite a tussle with big Beth Strong; biting and scratching every part of her body that they could reach. With a loud grunt of fury, Beth threw them off and lunged at Olivia, catching her around the waist.

"Got you!" Beth cried triumphantly.

"You've had it, Olivia Vertigo," said Zelda. "We're going to tie you to a tree, and very soon a vicious old beast is going to come prowling around here. You'll be in a very nasty mess by morning."

"You won't get away with this," cried Olivia. "My mom'll . . ."

"Your mom'll be too late," said Beth. "Naughty girls shouldn't go out at night."

Shrieking with laughter, Zelda drew a piece of rope out of her pocket. As she pulled Olivia's wrists behind her back, the moon was suddenly obscured by a huge black cloud. The cloud seemed to be falling to earth; it dropped toward them and now Olivia could see it was a gigantic bird.

The vast wings drove a rustling wind across the glade and Zelda and Beth gazed up in horror. All at once they were in the air; hooked up by the necks of their bathrobes, and dangling from the talons of a great feathered foot.

"Kraaak!" called the bird.

Olivia shrank against the bare trees and watched in horrified amazement. Beth and Zelda sailed into the night sky. Beth's head lolled forward in a faint, while Zelda's mouth was open in a silent scream.

Olivia tore up the bank and began to slither along the tunnel. The cats had joined her and filled the tunnel with their bright light. But when Olivia squeezed through the boarded entrance the cats remained behind.

"Thanks!" whispered Olivia.

She raced across the garden, not daring to look back. The door into the hall was still unlocked. There was no one about. Olivia crept up the stairs. As she entered her dormitory, one of the windows closed with a soft thud. Olivia could see a figure silhouetted against the moonlight.

"Who's that?" she whispered.

"Me," said Dorcas. "I was just shutting the window. It was freezing in here. Where've you been?" Dorcas was one of the endowed but Olivia had never seen any evidence of a magical talent.

"I've been to the bathroom." said Olivia.

"Did you see Emma? She's gone, too."

"Er — yes," said Olivia.

"Night then." Dorcas closed the curtains and got into bed.

For several minutes Olivia sat in the dark wondering about the window. Who had opened it? And where was Emma? They said Emma could fly. Was it possible that she and the bird in the ruin were one and the same? If it were true, then Emma would need a way to come back.

When she was sure Dorcas was asleep, Olivia tiptoed out of the dormitory and opened one of the windows in the corridor.

"Good luck, Emma!" she murmured.

The next morning, Olivia could barely keep her eyes open. Emma looked exhausted, too. The girls went down to breakfast together. They caught up with Charlie and Fidelio, just as they were going into the dining hall.

"You two look as if you've been awake all night," said Charlie.

"We have," said Olivia, grinning at Emma. "Tell you about it later."

In the first break the two girls found Charlie and Fidelio sitting on a pile of logs outside the ruin.

"What's the news, then?" asked Charlie.

Olivia told them about her adventure. Charlie looked at Emma. "The tollroc came to life, then?" he said.

"Of course," said Emma.

At that moment, Gabriel came running up. "Have you heard?" he cried, dropping on to a log. "Beth and Zelda were found wandering on the Heights in their pajamas. They're in a state of shock and can't remember how they got there."

"We know," said Olivia.

When she told Gabriel about the tollroc, he stared at Emma in disbelief.

"You don't eat gerbils, do you?" he asked gravely.

Emma shook her head and everybody laughed. But as the laughter died, a chilly draft crept down Charlie's neck and he thought of Henry.

"I can't wait until the weekend," he said. "Tonight, I may need your help."

Fidelio stared at Charlie. "You mean . . . ?"

"I'm going to visit Skarpo."

THE WAND

Charlie decided to use the art room for his visit to the sorcerer. The painting of Skarpo wouldn't look out of place among the other pieces of artwork, and if anyone caught him, he could say Emma had asked him to look at her sketches.

As soon as homework was over, he began to make his way up to the dormitory.

"What's the hurry, Charlie Bone?" asked a voice behind him.

Charlie turned to see Manfred strolling toward him.

"No hurry," said Charlie as casually as he could.

"I want a word with you," said Manfred.

"Now?"

"Yes. Now." Manfred came up to Charlie and stared at him.

Charlie looked away quickly. He couldn't afford to

be hypnotized when he was so close to rescuing Henry.

"Look at me!" Manfred demanded.

"I don't want to," said Charlie. "Anyway, you know I can play your mind games."

"Hm." Manfred stroked his chin, where a few wispy hairs were beginning to sprout.

"You've got a fine beard coming in, Manfred," said Charlie.

Manfred couldn't decide if Charlie was being rude or flattering him. "All right. You can go now. But try and keep out of trouble."

"Yes, Manfred." Charlie hurried away.

Why had Manfred stopped him? It was almost as if he were trying to slow him down.

As Charlie walked into the dormitory Billy Raven turned quickly from Charlie's bedside closet. He was holding the painting of Skarpo.

"What do you think you're doing?" said Charlie angrily.

"I was looking for something of mine," said Billy innocently. "I thought it might have got into your closet by accident. So I looked, and this fell out."

"It couldn't have. It was right at the back. You've been spying."

"Why are you always so suspicious?" said Billy resentfully. "I'm telling the truth."

"Give it to me!" Charlie demanded.

"OK. OK." As Billy handed the painting to Charlie he pointed to a dagger lying on Skarpo's table. "Look at that dagger. It's so bright. I bet it was as sharp as anything. I bet it killed a few people."

"I bet," said Charlie, grabbing the painting. "Just leave my stuff alone in the future."

"Sorry, Charlie." Billy smiled. "I didn't mean to be nosy."

Charlie hurried out of the dormitory. He waited for a few seconds to make sure Billy wouldn't follow him, and then he ran down the passage that led to the art room.

He was surprised to find his friends already waiting for him. Even Lysander had turned up.

"Gabriel told me what you're going to do," he said. "I'll stand by the door in case anyone tries to come in while you're . . . out of action."

"Thanks, Lysander," said Charlie.

They chose an empty space behind one of Mr. Boldova's large canvases. Charlie sat on the floor with the painting in front of him. Olivia and Emma knelt on either side of him, while Gabriel and Fidelio perched on a bench in front of him.

All at once, Charlie began to have doubts. He'd never done this before. How would he get out of the painting? He hadn't really thought it through. But somehow it was too late to stop.

Charlie took a deep breath. "OK. I'm going in."

"Hold on, Charlie," said Gabriel. "Just so we know — are you going to bring that weird-looking person into this room?"

"Skarpo? No, I hope not. I'm just going to ask his advice. Maybe I'll borrow something." Charlie was already beginning to feel dizzy. "I don't . . . ," he began, and then Skarpo looked at him, and he could hear the swish of the sorcerer's robes and the squeak of chalk on stone.

"Enter," said a voice.

Charlie's friends began to fade. A white mist drifted around him, obscuring everything except the sorcerer's bony face with its strange golden yellow eyes.

When the mist cleared, Charlie found himself in a chilly, candlelit room. He could smell burning candle grease, pine, spices, and ancient decaying things. The sorcerer's possessions were no longer merely painting objects. Now they were real; pages were rough and ink-stained, feathers were delicate, and velvet smooth, the earthenware bowls were pitted and chipped, and belts and straps had a worn, shiny look.

Charlie's eyes fell on the dagger. It was lying in front of a large open book, right at the edge of the long table. Candlelight made it gleam with life. The blade was so thin it was just a shaft of brilliant light.

"What is it you want, child?"

Charlie jumped. He'd forgotten that the sorcerer could see him, too.

"You know what that weapon is? It's magic, boy." The sorcerer's magnetic eyes glittered.

"You can see me," breathed Charlie.

"I can see your face. You've been peeping at me for days, you rascal." The sorcerer's voice had a lilt to it, but it was definitely not Welsh.

"I've come to ask for your help," Charlie said nervously.

"Is that so?" Skarpo smiled grimly. "Then it's the dagger you'll be after. It can pierce a heart and leave no mark at all. Not even a pinprick."

"I don't want to kill anyone," said Charlie.

Skarpo ignored this. "A mere touch and they're gone," he persisted.

Billy Raven had drawn Charlie's attention to the dagger. But Billy was no friend of Henry's and the dagger was the last thing Charlie would choose.

"I don't want the dagger," he said. "I want to rescue a friend."

"Someone wants it," muttered the sorcerer. "Someone wants it very much. They've been trying to reach it but they're not — how can I put it? They're not ac-complished magicians."

Ezekiel Bloor, thought Charlie. He scanned the table. What could be used to get Henry out of his dungeon? How could he possibly know what to choose? Skarpo was being deliberately unhelpful.

"Herbs?" the sorcerer suggested. "A poisonous po-tion?"

"No, thank you."

"Slip one of these fine feathers into your enemy's boot, and he'll be lame for a year." Skarpo gave a ma-licious chuckle.

"I don't want to make anyone lame." Charlie was beginning to lose heart. "I just want to rescue some-one."

"Rescue? Rescuing is no concern of mine. Destruc-tion is more to my liking. If you want someone maimed, or fatally wounded, poisoned, burned, van-ished, shrunk, driven mad . . . ?"

"All those things sound very useful." Charlie thought he ought to be polite, just to keep Skarpo on his side.

"But right now I just need something that will . . . move a rock."

It was then that he saw the wand. It had to be a wand, for it couldn't be anything else. A slim white stick lay behind one of the huge books. It was about half a meter long with a pointed silver tip. Charlie picked it up.

"You can't have that," said Skarpo sharply. "It doesn't belong to me."

"Whose is it, then?" asked Charlie. The wand was cool and smooth, and it seemed to fit into his hand as if it belonged there.

"I stole it," said Skarpo. "It belonged to a Welsh wizard. It'll be of no use to you at all."

"But I think it will," said Charlie excitedly. "I think it's just what I need."

"NO!" Skarpo made a grab for the wand.

Charlie ran around the table. "I'll bring it back. Honest."

"Give it to me this instant," roared Skarpo. "Or I'll turn you into a toad."

"No, I need it." Charlie ducked away from the sorcerer's long arm.

"Villain. Thief. You've asked for it!" Skarpo picked up a spear and swung it at Charlie's head. Paper, feathers, and herbs went fluttering off the table.

Charlie rushed for a low door at the back of the room. He twisted the handle but it was stuck fast. As he bobbed out of Skarpo's reach again, he closed his eyes and thought of his friends in the art room. "I want to be there — NOW!" he said aloud.

It didn't work. He was still in the sorcerer's cell. Skarpo was chanting now as he raised the spear, ready to hurl at Charlie. "Vile, creeping wretch, I'll burn your heart out," he cried.

Charlie cowered against the wall. There was no escape. Benjamin had warned him about this. Why hadn't he listened? "Help," he moaned.

The tip of the spear glowed like a red-hot poker, then suddenly burst into flames. As it flew toward him, Charlie bent his head and wrapped his cape around the wand.

The flaming spear never reached him. When Charlie looked up he saw two hands catch the spear and fling it back at the sorcerer. The hands were brown, with shining gold bracelets at the wrists; beyond the bracelets there was nothing, no sign of a body at all.

The spear struck the wall and then fell at Skarpo's feet. He screamed as the flames caught the hem of his long robe. Charlie didn't see what happened next because invisible arms tightened around him and tugged him away. Back, back through the wreaths of smoke that were filling the room.

"CHARLIE, COME BACK!"

Charlie blinked. His eyes were still smarting from the fire, but the sorcerer's room looked small and far-away. He was looking at it, but he wasn't in it. The painting was held by two brown hands. The hands that had saved him. Charlie looked up into Lysander's anxious face.

"You had us worried for a moment there, Charlie," said Lysander.

"It was your hands," Charlie murmured. "You saved me."

"Not me," said Lysander. "I had to call on my spirit ancestors. Good to have you back, Charlie."

"What happened — out here?" asked Charlie.

"It was amazing." Olivia poked her head in front of him. "You were rocking about and shouting, and we kept saying, 'Wake up, Charlie! Come out!'"

"But you wouldn't." Fidelio peered over Olivia. "So Lysander used his African language to call his ancestors. And then, all of a sudden, you stopped moving and something appeared in your hands. Just like that. Look!"

Charlie found that he was still holding the wand. It lay across his knees, smooth and pale, its silver tip glittering in the bright lights of the art room.

"What is it?" asked Emma.

"A wand," said Gabriel. "I bet it's a wand."

Charlie nodded. "Skarpo didn't want me to have it. He stole it from a Welsh wizard. I know what I've got to do now! I'll have to use one of the words in my uncle's book."

"You haven't got long, Charlie," said Olivia. "They're moving Henry on Sunday, and then we'll never find him."

"How are we going to get into the ruin?" Fidelio asked with a sigh. "They're watching us like hawks."

"If only Tancred would come back," Lysander murmured sadly. "A storm would be a good distraction."

"A storm would be great, but we can't wait for Tancred," said Charlie. "It'll have to be Saturday when we can get help from outside." He stood up and tried to hide the wand in the sleeve of his cape, but it was too long and stuck out beyond his hand.

"Give it to me," said Lysander. "My arms are longer."

Charlie held out the wand and Lysander fit it neatly into his sleeve.

"We'd better go now," said Emma. "Matron'll be on the warpath."

Charlie hid the painting under his cape, and the six children filed out of the art room.

As they walked back to their dormitories, Matron came rushing toward them, shouting, "Where have you children been? It was lights out five minutes ago."

"Sorry, Matron," Lysander said with a smile. "We were looking at Emma's work. And mine, actually."

Matron had "detention" written all over her face. The children waited to hear their fates. If they were given detention on Saturday, how could they possibly rescue Henry? Matron smiled triumphantly, "You'll all . . . ," she began.

But a voice behind the little group said, "It's my fault, Matron. I gave them permission. In fact I told them to come to the art room. Blame it on the art teacher, eh?"

Lucretia Yewbeam's smile of triumph faded as Mr. Boldova walked to the front of the group.

"Sorry about this, Matron," said the art teacher. "I lost track of time." He turned back to the children. "You'd all better run off now. And thank you for your excellent criticisms."

The six children scattered like dust as Mr. Boldova

asked the matron's advice about a very bad bruise he'd received while playing rugby.

"Good old Boldova," Gabriel whispered as the three boys crept into their dormitory.

"Where've you lot been?" Billy demanded.

"Wouldn't you like to know," said Charlie.

TANCRED AND THE TREE

At the top of the Thunder House, Tancred Torsson surveyed the wreck of his bedroom. He kicked a pile of shoes out of his way and sat on the bed, or what was left of it. The mattress lay on the other side of the room, and his covers were in a tangled heap under the fallen wardrobe.

Tancred was wearing his pajama bottoms and his green cape. Most of his clothes were torn or stained with food. He was tired of being angry, but he couldn't do anything about it. Little waves of fury kept spilling out of him, sending the air into a turmoil.

Mrs. Torsson put her head around the door. "Are you coming down to supper, dear?" she asked nervously.

"Do you trust me?" Tancred stared grimly at the floor.

"Well, it's been a bit quieter today," said Mrs. Torsson.

"Sorry about the headaches, Mom," said Tancred.

"You can't help it, dear. I know."

Tancred's mother scurried downstairs. There were days when she longed to live somewhere else, with a nice ordinary husband and a small, quiet son. But she loved her tempestuous family and, in spite of the headaches, she knew she could never be as happy with anyone else.

Tancred followed his mother downstairs and took his place at the kitchen table. Mr. Torsson was already digging in to a large portion of shepherd's pie.

Mrs. Torsson put a plastic plate in front of her son. She'd given up on china for the time being. "There," she said, spooning some pie onto Tancred's plate.

"It's about time you calmed down," Mr. Torsson told his son. "This stormy bout has gone on far too long."

Tancred's paper cup blew over. Luckily it was empty. "I can't help it, Dad," he said. "I've tried, but I can't."

"If you ask me, that hypnotizer's got something to do with it," boomed Mr. Torsson. "Manfred Bloor. He's put you into a real state, hasn't he?"

"I don't want to talk about it," said Tancred as the hood of his cape suddenly blew over his head.

"Control yourself," thundered Mr. Torsson.

The light above the table swung violently from side to side.

"See, you're not much better," Tancred remarked.

"I can direct the violence," said Mr. Torsson. "What we have is a very useful talent, but talents have to be focused."

"Yes, Dad." Tancred gritted his teeth, but the window behind him blew open with a loud clang. "Sorry," he mumbled.

And then, through the window, a curious sound could be heard. It was hardly more than a whisper, but it had a strange effect on Tancred. He found that he was listening to music that was like no other music in the world. He stood up, straightened his cape, and carefully pushed back his chair.

"What is it, Tancred?" asked Mrs. Torsson, surprised by his unusually calm behavior.

"I have to go," Tancred said gently.

"Where?" asked his father.

"Out there!" Tancred pointed through the window at the dark trees in the woods. He strode past his startled parents and left the house before they had time to ask any more questions.

The ragged moon threw a thin light through the trees, but Tancred didn't hesitate. He knew which way to go. Deep in the woods he found what he was looking for — the source of the haunting music.

It was a tree.

The tree was red. The leaves that covered its slender branches seemed to burn with an inner fire, and the glade where Tancred stood was lit by a golden glow. Deep lines scored the bark, where water dripped slowly down the trunk. Looking closer, Tancred saw that the water too was red; as red as blood.

As he listened to the tree's hushed song, he felt a great stillness overwhelm him. His storms were there, deep inside, but Tancred knew he could control them. His strange talent had lost its grip on him.

He left the tree but when he was almost out of the

woods, he looked back. The fiery light was gone and the song had ended.

"I kept your supper warm," said Mrs. Torsson as Tancred entered the kitchen.

"What happened out there?" asked the father.

"There was a tree, Dad. A red tree; it was kind of singing, but not any sort of song I've ever heard before."

Mr. Torsson frowned. "I've heard of a red tree," he said thoughtfully. "My mother told me a story when I was very young. Darned if I can remember it now. She said it was the Red King."

"Our ancestor!" said Tancred.

"My headache's gone!" murmured Mrs. Torsson.

Tancred smiled. "I'm going to see my friends tomorrow," he said.

"About time, too," said Mr. Torsson.

After supper, when Tancred was tidying his room, his mother appeared with a pile of clean clothes and sheets. She'd kept them hidden while he was in the grip of his storms, as she put it.

"You look so much better," she said. "Even your hair is lying down."

"I am better, Mom," said Tancred.

He had the best night's sleep he could remember. When he woke up, the mattress was still on his bed, and so were the sheets and blankets. He dressed quickly and had a very civilized breakfast with his family. Mrs. Torsson even served his bacon and eggs on a china plate.

•   •   •

Charlie didn't know Tancred was back until he went to the King's room that evening. He had just put his homework on the table when Gabriel came running in.

"Guess what?" said Gabriel. "I've seen Tancred!"

Charlie could hardly believe it. "That's fantastic!" He said happily.

Asa limped into the room. His bandages were off but the scars on his hands were still red and painful. "What are you two smirking about?" he snarled.

"Just a bit of good news," said Charlie.

The room began to fill up. Emma took her place next to Charlie, and Billy came hopping in after Manfred. Dorcas was next, and then, at last, Lysander and Tancred arrived.

"Hi, Tanc!" said Gabriel and Charlie.

"Good to see you back," Emma added quietly.

Before Tancred could reply, Manfred said, "Shut up, and get on with your homework. Tancred and Lysander, you're late!"

"Sorry, pal," said Tancred with a grin.

"I'm not your pal," snapped Manfred.

This seemed to annoy Manfred even more. He scowled at Tancred, but couldn't think of anything else to say.

Billy Raven gazed sadly at Manfred. "So sorry to hear your girlfriend's ill," he said, obviously hoping to earn a few sweets. Unfortunately, it had the opposite effect.

"What?" Manfred glared at Billy.

"Zelda," said Billy nervously.

"She's not my girlfriend," barked Manfred. "And I'd advise you to mind your own business, Billy Raven."

"Yes, Manfred."

Everyone put their heads down and began to work. In spite of the intense concentration in the room, Charlie was aware that, somehow, a weight had been lifted. There was a fresh and hopeful atmosphere. Now there are five of us, he thought. And only three of them. Dorcas was a puzzle. No one knew what her endowment was. Even when she was doing homework there was a smile on her face. Charlie liked to think that she was neither on one side or the other, but placed firmly in the middle.

He looked up at the painting of the Red King. Would the tree appear again? And could he go into this painting? Would he hear the Red King speak?

Manfred's voice cut into Charlie's thoughts. "Day-dreaming won't get you anywhere, Bone. Get on with your work!"

"Yes, Manfred." Charlie was about to look away

from the painting when he noticed a shadow fall be-hind the figure of the king. Gradually the shadow took shape. It became a face beneath a dark hood. And Charlie became convinced that this dark figure was blocking him. It would never let him hear the King's voice, or step any closer.

"Do you want detention, Bone?" shouted Manfred.

"No . . . no. Sorry, Manfred. I was just thinking. My homework's a bit difficult today." Charlie fumbled with his books.

"Just get on with it," grunted Manfred.

Charlie kept his head down until the clock struck eight, and they were all released.

Tancred and Lysander caught up with him as he hurried away from the King's room.

"Sander's told me everything," Tancred told Charlie. "I hope I can help with your cousin's problem."

"You bet you can," said Charlie. "Somehow I've got to get into the ruin. It must be on Saturday when I'm not being watched."

325

"That means you'll have to get in from the other side." Lysander looked doubtful. "It's very dangerous, Charlie. There's a deep gorge with a river at the bottom. You'll have to scale the cliffs and they're almost sheer."

Charlie didn't like the sound of it. "Maybe I could get in through a window in one of the towers, if there was a distraction." He looked at Tancred.

"A storm?" asked Tancred.

"That would be great."

"Do you want me to keep the wand, Charlie?" Lysander made a sweeping movement in the air.

"I think it would be safer with you," said Charlie.

"What are you three doing?" Dr. Bloor came marching up to them. "You shouldn't be lurking about here. Hurry along now."

"Yes, sir," said the three boys.

They dared not say anything more to one another. With a quick grin, Charlie left the older boys and walked up to his dormitory.

That night Charlie found it difficult to sleep. He

was haunted by thoughts of falling down steep cliffs and drowning in fast-flowing rivers. Next morning he was so preoccupied he nearly went down to breakfast in his pajamas. Luckily, Fidelio was waiting for him.

"You'll be in trouble if you go down like that."

"I can't think properly. I keep wondering what'll happen to Henry if we don't get him out."

"We will get him out," said Fidelio, though he sounded much less confident than usual.

Later that day, something happened that changed their mood entirely. When they went to the cafeteria for lunch, they were surprised to see Cook behind the counter.

As Charlie came up to get his portion, Cook bent her head over a pan of macaroni and said in an undertone, "I've had a message from Mr. Onimous. You're to go to the Pets' Café at two o'clock on Saturday."

"Why?" said Charlie.

"Move up, Charlie," Billy Raven whined from the line. "We're hungry."

Fidelio stepped back onto his foot.

"Ouch!" yelled Billy.

"So sorry, Billy," said Fidelio in a loud voice.

Taking advantage of the noise, Cook murmured quickly, "It's going to be all right. Mr. Onimous has the answer." She raised her voice and said, "Here you are, Charlie. Macaroni without the peas."

"Yippee!" said Fidelio, joining Charlie at his table. "Something for us veggies, at last." He lowered his voice. "I heard what Cook said, so cheer up, Charlie! All will be revealed on Saturday."

The next day was Friday. During the first break, Charlie and Fidelio managed to pass on Cook's message to Tancred and Lysander. Gabriel had already been told, and he passed the news on to Emma and Olivia. After all, it was they who had found Henry.

"You'll have to bring a pet," Gabriel warned the girls. "I can lend you a gerbil each; I've got plenty to spare."

"Actually," said Olivia. "I've got some very nice rabbits."

Emma accepted the offer of a gerbil.

That evening, Charlie wrapped the painting of Skarpo in his pajamas. He put it carefully at the bottom of his bag and then piled the rest of his clothes on top.

Billy Raven sat on his bed watching Charlie pack. The others had already left and the two boys were alone.

"Why are you taking that painting home again?" asked Billy.

"Because I want to," said Charlie. He used to feel sorry for Billy, all on his own in the creepy academy every weekend. But he was sure that spying had brought the orphan a great many rewards; bars of chocolate, late-night hot cocoa, fur-lined boots, and powerful flashlights, to name but a few.

"I'll be off, then," said Charlie, zipping up his bag. "Have a good weekend, Billy."

"I don't think you will," said Billy.

What did he mean? Charlie was too distracted by his own plans to worry about Billy's spiteful little digs.

He rushed down to the hall where Fidelio was waiting for him. The two boys were the last to leave.

On Friday afternoons, Dr. Bloor and Manfred always waited in the hall until the last pupil left the building. As Charlie and Fidelio walked toward the tall double doors, Dr. Bloor stepped in front of them.

"I want to see what's in your bag," the headmaster said to Charlie.

"My bag, sir?" Charlie was very glad he'd given Skarpo's wand to Lysander.

"Your bag, Bone. Empty it!"

"Here, sir?"

"Right here!"

"He'll miss the bus, sir," said Fidelio.

"This is none of your business, Gunn," barked Dr. Bloor. "Run along."

Fidelio didn't move. "I'll wait for Charlie, sir," he said.

Charlie opened his bag and turned it upside down. Clothes, shoes, and books lay in a pile on the floor. Manfred bent down and shook out every item of clothing and every book. Even Charlie's sneakers were investigated. As the head boy picked up Charlie's pajamas, the painting fell out.

"There's only this!" Manfred held the painting out to Dr. Bloor.

"Ah. A very fine work," said Dr. Bloor. "Nothing else? Look in the bag, Manfred!"

Manfred felt inside Charlie's bag. He ran his hands along the lining, shook the pockets, and lifted the board at the bottom.

"Please, sir. We're going to miss the bus," Fidelio said bravely.

"Then you'll have to walk, won't you?" snapped Manfred. "Nothing here, Dad." He threw the bag at Charlie. "All right, you two. Get out of here."

The two boys just managed to catch their bus, but as it traveled around the city, Charlie suddenly began to have doubts about his uncle. Suppose he were still in the hospital? Suppose his sisters had done something even worse? Paton had looked so ill when

Charlie last saw him. How could he possibly recover in time to help Henry?

Charlie ran down Filbert Street dreading more sad news.

When his mother opened the door of number nine, Charlie's worst fears were confirmed.

"What's happened?" breathed Charlie.

"Nothing, love." His mother kissed his cheek. "I just took the day off. Had some shopping to do."

Charlie stepped into the hall. "Is Uncle Paton . . . ?"

"He's up in his room. A bit sore, but nothing serious."

"Wow!" Charlie dropped his bag and rushed upstairs.

For the first time in his life, he burst into his uncle's room without knocking. Paton was sitting at his desk.

"Hello, Charlie!" said Paton.

For a moment Charlie didn't know what to say. He was so relieved, so overjoyed, in fact, to see his uncle. A hug would have been appropriate, he thought, but Uncle Paton might be embarrassed.

"I'm so, so glad you're better," said Charlie at last.

"Me, too. You should see my bruises. They're very impressive."

Charlie could see a cut and a large bruise on his uncle's forehead where the bandage had been. "Your head looks very, er, colorful."

Paton laughed. "That's nothing. The others are works of art!" He patted the arm of his rather shabby velvet jacket. Lowering his voice, he added, "They didn't finish me off, though."

"Do you think they really meant to?" asked Charlie.

Paton shrugged. "Who knows? With sisters like mine, anything is possible."

"Uncle Paton, I've got a lot to tell you," Charlie said gravely.

"I'll bet you have. Run along and have your tea and then we'll discuss!"

Charlie went down to the huge Friday spread Maisie provided to make up for the academy's meager rations.

"Doesn't your uncle look grand? Considering," said Maisie.

"Did they find out who did it?" Charlie asked tentatively. "I mean, will they be sent to prison?"

"It was a hired car," Amy Bone told him. "And the driver was a blonde in dark glasses. That's all they know."

A wig, thought Charlie. Uncle Paton knows, but he can't prove a thing.

He bolted his tea as fast as he could and ran up to see his uncle again. Paton had actually cleared a space on his bed for Charlie to sit down. He had never been invited to sit in his uncle's room before. The candles had been lit and the oil lamp gave the room a cozy glow.

Charlie told his uncle everything from the moment he'd discovered Henry's capture, to his escape from the sorcerer. Paton did not interrupt, though he gave a low whistle when Charlie described Olivia's night with the giant tollroc.

"And a friend of yours now keeps the wand you found?"

"Lysander," said Charlie. "I trust him. He saved me from Skarpo."

"But you have the book? You'll have to use Welsh to command that wand, you know. It's the only language it will understand."

Charlie nodded. He'd already learned some words, and repeated them to his uncle. *"Symuda'r gareg yma!"*

"Move that rock." Uncle Paton nodded approvingly. "But it's pronounced like this, Charlie. *"Sumidar gareg umma!"*

"I'll practice," said Charlie. "It's lucky that Miss Ingledew found the Welsh dictionary. It was lying in the gutter after your accident."

"It was very lucky. She's a remarkable woman, Miss Ingledew."

"Are you . . . friends again?" Charlie asked tentatively.

Paton went slightly pink. "I believe so." Then he gave a light cough and asked, "So what's your next plan?"

"Tomorrow, me and my friends are meeting at the Pets' Café. Mr. Onimous sent a message. He says he has the answer. But I don't know what that means. How can he rescue Henry?"

"The Pets' Café," Paton murmured. "The Pets' Café." He rubbed his chin thoughtfully. "Aha! I should have remembered." He gave a delighted chuckle. "There's an old passage, long forgotten. It's mentioned in one of these." He tapped a pile of books on his desk. "It leads underground, from somewhere in the old city walls, right into the center of the ruined castle. No one knows where it starts, but I'll bet you anything Mr. Onimous knows. He has a wonderful, underground, burrowing look about him."

"It's in the Pets' Café!" Charlie exclaimed.

"Without a doubt," said Paton. "Charlie, get a bag packed. Tell your mother you're coming to the coast with me on Saturday night."

"I don't understand," said Charlie.

"Tomorrow, you're going to get Henry out of that

pit. You'll bring him back to the Pßets' Café, and there he'll have to stay until nightfall. You'll come back here and tell me that all is well, and together we'll drive to the café and collect our poor lost relation."

"And where will we take him?"

"Ah — you'll have to wait and see."

AMBUSHED!

On Saturday morning, Benjamin Brown crossed Filbert Street to number nine. He had done this every Saturday for as long as he could remember. Runner Bean, as usual, raced across the road in front of him.

When Benjamin rang the bell he had to wait at least a minute before Charlie opened the door.

"Oh!" said Charlie, when he saw Benjamin. "It's you!"

"Of course, it's me," said Benjamin. "Why are you so surprised?"

Charlie felt guilty. He had completely forgotten about Benjamin.

"Come upstairs," he whispered. "I've got a lot to tell you."

Benjamin stepped inside. "Where's your grandma? She'll be cross about Runner."

"It's OK. She's gone out. She had a plotting look on her face. I dread to think what she's up to."

It took Charlie a long time to tell Benjamin everything that had happened. Benjamin sat motionless on the bed with his mouth open and his eyes getting wider and wider.

"Phew!" he said, when Charlie had finished. "You are going to let me come to the Pets' Café, aren't you?"

Charlie didn't see how he could leave Benjamin out. "Of course. And Runner Bean might be useful."

"Mom wants you to come to our place for lunch. We can sneak out the back afterward. And then your grandma won't know where you are."

Charlie thought this an excellent idea. His mother was at work so he ran down to tell Maisie where he was going, and then the two boys walked over to number twelve.

That afternoon, everything went according to plan until they reached Frog Street. Runner Bean gave a low growl and Benjamin saw a woman in red boots disappear around a corner. High Street was full of shoppers, so he didn't get a clear view, but the figure looked very familiar.

"I reckon your auntie's been following us," said Benjamin, "the one with the red boots."

"Venetia!" said Charlie.

Before walking down Frog Street he scanned the crowds for a glimpse of the Yewbeam aunts. There was a chilly wind and a lot of people were wearing hats and head scarves. He couldn't see any of his aunts or his grandmother.

"We'll have to risk it," he told Benjamin.

They dashed down Frog Street with Runner Bean bounding ahead of them.

"Welcome, Charlie Bone," said Norton, the bouncer, as the two boys entered the café. "It's all right, your friend over there is looking after your pet for you."

Charlie had forgotten about bringing a pet. He was glad to see Gabriel waving at him from a dark corner.

As he made his way toward Gabriel he saw that all the others had reached the café before him. They were sitting around one of the largest tables. Olivia had a white rabbit on her lap, and its mate was sitting

on Tancred. Gabriel had his usual assortment of gerbils, one of which was sitting on Emma's shoulder.
Lysander had brought a parrot in a cage and Fidelio
was holding a startled-looking cat.

"She's deaf," Fidelio explained. "On account of the
noise in our house, but her eyesight's terrific."

The cat bristled when it saw Runner Bean, but the
big dog ignored her and ran over to a group of dogs
by the window.

Tancred's yellow hair began to crackle. "Who's this?"
he asked, frowning at Benjamin.

"Benjamin," said Charlie. "He lives on my road and
I've known him forever."

"OK." Tancred's hair subsided. "Sorry, I'm just a bit
edgy."

"Who isn't?" said Gabriel.

"We're not, are we?" Olivia grinned at Emma.

"Not a bit," said Emma, pulling a gerbil from under
her collar.

"Hi there, Benjamin," said Lysander with a huge

smile. "Don't you take any notice of us. We're Charlie's school friends. I'm Lysander. He's Tancred. You just sit down and have a bite to eat."

"Thanks." Benjamin eyed the plates of food on the table and sat down beside Charlie. They both helped themselves to a large portion of chocolate cake.

"We didn't have to pay for anything today," Gabriel told them. "Mr. Onimous said it was a special occasion and to take as much as we wanted."

"I suppose it will be special — if everything works out," said Charlie, remembering why he was here.

"It will!" Mr. Onimous had suddenly appeared at Charlie's side. "We'd better make a start, Charlie my lad," he said. "Are you coming alone, or do you want to bring a friend?"

Charlie looked around the group of expectant faces. He didn't want to disappoint anyone.

"I don't want it to be me, if you don't mind," Benjamin said helpfully.

"Is he going into the ruin?" asked Gabriel, lowering his voice.

"He is," said Mr. Onimous.

"Then we'll be more use here." Gabriel looked at Lysander and Tancred.

"Fidelio, will you come?" asked Charlie.

Fidelio jumped to his feet. "You bet!"

Olivia gave a huge sigh. "I suppose I've done my bit."

"It's not over yet," Emma reminded her.

With a furtive look around the café, Lysander slid the wand out of his sleeve and handed it to Charlie. "Good luck," he murmured.

"Thanks." Charlie tucked the wand under his jacket.

Fidelio passed his cat to Gabriel and then he and Charlie followed Mr. Onimous to the back of the counter. They walked through a tinkling bead screen and into the kitchen.

Mr. Onimous showed them to a small door at the back of the kitchen, and then they were in a long passage lined with shelves of disgusting-looking pet food.

"Come along," urged Mr. Onimous as the boys gazed around them.

The shelves came to an end and the passage narrowed. They were now walking on a rough stone floor and this very soon became a path of hard earth. As Mr. Onimous scurried along he seemed more and more to take on the appearance of a mole or some other burrowing creature.

Charlie realized that the ceiling was now so low he could rest the flat of his hand on its damp surface. It was getting darker. When the light had almost petered out they stepped into a small round cavern. It was lit by a single lantern hanging from the ceiling, and all around the walls huge tea chests stood shoulder to shoulder with plastic sacks and wooden crates. There seemed to be no way out except the way they had come.

"Now what?" Fidelio whispered to Charlie.

Mr. Onimous had ears as sharp as a rabbit's. "Aha!" he said, making both boys jump nervously. "You're wondering where it is, aren't you? You think Mr. Onimous has led you into a nasty trap, don't you?"

Charlie gulped. "Of course not."

Fidelio asked, "Where what is?"

Mr. Onimous beamed, and then, with amazing speed, he spun a crate away from the wall. And there it was. A very, very small and ancient door. The little man's smile disappeared. His next words were spoken in such a solemn tone Charlie would never forget them. "Before you go in I want you boys to swear never to tell a soul about this door."

"I swear," said Charlie.

"I swear," Fidelio repeated gravely.

Mr. Onimous nodded. "Good." He reached inside his woolly shirt and pulled out a small key on a gold chain. Putting a pawlike hand on the door, he fit the key into the lock and gently turned it. With a light creak the door swung open.

"The cats are there," said Mr. Onimous. "They'll take you. Off you go now. I'm going to lock the door behind you. We can't take any chances."

Charlie peered into the gloom behind the door. He

could just make out the huge stones that formed the walls of a tunnel. A distant glowing light began to draw nearer and Charlie breathed, "I see them."

He stepped into the tunnel. Fidelio was right behind him. They walked in single file, treading softly on a smooth cobbled floor. Charlie had expected a rough, earthy burrow, but the tunnel had been carefully built. The large red stones fitted neatly together, even in the low ceiling.

"It's very old." Fidelio's hushed voice echoed down the tunnel. "I wonder who used it."

"Soldiers perhaps," said Charlie. "It would have been a secret way out, if the castle was under siege."

"And children," said Fidelio. "Now it's Henry's way out."

They could see the cats clearly now, but before the boys could reach them the three animals turned and began to hurry along the tunnel ahead of them.

Charlie and Fidelio began to run. The tunnel was far from straight and they had to make several turns before they could see a welcome speck of daylight in the distance. Instead of making for the light, however, the cats swerved away from the main passage and disappeared into a long fissure. The boys hesitated and then squeezed themselves into a tunnel that was so narrow they had to walk sideways. At the end of a very nasty journey they inched themselves past a pillar and stepped into an astonishing room.

The ground was paved with tiny squares of color. On a white background, lines of red, orange, and yellow radiated from a huge red circle. The walls were covered in frescoes; golden domes blazed beneath blue skies and tall robed figures paced through leafy arbors. The vaulted roof echoed the pattern on the floor, only here the central circle was open to the sky.

"It's the sun," murmured Charlie. "See, the pattern is like the rays of the sun."

"There's so much light." Fidelio gazed up at the tiny circle in the roof. "It must be a trick — or magic."

"It was on his shield," said Charlie. "The Red King's

shield was like a burning sun. It's his room. His own, special place. I don't think anyone's been here since he left."

"Not ever?" asked Fidelio.

Charlie shook his head. "I don't think so."

At that moment neither boy could have explained his feelings. The place affected them in very different ways. While Fidelio was uneasy and eager to move on, Charlie felt at home and deeply comforted.

"The cats have gone," Fidelio observed. "Now what?"

Charlie noticed a red-gold leaf beside his foot. How did it get there? Through the roof? He studied the ten pillars surrounding the courtyard. They were made of the same deep red rock as the rest of the castle, and there was only the space the width of a finger between the pillars and the wall. Except for two standing opposite to each other. They had entered the courtyard by a narrow opening behind one of the pillars. Charlie walked over to investigate the other.

Screened by the pillar, a small round window gave

onto a dark wood. Squinting through the window
Charlie could see a green glade beyond the trees. In
the center of the glade there was a black rock. The
three cats were sitting on top of it.

"It's here," cried Charlie. "Fidelio, it's here."

Fidelio ran over to Charlie. "What is?"

"The dungeon. There's a rock, just like Olivia said.
See? Where the cats are sitting."

Fidelio gave a low whistle. "You first, Charlie. I'll be
right behind you."

They scrambled through the round hole and
dropped to the ground. When they looked back all
they could see was a wall of ivy. No one would have
guessed what lay behind it.

Charlie led the way. The cats yowled encouragement as he knelt in the grass and called, "Henry?
Henry, are you there? It's me, Charlie!"

"Charlie?" From a narrow gap beside the rock there
came a sound of shuffling footsteps. And then Charlie
was looking into a pair of large gray eyes. "Good to see
you, Charlie," said Henry.

"Great to see you, Henry. Sorry it's taken so long. But we're going to get you out of there, right now."

"How?" The gray eyes looked anxious.

"Well, I've got something powerful here." Charlie drew the wand out of his jacket and held it above the eyes. "Can you see it?"

"But it's just a stick." Henry sounded disappointed. "That won't do it, Charlie."

Fidelio peered over Charlie's shoulder. "Actually, Henry, it's a wand," he said, "and wands can do anything."

"Oh! Who's this?" Henry asked.

"My friend Fidelio," said Charlie. "He's great in a crisis. Never panics. I think you'd better get away from there now, Henry. Just in case the rock moves the wrong way."

"I won't be able to breathe if it does that," Henry said in a scared voice.

"Don't worry. It'll work," Fidelio said confidently.

"If you say so."

The eyes disappeared and they heard Henry shuffle down into his dungeon.

Charlie stepped away from the rock. He held out the wand. "Suppose it doesn't work," he muttered.

"Of course it'll work," said Fidelio. "Think where it came from, Charlie. Believe in yourself."

Encouraged, Charlie flourished the wand in the air, and then, pointing it at the rock, he chanted,

Sumidar gareg umma!

The three cats leaped off the rock, but nothing else happened.

"Things like this never work the first time," said Fidelio. "Like our car. It always needs two goes."

Charlie repeated the Welsh words, pronouncing them exactly as his uncle had told him. The rock didn't move. A cold, panicky feeling clutched his stomach. Perhaps Skarpo had tricked him. He shouldn't have chosen the wand. It was useless.

"Useless, useless," Charlie muttered. "What are we going to do, Fido?"

"Try again," said Fidelio. "Only this time use a different kind of voice. You sound like someone pretending to be a wizard. A bit false. And too bossy. I bet a real wizard treats his wand like a friend. Try and sound more friendly, and more polite."

"OK." Charlie cleared his throat. Once again he pointed the wand at the black rock, and when he spoke the words, he tried to imagine that he was speaking to his uncle Paton; polite but friendly.

Sumidar gareg umma!

This time, as soon as Charlie had spoken, the wand became warm in his hand. It felt as if it were turning through his fingers. A red glow spread through the wood and its silver tip sparkled like a firework. With a sudden explosion of light the wand flew out of Charlie's hand and landed on the rock.

All around the glade, birds fluttered into the sky, calling anxiously. Fidelio and the cats rushed to Charlie's side as the rock gave a thunderous groan. There was a deep underground boom, a crushing rumble, and the rock slowly rolled backward.

The boys were so amazed they stood rooted to the spot, and then Henry's head emerged from a dark hole beside the rock.

"Hurrah!" he said. "I'm out. Well done, Charlie!"

They were shocked by his appearance. Never had they seen a boy so drained of life. His face was white and pinched and the circles around his eyes made him look like an exhausted owl.

Fidelio and Charlie took an arm each and helped Henry to climb the rest of the way out of the pit. He was a bit unsteady but so happy to be alive and free, he couldn't stop himself from doing a skip and a jump as soon as he was out.

Charlie looked down into the pit. It was hard to imagine how it must have felt to be trapped in that awful place for two whole weeks.

The wand had lost its strange glow and was once again a pale stick with a silver tip. Henry gazed at it in awe, as Charlie slipped it under his jacket.

"I'll tell you how I got it," Charlie said, "but not here. Let's go before someone comes snooping around."

They hurried across the glade and through the woods, but when they reached the ivy-clad wall, the round window seemed to have disappeared. Fidelio eventually found it by clambering up the thick vines and pulling aside a long curtain of leaves.

One by one, they wriggled through the window, and then dropped into the domed room. Henry gazed at the painted walls in amazement, "It's like the world in the Time Twister," he murmured, "the world of the Red King." He would have liked to stay longer but the others hurried him across the room. They squeezed past the pillar and entered the tunnel. The cats had followed them every step of the way and now lit the darkness with their bright coats.

As they made their way along the tunnel, Charlie told Henry about Skarpo, the sorcerer, and the stolen Welsh wand. Henry found all this rather hard to take in, so soon after his escape. It was easier for him to understand Fidelio's description of the Pets' Café and, after two weeks on little more than bread and water, he began to look forward to the delicious cakes that he would find there.

They had almost reached the end of the tunnel, when the small door into the café was flung open and a tall figure appeared. The boys stopped. It was difficult to see the stranger's face. And then Mrs. Onimous ran toward them, frantically waving her hands.

"Oh, boys," she cried. "It's no use. A dreadful thing has occurred. It's an ambush!"

"What?" said Charlie. What's happened?"

"Dr. Bloor and one of your aunts are in the café. They're watching every move we make."

This was very bad news.

"Maybe we could sneak Henry out while they're eating," Charlie suggested.

"Not a chance, dear." She peered down at Henry. "So you're the young traveler. What a thrill to meet you, dear. I'm Mrs. Onimous."

"How do you do?" Henry shook her hand. "I've been looking forward to one of your cakes," he said.

Mrs. Onimous beamed. "Then you shall have one very soon, dear. But you'll have to stay here for a bit, nice and quiet, while your friends come back with me."

"We can't leave Henry here!" said Charlie.

"You'll have to, dear. They saw you both come into the café. Your aunt has been asking where you were. I told her you were helping in the kitchen, but who knows if she believed me. She'll be behind the counter and nosing in the kitchen before we know where we are."

Mrs. Onimous took Charlie and Fidelio by the arm and drew them up the tunnel and into the store room. The last thing Charlie saw before she closed the door was Henry's pale, stricken face.

"I'm sorry, Henry," Charlie whispered. "You won't have to stay there for long. There'll be a storm, but you mustn't worry. It's to protect you. Wait for Mr. Onimous. He'll tell you when it's safe to come out."

"Good-bye, Charlie," said Henry.

Charlie shivered when Mrs. Onimous locked the door. Henry's words had sounded so sad and final.

"I didn't think I'd have to leave him in the dark again," he muttered, as Mrs. Onimous led the way back to the kitchen.

"It won't be for long," said Fidelio.

Charlie wasn't sure. How long would his aunts be watching the café? Who knew what could happen in the next few hours. When darkness fell, the beast would be about.

When the two boys walked back into the café they found Lucretia Yewbeam staring at them from a table in the center of the room. Dr. Bloor sat opposite her. Lucretia gave a nod and the headmaster turned his head in their direction. As the boys made their way over to their friends, they could feel two pairs of eyes watching them.

"We were getting worried," said Olivia. "Did you . . . ?"

"Yes," said Charlie.

"Shhh!" said Gabriel. "Let's get out of here. I've got a feeling there are spies everywhere."

The eight children filed past Dr. Bloor's table. Dr.

Bloor gave them a curt nod and Lysander said, "Afternoon, Dr. Bloor!"

Lucretia Yewbeam glared at Charlie and said, "Earning pocket money, Charlie? I hope you'll be putting it toward your school fees."

"What?" Charlie's jaw dropped. He couldn't think what his aunt was talking about.

Fidelio came to the rescue. "They pay us very well, Matron," he said. "We do the washing up and sometimes they let us make the sandwiches."

"Do they now?" said the Matron. "Pity you don't do more of that at home, Charlie. It seems that children won't do anything these days unless they're paid for it."

Dr. Bloor was about to agree when there was a loud yelp from the floor. Charlie had stepped on a hairless tail beside Dr. Bloor's foot.

"Look where you're going, boy!" barked the headmaster.

"Sorry, Sir!" Charlie realized that Blessed must have been dragged along to the café as Dr. Bloor's pet companion.

Aunt Lucretia had brought something in a cage, though it was impossible to guess what it was. The cage was made of thick wire mesh and all that could be seen was a large blue blob.

"Snake!" whispered Fidelio.

Charlie hurried on.

As they stepped out onto Frog Street, someone in red boots leaped out of sight around the corner.

"Aunt Venetia again," Charlie muttered grimly.

Lysander and Tancred sprinted up to High Street, but the red boots had vanished in a crowd of busy shoppers. However, when Charlie caught up with his friends he saw someone else. There, sitting on a bench, was Grandma Bone.

Charlie marched up to his grandmother. "What are you doing here, Grandma?" he asked.

"Why does one usually sit beside a bus stop?" she said coolly. "One is waiting for a bus, of course. You're very popular today, Charlie. Lots of friends, I see."

"Yes," said Charlie. He walked on.

When they were some distance from Grandma

Bone, Olivia's curiosity couldn't be contained any longer. "How did you get Henry out?" she begged. "Did the wand work?"

Charlie told them everything that happened in the castle.

"So he's stuck in the tunnel," groaned Olivia. "Now what?"

"The rest is up to my Uncle Paton," said Charlie.

They had reached the traffic lights and Gabriel spotted his mother, waiting in her Land Rover on the other side of the road. She had promised to give Lysander and Tancred a lift back to the Heights.

Before he crossed the road, Tancred turned to Charlie and said, "I think we're due for a storm. It'll get a few of these busybodies off the streets."

Charlie had just caught sight of Aunt Eustacia, watching them from the doorway of the pharmacy. "A storm would be great," he said.

"You're on," said Tancred.

As the three older boys crossed the road, Tancred's

hair stood up in stiff tufts and a cold breeze blew into Charlie's face.

Raindrops began to spatter the pavement.

"Good old Tancred," said Fidelio. "Let's get home before the storm gets going."

Charlie agreed to let everyone know when Henry was safe and then, as thunder rumbled in the distance, Emma and Olivia headed off to Ingledew's Books. Fidelio hurried away through a sea of umbrellas, and Charlie, Benjamin, and his dog rushed back to Filbert Street.

"I'll come over after tea," Benjamin called as Charlie leaped up the steps to number nine.

"See you!" Charlie let himself in and ran straight up to his uncle's room.

Paton was waiting for him. "Did it all go according to plan?" he asked.

"Almost," said Charlie. "But I had to leave Henry in the tunnel. Dr. Bloor was in the café, and the aunts were everywhere. Even Grandma Bone was watching us."

"Calm down, Charlie," said his uncle. "They'll have to give up soon. There's a old storm brewing out there, and my sisters hate getting wet. Mr. Onimous will take care of Henry. All we've got to do is wait."

"But for how long?"

"We should be safe by ten o'clock," said Paton. "I'll phone the Pets' Café to make sure all is well, and then we'll pop along and collect our Henry. It's going to be quite a night, Charlie."

Uncle Paton's dark eyes shone with confidence, so why did Charlie feel so uneasy?

"We shouldn't have left him in the tunnel," he murmured.

THE TIME TWISTER

Henry had fallen asleep. A crack of thunder woke him up and he scrambled to his feet. Charlie had warned him that there would be a storm, but he didn't expect it to sound like this. Another boom echoed down the tunnel, and something scurried through the dark behind him. One of the cats pounced. There was a squeal and the crunch of bones.

This was worse than being in the pit. Henry thought of the room where a red sun sent bright rays across the floor. It was a cheerful place and he longed to be there again.

"Why shouldn't I?" he said to himself. "They'll come and find me when it's time."

He set off toward the comfort of the bright room. Immediately as he moved away from the café door, the cats leaped around him meowing loudly. They seemed disturbed to find him walking in the wrong direction.

"I'm not going far," Henry told the cats. "Just to the sun room."

They followed him down the dark tunnels and into the room. When he spread his cape on the red sun and lay down, they relaxed and sat close to him, washing themselves vigorously.

Light from the hole in the domed roof began to fade. Soon the sky was inky black. The storm raged on, and lightning lit the patterned walls with sudden fierce flashes.

Undisturbed by thunder or lightning, the three cats curled up and went to sleep.

Who knows what made Henry do what he did next? Perhaps it was the sound that came from the round window? Some might have thought it was the wind, or raindrops falling through the branches. Henry thought he heard someone sobbing. It reminded him of James. He could never hear that sound without wanting to do something about it.

The cats slept on as Henry tiptoed to the round window and climbed out. He had only taken a few steps through the woods when there was a deep snarl behind him.

Henry ran. He tore around the glade where the dark pit gaped beside the rock. He mounted the wooded bank beyond the rock, while the beast stalked him through the trees, grunting hungrily.

Henry searched desperately for a way out of the glade. His fingers tore at dry rock, walls of ivy, and branches of thorn. All at once, a flash of lightning showed him a stone archway and he leaped through it. He found himself in a dark, damp passage where the ground was covered in thick, slippery moss. Stumbling blindly up a steep incline, Henry made his way toward the streaks of lightning that lit the far end of the passage.

The grunts and snarls of the beast echoed behind him as he crawled through a network of planks and then fell onto the stones of a large courtyard. Without looking back, Henry got to his feet and rushed through the huge arch that led into the garden.

As he tore across the wet grass the noise of the

storm intensified. A howling wind swept rain across the garden in torrents and, by the time Henry reached the academy he was soaked to the skin.

The garden door was unlocked and Henry thankfully leaped inside, slamming the door behind him. At the top of the stairs, on the other side of the hall, Billy Raven stood staring at him. The white-haired boy didn't say a word, he just watched impassively as Henry rushed for the nearest door: the door into the west wing. He didn't have long to hide. Billy wouldn't waste any time. In a few minutes the Bloors would know their prisoner had escaped and they would be searching the building.

Henry began to climb the stairs up to the music room. He had been safe there before. The music teacher was a strange man, but Henry knew he could trust him. The storm was now at its height. The whole tower rocked under deafening thunder, and lightning flashed continuously through every window.

Henry had almost reached the top of the spiraling stairs when there was a shout from below.

"He came in here!"

Two pairs of footsteps could be heard running up the tower steps. Henry leaped forward, missed a step, and tumbled back onto the floor.

"Hear that? He's up there!" shouted Manfred.

Henry picked himself up. He began to wonder if there was any point in trying to escape. They would find him in the end. He gazed hopelessly up the narrow stairs, and gave a sigh of despair. The next moment, his arm was touched by a slim, gloved hand.

Mrs. Bloor was standing beside him. An utterly changed Mrs. Bloor. Gone were her dark clothes. Now she wore a red coat and a brightly patterned scarf. She had a violin case tucked under her arm and in her free hand she carried a small leather bag. Her hair shone and her eyes were sparkling.

"It's time to go, Henry," she said, uncurling her crippled hand. "Look!"

Henry saw the Time Twister glowing against her dark glove. He looked away quickly.

"We'll go together," said Mrs. Bloor. "Take my arm and come this way."

Without thinking, Henry grasped Mrs. Bloor's left arm as she hurried through the door behind her. It led into one of the long, dark corridors in the west wing.

Mrs. Bloor began to run. "The time is perfect," she said. "There was a storm, you see, the night they broke my fingers. I can go back, now, to the way I was. I can leave before they catch me." She put on a sudden spurt and Henry almost tripped as he tried to keep up with her.

"Suppose . . . ," he said breathlessly. "Suppose you go back to the wrong place."

"I won't, Henry. I've been thinking so hard about where I want to be. I trust this ancient marble. I'll be five minutes ahead of them. This time I'll be through the doors and hailing a taxi before anyone knows I've gone."

"I don't think I can come with you," Henry panted.

"But you must."

A voice bellowed down the corridor, "Dorothy, STOP!"

"Faster, Henry!" cried Mrs. Bloor.

Henry felt as though his lungs were being crushed by an elephant. He couldn't keep running. He'd never breathe again.

"MANFRED, GET THEM!" roared Dr. Bloor.

As Manfred came bounding after the runaways, a short fat shape ambled across the corridor. There was a loud yell and Manfred tripped over Blessed. He fell headlong onto the floorboards, groaning and swearing.

"Blasted, wretched, hateful . . ."

While Manfred cursed the old dog, Mrs. Bloor swerved around a corner and under a low arch. Beyond the arch a flight of stone steps ascended to a narrow window.

"Bother," Mrs. Bloor panted as she mounted the steps. "I didn't mean to come this way, but there's no help for it. Come along, Henry."

Henry had by now let go of Mrs. Bloor's arm. He

was of two minds whether to follow her, but he didn't seem to have a choice.

"Come on, come on," she urged.

When she reached the top of the steps, Mrs. Bloor unlatched the window and appeared to leap into the air. Henry froze as a bolt of lightning lit the sky. Had his companion fallen to her death, or was she already twisting back through time? He scrambled up the steps and looked out.

Mrs. Bloor was standing in a wide passage between the roof and a long parapet. From the top of the parapet strange stone beasts looked out over the garden and the dark, faraway trees.

"Come on, dear," said Mrs. Bloor. "Don't be afraid." She was gazing at the Time Twister, and the glowing glass ball threw dazzling colors out into the night sky.

Henry couldn't help himself. He stepped toward her. Behind him came the thud of heavy footsteps.

Without taking her eyes from the Time Twister, Mrs. Bloor hitched the strap of her bag over her shoulder and grabbed a corner of Henry's cape. "A few more seconds," she breathed. "I can feel it, Henry. Soon we'll be gone."

She ran beside the parapet, tugging Henry with her, and laughing happily. Henry wondered what would happen when they reached the end of the roof. But they never got that far. Mrs. Bloor's red coat began to shiver under the fierce white lightning. Her pale hair sparkled and scattered in a burst of starlight.

"Henry," came a soft, disembodied voice. "There was something I meant to tell Charlie. I know where his father . . . but now it's too late . . . he'll never . . . oh, Henry, we're going!"

But Henry didn't want to go out there, to another world he didn't know. He'd only just got used to this one. Slipping out of his cape, he flung himself behind one of the massive chimneys that rose above the roof. From the chimney's deep shadow he watched Mrs. Bloor twist into a bolt of rainbow colors — and disappear. There was a gentle floating laugh — and then nothing.

The wind died and the thunder rolled away, but in

a last brilliant shaft of lightning, Henry saw Manfred Bloor standing by the parapet. He was looking up into the sky and calling out. It was a faint strangled cry and Henry could have been mistaken, but it sounded very like the word "Mommy!"

"Has she gone, then?" Dr. Bloor shouted from the window.

"They've both gone," said Manfred, blowing his nose. He picked up Henry's blue cape. "The boy left this behind. I dare say he won't be needing it where he's gone."

"Wherever that is," muttered Dr. Bloor.

"Great-grandpa will be disappointed," said Manfred as he walked away from Henry's hiding place. "He wanted to have a bit more fun with the little beast."

Henry shuddered. *What sort of fun?* he wondered.

Manfred stepped through the window and closed it with a bang.

A wan moon peeped through the rolling clouds. Henry moved out from the shadows and looked down into the garden. He had no idea how he was going to get away without being seen. The Bloors were bound to catch him before he reached the ruin. And even if he got that far, the beast would be waiting for him.

He ran to the window and found that it was locked. Cold and hungry, Henry thought of the Pets' Café and the cakes Mrs. Onimous had promised him.

"It just wasn't to be," he sighed.

He had almost decided to risk breaking the window when something swept through the air above him. A huge bird landed on the parapet, its great wings glistening with raindrops. Henry had never seen such a gigantic bird. Its beak had a cruel curve and each of its massive talons was like a shining scimitar. And yet Henry wasn't afraid. He sensed something friendly about the great creature, something almost kindly.

As he approached the bird it bent its head. Henry put his arms around the long feathered neck and closed his eyes.

• • •

At seven o'clock Benjamin went to see Charlie.

"I want to know what's happening about Henry," said Benjamin.

"I'm going to get Uncle Paton to ring Mr. Onimous soon," Charlie said. "It's horrible just waiting and waiting and not knowing what's going on."

Benjamin and Runner Bean followed Charlie up to his room. Grandma Bone hadn't come home and this was worrying Charlie. Was she still waiting outside the Pets' Café? Would she be lurking there when Uncle Paton drove around to collect Henry? And what of the Yewbeam aunts? Was Henry still safe in the tunnel? That was another worrying question.

After a while Charlie couldn't stand it any longer. He went to his uncle's room and knocked on the door. "It's me," said Charlie. "Uncle Paton, do you think you could call Mr. Onimous? I'm worried about Henry."

"Very well," sighed Paton. "If I can find my phone."

At that moment the front door slammed and

someone marched across the hall. Charlie recognized Grandma Bone's footsteps and ran back to his room.

A few minutes later Uncle Paton's troubled face looked around Charlie's door.

"I found the phone," said Paton. "I called Mr. Onimous. Henry's gone!"

"What!" Charlie stared at his uncle in horror. "But how? Did Mr. Onimous look?"

"He told me he went right to the end of the tunnel and out into the ruin. There was no sign of Henry. The poor little man is very distressed."

"Henry went into the room with the sun," Charlie murmured. "He'd feel safe there. But why didn't he come back?"

"We'll have to wait," said Paton. "That's all we can do. Wait and hope. My father will be waiting, too."

"You mean . . ." Charlie suddenly realized what Paton meant.

"Yes, I've told him about Henry. That's where I was hoping to take him, to live with his brother by the sea."

Waiting and hoping is a hard thing to do when you've already been waiting and hoping for almost as long as you can bear it. Terrible images kept springing into Charlie's mind. Henry being chased through the ruin, captured, eaten alive.

Benjamin stayed as long as he could, but after another half hour he told Charlie he'd have to go home or his mom would start to worry.

"OK," Charlie said gloomily.

As Benjamin turned to go, Runner Bean rushed to the window and barked.

"Shhhhh!" said Benjamin.

The big dog barked again. He stood on his hind legs and pawed the curtains.

"Shut up, Runner," said Benjamin. "Grandma Bone'll catch us."

Runner Bean looked at his master and whined mournfully.

"We don't go out through the window," Benjamin said impatiently. "Come on, Runner, this way."

"Ben!" Charlie jumped up. "I think there's something out there." He went to the window and drew back the curtains.

There was a large chestnut tree outside Charlie's window. Sitting on a wide branch was Henry Yewbeam. He waved at Charlie and mouthed the word, "Hello!"

Charlie dashed downstairs and out of the front door. He waited anxiously while Henry swung from a branch and dropped to the ground, then the two boys ran into the house.

"Upstairs," Charlie whispered as he closed the front door.

Henry quickly mounted the stairs, but before he reached the top, Grandma Bone came out of the living room.

"Who's that boy?" she demanded.

"Benjamin." Charlie was halfway up the staircase.

"Oh?" she looked suspicious. "I hope that dog's not in your room."

"Of course not, Grandma."

Charlie followed Henry up to the landing, while Grandma Bone walked across to the kitchen.

"In here," said Charlie, quickly drawing Henry into his bedroom. "This is Benjamin."

"Hello! I'm Henry." While Charlie closed the door Henry shook Benjamin's hand and then the paw that Runner Bean was eagerly holding up to him. "I'm very pleased to meet you both," he said. "Please don't be alarmed."

Benjamin realized he was staring at Henry with his mouth open. "I'm Benjamin," he said. "You look quite normal."

"He is normal," said Charlie. "He's just . . ."

"Out of time," said Henry. He sat on the bed and announced, "I'm free. I'm safe. The Bloors think I've gone back, so they won't be looking for me."

"I don't understand," said Charlie. "How did you get here?"

"It's a long story," said Henry and he began to describe his extraordinary adventure.

"You say a bird rescued you!" Benjamin exclaimed.

"It must have been Emma!" said Charlie.

Benjamin and Henry looked baffled, so Charlie explained.

"I'd like to thank all your friends," said Henry, "the ones who helped me."

Charlie told him there wouldn't be time to meet his friends. "Tonight Uncle Paton's taking us to a place where you'll be safe," he said. "We have to go before Grandma Bone finds out that you're in the house."

"Where will I go?" Henry looked worried.

"You're going home. To the house by the sea. And I'm coming with you. Just for the day. It'll be the very first time I've seen my great-grandpa."

Henry frowned. "And who's he?"

"He's your brother, James."

"James?" cried Henry. "Little Jamie? He's still alive?"

If it hadn't been for Runner Bean, Henry might never have seen his brother again. With a low, rumbling growl the dog stared at the door. Charlie pushed a startled Henry under the bed, and the door opened.

Grandma Bone stood on the threshold, glaring at

Runner Bean. "You're a liar, Charlie Bone," she said coldly. "You did have a dog in here. Get it out. Now!" She looked around the room, her long nose wrinkling like a pug's. "Who else are you hiding? What's been going on?"

"Nothing, Mrs. Bone," said Benjamin. "My dog's scared of storms so I brought him over here to take his mind off it."

"Storm's gone!" bellowed Grandma Bone. "Hadn't you noticed? Now, go home."

"Yes, Mrs. Bone." Benjamin shuffled meekly past the tall woman in the doorway. Runner Bean bared his teeth and directed one of his best growls at Grandma Bone's skinny ankles.

"Aaaah!" she shrieked, backing out of the door. "Get him away from me."

When Benjamin and his dog were safely out of the house, Grandma Bone looked in on Charlie and told him to get ready for bed.

"Yes, Grandma." He closed the door and ran to the

window. Benjamin had just reached the other side of the road when Charlie looked out.

"Ben!" he called. "Pass on the news, will you? Tell the others what happened?"

Grandma Bone gave up wondering about all the creaking and whispering that went on in the house that night. As far as she was concerned, Henry Yewbeam had disappeared into the past — or the future — so whatever was going on was all childish nonsense and she couldn't be bothered with it. She drank a stiff whiskey and went to sleep.

A JOURNEY TO THE SEA

Charlie told the rest of the household about Henry's arrival, and, one by one, they began to visit the boy from the past.

Paton came first. He stood in the doorway for a second, blinking speechlessly, and then he strode up to Henry, exclaiming, "My dear, dear fellow, I can't believe it. This is just too wonderful for words." He shook Henry's hand vigorously. "I've heard so much about you. My father idolized you, you know."

"Did he?" said Henry. "I suppose I'm your uncle."

While Paton was still chuckling over this, Amy Bone looked in.

"This is my mom," Charlie told Henry.

"And you're Henry." Mrs. Bone gazed at Henry as if she couldn't quite believe her eyes. "All that way," she murmured. "All those years, I should say. So it really can happen."

Was she thinking of his father? Charlie wondered. *Was*

she wishing that he too might come twisting through time to be with her again?

As Henry and Mrs. Bone solemnly shook hands, Henry said, "Mrs. Bloor told me she knew . . ." and then he seemed to change his mind.

There was no time to ask Henry what Mrs. Bloor knew because, at that moment, Maisie arrived on the scene.

"He looks a bit like Charlie, doesn't he?" she said.

"Mm. Just a little," said Amy.

Wherever Henry had come from, it didn't matter to Maisie; he was a boy in trouble and therefore in need of a hug. "You poor, poor thing," she cried, almost squeezing the life out of him. "You look half-starved. Come to the kitchen this minute and I'll cook up a feast."

"I don't think that'd be a good idea," said Charlie. "Grandma Bone might come down."

"Drat Grandma Bone," said Maisie. "What's she up to now? If she so much as lays a finger on this poor boy I'll give her a good wallop."

"Maisie, dear, please lower your voice," said Paton

in a quiet, but commanding tone. "If you want to help, you can bring a snack up to Charlie's room. And we shall need food and blankets for a long journey to the coast. I did mention it before."

"Yes, Paton," Maisie said patiently. "I hadn't forgotten."

"Come on, Mom, we've got work to do," said Amy.

The two women went downstairs to prepare a picnic basket while Henry chose some of Charlie's clothes to wear in his new life.

"It'll be so strange," he said to Charlie. "I was always the oldest. I took care of James. What's he going to make of it all?"

"I can't wait to find out," said Charlie.

At ten minutes to twelve, Charlie and Henry climbed into Uncle Paton's midnight blue car. They were followed by a pile of blankets and pillows and a huge basket of food.

"You help yourselves whenever you're hungry," said Maisie as she stuffed cushions behind their heads and tucked blankets around their legs.

Paton was already in the driver's seat glancing impatiently at his watch. He was a man of habit and he liked to leave for the coast on the stroke of midnight. As the great cathedral clock began to ring out across the city, he said, "Snuggle down, boys! We'll have breakfast by the sea."

The car doors were slammed and Mrs. Bone and Maisie waved and blew kisses from the curb, as Paton drove slowly up Filbert Street. In case of lamp accidents, he liked to keep to the side roads, and after driving down several badly lit alleys, they were suddenly deep in the countryside. Here there were no lights at all, except for the odd twinkle from a cowshed or a porch light.

Charlie was beginning to drift off to sleep when a question popped into his head. "You told my mom Mrs. Bloor knew something," he said to Henry. "What did she know?"

Henry yawned. "It was about your father," he mumbled sleepily. "Just before she disappeared she said there was something she meant to tell you. I think she knew where your father was."

Charlie sat bolt upright, throwing his pillow to the floor. "Didn't she tell you?" he demanded.

"No," Henry murmured. "She just vanished."

"What did she say exactly?" Charlie asked frantically.

There was no answer. Henry had fallen asleep, and Charlie didn't have the heart to wake him.

"Did you hear that, Uncle Paton?" said Charlie. "Mrs. Bloor knew where my father was — or is."

"I heard, Charlie. Perhaps it means that he isn't very far away. We'll find him one day. That's a promise."

Charlie thought he would never sleep after this amazing piece of news, but before he knew it, his eyes were closed.

Whether he was awake or dreaming, Charlie could never be sure, but at some time during their long journey to the sea, his uncle began to talk about the Red King. Perhaps Charlie had mentioned the vanishing tree he had seen in the snow, or the strange red tree that had appeared in the king's portrait, but Paton's words remained very clear in his head.

"I believe he is a tree, Charlie. That's what my books seem to tell me. When the king lived in the great forests with only the trees and his leopards for company, he became a part of the forest himself. Can trees move, you might ask? Who can say? Who is to know if a tree standing in a field at dawn, cannot later be seen in a castle ruin, or in the shadows of a great park? Perhaps, one day you'll find out."

When Charlie opened his eyes again, he saw a great sweep of gray sea. They were traveling along a narrow cliff road and light was beginning to fill the sky. He nudged Henry, who was still asleep beside him. Henry stirred and rubbed his eyes.

"Look!" said Charlie. "The sea!"

Henry looked out of the window. "I know this place," he cried. "We're nearly home."

"There's a few miles to go, yet," said Paton. "Let's have breakfast."

There was a shout of agreement from the boys and soon they were enjoying Maisie's feast. A cold wind was howling outside, and so they ate in the car, watching the huge foamy breakers crashing onto the shore below.

When breakfast was over they set off again. The road ran beside the sea almost the whole way and Charlie never tired of watching the waves, the tumbling cliffs, and the misty islands far out in the water. And then they turned a corner and Henry cried, "We're here!"

Ahead of them was a small bay where the sea was calm and blue. As they drove down toward the beach, sunlight spilled over the horizon and the water became a sheet of sparkling glass. It was like entering another country. Gone were the dark clouds and the winter wind. Gone were the wild waves pounding the shingle.

"What's happened?" said Charlie. "Everything's gone calm."

"Like a spell," breathed Henry.

They parked on a patch of grass beside the beach. On the other side of the road, Charlie could see a white house perched on top of a steep cliff.

"Is that it?" he asked Henry.

Henry just nodded.

They crossed the road and climbed two flights of whitewashed steps set into the cliff. Uncle Paton went first with Charlie following. But Henry hung back. He seemed to be afraid of what he might find in the house at the top of the steps.

There was a porch with a blue painted door at the side of the house. Paton let himself in and Charlie stepped in after him. They went through another door and into a room that seemed to be full of sunlight.

An old man came toward them. His hair was white and his eyes were gray, and although he was obviously very old, his face looked young, somehow, as though all his wrinkles had come from smiling and sea weather.

"I saw you arrive," said the old man, giving Paton a big hug. "So this is Charlie. Well, well, well! At last we meet!"

"At last," said Charlie, while his great-grandfather clutched him to his chest.

Henry was standing just inside the door. He was

staring at the old man. And then the old man saw him, and they just gazed at each other, without saying a word.

At last Henry said, "Jamie!" as if somewhere under all those wrinkles, he'd suddenly seen his little brother; the boy he'd left behind when he went to play his last game of marbles.

James Yewbeam still couldn't speak. His eyes had a glittery, tearful look, and Paton took Charlie aside while the two brothers hugged each other.

It was almost too much for the old man. He sank into an armchair and shook his head, over and over again. "I can't believe it," he said. "It's really you!" He reached into his pocket and brought out a small leather bag. "Look, Henry. I've still got the marbles."

Henry sat on the arm of his chair. "I'll teach you how to play Ring Taw," he said.

"About time, too," said James with a laugh.

And then another extraordinary thing happened. A door opened and Cook walked into the room. Or was it Cook?

"Cook?" said Charlie.

"Not Cook," said the woman. "I'm Cook's sister, Pearl."

"So that's why the sea was so calm," Henry murmured.

Pearl nodded and gave him a big smile. It turned out that Pearl had been James Yewbeam's housekeeper for twenty years. Ever since his wife died.

They all began to talk about Henry's future. How he would go to the local school beyond the bay.

"It's small and friendly," said Pearl. "Henry will fit in perfectly. He can start in the summer term, when Charlie's filled him in a bit about all these newfangled things like cell phones and videos and whatnot."

It was decided that Charlie would come to see Henry once a month, every time that Paton visited his father.

"And over the holidays, too," said Henry. "Charlie must come here over the holidays."

"Of course," said Paton.

Charlie had never had a vacation by the sea. It was

something he'd always dreamed about, but he'd never really believed it would happen. He looked through the window at the sparkling water and the sandy beach.

He didn't have to wait long to visit the beach. Old James Yewbeam had been awake all night, and now, after all the excitement he fell fast asleep in his chair. Paton went upstairs for a snooze before his long drive back to the city, and Pearl began to prepare a meal.

"You two should go down to the shore," she told the boys. "You both look as if you could do with some fresh air."

They didn't need any more encouragement. Charlie and Henry spent the rest of the day on the beach. They skimmed pebbles across the water, jumped over rock pools, and explored the caves that Henry knew so well.

All too soon night clouds began to roll in across the water, and Uncle Paton was calling the boys to supper.

They sat around a table in the bay window, where

they could watch the moonlit water. There were candles on the table but the rest of the room was in darkness. Old Mr. Yewbeam always removed the lightbulbs on Paton's visits. As Charlie dug into the delicious supper that Pearl had prepared, he couldn't help thinking of Cook in her little underground rooms, far away from the sea and the sun.

"I wish Cook could find a place like this to live," he said.

Pearl told him that Cook was very happy where she was. She loved keeping an eye on the children at Bloor's Academy. "We talk on the phone for hours," said Pearl. "And Treasure — that's her name — Treasure tells me everything that's been going on with you children of the Red King, and sometimes I think it's me who's missing out."

"But now you've got Henry," said Charlie.

"Now I've got Henry." Pearl's eyes twinkled. "And I can see that he's going to be quite a handful."

They all laughed at this, and then Uncle Paton stood up, saying, "Come on, Charlie. We've got to get you home, or you'll never be awake in time for school tomorrow."

"School," sighed Charlie. He wished he could have stayed a little longer.

The two brothers — one so old and the other still young — stood at the top of the cliff steps and waved good-bye as Paton and Charlie climbed into the midnight blue car. Charlie snuggled down in the seat beside his uncle and the car roared into life.

"I think Henry's going to be OK, don't you?" he said.

"OK?" said Paton. "He's going to be absolutely splendid. Well done, Charlie!"

PATON HAS A PARTY

Every year, on Uncle Paton's birthday, Grandma Bone and her sisters took a short trip. They hated having to buy presents or indulge in "nonsensical celebrations," as Grandma Bone put it.

This year, Paton's birthday was on the first day of the break. Maisie decided that before Charlie and his uncle set off for the coast again, Paton should have a real party for a change.

"We've never had a real party here before," she said. "But Charlie's new friends have got such interesting parents, we really ought to get to know them."

Invitations were sent out and, surprisingly, everyone accepted. Even the judge.

The party was kept secret from Grandma Bone in case she tried to put a stop to it. Maisie managed to hide the champagne under a sack in the pantry and the birthday cake was put in a crate marked CAULI-

FLOWER. Grandma Bone hated cauliflower so she kept well away from it.

On the morning before the party, Charlie carried his grandmother's suitcase down the stairs. Grandma Bone was right behind him when he crossed the hall to the front door. There was a bang and the sound of breaking glass. Charlie dropped the case and look around.

"Oh dear," said Grandma Bone. "That picture's broken again, and Paton's just had new glass put in it."

The photo of Henry and his family lay on the floor; the glass in the frame had smashed into a thousand pieces. Had Grandma Bone knocked it down on purpose? She had a nasty smile on her face.

"Well, it's good riddance to him," she said, pushing the frame with the toe of her boot.

Charlie didn't say a word. *If only she knew the truth,* he thought.

Once she was out of the house, everyone breathed a sigh of relief.

"To work," cried Maisie. "Let's make this old house like a palace!"

At seven o'clock, their work complete, Maisie and Paton, Charlie and his mother, waited for their guests to arrive.

Tancred and his parents came first. As soon as the Torssons walked through the front door, all the candles flickered violently. A few went out.

"Sorry!" boomed Mr. Torsson. "We'll try and keep the breezes to ourselves."

Maisie was delighted. "How clever," she said. "We could do with a bit of fresh air in here."

Benjamin and the detectives came next, and they were quickly followed by Fidelio and the singing Gunns, and Gabriel and his parents. Mr. Silk wrote murder mysteries and when he heard that Mr. and Mrs. Brown were private detectives he whipped out his notebook and was soon deep in conversation with Mr. Brown.

The Onimouses, the flame cats, and the Vertigos arrived at the same time. Olivia's father was a famous film director and immediately wanted to know if Mr. Onimous had considered a career in the movies. "I'm casting for *The Wind in the Willows* right now," he said.

"I'll consider it," said Mr. Onimous.

By eight o'clock the party was in full swing. Charlie thought everyone had arrived, but Paton told him that there was just one more guest to come. A few minutes later the bell rang. Charlie opened the front door and found Cook on the doorstep.

"Pearl's been keeping me up-to-date about Henry. It's a happy ending for him, after all."

"And Mrs. Bloor," said Charlie.

He took Cook into the kitchen where Gabriel Silk was helping to serve the drinks.

"There's just one thing I'd like to know," said Cook, sipping her glass of wine. "Where did Dorothy find that marble?"

"I gave it to her," said Gabriel. "Well, she asked me for it."

Charlie was surprised to hear this.

"Well, well," said Cook, "and where did you find it?"

"Mr. Pilgrim gave it to me," said Gabriel.

"Of course." Cook nodded slowly. "Mr. Pilgrim is a mysterious man."

"Where do you think Mrs. Bloor is now?" asked Charlie.

"She'll be in Paris, just as she always intended. She'll have gotten herself a nice little apartment and soon she'll be giving violin lessons. Maybe she'll join an orchestra. Who knows? She'll be playing her violin again, which is all she ever wanted. And she'll be safe." Cook looked at Gabriel. "Thank you, Gabriel."

There was a sudden loud bang on the front door. It came again. Someone wasn't even bothering to ring the bell.

BANG! BANG! BANG!

"Whoever . . . ?" said Paton.

Charlie followed his uncle to the front door.

Grandma Bone stood on the top step with her three sisters behind her.

"What's going on?" she demanded.

"We're having a party," said Paton coolly. "What are you doing here?"

"How dare you have a party in my house. Stop it this minute!" snapped Grandma Bone.

"Stop it!" said Lucretia.

"Everybody out!" said Eustacia.

"You can't have a party without our permission," said Venetia.

"SHUT UP!" said Paton. "I can have a party. In case you've forgotten, it's half my house."

"What's the trouble, Paton?" Mr. Torsson had come to see what the fuss was about.

"No trouble," said Paton. "Nothing I can't handle."

Whether Paton could handle it or not was beside the point. Mr. Torsson took one look at the four angry sisters, puffed up his cheeks, and blew them down the steps and clean across the street.

Grandma Bone narrowly missed being hit by a bus.

Charlie watched in awe and astonishment as the Yewbeam sisters picked themselves up, patted their hair, brushed their muddy clothes, and shook their fists at Paton and Mr. Torsson.

A loud thundercrack and a sudden cloudburst

sent them scurrying away down the street, shrieking and cursing.

"We'll pay for that," Paton murmured.

"But not tonight," said Charlie.

As soon as the four sisters were well and truly gone, Olivia Vertigo said, "Let's dance!".

"Yes, a dance!" cried Fidelio.

Before anyone could stop them they had moved the table in the dining room and rolled up the rug. Emma put some music on the CD player and all three of them began to dance around the room.

The other boys hung back at first, but then Maisie grabbed the judge around the waist and whirled him onto the dance floor. After that, no one else could resist the music. Soon the usually cold and cheerless room was full of swaying, bobbing figures. Uncle Paton even managed to persuade Miss Ingledew onto the floor. The room was so crowded they had to dance very close. Charlie noted that Miss Ingledew didn't seem to mind a bit.

He couldn't see his mother in the room and so he went to find her. She was sitting in the kitchen staring through the window. Little flakes of snow were drifting down from the sky, but Charlie knew his mother didn't see them.

"Dad will come back," said Charlie quietly.

When Mrs. Bone turned to him, she didn't look sad at all, in fact she was smiling.

"You know, Charlie, I'm beginning to believe you," she said. "After what happened to Henry, I can believe almost anything."

JENNY NIMMO

I was born in Windsor, Berkshire, England, and educated at boarding schools in Kent and Surrey from the age of six until I was sixteen, when I ran away from school to become a drama student/assistant stage manager with Theater South East. I graduated and acted in repertory theater in various towns and cities: Eastbourne, Tunbridge Wells, Brighton, Hastings, and Bexhill.

I left Britain to teach English to three Italian boys in Amalfi, Italy. On my return I joined the BBC, first as a picture researcher, then assistant floor manager, studio manager (news), and finally director/adaptor with *Jackanory* (a BBC storytelling program for children). I left the BBC to marry Welsh artist David Wynn Millward and went to live in Wales in my husband's family home. We live in a very old converted watermill, and the river is constantly threatening to break in, which it has done several times in the past, most dramatically on my youngest child's first birthday. During the summer we run a residential school of art, and I have to move my office, put down tools (type-writer and pencils), and don an apron and cook! We have three grown-up children, Myfanwy, Ianto, and Gwenhwyfar.

SNEAK PREVIEW OF

Charlie Bone and the Invisible Boy
BY JENNY NIMMO
CHILDREN OF THE RED KING SERIES   BOOK 3

A BEAUTIFUL GIRL ARRIVES AT CHARLIE'S HOUSE. HER EYES KEEP CHANGING COLOR. SHE LIVES WITH THE YEWBEAM AUNTS AND SEEMS TO HAVE A STRANGE POWER OVER THEM. HER NAME IS BELLE. SHE GOES TO BLOOR'S ACADEMY WITH CHARLIE, AND IS PUT IN THE ART DEPARTMENT.

EMMA FINDS A LETTER THAT MR. BOLDOVA, THE NEW YOUNG ART TEACHER, HAS DROPPED. IT REVEALS THAT HE IS THE OLDER BROTHER OF OLLIE SPARKS, WHO DISAPPEARED A YEAR AGO, MADE INVISIBLE BY AN ANCIENT BLUE BOA CONSTRICTOR. EMMA AND CHARLIE DECIDE TO HELP MR. BOLDOVA FIND OLLIE.

BILLY RAVEN SEES BELLE CHANGE HER SHAPE — SHE BECOMES A VERY OLD WOMAN. BILLY IS TERRIFIED. THE OLD WOMAN HAS COME TO HELP THE BLOORS CONTROL THE CHILDREN OF THE RED KING, AND TO MAKE SURE THEY DON'T RESCUE OLLIE.

CAN CHARLIE AND HIS FRIENDS RESCUE OLLIE AND MAKE HIM VISIBLE AGAIN?

SAMURAI KIDS

OWL NINJA

SAMURAI KIDS

OWL NINJA

SANDY FUSSELL

CANDLEWICK PRESS

THE SAMURAI KIDS

KYOKO A white-haired girl with pink eyes and extra fingers and toes. Her spirit is the Snow Monkey.

MIKKO A one-armed boy. His spirit is the Striped Gecko.

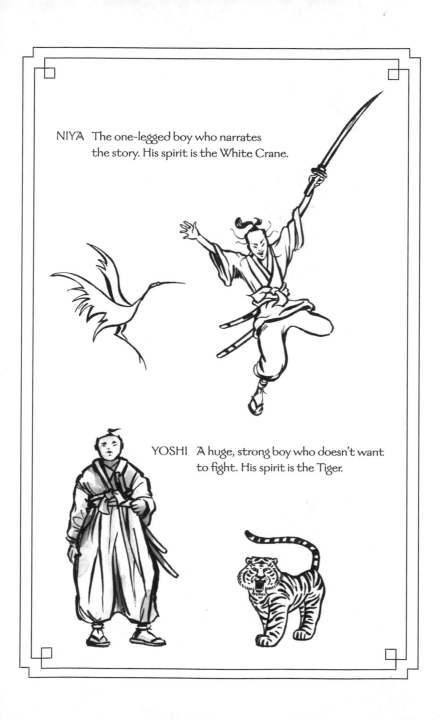

NIYA The one-legged boy who narrates
the story. His spirit is the White Crane.

YOSHI A huge, strong boy who doesn't want
to fight. His spirit is the Tiger.

TAJI A blind boy. His spirit is the Golden Bat.

NEZUME The last boy to join the Cockroach Ryu. His spirit is the Long-Tailed Rat.

THE TEACHER

SENSEI   Also known as Ki-Yaga the wizard. He
was once a famous samurai warrior.

CONTENTS

CHAPTER ONE
DRUMBEAT
1

CHAPTER TWO
BEWARE THE DRAGON
11

CHAPTER THREE
DEADLY SILENT
27

CHAPTER FOUR
HELL VALLEY
45

CHAPTER FIVE
WHAT THE GHOST SAID
59

CHAPTER SIX
THE BACK ROAD TO TOYOZAWA
73

CHAPTER SEVEN
GRANDFATHER'S STORIES
91

CHAPTER EIGHT
THE CASTLE WALLS
109

CHAPTER NINE
THE OWL HOOTS
127

CHAPTER TEN
INSIDE THE OWL DOJO
145

CHAPTER ELEVEN
THE FIRST SCROLL
165

CHAPTER TWELVE
IF THE SLIPPER FITS
189

CHAPTER THIRTEEN
THE SECOND SCROLL
209

CHAPTER FOURTEEN
FLIGHT OF THE CRANE
233

SEVEN VIRTUES
250

USEFUL WORDS
251

CHAPTER ONE

真

DRUMBEAT

"Someone's coming!" Taji yells.

I reach Taji first. Not because I'm the fastest. I'm good at many things, but running isn't one of them. It's hard to sprint with just one leg. I get there fast because I'm practicing sword thrusts only a hop away.

I peer into the valley and see a short, stocky figure making his way up the mountain path.

"Who is it?" Kyoko flops onto the grass.

Mikko, Nezume, and Yoshi arrive, pushing and shoving one another out of the way. Like an upended bowl of rice noodles, they land in a tangled mess beside me.

I've got really good eyes because in my heart I am the White Crane, able to spot a beetle on the ground from the air. My sight takes wing, soaring deep into the valley. But I don't know how Taji does it. How can a blind kid see at all? When I asked him, he laughed at me. "You have to listen, Niya. You are much too noisy to see with your ears."

It's true. I like to laugh and jump and yell. *Aeeeyagh! Aeeeyagh!* When I am practicing, the White Crane screeches out across the *ryu*. Even when I'm sleeping, Mikko has to poke me in the ribs because I snore louder than a pondful of frogs.

"It's Master Onaku," I announce.

"Why is the swordsmith coming?" Yoshi voices the question we all want to ask.

Master Onaku is Sensei Ki-Yaga's oldest friend, and it's always a special occasion when he visits. We usually spend days preparing the food. Sensei says a samurai kid must be able to wield his sword on the battlefield and a sharp knife in the kitchen. But we don't fall for that. The cooking isn't really about training. It's about Onaku's big, round stomach. The Sword Master loves to eat.

Last time, we prepared fish soup, three-egg omelette, and honey rice pudding, the finest dessert in all of Japan. My nose follows the imaginary smell as it curls into a smoke ring and drifts skyward.

"We should tell Sensei," says Nezume.

Puff. The smell disappears, but my mouth is still watering.

"I'll go," I volunteer. Maybe our teacher is in the kitchen.

But I can't even get up onto my foot before Sensei's voice meets me. "Tell Master Onaku I am waiting in the tearoom."

Sensei always handles important business there. My friends and I don't like the tea ceremony. Too many rules.

Most days, Ki-Yaga slurps his pudding and sucks the splatters from his long white beard, but during the tea ceremony, he doesn't make a sound and he doesn't spill a drop.

By the time Onaku is almost to the top of the mountain, we have made up many stories to explain his visit.

"He's bringing us extra swords," suggests Mikko.

Not likely. Last year, at our Coming-of-Age Ceremony, we were given new swords—the long *katana* and the short *wakizashi,* dual weapons of the warrior samurai. Onaku is a master craftsman. One of his swords would last two lifetimes, so it can't be that.

Kyoko looks concerned. "Maybe Mrs. Onaku is sick." Sensei is a great healer, and Onaku wouldn't trust anyone else to care for his wife. We hope that's not the reason.

"Perhaps he has run out of wine," says Yoshi.

It's the most likely explanation of all. Sensei's *dokudami* wine smells like rotten fish, but Onaku would walk up the mountain and back at the promise of a bottle.

"Hello, young Cockroaches," he calls as he draws closer. "How goes the studying and the practicing? And how is Niya's nose?"

It's an old joke. When I first came to the Cockroach

Ryu, I fell over many times during training. Twice I broke my nose. Then twice more Taji caught me unaware with the flat blade of his wooden practice sword and broke it for me.

"Our master is waiting in the tearoom," says Yoshi.

Onaku nods and hurries off to find Sensei. Something is wrong. Usually, the Sword Master will chat and joke for hours, telling us stories of the days when he was a boy listening at Ki-Yaga's feet. Sensei was old, even then.

Across the valley, a drumbeat echoes. *Thum. Thum.*

"What's that?" Nezume asks.

Ta-thum. Ta-thum. Thum.

Yoshi shakes his head. We all do. No one knows what it means, but we don't like it. It kicks hard against my chest and makes me nervous.

Yoshi puts his finger to his lips and gestures for us to follow. Yoshi is our leader, and I'd follow him anywhere. He has the spirit of a tiger—big and strong. When an earthquake rolled me off the mountain, he climbed through the darkness to my rescue.

Yoshi pads noiselessly to the tearoom. Crouching low behind Sensei's row of potted bonsai trees, he places his ear against the wall. We copy him, one by one. The wall is made of thin rice paper, so it's easy to hear every word.

"You were right, Ki-Yaga," Onaku says with a sigh. "It has happened just as you said it would."

I can see his blurred shadow, head bowed and shoulders slumped. Onaku looks old and beaten. The Sword Master is strong, and his spirit is tougher than twice-folded steel. What could make him clutch his head in his hands?

"Yes. Sometimes I really wish to be wrong." Sensei sounds sad. He places his arm around his friend.

Uneasiness surrounds us all. Things that were once solid are now wavering, hard to grasp. It's worse than when the mountain trembles, but that same air of foreboding hangs low over our heads.

I look at Yoshi, who shrugs. Yoshi looks at Kyoko, and she looks at Taji and Nezume. Mikko shakes his head. We haven't got a clue what's happening, but I know in my stomach that it's not good. Misery binds our worried faces together.

Even when a samurai is unhappy, he should never lower his guard. He'll be even more miserable if he's surprised by an enemy sword.

The door slides open, and we're caught by the
razor swipe of Sensei's steely gaze.

The door slides open, and we're caught by the razor swipe of Sensei's steely gaze. Our faces glow red and pink like the setting sun.

"Your walls have many ears, Ki-Yaga," Onaku says.

Sensei's face is like my calligraphy homework: impossible to read. "What have you heard?" he asks.

"Everything," Yoshi mumbles.

We look at the ground, hiding our sunset faces.

Yoshi scuffs his sandals in the dirt. "It was my idea. I'm responsible."

"Excellent." Sensei claps his hands. "A samurai must be a good listener. It gives him an edge even sharper than his sword. Now, Niya, how should a samurai listen?"

Our teacher always asks me the hardest questions. He says my brain needs more exercise than my leg. But I know this one because Taji taught me earlier.

"A samurai should listen with his eyes and see with his ears."

Sensei grins. First at me, then Taji. Finally, his smile collects us all. He's pleased because we are working together.

Last year, our team won the Samurai Trainee Games.

Before that, everyone laughed at us. Mikko with his one arm; blind Taji; Yoshi, who refused to fight. Me with my one leg and Nezume, who ran away from the cruel Dragon Master to live like an animal in the forest. They laughed at Kyoko most of all. "Freak girl," they jeered, pointing at her white hair, pink eyes, and six fingers and toes.

They stopped laughing when we won. We were no longer the students no other school wanted; we were the samurai kids everyone wanted to be. We made a lot of new friends. Except from the Dragon Ryu. It's hard to shake hands with your opponents when they have already gone home.

"What's happening?" asks Kyoko. "What does the drum mean?"

"Things I hoped you would never hear, Little Cockroaches," Sensei says. "For ten days, the drum will call the mountain *ryu*s to war. When it stops, the fifty-year peace will be over. The *ryu*s must pledge their allegiance to the Lord of the North or the Lord of the South. In times of war, a samurai must serve with his sword."

My stomach hurts, and the White Crane frantically batters its wings against my heart. The *ryu*s will fight on different sides.

I think of the Eagle Ryu. And the Rabbit. And all the others we competed against at the Samurai Trainee Games. The Games are real now.

Thum. Thum. Ta-thum.

The drum kicks even harder into my chest, and it hurts to breathe.

Will friends now be forced to fight as enemies?

CHAPTER TWO

仁

BEWARE THE DRAGON

"I won't fight." Yoshi plants his feet like the roots of a giant cherry tree. It would take an enormous wind to shift even one of his sandals.

"You don't have to." Sensei's words blow gently. The tree falls with a thud as Yoshi crumples, relieved, onto the grass.

We understand why our friend doesn't fight. It's not about strength or bravery. Yoshi is stronger than the rest of us pulling together. He carries a great weight around every day. When he was only seven, he threw his opponent from the wrestling ring. The boy hit his head on a rock and died.

"The drum is not calling to *us*," Sensei says. "The Cockroach Ryu isn't going into battle. We are not bound to any lord. My days of service were completed long ago."

The other *ryu*s belong to a *daimyo,* a lord they defend in times of trouble and war. In return, the *daimyo* looks after his samurai and their students. With its dilapidated buildings and old equipment, it's obvious our *ryu* has no lord to pay for its upkeep.

We have always been poor. But we are rich in honor. Once Sensei was the Emperor's personal bodyguard, teaching swordsmanship to the royal children. The Son of Heaven himself rewarded Ki-Yaga by releasing him from service. Now Sensei answers to no *daimyo,* not even the Emperor.

"I didn't want to fight either." Kyoko stretches her slender arms around Yoshi's broad shoulders. There's only one thing in the world that feels better than a stomach full of honey pudding, and that's a hug from Kyoko.

We all pile on top of her and Yoshi, to show our support, and poke and prod each other in the ribs.

"Get your foot out of my mouth," Mikko mumbles at me.

"What did you say?" I pretend I don't understand.

Aaargh. Nezume yelps and groans from somewhere underneath.

"If you don't move your bony elbow out of my ear, I'll chop if off. Then you won't have *any* arms," Taji threatens Mikko.

With a great roar, Yoshi shakes us all apart.

"See how dedicated my students are," Sensei says to Onaku. "Even now they do wrestling practice."

"I think they need a lot more." The Sword Master

We all pile on top of her and Yoshi.

smiles wider than the green tree frog we found swimming in Sensei's *dokudami* wine last week.

Everyone laughs. Except Kyoko. She's not even smiling.

"Someone pulled my hair," she complains, flicking the ice-white strands out of her eyes. "It took me forever to get it rolled into place. Look at this mess."

Samurai kids always wear their hair twisted into a topknot, pinned tight. But now Kyoko's hair swirls in a fall of snow, to hang like mist around her shoulders. "Who did it?" she demands.

I'm not stupid. I keep my mouth shut. Kyoko's hair might be soft and silky, but her fists are hard as rock. And when she kicks, her six toenails scrape like splinters of bamboo. I've already got a scar to prove it.

"One day this samurai girl will do great damage in the hearts of men. More than any of my swords ever did," says Onaku.

Kyoko hides her face in her hands, but I can see her smile shining through.

Ta-thum. Thum. Thump.

The drum doesn't frighten me anymore. It drifts over our heads, through the valley, to the next mountain peak. In my heart, the White Crane sleeps peacefully. It doesn't even raise its head to listen. I pull my jacket tight around my ears. It's autumn in the mountains, and when the sun moves down into the valley, the air grows cold with the promise of snow.

"Why do we keep training if we're never going to fight?" Mikko brandishes an imaginary weapon, finishing with a lethal thrust through Yoshi's chest.

Grrr. Yoshi growls a warning, and the pretend sword is quickly returned to its scabbard.

"What use are swords if we can't wield them in battle?" grumbles Mikko.

"Would you like to teach my students this lesson?" Sensei bows low to show his respect for Master Onaku.

Some men pay a year's wages for one of Onaku's weapons. They travel for weeks, then wait for days while the Sword Master creates the perfect blade for each hand.

A samurai's sword is his most treasured possession. He wears it on his belt, but it is always close to his heart and it sings into his soul. My sword shines bright and sings loud enough for Onaku to hear. Even now, when it should be listening politely.

"May I borrow your weapon, Niya?" Onaku asks. "I need to make a point."

We're all paying close attention now. *The point of a sword is very sharp,* as Sensei says.

Carefully, I draw the blade and pass it to the Sword Master. I keep the cutting edge inward because if I tip over and fall, Onaku might be killed.

"It is bad manners to face the blade outward," Sensei taught us. "It is even worse manners to slice a friend in two."

Onaku holds my weapon flat across both his palms. "My swords are not forged to carve sinew and muscle. They are not kitchen knives. See? A samurai sword is an object of beauty and honor, not a butcher's tool."

With the cutting edge facing his stomach, he returns the sword to me. "May blood never touch this blade."

I agree. Especially if it's my blood. I cautiously place my sword back in its scabbard.

"Look with your ears and you will see the blade sing," Sensei reminds us.

"That's not hard," says Taji. "Niya's sword is almost as noisy as he is."

"I've got a lot to say," I protest, poking out my tongue. "Mikko's loud, too. Sometimes I have to yell over the top of him."

Now Mikko pokes out his tongue. "But when you yell, Niya, even the trees tremble. You're noisy *and* dangerous."

I grin at the compliment. If an enemy hears me coming, he'll just run away.

Our life has always had a pattern of comfortable sameness. Breakfast and practice. Lunch and study. And after dinner, "More practice!" Sensei calls every hour until bed.

Only very old men can remember wartime. And only even older men, like Sensei, know what it was like to fight.

"What about Sensei's sword?" Nezume asks. "He carried it into many battles. It must have been covered with blood."

"People say he wielded the fastest sword in all of Japan. Sometimes his opponent could not even see the blade," Taji adds.

Onaku grins and winks. "Perhaps they could not see it because it was not there."

That can't be true. Not even Ki-Yaga would go into battle without a sword.

But Sensei is grinning, too. "Sometimes I think my students are deaf. Or they have memories like fishing nets. What is the most important thing I have taught you?" he asks us.

It's an easy question, and we don't have to think about the answer. It was one of the first lessons we learned.

"A true samurai doesn't need a sword," says Yoshi.

Sensei nods. "I am a good swordsman, but I am an even better teacher. I can teach the deaf to hear and the forgetful to tie knots in their nets."

Could it be true? Did Sensei fight swordless? The villagers say he is a wizard. They say some nights he turns into a *tengu* mountain goblin and they see his black crow shadow fly across the moon. My friends don't believe a word of it, but sometimes Sensei speaks inside my head, so I'm not as sure.

"What's that smell?" Onaku asks, wrinkling his nose.

It's hard to imagine any odor offending the Sword

Master. When he swigs Sensei's fishy wine, he doesn't even hold his nostrils closed. But Taji is the expert when it comes to smells. Without eyes, he finds other ways to see. And his nose never misses a sniff.

"It's Niya's slipper," he says with a laugh. "He trod in horse dung when he fed Uma this morning."

Mikko pulls my slipper off my foot and waves it in Kyoko's face.

"Yuck," she squeals.

"I washed it. Give it back." If I had another one, I'd throw it at him.

Sensei takes off one of his own slippers and hands it to me. He tucks his other foot behind him and smiles.

I am like you, the wizard whispers inside my head. *I do not care if I have only one slipper.*

The game is over, and Sensei is still looking at me, his bright eyes drilling deep. He has another lesson for me to find.

Ta-thum. Ta-thum. Thump.

The drum leads me to it. We're not out of danger yet. The Dragon Master is looking forward to fighting us, and for him, the war is a convenient excuse. He has a score to settle.

"The Dragon Master won't like it when he finds out we're not going to war," I say miserably.

Sensei nods. "I do not believe blood must be spilled to solve a problem, but the Dragon Master thinks differently."

Taji shakes his head, confused. "Why would a teacher want to lead his students into war?"

"Why would he choose to risk their lives?" Kyoko is puzzled, too.

But Nezume understands the Dragon Master. "He doesn't care who he hurts. He sees glory in any victory, and he'll do whatever it takes for his side to win. Especially if he is given the chance to fight against us."

No one argues with that. Nezume would know. He studied at the Dragon Ryu for two years, and the Dragon Master's cruelty is written in the scars across his back.

"Dishonor and stupidity go together," Sensei says sadly. "The Dragon Master's brain is as empty as Niya's other slipper."

He means the one I haven't got.

"We have to do something. We can't stand back just because we don't have to fight. No one should have to. Not even the Dragons," insists Yoshi.

Sensei nods in agreement. "All war is about nothing important. When something is nothing, it is not worth fighting about."

Ki-Yaga is a Zen master. They're experts at Nothing. And I'm good at Zen, too. I think about nothing all the time.

Ta-thum. Thump. The drum dares us to make it stop.

"Only the Emperor or the Shogun can silence a war drum," Taji says.

"The Shogun is away in the far north, but the Emperor is in winter residence at Toyozawa Castle. We will go there and ask the Emperor, the Son of Heaven, to help. But we must be careful." Sensei frowns, his brow wrinkling like rice paper. "Not everyone will want to see this war end before the first sword stroke. The mountain lords will insist on the right to settle their differences with the sword."

"And the Dragon Master will do all he can to make certain the bloodshed begins," says Onaku. "He will see Ki-Yaga's peacemaking as an attempt to deprive the Dragon Ryu of its chance to win great honor and distinction."

We understand that. Beware the Dragon. But we're also excited to be going on a journey.

I can't wait to see the castle again. Many years ago, when I was too young for school, my father and mother took me to see the Emperor honor the great samurai warrior Mitsuka Manuyoto. Now Mitsuka lives as a hermit beside the ocean, but when he was a boy, he studied at the Cockroach Ryu and slept in my bed. His name is scratched into the wood above my pillow. I carved my name beneath it. His writing was as poor as mine.

I remember the castle. Food, singing, dancing, and music.

But the only music now is the drum.

Ta-thum. Thum. Thum.

Ten days to war.

"We leave at once, before the Dragon Master realizes what we are trying to do," Sensei announces. "We must ask the Emperor to move quickly."

But it might not be possible for him to move quickly. Our Emperor is even bigger and rounder than Onaku. Maybe he could sit on the Dragon Master. Imagining the Dragon Master squashed flat, I smile wider than the drunken tree frog.

Sensei's brilliant eyes search my face. *Is the wizard reading my mind?* I practice Zen thoughts and think of nothing. But it doesn't help. Sensei doesn't stop at nothing.

"Taji and Kyoko will pack food for the journey," Sensei instructs. "Yoshi, Mikko, and Nezume will gather clothes and weapons."

"I'll help with that," Onaku volunteers.

"Niya will go and catch Uma."

Once we would have drawn bamboo straws to see who had to go near his snarling teeth. That was before I discovered he liked honey rice pudding as much as I do. Now we're the best of friends. But we can't load our goods on his back, we'll have to carry everything ourselves. Uma is a proud warrior horse. He'll let us ride, but he won't cart raincoats and rice cakes. Not for all the pudding in Japan.

By the time the sun sinks low into the valley, we're packed and ready to leave. Sensei goes first, leading Uma through the dusk, down the path to the village. When

Yoshi and I walked this way alone, I saw shapes shifting in the darkness. Wolves. *Tanuki* dogs. But here with my friends and our ferocious horse, there is nothing to fear. Not even Grandfather's ghost stories could frighten me now.

Our spirits shine bright in the deepening gloom. Yoshi, the Tiger; Taji, the Golden Bat, who doesn't need eyes to see; Mikko, the Striped Gecko; Kyoko, the mischievous Snow Monkey; Nezume, the Long-Tailed Rat; and me. I am the White Crane, spreading my wings over them all, a cloak against the thump of the drum.

Night turns the trees gray and spectral. It's a four-hour journey to the village, but it will take longer traveling with Uma. The ground is uneven where last year's earthquake has refolded the path, and it's easy for a horse to stumble if we move too quickly.

I walk second from the end. Not because I'm slow—even with one leg I can travel as fast as the others—but because Onaku brings up the rear and I like to talk to him. I like to hear about the adventures he and Sensei had together.

"The Emperor will be pleased to see Ki-Yaga," I say.

"Maybe there will be a welcoming parade when the Son of Heaven hears we are coming."

Onaku lifts one eyebrow, then the other.

"The Emperor was so pleased with Sensei's service that he rewarded our teacher with his freedom," I continue. "He was the only royal bodyguard ever to receive such a great honor. Maybe there'll be fireworks."

Onaku grins, and his belly begins to jiggle as the laugh works its way to his face. "Is that what Sensei told you?"

"Well, not exactly. But I thought . . ."

Onaku's laugh erupts over my words. "I remember it a little differently. The Emperor yelled so loud that his words are still stamped inside my ear. His face went purple, and his eyes bulged bigger than a bubble-faced goldfish. 'If I ever see you around here again, Ki-Yaga, I'll chop off your head' was what he said. As I recall, Ki-Yaga and I left very quickly."

CHAPTER THREE

DEADLY SILENT

Half a moon lights our way forward, the drumbeat pushing against our backs. We keep going.

The path has narrowed now, forcing us to walk in single file. It's cold, but that's not why I'm shivering. Samurai kids wear many layers of clothing. I could walk through the snow and not feel a single icy drip. I'm worried about what might happen to Sensei when we reach the castle.

Even I can't yell louder than the rising night wind and the pounding drum, so I send my question down the path, echoing from friend to friend.

"Ask Sensei why the Emperor wants to chop off his head. Pass it on," I whisper to Nezume, walking in front of me.

"I'd like to know that, too. Sensei's head belongs where it is," Nezume says.

He repeats my question to Mikko.

Mikko tells Taji, and I just catch Mikko's muffled words. "Ask Sensei why the emperor wants to drop his head. Niya needs to know."

I never said that! But a whispered message has a life of its own, and like the bamboo snake, it sheds its skin and changes as it wriggles on. I hear Taji's voice. Then

Kyoko's. Finally, Yoshi's words bellow through the darkness. "Why does Niya want to know that?"

"Know what?" Sensei's voice rises to hang like a question mark.

The path has widened, and now we're close together again. I could have saved a lot of trouble and asked Sensei myself.

"Niya needs to know why the Emperor wants you to drop dead," Yoshi says.

It's not what I said at all. Still, it's near enough.

"Is it true, Sensei?" Kyoko is worried, but Sensei laughs.

"Yes. The Emperor was very angry. But there is a long line of men waiting to collect my head. Some, like the Dragon Master, would even push the Emperor out of the way to get it." Sensei laughs again. "But I have more important things to worry about. Yoshi's stomach is rumbling as loud as the war drum. There is a cave just below the next bend where we can eat and rest. I'll tell the story then."

Yoshi is much bigger than the rest of us, and he loves his food almost as much as the Sword Master does. We always tease him about it.

"Better get in quick." Mikko winks at Nezume. "Otherwise Master Onaku and Yoshi will eat everything. Rice-paper wrapping and all."

Cheeky Striped Gecko. The wrapping is meant to be eaten.

"I'm so hungry, I could eat a handful of lizards and maybe a long-tailed rat or two." Yoshi grins and bares his tiger teeth.

I'm hungry enough to eat a horse.

Uma snorts a warning in my direction. Now even the wizard's horse is inside my brain. I must be light-headed from lack of food. We didn't eat before we left, and the time for dinner has long passed.

"A samurai must learn to overlook the hunger in his gut and concentrate on his head. He cannot worry about food in the middle of battle," Sensei taught us. "And if he does, he may not have a head."

I have always been attached to my head, so I try to ignore my stomach.

The entrance to the cave is narrow, and inside, the space is smaller than the *ryu*'s tiny kitchen. But no one complains. We feel warm and safe, wedged tight. Even the sound of the drum is muffled into noiselessness. If only the beat didn't continue echoing its warning inside my head.

Mikko and Kyoko unpack egg rolls and noodle cakes. Yoshi passes the bowls, and Nezume places the water bottle in the center. Taji lights the tree-wax candles and holds the last one close in front of his face.

"What are you doing?" Nezume asks.

It's a good question. We need the candlelight, but it makes no difference to Taji. He's always in the dark.

"Can you see something?" Kyoko looks hopeful.

Long ago Onaku told us the story of an old blind villager. One morning he opened his eyes and the blindness was gone. Every night we wish for the same miracle for Taji, but every morning he is still blind. Sensei says it doesn't matter. Taji already sees better than the rest of us staring together.

"Sometimes I can see gray in the black." Taji moves the candle to-and-fro.

"Is that a good sign?" Kyoko asks Sensei.

She wants to know if it means Taji might see one day.

Sensei nods. "It is a very good sign. There is no black and white in the world. Only black and gray."

But I want Taji to see all the colors of our world, not just its shadows. I want to show him the pink and orange of the sun rising over the mountains. The bright white of Kyoko's hair. And the blue blazing in Sensei's eyes.

Our conversation fades into a quiet camaraderie of food and thought, until the silence is finally big enough to hold Sensei's story. He places his chopsticks across his bowl. His words grow large to fill the spaces between us, drawing us even closer to one another.

"Many years ago, before you were born, when even Onaku was a young man, I was the Emperor's bodyguard. I taught swordsmanship and zazen meditation to the castle children. I protected the Emperor's life with my own."

Our legs are folded, but our backs are straight and proud. Once Sensei taught princes and princesses. Now he chooses to teach us.

"Assassins are masters of disguise. They sneak beneath the night. They hide in small spaces," Sensei says.

Like a ninja! I remember what my father told me about them. They are ancient enemies of the samurai. They kill in secret, their dishonorable deeds cloaked in darkness. They don't even carry proper swords. They're worse than the Dragons.

"Some assassins are very hard to see. The one that crept to murder the Emperor was almost not there. But I watched with my ears and killed him before he could strike."

"It was a ninja," I announce. "They're experts at hide-and-sneak. The ninja are without honor." I'm pleased I worked it out first. Sensei always says my brain is a good athlete. It doesn't need two legs to run.

But our teacher doesn't look impressed this time.

"The ninja are not enemies of the Cockroach Ryu. You mustn't judge too quickly, Niya. If you stick your foot in your mouth, you will fall flat on your face."

Chastened, I nod respectfully.

"The Emperor must have been very grateful. You saved his life," Mikko says, rescuing me from our teacher's frown.

Sensei shakes his head. "At first, the Emperor wished *himself* dead. The assassin was his youngest brother."

Kyoko gasps.

Sensei killed a member of the imperial family. The penalty for that crime is death. There's no excuse at all. Yet somehow Sensei is still alive.

Ki-Yaga is a wizard. I'm sure of it now. It's the only possible explanation.

We sit in stunned silence. We know what should have happened next. To avoid dishonor, a samurai must slice his stomach and spill its contents onto the bamboo matting. It is called *seppuku.* The practice is forbidden under the new laws, but Sensei is a samurai of the old ways and the Emperor would have expected this private show of respect.

But Sensei couldn't have sacrificed his stomach. No wonder the Emperor wants his head.

"The Emperor left my death sentence open until another time. Then he banished me from his presence. Onaku has already told you the end of the story."

Yoshi is quick to defend our teacher. "There was no dishonor in what you did."

"You had no face to save," I agree.

Sensei grins. "Only the contents of my last meal. Steamed fish and seaweed rice, I think. Do you remember, Onaku?"

The Sword Master nods, patting his belly. "It was very

tasty and worth keeping. You made the right decision, Ki-Yaga."

"Do you think the Emperor still wants to cut your head off?" Kyoko's face wrinkles with worry.

"One cannot be sure. Few debts are never collected," Sensei says with a shrug. "We have a long way to go before we find out. Come, Little Cockroaches."

He claps his hands and Nezume jumps, knocking some of his rice onto Yoshi's plate.

"Thanks," Yoshi says, between hurried extra mouthfuls.

My appetite is gone. I'm much too worried about Sensei to eat.

Taji and Kyoko pack up the leftover food as Onaku helps himself to the last egg roll.

The sound of the drum fades as we descend toward the valley, but the echo of it still blasts and batters inside my head. War is marching to the mountains, and if we fail to stop its advance, many of our friends will die.

It's very late by the time we reach Onaku's home at the edge of the village. Mrs. Onaku is waiting at the door.

"Quickly, inside," she says, looking beyond us into the darkness. "Strangers passed through the village this afternoon. We'll tether Uma inside the smithy."

A night surrounded by armor and swords is a dream come true for an old warrior horse. Uma bares his teeth in a wet, wide smile.

Onaku isn't worried by the falling spray of spittle. He has other things on his mind. "Is there anything to eat, good wife?"

"I have supper prepared," she replies, smiling. "But first I must look after these children. They are exhausted. Especially Niya."

"I'm all r-r-ight," I stutter and mumble, struggling to breathe.

Yoshi prods me in the ribs. My friends know what the problem is. Mrs. Onaku smells like cherry blossoms, and her voice runs like honey to clog my thoughts until I can't think at all. Whenever she speaks to me, the goldfish in my stomach flip and wriggle and my face goes bright red.

Fortunately, she never notices.

"I've put the boys in this room." She opens a screen door, delicately painted with samurai battle scenes. All the warriors on the wall have Onaku's face but none of them have his stomach. Mrs. Onaku is a skilled painter and a loving wife.

Onaku knows how lucky he is.

"I am no good at zazen," he told us. "When I close my eyes, her face fills my thoughts. Until there is no room for Nothing."

If I had a wife that looked like Mrs. Onaku, I'd never close my eyes.

"Kyoko can come with me," she says. "I'm sure she needs a break from your smelly boys, Ki-Yaga."

Mikko grunts and Taji makes a face. After wrestling practice, Kyoko smells as much as we do. Sometimes worse. Our Snow Monkey hates bathing in the icy waters of the *ryu* river.

"I'll bring supper in soon," Mrs. Onaku promises.

My mouth waters. She's a wonderful cook. No wonder Onaku has a big stomach.

"Where's Sensei?" Taji asks. Trust Taji to notice what we didn't see. Sensei and Onaku have slipped away.

"They have much to organize for tomorrow. And to

help, you should eat and get some sleep." Mrs. Onaku smiles, and I silently promise to eat and sleep forever.

Supper is honey rice cakes with plum juice. It's gone quickly, and I'm alone in the dark with my friends.

"Hey, Niya! Would you like Mrs. Onaku to tuck you in?" Mikko teases.

I throw a pillow at him and grin as the thwack finds his head.

"I'm worried," Nezume whispers into the darkness.

He always is. Like the long-tailed rat, his nose twitches and his eyes shine anxiously.

"Me too," admits Mikko. "What if we can't stop the war? What if Sensei dies trying?"

"There's nothing to be concerned about." Yoshi's voice is calm and authoritative. "Sensei's head wields more power than any sword stroke."

We already knew this, but we feel better now that Yoshi has reminded us.

Especially Nezume. "Thanks, Yosh," he says.

"Rise and shine, Little Cockroaches."

Blearily, I open my eyes. The only thing shining is Ki-Yaga's bamboo torch.

"It must be the middle of the night," Mikko moans.

"Five hours of sleep. The perfect amount." Sensei's voice booms in our ears.

Five is Sensei's favorite number. He teaches us about Godai — the five tiers of Zen. Earth, water, fire, wind, and sky. The most powerful of all is sky, where the White Crane and the black *tengu* take flight. But sky is also void. It's no surprise that Nothing should be so important.

We dress as quickly as we can. Underwear, trousers, jacket, kimono. Layer after layer tied together. It makes us look noble and proud, but it takes forever to put on. Not good for a quick getaway.

"Watch out!" Taji ducks as Mikko's *obi* sash flicks past and slaps me in the face.

"Why are we leaving now?" grumbles Nezume. "It's still dark."

"My tearoom walls are not the only ones with ears," Sensei says. "When the mountain lords hear that the Cockroach Ryu is empty, they will be suspicious. Each will think we have joined the forces of the other, and they will send spies to find out what we are planning."

"Will they send the Dragon Master?" Nezume asks nervously.

"As soon as he realizes we serve no lord, he will know what we intend to do. And he will quickly work out where we are going. He will follow us, but for his own purpose." Sensei frowns. "Some people would be happy if we disappeared on our way to the castle."

"We're not scared," Taji says.

"Definitely not," agrees Yoshi.

Nezume, Mikko, and I add our support. My face is brave, but inside my heart, the White Crane hides. It's not as brave as I'm pretending to be.

The Sword Master and his wife have risen, too. Kyoko is waiting with them, holding Sensei's favorite traveling staff, the one with the owl feathers tied at the top.

"I wish I could come with you," Onaku says. "I would like to see the castle again, and I have a package to deliver."

"We need you here, old friend. Who else could I trust with Uma? I will see that the Emperor gets his new sword."

The village streets are quiet and empty.
Darker than old cherrywood.

Onaku hands Sensei the package. Two sword handles protrude from the end. *If one is for the Emperor, then who gets the other?* The last time we carried a spare sword, we found Nezume in the forest and gave it to him. Now he's one of us. But this time, the second sword is too large for another samurai kid.

Mrs. Onaku grips her husband's arm tight. She knows we're heading into danger, but she trusts Sensei. We all do.

Sensei raises his hand to signal good-bye, and Onaku nods. The most important conversations between friends don't need words.

Sensei turns and strides quickly into the night. As usual, we hurry to keep up.

The village streets are quiet and empty. Darker than old cherrywood.

"Where is everyone?" Taji asks.

"Asleep in bed," Mikko mutters. "Where we should be."

Nezume sighs. "Even the drummer isn't awake yet."

"No. It's something deeper than that," says Taji. "The village is almost empty. Listen. There's nothing at all. Where are the snuffles and the sounds of sleep? It's too quiet."

"Sometimes it is what you don't hear that matters most," Sensei agrees.

Where did they all go? A whole village can't just disappear.

Sensei hears every question, even the ones I haven't asked yet. "Some have answered the drum and marched to war. Others have hidden far away."

Now we're quiet, too, thinking of the villagers who might never return if we fail.

Once the village was alive with noise.

Now it's dead silent.

!

CHAPTER FOUR

忠
誠

HELL VALLEY

Sensei leads us west, toward the castle. Beyond that stretches the ocean. Even in the early morning gloom, I know I've been this way before. This is the direction toward my home.

Many years ago Father and Grandfather brought me along the same path to the Cockroach Ryu.

"I am going to be a samurai warrior," I yelled up the mountain. The White Crane shrieked in echo.

Waving my crutches with pride, I puffed out my chest. "The great Ki-Yaga wants to teach me."

"I thought he was dead," Grandfather grumbled and wheezed. "He probably will be by the time we get there. I might beat him to it."

Sensei might be old, but he walks fast. We hurry behind him, pushing and shoving each other along. Giggling at Taji's silly voices. Laughing at Mikko's jokes. Samurai kids are not skilled at sneaking. We wouldn't make very good ninja at all.

At the fork in the path, Sensei turns left.

I try to keep my voice still, but the quake in my stomach rises to shake my words.

"Are we going into the Jigokudani Valley, Sensei?" I ask.

Now Nezume's worried, too. "What's wrong with the valley?"

"Nothing that bothers me," Sensei says.

But there's plenty for the rest of us to be nervous about. They don't call it Hell Valley for nothing. Boiling mud. Thick steam mists to get lost in. Great cracks in the ground to fall through. And most terrifying of all, the restless souls of the dead. If we die here, who will save the mountains from war?

Yoshi moves to walk beside me. "Your face has turned white."

Mikko thinks it's funny. "You look like you've seen a ghost, Niya."

I haven't yet. Ask me later. We'll be surrounded by them.

"My grandfather told me the valley is haunted by demons," I tell them. "Transparent shreds of flesh hang from their limbs. Their eyes burn like molten rock. They like to play tricks. And when they tell the future, it always comes true." My voice quivers and cracks.

"One day Niya will be a better storyteller than I am." Sensei places his arm around my shoulder. "Already he can frighten his friends with just a few words."

His praise lifts my spirit high, and the White Crane forgets its fear, soaring bravely into Hell Valley's gaping mouth.

"Since when did we care how people look? Do we worry about a missing arm? Or leg? Or slab of flesh?" Sensei plants his staff in the soft ground. "Dead people are usually very polite. They like to say hello and talk about the weather."

Mikko giggles and nudges Yoshi, but Sensei doesn't laugh. "Some ghosts play tricks because they get bored," he says. "Death is monotonous. But every spirit I've spoken to tells the truth. Their sense of honor is not dead, only their bodies."

"You talk to ghosts?" Kyoko's mouth drops open.

"All the time. I am very old, and many of my closest friends have died. It would be rude to ignore them." Sensei's eyes twinkle. "I hope you won't stop talking to me when I die."

Mikko sticks his thumbs into his ears and waggles his fingers. "*Whoooo-ooo*, I'm a ghost," he wails. "I want to talk to Kyoko."

We laugh, and Kyoko kicks Mikko in the shins. But I'm not so sure Sensei was joking. If he really is a *tengu* goblin priest, he would have conversations with the spirits all the time.

As for me, I don't think I could trust anyone I could see straight through. No matter how well mannered they are.

"Phew. What's that smell?" Taji interrupts my thoughts, his nose toward the valley.

Yoshi sniffs. "I can't smell anything."

Neither can I, but that's not surprising. Taji's nose is always first to the finish line. "Smells like . . ."

"Niya's slipper?" suggests Mikko.

Taji pinches his nostrils tight. "It's worse than that."

"Dead fish." I grin, whacking Mikko across the shoulder with an imaginary bundle of them.

"Oh, yuck." Kyoko wrinkles her nose in disgust as the smell grows stronger.

Choking and sputtering, I struggle to breathe. The White Crane isn't brave anymore. Hiding its head under a wing, it refuses to come out.

"*Aaaah.* Sulfur. More pungent than a bottle of medicinal wine," Sensei says, inhaling deeply. "Even the bravest tracker would hesitate to follow us in here."

No one would think we would dare enter this valley.

"Chop, chop, Little Cockroaches. The drum is still beating even though we can no longer hear it. We have only nine days left. No time to hesitate." Sensei takes another step, and the mist reaches out to swallow him whole. "A samurai warrior must not allow himself to be beaten by his nose," he calls.

"A good student doesn't hesitate to follow the teacher. How far will you follow me?" Sensei once asked.

"All the way to hell and back," Yoshi answered for us. "We are very good students."

Now the time has come to prove it.

I can put up with the smell, but I can't forget the ghosts. I don't want to be at the end of the line anymore. Yoshi understands, already moving into place behind me. "Thanks, Yosh," I whisper.

We all feel safer with Sensei and Yoshi. Taji links his arm through mine. The earth is warm on the soles of our sandals, and early morning sun gently thaws the night from our backs. Steamy mist thickens into imaginary faces, but Sensei is right: these ghosts are not bothering us. They look, laugh silently, and dissolve away. They were never really there at all.

We all feel safer with Sensei and Yoshi.

"Would the Dragon Master follow us here?" Nezume's eyes scan the sparse clutches of trees.

It's his greatest fear that one day he will have to return to the Dragon Ryu. The Dragon Master didn't want Nezume until Sensei claimed him as a Cockroach. Now every month the Dragon sends a letter demanding the return of "his boy." Each time Sensei gives the same reply: "Poor handwriting. More practice needed."

"The Dragon Master will not find us here," Sensei promises. "I do not need to see him to know his thoughts. They never change. He will already be on his way to thwart our plans, but as always he travels a different path from me. We'll meet him at the castle."

Sensei smiles as if he's going to meet old friends. But the Emperor and the Dragon Master are powerful foes. Ki-Yaga will need more than a tree frog grin. He'll need two heads, one for each enemy to keep.

We've been walking for half the night and all the morning. Muscles hurt, eyes ache, and the thick air clogs our throats. We are no longer laughing and jostling. Instead, we drag our tired feet through the sticky mud. Grandfather's stories of this place can't be right. Not even dead souls would hang around here.

The trees have shrunk and thinned. Grass has given way to stone. In the beginning, the Tateyama Mountains were born of fire. Now their volcanic heart pulses where patches of mud bubble like thick rice porridge. But no one would come running for a bowl of this foul-smelling sludge, no matter how hungry they were.

"Walking is so boring," Mikko moans.

"A shortcut would be good," adds Nezume.

When we found Nezume on our way to the Annual Trainee Games, he showed us a quicker way into the mountain. Now the Long-Tailed Rat knows all the tracks and trails around the *ryu,* but this valley is a strange, alien place.

The mist wraps across our eyes like a *hachimaki* headband.

"I can't see very well," Yoshi complains.

"Lucky you," laughs Taji. "I can't see at all."

Even Taji's humor can't lift our spirits out of the mud. The White Crane's wings are wet and heavy. The Rat's tail is covered in slime, and the Tiger's fur is matted.

"There's nothing but mud and rocks," Kyoko grumps.

"Then we will walk another way," says Sensei. "It is good to practice."

I groan. There are thirty-three ways to walk, and Sensei makes us learn every one.

"We will walk like a wild cat," he announces. His long legs stretch out in loping strides. We pad after him, but it's not easy to copy.

"Your choice next, Nezume," Sensei instructs.

"Walk like a mouse."

Of course a Rat would say that.

We take small, soundless steps. It's hard with only one leg, but Sensei doesn't let me complain.

"When a one-legged boy creeps, he makes half as much noise," Sensei told me once. "One leg is not an excuse. It is a reason to be proud."

Now it's Mikko's turn to choose.

"Walk like a wild boar," he shouts.

Boars *like* mud. Crashing and blundering, we make more noise than Black Tusk, the wild boar who once stalked the forests around the *ryu* — until Sensei cooked roast pork for dinner. We're making enough noise to wake the dead. I scan the trees, just in case.

My foot aches. My shoulders hurt.

"Are we stopping to rest soon, Sensei?" Yoshi asks.

"I see I am not the only mind reader. Excellent." Our teacher points to a pool of water just ahead. "We are almost there."

We forget our sore muscles and race ahead to look.

"This is a heated mineral pool," Sensei says, easily catching up to us on his thin spider legs. "The water springs from the warm soul of the earth to heal tired joints and cold bones."

"Have we got time for this?" asks Taji, wistfully. He wants to swim, but the drum is pounding inside his head, too.

"After we rest here, we will be able to walk much faster," Sensei promises.

That's all the encouragement we need.

Nezume kicks off his sandals and dips a toe into the pool. A grin ripples across his face.

Kyoko cups a handful of the water, and her Snow Monkey spirit smiles mischievously. "You try it." She flicks the water into my face and up my nose. "That's for pulling my hair yesterday. Now we're even."

I should have known I couldn't outsmart her.

"The ninja come here often," says Sensei. "Unlike

my samurai kids, they love to bathe. A clean person has no odor and cannot be identified when disguised. We can learn much from the study of the ninja arts."

Sensei said the ninja are not our enemies. I trust him, but the ninja are not my friends, either. I'm not ready to learn anything from them yet. How can it be right to sneak and deceive? When I draw my sword in battle, the White Crane will screech and I'll shout my name proudly for all to hear. Grandfather says the ninja are part demon and part man, part magic and part trickery. They would fit right in in Hell Valley.

"Are there ninja here now?" Yoshi's eyes comb the straggly-haired trees. "I'd like to meet one."

My eyes follow his. "I don't see anyone."

And I don't want to meet one.

"There's nowhere for a ninja to hide here," says Nezume.

Sensei points to the nearest rock. "A ninja doesn't need to hide to conceal himself. Does a moth hide away when camouflaged against the tree trunk? The ninja way is one of *budo,* of blending into his surroundings. Are you sure that's really a rock?"

"I'll check," Mikko volunteers with a grin. He gives it a kick.

56

"*Ow-aw.* It's a rock!" he yelps, hopping around as if he were me.

"What about that one?" Sensei points again.

But Mikko cannot kick rocks all the way to the castle.

"I think there were five ninja following us." Taji listens and sniffs. "But they are not here now."

"I'm sure they have better things to do than watch my students wash." Hanging his sword and staff on a tree branch, Sensei throws his kimono, jacket, and trousers onto a large flat rock.

Sensei is chopstick-thin, like rice paper stretched over chicken bone. This time I'm not fooled by what I can see. The Dragon Master is younger and strong as an oak tree. But when he challenged Sensei at the Games, our teacher whirled his bamboo staff and that oak tree crashed into the dirt.

The first pool flows into an even deeper one, wide enough to swim and play in. Sensei steps into the shallows, then wades out until only his head is showing.

Carefully, we place our swords in the tree, too. Then we toss our clothes on top of Sensei's jacket. Shivering in my long undershirt and loincloth, I throw my crutch down as well. But I miss the clothes, and it bounces off the rock to land in the stringy branches of a small tree. It's the perfect place for anyone or anything to hide. I have to go get it, but I stall by pulling on my robe and grabbing my sword.

"Do you want me to come with you?" Mikko calls from the water. Mikko and I tease each other all the time, but we know when to stop. That's how the lines of friendship are drawn: in exactly the right place.

"I'm okay," I call, already halfway to the tree. Taji said the ninja had gone, and so far I haven't seen a single ghost.

Except for the one sitting on the bottom branch, holding my crutch.

CHAPTER FIVE

WHAT THE
GHOST SAID

Red-hot eyes burn through me. The White Crane cringes and pulls its wings in close, away from the heat. My stomach cramps tighter than a tangled kite string.

"Nice weather, isn't it?" The ghost's words whistle through missing teeth.

I shiver. "Very n-nice."

"You should be more careful." It passes me my crutch. "Dead people don't like to be hit in the head with lumps of wood. Didn't you see me sitting here?"

"S-s-sorry. Thank you."

The ghost nods, accepting my apology. "Some people don't even believe I exist. Like your friends. They can't see me because they won't look. I don't like being ignored." Angry now, its voice hisses like steam. "Nobody wants to fade away to nothing. Not even a ghost."

Sensei told us that a samurai warrior must stand straight and still when he looks into the face of death. Now I understand why. It's easier to stand still when you're scared stiff.

"Would you like it if people looked straight through you?" the ghost demands.

I shake my head politely, trying not to stare. But my eyelids are frozen open in fright. Grandfather told me that ghosts like gruesome meals. In Grandfather's stories, their caves are littered with the bones of kids just like me. My teeth chatter.

"Are you cold?" Its voice curdles, sour as overheated milk. "If you take my hand, you'll feel warm."

I can see only two fingers and a shard of broken bone. The hand is a lump of melted flesh.

I'm not touching that.

Fiery eyes spit and crackle, but I'm shivering so hard that my head shakes without me. "N-no. I'm fine. Thank you."

The ghost nods approvingly in Sensei's direction. "Ki-Yaga always teaches his students good manners."

Looking up, Sensei waves. I should have known he could see what was happening. The wizard sees everything, even with eyes closed, asleep under the old cherry tree back at the *ryu*.

Fear is nothing to be afraid of, Sensei whispers inside my head. *And except for a little leftover skin and bone, a ghost is all hot air.*

Braver now, the White Crane unfolds one wing. I place my hand on my sword. Onaku's blade cannot cut through what is hardly there, but with my fingers around the hilt and Sensei's words in my head, I feel less afraid.

I'm not out of the trees and into the pool yet. The ghost grins, its mouth a grotesque cave of bones. "I have a message for you."

I don't want to know.

It leans closer, hot breath in my ear. My heart beats like the mountain drum. *Thum. Ta-thum. Thum-thum-thump.* I'm afraid to listen, but there's no escape.

"You need only one slipper." The ghost's voice cackles softly, embers in a dying fire.

"What?" The ghost is making fun of me! My blood bubbles in anger. I'm not afraid anymore. No one likes to be made a fool of. Especially me. The other *ryu*s always jeer and call me silly names. Hopscotch. Frog foot. I'm glad I whacked the ghost in the head with my crutch. I'd like to do it again.

But now the branch is empty. All that remains is the faint smell of scorched wood.

"Come back," I yell, swinging my crutch like a sword. "Who are you to laugh at my one leg when your body is barely there? You're nothing but a pair of firefly eyes."

A Cockroach is not afraid of other bugs.

"What was all that yelling about?" Nezume asks moments later when I climb into the pool, my crutch safely leaning against our clothes.

Kyoko giggles. "Niya likes to talk to himself."

"So who was he waving his crutch at?" asks Mikko, snickering.

I'd do more than wave my crutch at him, if it wasn't resting out of reach. "Didn't you see anything?" I ask.

My friends shake their heads.

"Niya was talking to ghosts." Mikko laughs at his joke, and Nezume joins in, even louder.

Sensei says nothing, but his face has words written all over it. My friends can read the whole story there. It's not a joke. Their eyes grow as wide and round as rice balls.

"Were you scared?" Kyoko's eyes are biggest of all.

"No. I stood straight and still like a samurai warrior. I stared death in the face." Even Mikko looks impressed. "I shook my crutch, and it ran away."

It's almost true. Most of the time I was so terrified I couldn't move. But in the end, I did shake my crutch. They all saw that.

"What did the ghost say?" Yoshi asks.

Embarrassed, I stare down at my foot. "It said, 'You need only one slipper.' "

"I could have told you that without even looking," Taji says with a hoot.

Kyoko tries to hide her giggle behind her hand, but Yoshi guffaws loudly. Nezume and Mikko slap palms. Even Sensei thinks it's funny.

When the ghost laughed at me, I was insulted. But when my friends laugh, it sounds different. It makes me smile and forget my anger.

"The dead like to play games, but they are also very knowledgeable. The ghost has given Niya a special message," Sensei says. "Sometimes the information we need is right under our foot."

"But what does the message mean, Sensei?" asks Yoshi.

"It means Niya has a task to complete. And he only needs one slipper to do it."

"Maybe Niya will stop the war with his smelly old slipper," Mikko teases.

I wish it was that easy. I would give my remaining foot to ensure no one dies.

Inside my head, the wizard is whispering again: *I am very proud. You have passed an important test. None of my other students were ready.*

The pool soothes my aching muscles, but Sensei's words warm my heart. I want to ask more questions. Why am I being tested? What task must I complete? And why do I need to be told what I can see every morning when I put my slipper on? But there's an even more important question I need to ask Sensei. "Are you worried about what will happen when we reach the castle, Master?"

I know *I* am. What would we do without Sensei? Yoshi is a good leader, but he's not a teacher. And we still have so much to learn.

"There is nothing to fear. The Emperor is wise but very superstitious, and he knows that if he chopped off my head, I would haunt him for the rest of his life." Sensei smiles. "He would never enter Hell Valley. One word from a ghost and the Son of Heaven would die of fright."

"I could stay here forever," Kyoko sighs. Her long white hair floats like water lilies on the surface of the pool.

Taji sinks low until only frog eyes show above the water. "The ninja are smart to come here."

Not even I would argue with that. The waters of the river near the *ryu* are freezing cold, except in the middle of summer. But the mineral pool is the color of tea and just as warming.

Nezume pulls my foot out from under me, and I sink toward the bottom. When I surface, thrashing and sputtering, I spit water in Nezume's face. Despite appearances, mineral water is not good to drink—it doesn't *taste* a thing like tea.

"I like the feel of warm mud between my toes," says Nezume. "Maybe I would like to be a ninja."

I shake my head. "The ninja sneaks around in the night, but the samurai calls his challenge loud and brave, looking his opponent in the eye."

Sensei smiles knowingly, like the cat that swallowed the crane. "If you are hungry for an extra rice cake and there is only one left over, what do you do? Do you wave your sword and shout for challengers?"

I remember the honey rice cakes we had for dessert two nights ago. Especially the last one I ate in secret as I sat on the *ryu* kitchen floor in the moonlight. Sensei knows what I did. I sneaked in, just like a ninja.

"Sometimes ninja skills might be useful," I admit.

Taji pokes me in the ribs. "Next you'll be throwing *shuriken* stars."

Shuriken stars are small metal shapes the ninja use to throw or stab. They can be tossed at the eyes, hands, or feet, and they're used to distract a warrior from his sword. I lean back against the edge of the pool, warm water lapping against my chin.

Someone pulls my hair. Hard.

I ignore it. Then it happens again, even harder.

I whirl around to face Kyoko. "You said we were even. Why are you pulling my hair?"

"I didn't do anything." She grins. "Although I wish I did. Maybe it was ninja fingers."

"Or a ghost. *Whooooo . . .*" Yoshi teases.

Another tug. This time I'm faster and find myself looking at a bunch of tiny faces with more wrinkles than Sensei and breath worse than one of Uma's after-dinner belches.

"Snow monkeys!" Kyoko shouts excitedly.

She was born in the snow-covered mountains of northernmost Honshu. Her superstitious parents left their white-haired, six-fingered child on the mountainside to die. The snow monkeys came and

"Snow monkeys!" Kyoko shouts excitedly.

took her to their home—and that's where Sensei found her, climbing trees before she was old enough to walk.

"Look, Sensei, there are five. It's a family." Kyoko reaches out to link fingers with the mother.

"Five is a good number. My favorite," Sensei says, gently removing a young monkey from the top of his head.

Two bigger monkeys fight over who will pull my hair next. They chatter and screech. They chase their tails around the pool and stick their noses in our clothes.

Nezume laughs. "They're checking to see who smells the worst."

"That'll be Niya. You don't have to be a ninja to smell him coming," Mikko teases.

I've only got one foot, but it kicks twice as hard. Even underwater.

"Er-er-ergh," Mikko groans theatrically and does a dead-fish impersonation, floating on top of the water.

"I do not smell. And no one can tell who a person is by sniffing," I insist. "Not even a ninja. Or Taji. Or a monkey."

The smallest snow monkey pushes its way into my armpit to prove me wrong.

"Every person has their own odor." Taji smiles. "You know that." He blows a kiss to remind me. Mrs. Onaku smells like cherry blossoms.

"The ninja have many secrets worth learning," Sensei says. "Before I came to the Cockroach Ryu, I trained with a ninjutsu master for more than a decade."

Sensei is a samurai and a ninja? Wait till Grandfather hears about this. It'll make a great story.

"I learned to move with the wind, to disappear in the mist, and to run up the cherry tree. How do you think I manage such things? Did you think I could do magic?"

I *know* he can. I know because he's always practicing on me. Maybe I could learn a little ninja magic too. Then when Kyoko throws things at us, she won't be able to escape by climbing Sensei's cherry tree. I'll be able to run up after her.

"You would make a good ninja, Taji." Sensei's praise fills Taji's unseeing eyes with pride.

"What about me?" I ask. Before, I mocked the ninja. I only wanted to yell and wave my sword. But now, suddenly, I want to do more. I want to sneak and sniff and fade into the night. Like Sensei.

"You are an excellent student, Niya. Even ghosts want to teach you a lesson. You could learn to be the greatest ninjutsu samurai ever."

Even better than Sensei? *Not likely.* But in my heart I accept the challenge and the wizard nods.

"Are there any ninja girls?" Kyoko asks.

Sensei smiles. "Many more than samurai girls."

Kyoko is the only samurai girl we've ever heard of.

"There are?" Mikko grins and whistles. "Then I think I might be a ninja, too."

Sensei closes his eyes and twists the water from his long white beard. We wait for his words of wisdom to fall with a splash. Even the snow monkeys are quiet now.

"We must learn to open our eyes and ears to new things if we are to stop the war drum. Our first battle is not far away."

Yoshi looks alarmed. "I thought we weren't fighting."

"Not every conflict is settled with a sword. At the castle, a word can send a head rolling across the floor," Sensei says.

The White Crane cowers. Is Sensei talking about his own head? He smiles at me, but I don't feel reassured.

"Our path to Toyozawa is very rocky," Sensei continues.

"I know." Mikko grimaces. His foot still hurts from kicking rocks.

Sensei stretches his arm out, palm down. *"Chi,"* he says.

Yoshi places his hand over Sensei's and Taji adds his next. *"Jin."*

Then Kyoko. Mikko. And me. *"Yu."*

Chi, jin, yu.

Wisdom, benevolence, and courage.

Our wet hands form a mountain where the code of the samurai binds us together. Ancient powerful words, stronger than rock and sharper than any sword. Standing together, samurai kids are not afraid of anything. I'm even braver than the Emperor of Japan. Not even the most fearsome ghost in Hell Valley could frighten me now.

CHAPTER SIX

礼

THE BACK ROAD
TO TOYOZAWA

"Drop," Sensei yells.

We do, without hesitation or thought for rocks, mud, and puddles. We sit cross-legged and still and wait for the next instruction. We've been doing this training exercise since our first day together at the *ryu.* A samurai cannot choose where to fight his battles, so Sensei doesn't let us pick where we practice. Anywhere will do. Even in the middle of the back road to Toyozawa.

I watch Sensei's eyes, searching for the moment when he will command us to jump up and draw our swords. Flickering eyes mean your opponent is thinking. When a man makes a decision, his eyes stop moving. He doesn't need to think anymore. He knows.

"The samurai who draws first is very slow," Sensei taught us. "He draws first because he needs a head start. The true swordsman waits until the last moment, then unsheathes so fast that he catches his opponent in mid-swing."

My leg aches, but I don't move. Beside me Nezume crouches motionless, coiled to spring at Sensei's next word. Like his spirit totem, the Long-Tailed Rat, Nezume radiates nervous energy. Nose twitching, ears wriggling. He'd flick his tail, too, if he had one.

Nezume has the fastest sword in the mountains; he always draws last and slices first. No wonder the Dragon Master wants him back. He doesn't want Nezume on our team at the Games next year.

"Draw!" Sensei bellows.

I'm on my foot in an instant, sword in hand. Yoshi is standing too close, and I catch him on the elbow by accident. It's a good thing we are using our wooden swords for practice, or Yoshi would have nothing to lean on next time he lies out on his rock overlooking the valley. But it's my error. To bump against another samurai is a great insult. Honor demands a duel to the death. Luckily, to bump against a samurai kid is not as dangerous.

Yoshi pokes his tongue out at me, raising his sword in triumph. "Niya loses a point."

We don't really keep score. Sensei doesn't believe in awarding prizes. When we asked for merit scrolls like the other *ryu*s have, he gave each of us a blank piece of rice paper.

"This contains everything I have taught you," he said, presenting my copy with a flourish and a smile.

I grinned back. "Then I am an excellent student, because I have learned it all."

Awards look good, but they mean nothing. Still, we did like winning the trophy at the Annual Samurai Trainee Games. And there is one reward worth striving for. When Sensei beams at us with pleasure, we glow warm and proud.

"Stop," Sensei commands.

We turn to stone, like statues blocking the road. Sensei usually waits until one of us moves. Usually Kyoko will giggle or Nezume will twitch his nose, but sometimes it takes hours. This afternoon, Sensei doesn't have the whole day to wait. *Ta-thum. Thum. Thump.* Inside my head, the drum throbs against my temples. Time is running out. Only eight days left.

"Go!" Sensei yells.

We take off running. The road winds through the rice fields where the only people we'll see will be farmers, too busy to notice an old man and his students. It takes a lot of rice to feed a castle town and to pay its samurai soldiers. Once the samurai lived on country estates, but peace has made the daimyos nervous and they like to keep their armies close. Now most of the samurai live in houses in the town or castle keep, their wages paid in rice. Their jobs are to wait and practice.

No wonder Sensei makes us train so hard. We are practicing for a life of practice.

"More practice," Sensei yells. "Run like the tiger."

Yoshi *is* the Tiger, and with great loping strides, he hunts down Sensei. The rest of us chase along behind. We're covering ground quickly now. At this pace, we might even reach the castle town by midnight.

My father is a town samurai. He collects his samurai rice and lives in a comfortable house with a garden. But sometimes I know he wishes for the days of Grandfather's youth, when samurai slept in fields. One winter, Grandfather told us he slept in the snow. "*Brrr!* Too cold for me. I'm glad we don't do that anymore," Father said. But he doesn't want to grow old counting rice, either.

Sensei slows to a brisk walk. "Soon we will reach the river," he says. "We'll stop and catch fish for dinner."

None of us are fooled by that. He means he'll sleep on the riverbank while we hold the rods. Fishing is so boring. Mikko groans and Nezume moans even louder.

"I can't see the point of fishing," Taji complains.

Kyoko giggles. It's a good joke because Taji can't see anything.

"It is a waste of time," I agree. "I thought we were in a hurry."

"The war will not outrun the drumbeat, and we do not want to stand before the Emperor without the skills we need. All samurai warriors have time to fish," Sensei insists. "It's always good practice."

Not more practice.

Even Yoshi rolls his eyes, but Sensei continues. "It keeps the brain focused. If a samurai allows his brain to wander off, when it comes back, there will be no head left to hold it. Fishing teaches the mind to stay in one place."

I'm not convinced. Fishing puts my brain to sleep. And I'll bet it does the same for Sensei. That's probably why he lies there snoring while we cast our lines.

Sensei's smile flashes in my eyes like sunlight on fish scales. He knows what I'm thinking.

When we reach the place where the road crosses the river, Sensei stops to talk to a lone man fishing on the bridge. He bows low and exchanges a bottle of wine for a bucket of bait. The only way to catch a river sweetfish is with another of its kind. Sweetfish are too smart to swallow a hook but foolish enough to chase the bait fish.

The road soon veers from the flat, open fields to the protection of trees.

"Stop!" Sensei yells.

Yoshi crashes into me. I stumble against Mikko, who tips over. He falls, dragging Taji and me with him. Kyoko loses her footing, and Nezume lands on top of us all.

Only Sensei is still standing.

"We thought you said 'drop,' " Mikko says sheepishly.

"I can't hear anything. Someone's elbow is in my ear," Taji complains.

"Sorry," Yoshi and Kyoko chorus.

Poor Taji. One elbow in each ear.

"We have found the perfect spot," Sensei announces over the noise of arms and legs untangling.

Nezume removes his foot from my face, just in time. I was about to bite it.

"Are there lots of fish here?" he asks.

"Even more important. There is a tree," Sensei says, settling back against it. "Fish swim all over the river, so it does not matter where you throw your line. A tree is much harder to catch. You must find a place where one is already standing still."

That's true, but I'd rather chase trees than fish any day.

Sensei unties the long bundle from his back and takes out our rods. My mouth waters. Fresh sweetfish taste much better than two-day-old rice cakes, cold omelette, and gluey noodles. Sensei will let us light a cooking fire this evening. Last night, on the edge of Hell Valley, we slept on warm volcanic rocks around the hot springs, but our food was stone cold. Sensei said flames might attract attention. Here on the road, many fires burn through the night. One more won't be noticed.

Inside the bucket are six small sweetfish, one for each of our hooks. The first fish is the bait to catch the second. Then the second fish becomes the bait to catch the third. That's if any of us get up to three. Sweetfish are not easy to catch.

I cast my rod into the river wearily. I'm tired of this already.

"Look, Niya." Mikko points to a bird upriver at the far water's edge. It's a white crane.

We creep closer. Head bent slightly, the crane stands

perfectly still, black eyes staring into the water. Even the crane must concentrate when fishing. At the last moment it strikes, faster than a samurai sword stroke. When it lifts its beak out of the water, a bright silver fish struggles in its mouth.

"Why can't you do that?" Yoshi teases me. "Then we wouldn't have to stand around fishing so long."

I would if I could. Anything to spend less time fishing.

My friends drift back toward Sensei and their rods. But the white crane holds me in place. It turns and looks. Standing straight and still, I raise my arms high.

"Aye-ee-yah." I am the White Crane.

Aye-ee-yah. The other crane screeches in response, opening its wings wide and lifting itself into the sky. I watch it wheel over the river and head toward the town, the castle, and the ocean. My thoughts soar after it: *I'll see you there. I can't fly yet, but I'm coming, too.*

"It's very beautiful." Kyoko's voice makes me jump. Not easy on one foot.

"So graceful," she sighs. "Can I tell you a secret? You mustn't tell anyone. Not even Sensei."

"Okay." It's easy to agree. Whatever it is, Sensei already knows. He always does.

Kyoko smiles. Hesitates. Then blurts, "Sometimes I wish I was beautiful."

I don't know what to say, because she already is. I try to remember the words from one of the haiku poems we studied. That would help. But I always fall asleep in poetry class. It's even more tedious than fishing. But right now I wish I'd paid more attention.

Kyoko shifts uncomfortably in the silence. "Forget what I told you," she says, reaching out to grab the front of my jacket and twist it tightly. "All right?"

"Okay," I agree again. It's hard not to, with her fist in front of my nose.

"What did I say?" she demands.

"When?"

It's the right answer, and Kyoko lets go of my jacket. "Thanks, Niya." She turns and runs to join the others. A samurai girl is much harder to understand than any haiku.

"Got one," Yoshi booms.

Not even Sensei could sleep through that, but his wizard eyes stay closed. They'll open like magic the moment we have just enough fish. They always do.

"I've got one, too," Nezume shouts.

It's still another hour before we've caught enough. Kyoko strings the last one onto a long stick. Sensei's eyes snap open.

"More walking, more practice," he says, jumping to his feet and rapping his staff on the ground.

The last few days we have traveled the back road, skulked through the late afternoon or walked in the darkness. It's dusk now. The road is almost empty because closer to town, it's no longer safe. This is the hour when merchants and travelers hurry to their lodgings before the gangs of outlaws and robbers slink from the shadows. But samurai kids aren't scared of anything except haiku lessons.

Here the road is paved. It's easier for me to walk on the cobblestones, and the clip of my crutch has a familiar ring. I was born in a town, but none of my friends have even seen a road before. Their homes are in small villages with dirt paths and mountain tracks.

Taji tips his head sideways, the way he does when he's listening hard for something. Have the ninjas and spies finally caught up with us? Sensei isn't worried. He strides, whistling, his long legs hurrying us along. I decide not to worry, either. I'll find out soon enough.

"Halt!"

Ten men block our way, roadside cutthroats whose swords glimmer, dull and greedy.

Sensei says nothing, eyes measuring the man in front of him.

"Give us those sweetfish and everything else you have," the leader says, "or I will slice you and the kids where you stand."

We move as one to protect our teacher and defend our honor. But Sensei waves us back, his gesture telling us to sit on the grass and wait.

"Do you have any more men to help you?" our master asks politely.

The man sees an old fool when he looks at Sensei. It's his first mistake.

"Why?" he growls, amused.

"Because I have you outnumbered. It would not be a fair fight when you have only ten men to fight against me."

Ki-Yaga is a master swordsman who could cut down this band of vagabonds blindfolded, with one arm tied

Ki-Yaga is a master swordsman who could cut down this band of vagabonds blindfolded.

behind his back and one leg tucked up. He draws his blade so fast, it is only a flash of light until it rests, point hard against the big man's stomach.

This bunch is not stupid after all. The big man sees what he is up against. He bows low and edges back into the forest, taking his followers with him.

Sensei tucks his blade into his sash and waves us forward. We hurry to keep up.

In a small cleared area nearby, Sensei stops.

"Shouldn't we keep walking?" I ask. I see danger everywhere now.

"Time for dinner," he says. "Not even I can stop a war on an empty stomach."

Or without a head. Suddenly, I'm not in such a hurry to reach the castle. We quickly gather branches and sticks. Our teacher eyes them with a smile.

"No, not now," I groan. Sometimes I can read Sensei's mind, too. He thinks we should do *bo* practice. Fighting with sticks. It's all about dodging, ducking, weaving. And one well-timed blow.

"A samurai may not always have his sword," Sensei teaches us. "But he can always find a stick."

We don't argue. Once Mikko did. "A samurai can't

always find a stick. There are no sticks here in the classroom," he had said.

Sensei then picked up the broom and Mikko ducked. *Bo* training had begun.

While we practice, Sensei cooks. After dinner we lie back under the stars and dread the night's walk ahead.

"I am so tired, I think I will sleepwalk to the castle." Yoshi yawns.

"It's safe here," Sensei says. "We can stay tonight."

We're almost used to sleeping in the day, but rest seems more comfortable and familiar under a blanket of darkness.

"Dream deep, Little Cockroaches. I am going for a walk." Taking his staff, Sensei heads in the direction of the river.

Our master often walks alone at night. The others know what I think of that.

"Sensei's gone for his evening fly around the mountains." Mikko jabs me in the ribs.

"It might be true," I say. "I'm not the only one who thinks so. Down in the village the old women say Sensei is a *tengu*."

"Old wives' tales. Now Niya is an old woman." Yoshi laughs.

My friends are probably right. A *tengu* is a mountain goblin priest, a samurai who has fallen from grace. But Sensei is good, kind, and wiser than the mountains.

"What could Sensei have done?" Kyoko asks. "It would have to have been something truly dreadful."

"The most dreadful," agrees Nezume.

We know what that would have to be. Every samurai kid does. It's the first thing a father teaches his child. "The most dishonorable thing a samurai can do is to share the sky with the man who killed his father."

"It can't be that," Yoshi says. "Sensei would not hesitate to avenge his father's honor."

And he would never shirk his duty. Even though he teaches us that our swords should not be used for killing unless absolutely necessary, we know that Sensei has killed many men in battle.

"Go to sleep," Taji grumbles. "Why are we even discussing this? Sometimes I think you have bean sprouts for brains, Niya."

Yoshi chuckles. I've always been the quickest thinker, and my friends are proud of that. But it doesn't stop them from giggling at me. Laughter between friends is a double-edged sword, held carefully so it does no harm.

The night quickly fills with snuffles and snores. Except mine. Sleeps runs ahead of me, and no matter how fast I hop, I can't catch up to it. Under the full moon the White Crane is restless. I pull my blanket over my head, but it doesn't help.

Hours later Sensei slips noiselessly back to settle against his cherry tree. In the moonlight I see his closed lids.

"Are you having trouble sleeping?" he asks me.

"Yes, Sensei," I admit.

"Then you must ask the question that is keeping you awake. Only then will you be able to sleep."

It's not easy to ask. "Can you fly, Sensei?"

"Everyone who dreams can fly," he answers.

The White Crane nods drowsily.

"Can you sleep now, Niya?"

"Yes, Master."

I close my eyes and dream I can fly.

CHAPTER SEVEN

GRANDFATHER'S
STORIES

Last night I dreamed I soared above the fields, over the town, and across the ocean. But when I woke this morning, the castle was still a day's walk away. Sensei sets a fast pace, and we hurry along behind, telling stories about all the things we'll see and do when we reach the Emperor's court. No one mentions the terrible things that might happen.

Instead of taking the quickest route, Sensei veers right, onto a lesser road. Here the cobblestones are overgrown with grass and the road is empty. Safe.

"This is the way to my home," I announce excitedly.

"Why are we going there?" asks Taji.

I shrug. "I don't know. Maybe Father invited us."

"Ask Sensei," Kyoko suggests. My friends are listening closely, but Sensei strides ahead, out of earshot.

He doesn't need ears to listen. "I must ask Niya's Grandfather for news of the castle. It is an advantage to know before we arrive."

Ha! Sensei doesn't know everything after all.

But the wizard does know what I'm thinking and his blue eyes drill into mine.

"A samurai must be prepared. Swordsmanship is not

everything. In battle it is sometimes useful to know on what day your opponent was born."

We wait for Sensei's lesson to solve our puzzled faces.

"Even the fiercest warrior will hesitate and smile if you yell 'happy birthday,'" Sensei says, swinging an imaginary sword to make us duck. "He who hesitates has lost. And often what he has lost is his head."

It's hard to believe that Grandfather knows any useful information. He is not wise like Sensei. He stands straight and his eyes are clear, but his mind is bent and muddled. Wisdom came with age, but it left with even older age. Sometimes, for no reason, Grandfather laughs in the middle of a sentence. And sometimes he disappears for days.

"Where has Grandfather gone?" I would ask my father.

He'd smile and say, "Our Eldest One is like the wind. He blows out and he blows in."

Father never seemed worried, and he was right. The wind always returned. And so did Grandfather.

"My grandfather will not be much help," I confess. "He tells many stories, but they're not all true."

Sensei grins. "Like the tale of the imaginary ghosts

of Hell Valley? The best place to hide a fact is behind a screen of fiction."

Grandfather *was* right about the ghosts. I think back over all the other stories he told me. Shape-shifters. Wizards. *Tengu* goblins of the mountain. Maybe *he* can tell me a story about Sensei.

"I can't wait to meet your sister. I'm bored with boy talk." Kyoko covers her ears, pretending to be in pain.

"You'll be disappointed," I yell. "Ayame talks endlessly about dolls and spends all day changing their kimonos and braiding their hair."

I laugh at the faces Kyoko makes. My sister, Ayame, is soft and fragile like a flower. She's not like Kyoko at all. Ayame couldn't kick her way out of a rice-paper bag.

"As long as the pillows are fluffy and my bed is warm, I don't care how many giggling girls I have to put up with," Mikko says. "I'm tired of sleeping on the ground."

"I can't wait to see the town. What's it like?" asks Yoshi.

"People rush everywhere. They are busy like bees, packed tighter than honeycomb in the hive," Sensei says.

The others gather around, hanging on every word.

"When I went to bed, I could hear the people next door snoring," I tell them.

Nezume laughs. "I bet they could hear you snoring ten houses away."

"I don't snore," I insist.

But when Sensei nods, I decide not to protest so loudly.

"I thought we didn't want people to know where we were," says Taji. "Why are we going into such a crowded place?"

It's a good question. Walls have ears, and a town is nothing but rows and rows of listening walls.

"If you don't want to be found, where is the best place to hide?" Sensei asks.

Taji knows that, of course. "Where no one would look."

Pleased, our teacher claps his hands. "Excellent. No one would ever expect us to go to Niya's home."

It's true. Not even I did.

"The ninja will," Yoshi teases. "I bet they're watching now."

Mikko brandishes his sword at the nearest rock. "Come out and show yourself."

"The ninja creep like the wind. No one can hide from that," Sensei agrees. "But we have nothing to fear from them either."

My thoughts are warmed by the fire waiting for us at home. Around me my friends chatter about market stalls and how many types of sweets the vendors might sell. Their cheeks are full of imaginary balls of cherry blossom gum.

But one question bothers me. "Do Mother and Father know we are coming, Sensei?"

My parents are very proud that the great Ki-Yaga chose to teach me. But Mother has a voice like a bird and she never stops singing. If she knows we're coming, it will be all over the tearooms, from one end of Japan to the other. Everyone will know where we are.

Sensei smiles into my eyes, and his voice is a shadow against my ear. "Your grandfather will tell them when we are closer."

How can he? He doesn't know.

I will tell him, the wizard whispers inside my head. *Just like this.*

It's almost midnight when we reach the edge of the castle town. I guide my friends through the dark, narrow streets toward my home. We trudge past rows of houses, stacked and packed like origami boxes.

The way of the warrior is a long walk. So many paths to travel — Buddha, Tao, Zen. We walk in never-ending circles until our brains spin like goldfish swimming in a bowl.

"When you have lost your place in the world, you are enlightened and your mind will triumph in battle," Sensei taught us.

That's good news for me. I've got a terrible sense of direction, and I get lost often. I'm on the fast track to enlightenment and victory.

But tonight our walking is almost over.

"Are you nervous?" whispers Kyoko.

"Just a little." I haven't seen my family for years.

Yoshi puts his arm around my shoulders for support. Friends make the best crutches.

Memories rewind inside my head. Father painting. Mother's song as she sweeps. Ayame playing with her dolls and Grandfather dozing in the garden.

"Here we are." I knock gently, and Mother opens the door. Her arms wrap me up like a present.

"Welcome, Ki-Yaga." Father bows. "My home is yours tonight. I am proud to have so many sons and daughters." He nods in my direction, a small nod, hardly noticeable. But I understand what it means. He's especially proud of me. The White Crane preens, fluffing its feathers.

"Your house is huge," Kyoko whispers.

It never seemed that way to me. Our house being on the outskirts of town means that Father is not an important samurai. Not influential or wealthy enough to live inside the castle walls. But the buildings of the *ryu* have only one room and my house has seven. More rooms than Kyoko has ever seen.

Father ushers us into the main room, where Grandfather and Ayame are waiting. My little sister wears a pink kimono and shimmers like a spray of cherry blossoms.

Sensei and Grandfather bow low, scraping their foreheads on Mother's perfectly swept floors.

When I used to laugh at her constant dusting and cleaning, she scolded me.

"We must do things many times to get them right," she said.

And now I understand. Over and over. Round and round. Many paths lead to enlightenment, and my mother sweeps hers clean.

"Our home is bright and shiny," I whisper in Mother's ear. "I am happy to be here."

When Mother smiles at my compliment, the house is even brighter than before.

Grandfather claps his hands. "Now we are together, we must share tea. Ayame will serve us."

"Yes, Eldest One." She bends gracefully.

Kyoko raises an eyebrow in my direction as Ayame leaves to begin the preparations. This is not the irritating little sister I left behind. Tea making is an ancient and sacred ceremony. It requires special skill. Sensei doesn't let any of us touch his tea utensils.

"You are not yet ready," he had said. And he was right. We didn't want to waste our time pouring hot water on dry leaves. But if Ayame can do it, then maybe I can, too.

Sensei nods at me and smiles approvingly into my thoughts.

The entrance to the tearoom is so small that we have to kneel to pass through. Respectfully, Sensei stops in front of the scroll alcove to read the words especially placed there:

The rat scuttles, the big cat creeps, the monkey dashes,
The bat glides, the white crane soars, the lizard darts,
And the owl hoots
In the middle of the night.

We recognize ourselves, but who is the owl?

"Sensei must be the owl," Yoshi whispers. "He's wise."

Nezume agrees. "And he sleeps all day."

"And flies at night, if you ask Niya," adds Mikko.

"*Shh,*" Mother reminds us.

Pausing, Sensei admires the kettle and the hearth. The tea ceremony is a ritual of rules. Even getting to the mat is hard. You have to shuffle slowly. It's bad manners to tread on any lines between the tatami matting squares. When we were little, we used to yell, "The ghosts will get you if you do." But it wasn't ghosts we had to worry about. If you stepped on a line, Father would bellow. Just as scary.

First, Grandfather is seated. Then Sensei, the guest of honor. Father and Mother sit on either side of Sensei. We let Yoshi go next, because he's our leader. Feet tucked under, we rest back on our heels. Samurai kids have been doing this since the day they were born. It's easy, even with one leg.

Grandfather gestures for Ayame to begin. In the moonlight, her eyes glow bright and serious. Placing the tray on the ground, she slowly removes the cloth cover to reveal the tea bowl and tools of my ancestors.

Reverently, Ayame wipes the bowl. Three scoops of tea for each of us. She blends the paste and adds the remaining water. Her hands swirl like magic. Around and around the path.

Grandfather sips, wipes the rim, and hands the bowl to Sensei. Sensei sips, wipes, and passes it to Father. Another circle. Around again. We all take turns. Finally, Grandfather passes the empty bowl to Sensei to admire one last time. Cracked in many places, it has been carefully glued with lacquer and painted over with gold. It's an expensive way to repair an old pot. But I wouldn't dare tell Father that.

When Sensei makes tea, we are allowed to ask questions.

I remember the time I asked, "Why is the tea ceremony so slow?"

"To allow us enough time to treasure each moment," answered Sensei.

I didn't understand and wished it was over. I pinched Mikko sneakily. He pinched me back so hard I spilled my lukewarm tea all over Yoshi. Then Kyoko giggled. Nezume and Taji chuckled.

But Sensei rolled his eyes and said, "We will practice washing up."

Now with all the people I love around me, I finally understand. The room is filled with treasure, and I want this moment to last all night.

But it can't. The drum doesn't stop for cups of tea. There are only seven days left before the war begins. *Ta-thum. Thum. Thump.* Ayame folds her hands, and the ceremony is complete.

We leave the room with our hearts warm and full. Our bellies are still empty, but Mother has supper ready. Steaming noodles in fish broth. Nezume's nose twitches, and Yoshi's stomach growls.

"Your daughter shows much skill," Sensei tells Father and Mother.

My little sister glows pink and proud beneath his praise. My friends and I know exactly how she feels. Sensei's approval is even better than seconds for dessert.

"You should study tea making with a master," I say, impressed.

Ayame shakes her head. "This is enough learning for me. I only wish to pour tea for my husband and his honored guests. I am not going to be a scholar. I'm going to be a rich man's wife."

Someone to keep her in pearls and pink kimonos. She's still a little girl after all. I bet she's got dolls tucked in her sleeves.

"What sort of man would that be?" Sensei smiles. "A samurai swordsman perhaps?"

"A court administrator," says Ayame. "They have big houses filled with gold."

Mikko sputters. "What's wrong with a real samurai? Why would you want to marry a warrior who wields a writing brush?"

Ayame giggles.

I hate writing, but I love listening to stories. Sensei settles back cross-legged, ready to tell one. "When Grandfather was younger, he came on a pilgrimage to the Cockroach Ryu."

Grandfather never told me this story.

"I asked him a *koan*. Like I ask all my students. 'What was your face before you were born?' I said. Your grandfather would make the strangest faces, but he never found the answer." Sensei grins. "Would you like to tell him, Niya?"

"The boy always was twice as clever as me," Grandfather says proudly.

I beam at our Eldest One. I am made in his image, but I never knew it until tonight.

"Before I was born, my face was my grandfather's."

Ayame clicks her tongue, unimpressed. "Any mirror could tell you that," she says. "You've always looked like him."

After supper Grandfather and Sensei retire to the tearoom to drink another cup. Through the rice-paper wall, we can see them huddled together, heads almost touching.

When Yoshi gestures to the partially closed screen, we don't hesitate. Sensei told us that samurai kids need to be good listeners, and he's always telling us to do more practice.

Through the rice-paper wall, we can see them huddled together, heads almost touching.

"Which way does the wind blow, old friend?" Sensei asks.

"Is your grandfather a ninja?" whispers Taji.

I shake my head. "Of course not. He couldn't sneak past a rock."

"The wind blows many ways," Grandfather replies. "The Dragon Master has not reached the castle, but your friends are already inside."

What friends? We thought Sensei had only enemies waiting for him.

"The streets of Toyozawa are filled with rumors of your return. I have whispered many myself. The Emperor is expecting you to appear any day now. But even more important than that, what happened in Hell Valley? Did the ghosts give you any advice?"

"Not this time. I must try to wait patiently until they are ready to help me. They chose to speak to Niya with a message about using one slipper," says Sensei. "I'm glad you wrote to me about your grandson. The Dragon Master was a fool not to accept him as a student."

"Dragons have big, fast wings but small, slow brains. No wonder I never fit in when I studied there." Grandfather chuckles. "Buddha taught that we are born as Cockroaches so we can work our way up to being reborn as Dragons. Just goes to show that no one is right all the time."

It's a good joke, but Sensei doesn't laugh. "I, too, make mistakes," he says sadly.

Grandfather's voice softens. "It is the way of the Tao. There cannot be light without dark. There cannot be good without evil. Not even in one man."

"Who is he talking about?" Kyoko whispers.

"Maybe it's the Emperor," says Yoshi.

"Or the Dragon Master," Nezume suggests.

Or Sensei. Our teacher is wise and kind, but what if he really *did* do something evil? Good and evil in one man. It's the perfect description of a *tengu* goblin priest. Why else would Sensei need advice from the ghosts of Hell Valley?

The door slides open, but this time we're not ashamed to be caught.

"We are practicing gathering information," announces Yoshi.

"Excellent. Then I do not need to repeat anything," Sensei says. "But now it is time for your ears to sleep. Good night, Little Cockroaches."

I lead the way to my room, where Mother has laid seven mats on the floor.

"Your sister is very beautiful," says Nezume. "Like the moonflower."

Mikko sighs. "Like a lotus blossom."

"And what am I?" Kyoko asks. "Bamboo grass?"

Remembering Kyoko and the crane, I know it's important to say the right thing. I want to tell her how beautiful she is, but once again, I can't find any words.

Luckily, Yoshi knows what to say. "You are *yukika*. The snow flower."

"Not an ugly snow monkey?" There's a smile in her voice now.

Taji leans over to give her a hug. "Snow monkeys are cuddly."

"So why doesn't anyone make eyes at me?" she demands.

It's a challenge that answers itself. She would beat us up if we did.

"You are our sister," Yoshi says. "We look at you and we feel proud."

I keep my mouth shut. I know how I feel when I look at my sister. And it doesn't feel at all like that when I look at Kyoko.

CHAPTER EIGHT

真

THE CASTLE
WALLS

At sunrise we take our leave. We will travel along the main road now. There's no need for secrecy anymore. No one would dare harm those whom the Emperor is expecting.

But none of that matters if we can't convince the Emperor to stop the drum before the war begins. And if Sensei loses his head first, he won't even get a chance to speak. What will we do then?

I know what Sensei would say. "We will worry about that when we get there. Why waste time on what might never be?"

I try, but I can't stop worrying.

"You should reach the east gate by midday," says Father.

My grandfather grins. "Ki-Yaga doesn't need a gate."

"Sensei's going to fly over the walls," Mikko murmurs, elbowing me in the ribs.

I'd like to poke him back, but Father is watching and he wouldn't approve. The White Crane lifts its head high, ignoring the lizard at its foot.

I'm the last to say good-bye, lingering for one final kiss from Mother and a hug from Ayame. The men in my family are more reserved. But when Father and

Grandfather gaze at me with pride, it feels just like another hug.

Beside me Mikko dawdles with a whispered message for my sister. "I'll be back with a bag full of gold. And a writing brush. Just you wait."

She answers softly, "I think I will."

Now I can tease Mikko. I'll poke *him* in the ribs this time and clutch theatrically at my heart. But if he did marry Ayame one day, we'd be related. The laughter bubbling in my throat drains away. I think I'll help him fill that bag with gold.

"Chop, chop, Little Cockroaches," Sensei calls to us.

Grandfather raises a hand in farewell, his fingers stained with black smudges. He likes to play with fireworks, and once he set the roof ablaze. But I'll never think of him as doddery ever again. I saw the respect in Sensei's eyes, and I heard him ask Grandfather for advice.

This morning other people share the road around the edge of town. Women with straw baskets on their backs and children on their hips. Men going to work in the fields. The occasional ox and one barking dog that follows us until Sensei waves his staff and growls.

"I liked your family." Kyoko sighs. "I wish I had one like it."

"The Cockroach Ryu is a family," says Sensei. "You have more brothers than any sister should have to put up with."

"That's true." She laughs. "What about you, Sensei? Do you have any brothers or sisters?"

It's hard to imagine Sensei as a young boy, wrestling with a brother or pulling a sister's hair.

"I had a sister once. She's dead now."

That's sad but not surprising. Sensei is very old, and his sister would be old, too. We wait for Sensei to tell us about her. There's usually a story, but not this time.

The silence is interrupted by two women arguing on the roadside. One yells, waving a plum in the other's face. The second shouts, brandishing a peach. If fruit was a weapon, both women would be in slices.

"Old, wise one," they call to Sensei. "Help us, please."

Sensei bows low. "How may I assist?"

"I say a plum is worth more than a peach," declares the first woman, handing Sensei a plum.

"I say a peach is worth more than a plum." The second places a large yellow fruit in Sensei's other hand.

Before Sensei can speak, they begin arguing again.

Sensei drops both pieces of fruit in the dirt, grinding them into dusty pulp with his sandals. No longer bickering, the women stand openmouthed. Sensei has worked his first piece of magic. He has made them stop and listen.

"If you do not want each other's fruit, then neither has value. But if you do, one is not better than the other. You must trade with honor."

Bowing to Sensei's wisdom, the women fill his arms with fruit. We continue on our way with sticky peach fingers and red plum-juice mouths. Sensei was right, of course. One is not better than the other.

The road echoes with the stomp of marching feet. A procession is coming. *Thump. Thump. Ta-thum. Thump.* A drum beats loud and insistent, in ominous time with the one in my head. "Come look," it pounds. "Hear my noise. See how important my travelers are." As the group draws nearer, red and gold banners flash against the sun. Their master swaggers in front.

Nezume gasps.

It's the Dragon Master. He holds his head high and is oblivious to the dust and traffic around him. Six of his

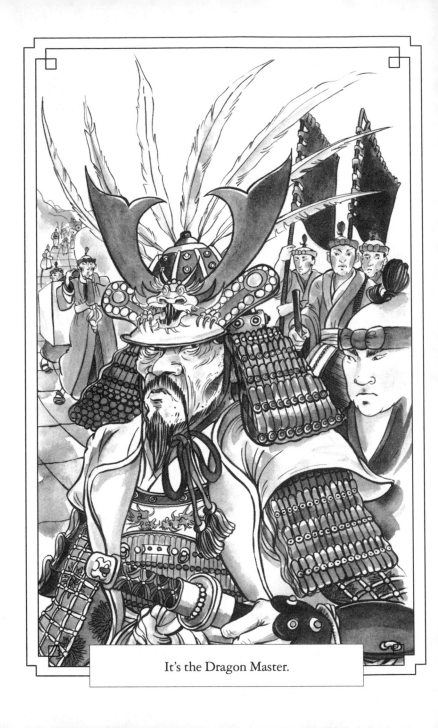

It's the Dragon Master.

students follow with bags, weapons, and boxes of all sizes. They are big and strong and carry the load effortlessly. Their faces echo their master's haughty disdain.

People stop to stare. The tallest Dragon boy raises his sword high, and the crowd cheers.

Sensei shakes his head. "A sword is not a flag to be waved in the wind."

The crowd roars again.

"Some people are easily fooled," says Sensei. "All that glitters is not gold. Sometimes it is just shiny rubbish."

The procession is almost out of sight now. The arrogant master and his students didn't even notice us. Perhaps it was best the Dragon Master didn't lower his gaze to meet Sensei's eyes. Imagine the sparks then. The grass would be burning.

Ta-thum. Thum-thum. Thump. The drum is only an echo, but its message is loud and clear. Six days to war.

Yoshi sighs. "Their uniforms *were* splendid."

I don't like to admit it, but he's right. Our drab brown robes are covered with dust and splattered with mud.

"Did you see all the feathers on the Dragon Master's helmet?" asks Nezume.

He wants one like it, and so do I. Our bare heads are thick with grit from the road.

"Did you see the size of the broadsword the last kid was carrying?" I ask.

It's hard not to be impressed.

Sensei thumps his staff on the ground to call us to attention. "Weapons should be avoided wherever possible. Or chosen carefully for the task. Size does not matter. Would you use a hatchet to remove a fly from the face of a friend?"

I grin. "I might if it was Mikko bugging me."

"If there was a fly buzzing around, it wouldn't be on my forehead. It would be on your smelly slipper," he retorts.

I swipe at him, and he dodges, laughing, just out of reach.

Giving in to temptation, I take off my slipper and throw it.

The others prefer to walk in sandals. But sometimes, when we have been traveling a long time, I find my slipper more comfortable.

"Perhaps we should leave Niya's slipper alone." Sensei's eyes twinkle as he hands it back to me. "The spirit messenger said it is fated for great things. But right now, it is destined to walk some more."

Sandals and slipper slap against the road. Nobody notices *our* little procession. Outwardly, there is nothing golden about us. Sensei teaches us to shine inside.

"The Dragon Master will get to the castle first," Nezume says. "What if he turns the Emperor against us?"

Sensei shakes his head. "At the castle, there are many procedures and protocols. The Emperor must set an example by following his own rules. He will wait for us. And besides, it is bad manners not to do so. Even the Son of Heaven does not want to be in trouble with his teacher."

What about the Emperor's decree that if Sensei returns he must forfeit his head? There's nothing polite about that. I've always hated rules. Now more than ever.

But Sensei doesn't seem worried about the future of his head. He leaves that to me. We walk along, kicking dust in the Dragon Master's footprints. Sensei whistles, tapping the ground with his staff. He nods politely to a fat man with a mat under his arm and calls a greeting to a farmer working in a field beside the road.

Father was right. By midday we have reached the

castle wall. And Grandfather was right, too. There's not a gate to be seen.

The wall stretches high to tug the clouds into place around its turrets and towers. Along the base of the wall runs a moat. We stop underneath a giant cherry tree. But Sensei's usual space in the shade is already taken by a large dirty man, asleep in the ragged remains of a red kimono and jacket—snoring there without his trousers on. We don't know which way to look. Sensei makes it even harder when he sits down next to the tramp.

"Wake up," he bellows into the man's ear. "Lunch has arrived."

Seaweed-green eyes snap open. "Good." The tramp smiles at Sensei. "I haven't eaten for three days. I am hungry enough to eat my bamboo hat."

I can't see a hat anywhere. Maybe he's eaten it already.

Dutifully, we unroll the lunch Mother packed and spread it on the grass. Sensei's new friend eats so fast, even Yoshi has trouble keeping up.

Leaning back against the tree, the big man burps loudly and looks up the wall. "It's a long way to the top."

"Always is," Sensei agrees.

Like a flea-riddled dog, the tramp scratches his ear so hard, his knees shake. I shift a little to the left so any dislodged fleas don't jump onto me. Cockroaches and fleas don't get along at all.

"Are you going in tonight?" the tramp asks.

"As soon as it's dark," replies Sensei. "I have business to complete before I let the Emperor know we have arrived."

We look up at the wall, amazed. The swim across the moat would be freezing cold, but the climb is impossible.

"How are we going to get over that wall?" Nezume shakes his head.

Maybe the Snow Monkey could scale it, but the rest of us haven't got a chance. Unless Sensei really can work a little magic.

The wizard smiles and waves his bamboo wand. "I have arranged for some expert help."

"Who?" we chorus.

The tramp bursts into a spasm of guffaws, spattering bits of rice all over Yoshi. Politely, Yoshi wipes the food spittle from his jacket and his cheek.

"Only a ninja can climb a wall like that," the tramp

says. "What are you teaching these students, Master, that they don't know such obvious things?"

Sensei sighs. "They are still learning to listen. I have taught them Nothing, and it is all they know."

The tramp burps again. "Nothing is enough, Master."

Sensei rummages in his pack and pulls out a pair of trousers. They must have belonged to Onaku. Sensei's skinny pants would never fit this huge man. How did Sensei know to bring Onaku's trousers?

Fully clothed, the tramp nods his thanks before closing his eyes to sleep and snore again.

"Who is he?" Kyoko whispers.

"A *ronin*," says Sensei. "A wandering samurai who serves no lord but chooses to travel his own path. A lot like us."

Mikko gently lifts the *ronin*'s jacket. "Phew. It wouldn't take a ninja to smell this vagabond coming. If he's a warrior, where's his sword? All he has is a student's wooden *bokken*."

Taji wrinkles his nose. "Perhaps he lost his samurai sword."

It's almost unimaginable. But if anyone could do it, it would be this scruffy man.

"Maybe he is not deserving enough," Nezume suggests.

Sensei's eyes dance. "Perhaps he does not need one. He might be a better swordsman than any of us."

Not likely. This man is no skilled samurai. He's not even a worthy opponent. Mikko could easily beat him one-handed. Even on one leg, I'm sure I could too.

"All that glitters is not gold," Sensei reminds us. "And all that smells is not rubbish."

While we play games to pass the time, Sensei joins the *ronin* in a snoring bout. Sensei is a champion snorer, but it's a close competition and we quickly lose interest in judging it. Kyoko draws a grid in the dirt. I'm an expert at hopping games. Throwing a stone, we jump from square to square, avoiding the lines. It's good practice for getting across the mats to the tea ceremony.

Late in the afternoon, Sensei wakes. With his staff he raps our new companion across the knees.

"Dinner?" the *ronin* asks hopefully.

Kyoko lays out the remains of our food and we race our guest to the last honey cake.

The *ronin* belches appreciatively. "Now I will tell you a story in return for your hospitality. Would you like to hear what happened to my trousers?"

We nod, shifting ourselves into a storytelling circle. The White Crane bends closer. It loves a good story.

"Listen and learn, young samurai. I am about to tell you a tale of great strategy."

Losing your trousers doesn't sound like much of a strategy to me.

"On the way to the castle, I was challenged by a renowned swordsman, victorious in his last fifteen duels. I did not want to hurt such an esteemed opponent."

It's hard to imagine his opponent was in any danger. Kyoko swallows a giggle and Sensei glares, but the *ronin* doesn't notice. Like all good stories, this one has a life of its own. It doesn't need to feed off the faces of its listeners.

"I required a strategy to disorientate my opponent. Something to make him hesitate."

"Because he who hesitates has already lost," Taji says.

The *ronin* chuckles, scratching the stray whiskers on his chin. "It seems your students have been listening, Master. To distract my worthy adversary, I decided to take off my trousers."

That's not so silly after all. It's enough to make anyone stop and stare.

"My opponent refused to fight someone he thought was an idiot. He went away. So I notched a victory on my scabbard, and my respected foe survived unharmed. But no plan is perfect, and while I was congratulating myself, a gust of wind blew my trousers into the nearby lake. They sleep with the sweetfish now."

"Your opponent was very fortunate. It was his lucky day," Sensei says.

What? Sensei thinks this ruffian would have won? He's got to be kidding.

"My lucky day, too. I didn't need my pants or my sword that morning," the *ronin* says. "Sometimes it is not what you have but what you don't have. So I gave my sword away to someone who needed it more."

That sounds like something Sensei would teach. And Sensei is nodding, pleased, as if he was somehow involved.

"Everything is not as it looks," he says. "The easiest opponent is the one who thinks he has already won."

Like the Dragon Master?

Sensei nods inside my head. I'm getting used to it now.

"I wouldn't mind fighting if I didn't have to use a sword or hurt anyone," Yoshi says.

"As long as you keep your trousers on. We don't need your lumpy legs to look at," teases Mikko.

"Sometimes it is good to be blind." Taji laughs. "There are some things no one should have to see."

Bellies full, Sensei and the *ronin* are soon snoring again. We wait excitedly for the adventure that tonight promises. Just a few hours to go, but the time crawls like a caterpillar.

"What if this tattered tramp really is a famous swordsman?" I whisper.

Nezume shrugs. "Like who?"

"Sensei seems to know him. He might even be Mitsuka Manuyoto."

The others giggle and guffaw, Mikko loudest of all.

"You think Sensei is a *tengu* and some old vagabond is the celebrated swordsman Manuyoto. A national hero who saved the Emperor from even more assassins than Sensei? Sometimes, Niya, you have mung beans for brains."

My friends laugh even louder, waking Sensei and the *ronin*.

"*Mmmh.*" The *ronin* yawns. "Is there any leftover supper?"

"Eating must wait. There is work to do." Sensei rises, shaking his long, skinny arms. He stretches his legs and touches his toes.

The *ronin* lumbers to his feet, looks down, and decides to stay upright.

Long, deep shadows have draped across the castle town. An owl hoots. A bat screeches. Night clambers over the walls and just behind it, a small dark figure.

CHAPTER NINE

仁

THE OWL HOOTS

Darkness chases the ninja down the wall. We strain to see his shadow disappear against the night. We struggle to listen. But all we hear is the muffled *bok-bok* of frogs in the weeds. Not a ripple breaks the water until the ninja emerges to shake himself like a wet cat. He runs toward us on silent feline feet.

Bowing low, he doesn't rise until Sensei taps him on the shoulder.

"Master," the small but familiar voice says.

Before I can fit the words to a face, the sword on the ninja's belt calls out to me. Izuru, the blade of my childhood.

Last year, I gave it to the young village boy who was carried to the *ryu* with a broken leg. While Sensei straightened the bone, the boy bit hard on the hilt of my sword. Once his teeth marks were on the leather, I knew where Izuru belonged. I was ready to wear the *katana* and *wakizashi* of the warrior samurai, and it was time to let Izuru go.

I know I did the right thing. I can hear it in Izuru's song.

The boy turns to me. Up close, in the gray gloom, I can see him clearly. He's wearing a dark indigo-blue suit, the night uniform of the ninja. His body and face are covered except for his hands and a narrow slit across his eyes so he can see.

Taji has recognized the voice, too. A voice is like a face in his memory.

"Hello, Riaze," he says.

"Hello, Little Cockroaches." Riaze bows to each of us in turn, including the *ronin*.

We all bow our response. It's a well-coordinated movement, perfectly timed to avoid a lot of head knocking and forehead rubbing. We learned this the hard way. The first time we bowed together, I received a lump the size of a duck egg. And Mikko had one even bigger.

Riaze touches the sword at his side. "I am taking good care of Izuru. I have not drawn it once in a fight. But I have taken it out of the scabbard many times to admire the blade and listen to its song."

"Thank you," I say, bending as deeply as I can.

Some things are really important, and this is one of them. A samurai kid never forgets his first sword. Even when he grows old enough to carry a longer, sharper blade by his side, he still keeps the memory of his first sword in his heart.

"Why didn't you return to the *ryu* to study with us?" asks Kyoko.

"I was greatly honored when Ki-Yaga offered to instruct me, but I was called elsewhere." Riaze grins. "It seems Sensei has come to teach me anyway. Before he begins, I must do some teaching of my own."

Riaze unstraps a bag from his back. Crouching, he empties the contents onto the ground and we drop to our haunches beside him.

First, he hands each of us a ninja-blue jacket and baggy trousers.

"Put these over your clothes. Brown is easy to see in the shadows, but blue will make you invisible."

Now the *ronin* has two pairs of trousers when this afternoon he had none.

"Are you coming with us?" Yoshi asks him.

"I wouldn't miss this for anything. Why else would I wait around for three days outside the castle wall?" His teeth gleam bright through the shadows.

"You are much appreciated," says Sensei. "We need all the help we can gather."

The *ronin* bows. "It is always an honor to wait for you, Teacher."

"That's not what you used to say." Sensei laughs. "I believe you once called me a slow old turtle, and I had to chase you with a stick to prove it wasn't true."

It's hard to imagine Sensei chasing this great bear around. Before we can ask for the whole story, Riaze holds up a metal bar with straps and spikes.

"With these ninja climbing claws on your hands and feet, you will be able to scale the wall like monkeys." He winks at Kyoko.

Kyoko slips a hand claw on, adjusting the straps and making room for her extra finger.

"Have you worn these before?" Nezume asks.

She shakes her head, flexing her knuckles. "It's easy to see how they go."

Not for me. I turn the metal band over and over. It won't fit my hand at all.

"That's a foot claw," says Riaze. "I'll show you how to put it on."

My leg is soon a lethal weapon, metal prongs protruding from the bottom of my toes. I imagine kicking an opponent. I wouldn't need two feet to fight if I had a spiky slipper.

Not a bad idea, for a ninja, Sensei teases inside my head.

I'm used to hearing his voice there now, and I like it. It's a special bond between us.

Before I have one handpiece in place, Sensei is ready. He's worn this climbing equipment before! And so has the *ronin*. He's already dressed and helping Taji with the buckles.

From the smaller bag hanging on his belt, Riaze removes a bundle of bamboo tubes. He gives us one each.

"We'll use these to cross the moat underwater. For many months my ninja clan has been piling stones in the ditch here to build a ridge across the bottom. If we walk along it, the water will flow just above our heads."

Riaze demonstrates how to use the bamboo tubes. "One end of the tube goes in your mouth, and the other sits above the waterline. If any water splashes into the tube, blow hard and it will clear."

Now I know why Sensei came to this section of the wall. And I know it's not coincidence that the *ronin* was waiting in the same place. They came to meet at the underwater bridge.

"This is how the ninja move across a river unseen. We do not splash and splutter like the swimming samurai." Riaze chuckles.

"I thought the ninja could walk *on* water," Taji says.

I've heard that, too. My father believes they have special shoes that glide across the surface, as if by magic. My grandfather says it is a good story and repeats it whenever he can.

Riaze laughs even louder. "That's just a myth. But words are powerful weapons. With each telling of the story, our imagined supernatural powers grow more believable. It's easy to fool a superstitious man, even a samurai or an emperor. Some men think we can vanish into thin air."

That sounds reasonable to me. Riaze disappeared when he was climbing down the wall. I saw it with my own eyes.

"It is hard to fight or track an opponent you can't see," Taji agrees. "You have to listen very hard."

The *ronin* slaps his hand against his leg. "I don't like listening anytime. If you can't beat them, join them, I say."

"Is that what we're doing, Sensei?" Yoshi asks.

Our teacher nods. "The way of the warrior has many paths to be walked many different ways. To silence the war drum, we must also creep on ninja feet."

Or in my case, hop on a ninja foot. Preferably with spikes on it.

"I will walk in samurai sandals," says Riaze. "I'm proud to carry Izuru by my side, and all my friends are envious. No ninja weapon compares to a samurai sword."

Sensei was right. We have much to learn from one another. We won the Annual Trainee Games because we worked together as a team. Inside the castle wall, a greater challenge is waiting. We must convince the Emperor to stop the war before he chops off Sensei's head. But this time our team is even stronger. We have two new members. Izuru chose Riaze many months ago, and I suspect Sensei chose the *ronin* long before that.

Riaze is looking in his belt bag again. Ninja might not wear magic shoes, but the bags they carry are full of tricks. What else could he possibly have in there?

He extracts a small bamboo cylinder. "You will like this best of all."

"What's it do?" Kyoko asks.

"It warms your heart. More than any kiss ever will."

As Kyoko reaches to take the cylinder, Riaze brushes her clawed hand against his lips.

Kyoko giggles, and my glare slices through the darkness between them.

"The tube *is* warm," she says, surprised.

"We pack embers inside layers of bamboo. It will generate heat for hours," Riaze promises. "And it's useful if you want to burn down a building."

The ninja use fire to flush out their victims. Father once said that a ninja can shoot flames from the palm of his hand. But Grandfather said, "All fires begin with a little spark. There's no magic in that." He knew about the ember cylinders. I should have paid more attention to Grandfather's stories. For years his wisdom was right under my nose and I never once breathed it in.

"There is a waterproof pocket inside your jacket," Riaze informs us.

I place the cylinder in it carefully. Warmth spreads through the pocket, across my chest.

But Mikko has other worries on his mind than being wet and cold. He's looking up anxiously. "It's very high."

"But not as difficult as it looks," Sensei reassures us. "The wall is pitted with handholds."

How does he know that? Maybe he can fly.

Or maybe he's climbed it before.

"I have left a grappling hook at the top of the wall. It's holding a rope ladder you can use," says Riaze. "Stick close and flat against the wall. We call it lizard walking."

Our Striped Gecko doesn't look convinced.

"Don't worry, Mikko. The ladder will help you climb like a ninja." When Riaze came to the *ryu,* it was Mikko who held his hand and made him laugh to forget the pain. Now it is Riaze's turn to help.

"You'll be all right," Nezume says, belting Mikko on the shoulder. "One arm never bothered you before. And it won't this time."

Mikko shakes his head. "It's not that." He pauses. "I'm afraid of heights."

"But you stand on the edge of our mountain looking into the valley," says Kyoko. "It makes me dizzy to watch."

"That's different. I feel safe because we're all standing there. I know Yoshi would reach out and grab me."

"Then I'll go last," says Yoshi. "And if you slip, I'll catch you."

Kyoko giggles. "Squashed Yoshi."

"The biggest problem is owls," Sensei says. "They

have nests all over the wall and their beaks are sharp. If you put your finger in the wrong place, you might lose it."

"I've got a spare finger, anyway." Kyoko shrugs.

The White Crane isn't scared of other birds either.

"I heard an owl calling earlier," says Taji. "I listened hard but I couldn't hear its wings."

"That's because it was me." Riaze puffs with pride. "I am a member of the Owl Ninja Clan. *Tu-whit. Tu-whoo.*" He hoots, soft and familiar, into the night.

In my memory an owl answers. Grandfather's tearoom scroll. The Crane, the Bat, the Lizard, the Tiger, the Rat, the Monkey. And the Owl. It's not Sensei at all. It's Riaze. Was Grandfather sending me a message?

"Time to go," the *ronin* reminds us. "We need to reach the Owl Dojo before midnight."

It's easy to walk with a claw on my foot. We follow Riaze into the moat, gasping as the icy water clutches our throats. It crushes against my chest until the fire in my pocket forces it to let go. I hop as fast as I can.

The ridge across the bottom is narrow and uneven. I concentrate carefully. My thoughts hold my mind in place, but my foot slips. Cold water fills my breathing tube. I am gasping and sputtering; the world around me turns to bubbles. I want to scream, but I force myself not to panic. A boy who has faced a ghost is not afraid of drowning. It's like I'm dreaming—I see the world through Taji's eyes, all gray and black.

Om-om, Sensei says inside my head. My waterlogged brain struggles to stay awake. *Om-om,* I force myself to answer.

The *ronin's* strong bear arms lift me back onto the ridge. I try not to gulp as I blow out to clear the tube. My aching lungs stretch and snap back into shape. My friends are ahead of me and don't even know what has happened. I'll have a good story to tell tonight at the dojo.

Riaze and Sensei reach the wall first. Sensei climbs like a spindly-legged garden spider. Kyoko follows quickly, but Riaze stops to help Mikko onto the first rung of the ladder. I'm just behind Nezume, Taji, and Yoshi. And the *ronin.* Like a column of ants, we scrape a trail up the wall.

Sensei is first to the top. His arms are skinny but strong—thin strands of unbreakable bamboo. The *ronin* is last. His arms are short but strong—bolts of bamboo

Sensei is first to the top.

matting. Climbing is all about arms, and I've got two of those. But it's hard with only one foot to rest against.

Like a sky ninja, the pale moon creeps from behind the clouds. I can see all the way to the castle keep. In the middle of the compound stands the main building where the Emperor sleeps. Four smaller buildings surround it, connected by passageways. Somewhere inside, Sensei will confront the Emperor and speak out against the drum.

The White Crane likes it up here. It shakes its feathers, itching to fly.

"Someone's coming," Taji whispers.

"Which direction?" asks Riaze.

"East."

"Everyone flat against the top of the wall." Dropping quickly, Riaze shows us how.

Crunch. Crunch. Crunch. The sound of samurai boots draws closer. The White Crane huddles paralyzed with fear, and the goldfish in my stomach hold their breath. *Ta-thum. Thum-thump.* My heart beats a reminder: six days to war.

Directly below me, two soldiers stop to argue. They smell as if they've been drenched in *sake* and rolled in warm mouse droppings. It's worse than the sulfur steam of Hell Valley.

In front of me, Nezume wriggles. He's not good at keeping still. He's usually the first to move when we practice statues.

Tsst. A small stone drops to the ground. *Tsst.* Another follows.

"What was that?" the first soldier asks.

"I didn't hear anything."

The first soldier looks along the wall. "I heard something. We should check."

"Do it yourself, Jungo. I'm not listening to you anymore. That's how I got into this trouble in the first place," the second soldier grumbles. "If you hadn't convinced me to gamble against the captain, we'd be home drinking hot *sake* instead of doing extra guard duty."

"Shh. Stop whining, Shouji, and let me listen," Jungo says.

"It was probably an owl. The place is riddled with the scraggly, stinking things."

"Tu-whit. Tu-whoo," Riaze hoots in protest.

"Hear that? What did I tell you, noodle-head? The

only thing threatening to attack the castle has claws and feathers," says Shouji.

Riaze rustles in his belt bag. It's a sound as soft as owl wings, but I'm a good listener.

Ssst. Pfft. A white cloud of smoke balloons to envelop us all. Another ninja trick.

"This ocean mist is thicker than day-old miso soup. Do you still want to go owl hunting?" Shouji sneers.

"Nah. I suppose you're right."

The two soldiers grumble their way into a farther corner of the night.

"Ninja are always pleased to see the castle defenses in the safe hands of the samurai," Riaze taunts. "It makes our job easier."

The *ronin*'s teeth flash a grin into the darkness, and Sensei snorts in mock indignation.

"It would be different if it was me. I could do it one-handed," Mikko boasts.

He'd have to. It's all he's got. But he wouldn't be doing it alone. The Cockroach Ryu is a team. We stick together like rice and honey.

After Riaze is sure the soldiers have left, he hauls the rope ladder up and drops it down the other side. As we near the ground, a ghostly-white shadow swoops low over our heads. Somewhere nearby, a mouse squeals.

"The owl strikes, silent and deadly," Sensei says, dropping expertly to the ground.

Yoshi lands on all fours, like a cat. I collapse with a thump to provide a soft cushion for Mikko, who lands on top of me. There's nothing graceful about our entrance, but only the moon is watching. It winks and returns to hide behind the clouds.

"Keep the climbing claws," says Riaze. "You might need them again one day."

Mikko won't like it if we do. And I would rather fly.

We edge along the dark shadowed streets, around corners, through narrow gateways. Around and around, until I'm hopelessly lost.

"*Yeow*. I stepped on a rock," Yoshi whispers through clenched teeth. "I can't see a thing."

"Me neither. How am *I* expected to find my way?" Taji laughs.

"The road is curved so that even in daylight attackers cannot see very far ahead," says Sensei. "But now that you are trainee ninja, you don't need eyes to see where you must go. More practice, Little Cockroaches.

Tomorrow your training begins at the Owl Dojo. We have many challenges ahead, and you will need new skills to meet them."

Oh, no. Back to school.

Mikko groans, and the *ronin* laughs.

Pressing his fingers against his lips, Riaze leads us through the maze to a small wooden entrance.

Yoshi reads the words above the door: "Kitchen staff."

"The best place for a ninja clan to hide is under the Emperor's nose," Sensei says approvingly.

"Owl Ninja are also the castle kitchen hands. My miso soup will make your mouth water," Riaze brags.

"Tu-whoo, tu-whoo," he calls softly.

The door creaks open. Just wide enough for the face behind it to see what the owl has dragged in. Just enough for the smell to reach out and tug at our tastebuds.

Hot miso soup. *Mmmm.* I can't help it. Drool pools in the corners of my mouth.

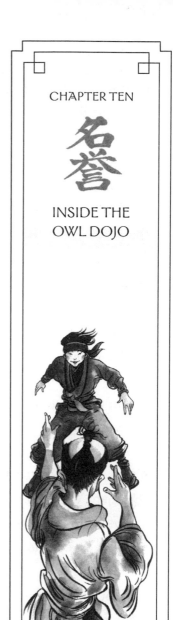

CHAPTER TEN

名誉

INSIDE THE
OWL DOJO

Last night was a tired blur of welcoming smiles, my tale of almost drowning, a hot bath, and the best miso soup ever. This morning I'm hungry again and hoping for another bowl.

In the dojo dining room, we are quickly surrounded by familiar faces from our mountain village. One of them makes the hair on the back of my neck bristle. It is the face of a dead man. Black eyes lurk behind shaggy eyebrows. Gray furry hair covers his chin and cheeks. His mouth curls, almost into a snarl. I'd never forget a face like that.

We accompanied Sensei to his funeral two years ago. Women howled, banging their rice cooking pots. The bright red coffin was lowered into the fire, and that night we sent a flotilla of lanterns down the river. Without a proper farewell, a soul wanders for eternity — like the ghosts of Hell Valley. But everything was done right for this man. Why can't his spirit rest in peace?

Goose bumps crawl across my chest as the ghost's wolf-like stare hunts me down. But then he grins, and there are no pointed rows of teeth — just a smile.

"Your face is pale, young Cockroach. I am surprised you remember my mock funeral."

"Niya has a memory like a steel boar trap and the fastest brain on any number of legs." Sensei beams proudly.

My goose bumps are gone now. I pretend they were never there at all.

"I'm used to talking with *real* ghosts," I brag. Yoshi stomps on my foot, reminding me to be polite, but I continue. "When we passed through Hell Valley, a ghost chose to speak with *me*."

"Then I am pleased to have such a famous person in my dojo," the man says with a chuckle.

The wolf man is the Ninja Master! I wish I'd listened to Yoshi's stomp.

I bow, low and humble. "I meant no disrespect. It was only half a ghost, not very frightening at all."

The Ninja Master nods, pardoning my insolence. "When I was chosen as clan leader, I had to disappear from my old life. Death is the ultimate vanishing act."

Ninja are famous for their tricks, and this master is a great magician.

His hypnotic stare binds me tight, piercing deep into my heart. The White Crane looks into the Wolf's eyes, unafraid.

Satisfied with what he finds, the Wolf releases us both.

"I am honored to have Ki-Yaga return to the Owl Dojo. It will be a privilege to teach his students."

I know I can trust this man. He could have swallowed my soul, but he chose not to. And there's something more: I recognize the wolf Yoshi and I saw on the mountain track just before the earthquake that almost killed me. Even then, the ninja were watching over us.

The Ninja Master places his hand on my shoulder. "Let us share breakfast and after that"—he laughs—"more practice."

Sensei nods his approval, but my friends and I groan. Around us, the Owl Ninja trainees echo our opinion. Ninja and samurai are not so different after all.

We're lucky the ninja of the Owl Dojo work as castle kitchen staff. They cook a wonderful breakfast.

"Never eat a big meal before a battle," Sensei taught us. "Sometimes in combat, a samurai sees things that make him glad his stomach is empty."

But we're only training today, so we pile our plates high.

"This is the best fish I've ever eaten," says Taji.

Yoshi belches. "These are the best *three* fish I've ever eaten."

We all murmur appreciatively, except the *ronin*. His goldfish cheeks are stuffed too full to make any noise.

After more breakfast than I've ever eaten before, an elderly ninja leads us in meditation and warm-up exercises.

"How can he teach us?" Kyoko whispers. "He's so old. If he stretches anything, it will snap in two."

Coughing softly, Sensei reminds us to be respectful or his old arms will teach us a lesson with his traveling staff.

A ninja needs to be flexible. Limb by limb, we stretch everything. By the time we've finished, I feel twice as tall as before.

The Ninja Master arrives to watch our progress. "Today each Cockroach student will learn a different skill," he announces. "Then, together, you will be expert at them all."

We're used to that. We have never been expert at anything on our own. Blind eyes, one leg, one arm. But our team is strong, with many arms and legs, able to see in the dark.

"Ki-Yaga and I have agreed on what each trainee needs to know. Yoshi will study concealment and disguise, learning to transform into other things and other people."

"He's going to be a ninja rock," Mikko teases.

Yoshi growls gently. "Kick me and you'll be sorry."

We laugh, but it's an excellent choice. Yoshi is already a rock. We lean on him all the time.

"Taji will learn espionage. Ninja have ways of listening that the samurai have never heard of," the master says. "Kyoko will train in the garden with our women."

Dark clouds thunder across Kyoko's face. "I'm just as good as the boys." She glowers, eyes flashing like lightning.

"The master did not say any different," Sensei intercedes. "You might be surprised at what you learn. If you leave your mind open, anything can fly in."

I always try to keep my mind open wide. Maybe *that's* how Sensei flies in so easily.

"A girl who can fight like a boy is the perfect surprise weapon," the Ninja Master says. "She will make the warrior hesitate and . . ."

"He who hesitates has already lost," we all chorus, including the *ronin*.

150

"You have taught your students well, Ki-Yaga."

Sensei nods, pleased with us and with the Ninja Master's praise.

"I will teach Nezume to fight with a ninja dagger, and Mikko will learn to use explosives. Niya will practice unarmed combat." The Wolf grins, sly but wise. "Maybe his slipper will learn new tricks."

Good. I grin, too. Then I'll be able to try those tricks out on Mikko.

Sensei eyes the cherry tree in the courtyard. "I think I will practice as well."

"I'll snore at your feet and learn from you," the *ronin* says. "It will be just like the old days."

We turn eagerly, hoping for the story. But somewhere a gong sounds, and we know what that means. No more chatter. Practice has begun.

"My name is Ako," my opponent says. He's smaller and thinner than me, but I'm not fooled by that. "I am also called Rice Boy," Ako continues, "because I make the best rice porridge in Toyozawa. And there is one more reason but I'll demonstrate that later."

I search his face for clues. But the ninja are masters of disguise. All I find is a smile.

Ako tucks one leg up and hops forward. He falls flat on his face but rises quickly, ready to hop again.

"Are you making fun of me?" I ask.

Ako looks offended. "A ninja would never insult a guest."

"Then why are you pretending to have one leg?"

"I want to fight like you. If I can manage on one leg, it doesn't matter if I fall and break an ankle."

I never thought about that before. What if I broke my ankle? The question answers itself. Yoshi and Mikko would argue about whose turn it was to carry me.

Ako and I begin to wrestle. Sometimes Ako wrestles me to the ground, and sometimes I topple him. But most of the time he stumbles and we crash together. It's not easy, but Ako refuses to give up, persisting until he can balance on one leg. Not as good as the White Crane but much better than Taji and Mikko.

"May I borrow your slipper?" he says. "I think it would be harder to fight with a shoe on."

"You are right," I agree, "but my slipper probably won't fit you."

It does. Perfectly. Now I have the advantage as my bare foot grips the floor.

We lock arms with a grunt.

Crash. Clunk.

We untangle legs with a giggle.

Riaze appears, raising his eyebrows at us. "Do you want to go and see what the others are doing?"

"We're supposed to practice wrestling," I say.

"We could practice stealth," suggests Ako. "All ninja have to learn that."

Riaze, Ako, and I sneak into the garden, where Kyoko is throwing *shuriken* stars. When Kyoko kicks me during unarmed fighting practice, I often see stars, but not like these. Each star has four razor-sharp points, and according to Grandfather's stories, sometimes they are dipped in poison.

At the far end of the garden, a woman stands holding a wooden pole. Kyoko swings her arm, and blades of metal spin across the open space to splinter the wood in the woman's hand. The woman doesn't flinch, but I do.

"What are you doing here?" Kyoko calls.

Riaze, Ako, and I sneak into the garden, where
Kyoko is throwing *shuriken* stars.

I wave her over. "We're sneaking up on everyone."

"Come with us, and I'll show you how I broke my leg. You can try the climb," offers Riaze.

Kyoko can't resist a climbing challenge.

Riaze points to a thin bamboo string swinging high between two trees. *I'm not trying that,* I think. But Kyoko is already running toward the nearest trunk. She scrambles across on all fours and drops to the ground.

"Too easy. How could you possibly fall?"

"Hmph," Riaze snorts. "I'll show you."

He walks the string like a tightrope. Kyoko wants to try it that way, but black smoke is billowing from the hut at the other end of the garden. That's where Mikko is. We race to see what he's burning.

In the middle of the room, Mikko is filling an eggshell with dark powder.

"Look," he calls. "I'm mixing sand, pepper, and nettles. When I throw this in someone's eyes, they'll be blinder than Taji. Do you know what else I learned this morning?"

We shake our heads. I've never seen Mikko excited about learning anything.

"I can make a wall of flame, but I can't show you."

He grins sheepishly. "I burned a hole in the wall last time."

"Then you are almost as good as Grandfather," I say. "He set the roof on fire twice, and once he even singed his own beard."

"Has Mikko finished his lesson?" Ako asks the teacher.

The ninja nods, looking relieved that the instruction is over. Winking at me, Mikko slips the eggshells into his pocket, unnoticed by everyone else.

We're looking for Taji next, but he finds us first. He's finished learning to listen and is practicing with a bamboo cup against the dojo wall. "I heard you coming," he says, laughing. "But I didn't need the listening cup to hear Niya."

"You won't hear me anymore. Ako and Riaze are teaching me to creep like a ninja."

"I'll believe that when I hear it," Taji says.

The White Crane is learning to fly on owl wings, but the Golden Bat already knows how to swoop without a sound.

We need Taji's help to find Yoshi. He's sitting motionless, not making any noise at all. Yoshi has been practicing like this for years. Every day he sits on his rock overlooking the valley, thinking about the time years ago when he accidentally killed another boy. But ever since he shared the story, he doesn't spend as much time sitting alone.

"Would you like to see something dangerous?" Riaze asks. "It's in the next room."

We nod eagerly. Samurai kids race toward danger. Except when they don't know where they're going. The dojo is a maze of rice-paper walls, and they all look the same to me.

"There it is." Ako points to a raised platform in the middle of the room.

Why would a room need two floors? And what's so dangerous about that?

"This is a nightingale floor," Riaze says. "It sings."

"Like a sword?" Nezume asks.

When Riaze steps onto the wooden floor, the boards creak softly. "No. This is not a song you ever want to hear."

"Its notes are meant to rouse sleeping samurai guards," says Ako. He draws an imaginary sword across his neck. "One dead ninja."

"And if the samurai don't wake up?" Yoshi asks.

"One dead samurai," says the *ronin* from the doorway. Sensei, the Ninja Master, and Nezume are with him.

Are ninja and samurai enemies? Or friends?

You must decide for yourself, Sensei answers me.

"Even the Emperor now sleeps surrounded by a nightingale floor," says the Ninja Master. "We haven't yet found a way across."

Nezume turns, hand on his sword. "Do you want to kill the Emperor?"

"No. The Emperor is a good man, and I would defend his honor. But we must be prepared for the day when this floor lies between us and our enemy."

"A samurai doesn't like to sneak and kill," I say indignantly.

Riaze laughs. "That's why he hires a ninja to do it for him."

I'm about to argue, but Sensei and the *ronin* are nodding. *It's true!*

Yoshi steps onto the floor to stand beside Riaze. He has made his decision. And he's right. These ninja are our friends. One by one, we follow his lead until we're all standing in the middle of the floor and a flock of nightingales cries out in deadly song.

The sound is familiar, and the White Crane shakes its head, trying to remember. Sensei says that sometimes you need to tip your head sideways so you can look at a problem differently.

Or tip your ear so you can hear at a different angle.

Kyoko places her ear against the floor. "I know that sound."

Taking her *shakuhachi* flute from her pocket, she begins to play. Her six fingers play the bamboo flute until it sings in tune with the creaks and sighs of the floor.

When she stops playing, the Ninja Master bows low.

"I am in your debt," he says. "You will save many ninja lives."

The ninja are masters of deception, but they had nothing to hide behind when they stepped onto the nightingale floor. Now they can play Kyoko's song. Slumbering beneath the sound of a flute's lullabies, no one will hear the ninja creep.

We came here to end war in the mountains, and now beneath the castle wall we are ending another conflict, as samurai and ninja work together.

Sensei grins proudly. *I am such a good teacher.*

Yes, I answer. *And we are such good students.*

It's hard to listen when Sensei laughs inside my head. The Ninja Master is speaking again. "Let us celebrate by shouting," he says.

We shout to release *ki.* Sensei teaches us that *ki* is a powerful spiritual energy, stored in the stomach and more potent than one of Yoshi's belches. A great shout can startle an ambush or frighten an adversary. And it always feels good to yell.

"Yoh-oh-oh-oh," the Ninja Master's voice howls across the room. Nezume shivers, and Taji covers his ears.

Yoshi roars. The *ronin* growls. And the White Crane screeches. *Aye-ee-yah. Aye-ee-yah.*

Slowly, Sensei raises his arms. The room begins to quiver like an earthquake. The nightingale floor creaks and groans. Even the air trembles.

"Banzai!" he bellows.

When he lowers his arms, the world stills.

"That felt good," he says. "Now I am hungry enough to eat a horse."

He's lucky Uma didn't hear that!

After lunch our time is our own. But we know what we need to do. More ninja practice.

Sensei and the *ronin* are already practicing under the cherry tree again. I would like to learn to sleep and watch at the same time.

You will, Sensei whispers. *The skill is strong in your family.*

No, it's not. When Father sleeps, he doesn't hear a thing. Not even Ayame and me arguing. And we're louder than a throng of pitta birds.

Sensei shakes his head. He doesn't mean Father. *Who is always asleep in the corner?*

He means Grandfather!

"Come with me now. I will show you my special talent," Ako says. "Do you want to know why I am called Rice Boy?"

He leads us to a room where the floors shine with wax. "Watch this." He runs across the room, without slipping.

"You try," he dares us.

Nezume accepts the challenge first and lands on his backside. Mikko slides in behind him.

"I'm impressed, but what's that got to do with rice?" I call from the safety of the doorway.

Ako returns at full speed to stand beside me. Taking

a handful of rice from his pocket, he strews it over the floor. More slippery than ice! He runs across the room again, feet flying and skidding on the grains. But he doesn't even stumble. He makes it look easy.

But it's not. Riaze follows, almost making it to the middle before he drops with a thump. Yoshi slumps beside him, and Nezume tumbles on top of them both. The rest of us skid to form a heap of flailing arms and legs.

"Yoh. Yah." Yelling, Ako launches himself on top of the pile. But we don't need to shout. The room is filled with the most powerful *ki* of all—friendship.

Nightfall is our signal to leave.

"I have a parting gift for each of you," the Ninja Master says.

Riaze and Ako step forward, their arms piled high with belts and daggers.

Once I would have sneered at ninja weaponry. But we have learned many things at the Owl Dojo, and one of those things is respect. The ninja blade might not sing like a sword, but it speaks powerful words of fellowship.

"We thank you, Master," Sensei says. "My students will keep your secrets safe."

The ninja have numerous places to hide their secrets—pockets filled with stars, knives in their boots, black powder in the end of their walking sticks, and scabbards with false bottoms. But a samurai uniform, with its layers of folds and wraps, has just as many perfect hiding places.

We bow low, proud to scrape our foreheads in the dust of the dojo floor.

"Return with honor, Little Cockroaches," the Ninja Master calls after us as we follow Sensei into the dark street.

Tu-whit. Tu-whoo.

"See you in the castle kitchen," Riaze says, hooting with soft laughter.

The air echoes with the noise of owls. And one lone wolf howl.

CHAPTER ELEVEN

忠誠

THE FIRST SCROLL

It's hard to sleep with all the shouting.

"Get up, old man!" the soldier bellows. "You can't lie here. You're blocking the castle keep gateway."

Sensei yawns, loud and wide. "Pardon?" There's nothing wrong with his ears. Ki-Yaga can hear a crane feather rustle, but sometimes he likes to pretend.

"Where did you come from? There's no record of you or your companions entering the main gate." The soldier grabs Sensei's traveling stick. That's not a good idea.

Slowly, the *ronin* opens one eye. He doesn't want to miss the fun.

Sensei's long, skinny leg strikes to trip the soldier.

Clump-fmp.

Standing, our teacher is suddenly taller, louder, and more frightening than the ogres in Grandfather's stories.

"I am Ki-Yaga. Master of the Cockroach Ryu. Former Imperial Teacher and Royal Bodyguard. The Emperor is expecting me, and while I do not expect much in return, I deserve better treatment than this."

Ki-Yaga's name has always opened doors. And now that it has been mentioned, the gates to the castle keep swing apart.

Kneeling, the soldier waits bare-necked for Sensei to draw his sword.

Instead, Sensei gently taps the man on the shoulder. "We all make mistakes," he says.

I want to ask Sensei about his mistake, but this isn't the time.

"My humble apologies, Sensei." On his feet again, the soldier takes charge. "We were instructed to watch for your arrival, but I did not expect to find you already inside the main gate." He barks an order, and guards rush to escort us through every gate between here and the Emperor's residence.

Beard flapping and cloak flying, Sensei strides between the soldiers. He's enjoying this! And so are we. The *ronin* puffs out his chest and swaggers, hand on his wooden sword. Kyoko giggles, waving to the people who line the streets and stare. If I had a drum, I would beat it proudly. *Ta-thum. Thum-thump.* We've come to stop the mountains from going to war.

At the entrance to the main building, a man is waiting. He wears a richly brocaded jacket and long baggy pants that drag across the floor. His snake-green eyes glitter with intelligence and authority. This is a man with an important job. Maybe the Emperor chose him especially to keep an eye on Sensei's head.

"Honored guests." The green-eyed court attendant bows. "The Emperor has asked me to greet you on his behalf. I will show you to your quarters. If there is anything you need, ring this bell to summon a servant boy."

He hands Sensei a gold bell. "Hot baths and clean clothes are waiting for you." His gaze slides down his nose to tell us our cockroach-brown traveling robes will not do here in the Emperor's compound.

We follow the attendant to a small building in the Imperial Garden.

"Breakfast will be delivered shortly. The castle has an excellent kitchen," our guide says.

We already know that. If I'm lucky, the meal will be Riaze's miso soup and Rice Boy's porridge.

The attendant's eyes narrow as he searches Sensei's face. "I have heard that you mysteriously appeared on the castle keep steps."

Sensei says nothing. The silent tension wraps itself around our throats. Mikko coughs, and the *ronin* scratches his neck.

Suspicious eyes drill even deeper. "Perhaps our guards were asleep or drunk when you passed through the main gate."

I don't like the sound of this. Someone could get into serious trouble. Maybe even lose a body part.

"Sir," I say, bowing low. "Do not punish the soldiers. No one can see Sensei if he does not want them to. Not even we can find him when he chooses to hide from our constant questions."

The man laughs, and the tension releases its fingers from our necks. "The deeds of Ki-Yaga are famous. I have heard he can walk through walls and disappear into the night. But I see he has worked even greater magic. He has taught his students honor *and* good manners. Unlike some others, constantly ringing their bell."

That sounds just like the Dragon Master and his students.

Bowing, the attendant takes his leave. The slap of silk against the floor tracks his departure. Sensei says the Emperor is afraid of assassins. He wants to ensure he can hear everyone coming and going. Especially those on their way across his nightingale floor.

Tap-tap. Tap.

Nezume opens the door cautiously, hoping it's not the Dragon Master.

It is another attendant, older and taller but with the same baggy trousers.

"I have a message for Ki-Yaga, sensei of the Cockroach Ryu," he says, eyes round and respectful. Our teacher is a living legend, the most famous samurai to still have his head on his shoulders. At least for now.

The attendant hesitates. It's not good news. But Sensei smiles encouragingly.

"The M-m-aster of the D-d-d-ragon Ryu sends you a greeting," the attendant stutters. He stares at the bamboo matting. He looks at his slippers, and he even stares at my one foot.

"Please continue," says Sensei. "I will not hold you accountable for another's rude words."

We know the message anyway. *Beware the Dragon.*

The attendant swallows loudly, but he speaks in an embarrassed whisper. "How many cockroach wings can a dragon's breath singe?"

It is a great insolence for the Dragon to threaten a man under the Emperor's roof. But Sensei is not insulted. His eyes gleam.

"The Dragon Master is finally wise enough to consult the bugs."

My eyes twinkle, too. This is a traditional saying that Grandfather uses all the time. If you need to know something, ask the bugs. Bugs can sense shifts in the world around them and predict what might happen next.

This Cockroach predicts that Sensei will wield his words like a sword and cut the Dragon's ears to kite ribbons.

"Tell the Dragon Master that I do not have time to teach him to count. I suggest he use his fingers and toes," Sensei says.

The attendant leaves, grinning. We bathe quickly and eat breakfast even faster. The Owl Ninja truly are excellent cooks.

"Will the Emperor still want to punish you, Sensei?" Kyoko is worried.

"Only when I least expect it," says Ki-Yaga.

"Are you expecting it today?" I ask.

Sensei picks a rice grain from his teeth. "No, I am not."

Now we're all nervous.

Tap-tap. Another knock.

"The Emperor is ready to see you," the attendant announces.

Sensei teaches us that seeing is not important. You must feel. It is too late when you see an army approaching, but if you feel the ground shake, you will expect them before they arrive. You will have the advantage and be prepared.

"You must learn to be like Taji," our master says. "Taji is not distracted by what he can't see."

Wiping his hands on his beard, Sensei is ready to go. But the *ronin* is still eating.

"Aren't you coming?" Yoshi asks him.

"I'll wait here," he answers. "I have no interest in bowing to the Emperor with my stomach only half full. I am loyal to my teacher and will come running when he needs me. But he does not need me now."

Yoshi would like to stay and help him eat but Sensei hurries us along. "Chop, chop, Little Cockroaches."

It's tricky to hop in long, trailing trousers. The Emperor will have no trouble hearing me approach; I'll probably trip at his feet. Two soldiers escort us into the waiting alcove. The Dragon Master is already there. His cloak gleams with gold embroidery, and his helmet is plumed with owl and crane feathers.

We wait in opposite corners, gazes slicing across the room like sword swipes in a battle.

"Someone should stuff an explosive inside his helmet," Mikko whispers.

Grinning, I remember the hole in the Owl Dojo wall. But Sensei doesn't think it's funny. He shakes his head to remind us of our manners.

Two Dragon kids stand beside their master. We recognize the largest boy. He purposely broke Kyoko's hand at the Games last year.

"I'd like to break *his* fingers," Yoshi mumbles through clenched teeth. He could do it, too. He's bigger and stronger than the Dragon boy.

Mikko is small, but his one hand is very powerful. "Let me," he mutters. Mikko could crush even Yoshi's fingers if he wanted to.

"No," counsels Sensei. "It is not an eye for an eye and a hand for a hand."

Nezume fidgets nervously. "Why must we wait so long?"

"The Emperor will be consulting his advisers to make

sure this is a lucky day for making important decisions," Sensei says.

How can a day be lucky? If it's lucky for us, it's not lucky at all for the Dragons.

"His Excellency is ready to receive you," an attendant proclaims.

The two soldiers usher us into a larger room where the Son of Heaven sits on a golden throne, swathed in layers of yellow silk. Biting my lip, I hide my disappointment. The man behind the expensive wrapping doesn't look impressive at all. He is short and round like a rice dumpling, and his fingers are too pudgy even to hold a sword.

Then he smiles.

Sensei is always right. It is not what you see that matters, but what you feel. When the Emperor smiles, the sun reaches down to pat each one of us on the back. The White Crane opens its wings to the warmth.

Grandfather likes to tell stories about the Emperor. "The Son of Heaven makes the crops grow and the rice flourish. But his displeasure can fill the sky with thunder, and when he is angry, lightning shoots from his fingers."

He wouldn't need to hold a sword, then. Maybe he's a ninja.

But in the final battle, great power cannot overcome great fear. Good-luck charms hang from vantage points all over the room. Beside the throne candles burn. Only a brave ghost would dare set foot in this room filled with talismans to keep the spirits away.

Removing his helmet with a flourish, the Dragon Master bows.

"Welcome," the Emperor says.

When Sensei bows, it is a simple gesture of great respect, like rice stalks bending in the breeze.

The Emperor stands. "Teacher," he murmurs, kneeling to touch his forehead against Sensei's feet.

"I would like to introduce my newest students," says Ki-Yaga.

We stand tall and proud. The Emperor is puzzled by what he sees. A one-legged boy leaning between a one-armed boy and a bigger, broad-shouldered one. A white-haired girl holding the hand of a blind boy. Another boy nervously watching the door.

"Are these the students who won the Samurai Trainee Games?" he asks.

"Welcome," the Emperor says.

Sensei nods.

"Cheats," a Dragon kid hisses.

The Son of Heaven is not as wise as Sensei, but he is not foolish.

"I see you have chosen *your* students carefully, Ki-Yaga. You always did." He bows to us. "It is a great honor to share your teacher.

"As you know," he says, resuming the throne, "the Shogun requires me to adjudicate on local matters such as those you bring to the castle court today. You may present your claims. Who will speak first?"

Sensei doesn't move, but the Dragon Master pushes forward. We remember what our teacher has taught us. The slow swordsman needs to go first, to get a head start. A duel of words has begun, and the Dragon Master is behind already.

His voice booms. "I bring a request from both the Lord of the South Mountains and the Lord of the North Mountains. They cordially remind the Son of Heaven that it was his father who sanctioned the Shogun's grant of their daimyo lands. They ask to be allowed to fight their own battles. To wage their own war."

"You have this in writing?" The Emperor leans forward.

Nodding, the Dragon doesn't even try to hide his smirk. He thinks he has won. But Sensei has not opened his mouth yet, and his wisdom can cut through ten rolls of matting.

"I have it here, tucked in my belt."

When the Dragon Master moves to open the scroll, the Emperor raises his hand. "I will hear Ki-Yaga speak now."

The Dragon puffs and blows, but Sensei's voice breathes gently. "I ask the Emperor to intercede and stop this war before death strips the mountains. I do not bring a scroll. I keep my words where all important things belong, between my heart and my sword."

"Does anyone else wish to speak before I make my decision?" The Emperor's gaze includes us, and Yoshi steps forward.

"I would like to ask the Dragon Master a question. Why would any master want his students to fight?"

The Dragon's chest bloats with pride and the opportunity to teach Ki-Yaga's Cockroaches a lesson.

"Because *my* students will emerge victorious and win great honor."

Nezume shakes his head. "They will be covered in blood."

"Or even worse," Sensei says, "they will be covered in cloth."

Dead.

BONG.

A gong sounds and the Emperor rises. "I have other business to attend to. I will think upon your requests and view the scroll in the morning."

BONG. Another gong sounds to dismiss us. The Dragon Master shoves past with a swish of red and gold. But Ki-Yaga waits.

"I have a gift from Sword Master Onaku." Sensei takes a package from under his robe, offering it to the Emperor.

Short, fat fingers grip the hilt perfectly. The sword sings, a song fit for its king.

"Not even an Emperor's riches can pay for a weapon like this," the Son of Heaven says as he caresses the hilt. "Tell Onaku his gift is gratefully accepted. Perhaps your students would like to spend some time with my son in the Imperial Water Garden?"

The Dragon kids aren't invited!

We know the way. We saw the water lilies from the window in our room.

"I'll meet you there." Taji winks. He's going off on his own to listen in and spy out information.

But before he can leave, the Emperor's scream cuts through our plans. His face whiter than Kyoko's hair, the Emperor points to where the three candles closest to the throne are no longer alight. Four still burn, but this is the worst number of all, a disastrous omen. The Emperor collapses on his throne.

Quickly, Sensei moves to relight the candles. "It is only a warning," our master says. "You have been given the opportunity to prevent many deaths."

Sensei waves us away and we're glad to go, eager to play in the garden. The Emperor is in good hands. Sensei is a renowned healer who can set broken pieces of both body and mind.

The Imperial Water Garden is huge, with an enormous pond covered in pink and white flowers. In the middle of the pond is an island, and standing at the water's edge is a boy about our age.

We hurry across the wooden bridge.

"I am pleased to meet you," the prince says. "I hear you wiped the tatami mats with the Dragon Ryu at the Samurai Trainee Games. I wish I'd seen that."

He smiles. The Grandson of Heaven commands the sun, too. I already like this boy a lot. Kicking off our sandals, we sit at the water's edge, letting the koi nibble our feet. It's peaceful here. Our *ryu* garden is full of cabbages, chickens, and stones. There's nothing restful about hard work and calloused hands.

"I am learning swordsmanship, too," the prince says.

Mikko grins. "We could have a practice match. Just for fun."

"I don't know," the prince says hesitantly. "It wouldn't be fair to fight a one-armed opponent."

"You could tie up one hand," Mikko suggests. "What about a wager? If I win, you owe me a gold piece."

The prince wouldn't stand a chance, even with both hands.

"Don't believe him. It's a trick," says Kyoko, glaring

at Mikko. "He could win with no hands and the sword between his teeth."

"Sorry," Mikko apologizes. "But there's a girl I like, and I need to bring her a belt full of money."

The prince winks. "I understand that."

I'm not sure I like the way the prince looks at Kyoko when he says it. Before I can pull my thoughts together, Yoshi changes the subject.

"We came through Hell Valley on our way here, and a ghost spoke to Niya. Sensei says you know a lot about the spirit world."

Trust Yoshi to know what the prince is interested in. Sensei would be pleased. A good samurai is always prepared.

"I wish I could go into the valley. Father says it's too dangerous. He is afraid, but I am not." The prince's eyes shine with excitement. "I've spent years studying but have never seen anything. Ghosts, goblins, shape-shifters, *tengu* . . ."

Mikko pokes me in the ribs, and my friends erupt in giggles.

"Supernatural beings should not be laughed at," the prince says. "Even my father cannot dictate to the other world. Emperor and subjects bow fearfully before the spirits."

"Three candles went out in the throne room," I say. "Your father was very upset."

The prince is not surprised. "When he was a boy, my father was visited by a fearsome goblin—a *tengu* priest from the mountains. The stories that priest told still give my father nightmares, and ever since then, he has slept with two samurai guards at his feet."

"What are the stories?" I ask.

"My father refuses to repeat even one, no matter how many times I plead."

"Niya thinks Sensei is a *tengu* priest," Mikko says, laughing.

The prince doesn't join the laughter. "It's possible," he says thoughtfully. "Some *tengu* are consumed by the darkness, but others give their life to teaching those with a special need."

I like him more than ever. Even if he stares at Kyoko.

"Everyone has goodness and evil in their heart," explains the prince. "We all try to hide the evil so our goodness shines brightest."

Sensei is very good. He could easily outshine a great evil.

"You know a lot about these things," I say admiringly.

"It's not easy being a prince. I don't have any friends, so I read a lot."

It's not easy being us either. But we've always got one another.

The prince pulls a gold coin from his pocket and offers it to Mikko, who shakes his head.

"Take it," the prince insists. "Then you can invite me to the wedding. I am invited many places but never as a friend."

"Thanks. I will." Mikko pockets the coin. "She's the most beautiful girl in all of Japan."

Mikko needs his eyes tested. My sister isn't even a little pretty.

Looking into her reflection, Kyoko sighs deeply. "The Dragon kids say I'm ugly. Who would marry me?"

Someone very lucky, I think.

"I would," volunteers the prince.

I don't like that idea much, but Kyoko is as beautiful as a princess.

Cranky ducks interrupt my thoughts, quacking and

complaining as Taji races across the grass toward the bridge.

"He should slow down. He might trip." The prince looks worried.

Yoshi shakes his head. "Not even if I stick my foot out." He pokes his foot out to prove the point, and Taji skids around it, careening into Nezume.

"I've overheard something really important." He hesitates, unsure whether to trust the prince.

"It's okay. Our new friend has the heart of a Cockroach," says Yoshi.

We never question Yoshi's judgment, except when he's deciding who gets the leftover serving of pudding. But this time it's got nothing to do with dessert.

"The Dragon Master's scroll will be stolen tonight," Taji confides. "While the master and his students are completing their evening exercises, the kitchen boy will deliver their meal and steal the scroll. Without it, the Dragon Master can't prove whom he speaks for."

But Sensei can. He always speaks for himself.

We wish we could tell the prince about the ninja in his kitchen, but it's not our secret to spill, and we promised the Owl Master we would keep it safe.

"Sensei is coming now," announces Taji.

The prince looks at me as Sensei rounds a corner. I shrug. I don't know how Taji does it either.

"Master," the prince stands and bows.

"Grandson of Heaven." Sensei returns the bow. "I have come to meditate in your garden. I hear you have many wise old cherry trees."

"It would be an honor for you to rest beneath their branches," says the prince.

Sensei looks tired. And he looks sad. Perhaps it took all his strength to calm the Emperor's fears. Or maybe he is worried about tomorrow. I hop with him to the oldest, wisest cherry tree, waiting while he settles back against its trunk.

"Are you sad, Sensei?"

He sighs. "I have lived a long time. Longer than any man should."

Are you a man? I want to ask.

"When you have lived as long as I have, you gather many memories. And some are very sad," Sensei says. "Some, I would even give my left leg to change."

Understanding, I nod. I have many happy memories,

and I would not trade a single one of them. Not even for another leg.

"Niya," Kyoko calls, "come and feed the koi."

The moment snaps like a frayed piece of bamboo. Sensei closes his eyes.

"Rest well, Master," I whisper.

Sensei snores. And inside my head, he smiles.

CHAPTER TWELVE

義

IF THE
SLIPPER FITS

Bash. Bash. BASH.

No gentle tap this time. The pounding demands that we open the door right away, before the rice paper rips. Even Yoshi stops mid-breakfast, rushing to answer the knock.

The attendant has run all the way to deliver this message and is gasping for breath. "The Emperor requires an audience with Ki-Yaga." Words tumble and drop so fast that my ears struggle to catch them. "Immediately."

It's not a request. It's a command.

"Chop, chop, Little Cockroaches." Wiping a stray noodle from his beard, Sensei heads out the door. We don't even stop to change into our castle finery. This time the *ronin* comes, too, pausing for one last mouthful and to tuck his wooden sword into his belt.

"What do you need that for?" Mikko asks.

"A stout piece of wood is always useful. Perhaps I will wave it around to make a point."

The point of a wooden sword is rounded and blunt, but even a floorboard would be a convincing weapon in the *ronin*'s giant hands. He might not have the skill and grace of a swordsman, but he has the strength of a huge bear.

Sensei strides along beside the attendant, whistling, the way he does when he's looking forward to something. But I know it's not good news. Good news is more polite. It waits until after breakfast.

Loud and angry, the Dragon Master's voice gusts along the corridor to buffet our ears. Nezume moves closer to Sensei. Our master is not afraid. "The castle's heating is working well this morning. The hallway is full of hot air," he says with a chuckle.

The Emperor's voice rises to quell the Dragon's fire. "I will wait to hear what Ki-Yaga has to say."

When Sensei steps through the doorway, the hush falls like a noose around us. The Dragon Master and his students are standing before the throne. Turning, the Dragon's glare swipes razor-sharp across the room. But our teacher bows effortlessly beneath it.

"How may I be of service?" Sensei asks the Emperor.

"You've caused enough trouble." The Dragon Master has forgotten his court manners, raking a long red fingernail just beneath Sensei's chin. "You took my scroll."

Sensei shrugs. "I have not seen it. But like the Emperor, I was hoping to check its authenticity this morning."

"You can't trick me this time." The Dragon Master smirks. "I've got proof."

He turns to the Emperor. "When I finished my exercises, our evening meal was on the table but the scroll in the adjoining room was gone. There was only one person who came into our rooms. The castle kitchen boy stole it for *him*." The red nail stabs at Sensei's chest, and the Dragon boys snicker. "Who else but Ki-Yaga would benefit from such a crime?"

Sensei nods. "It is true I have often benefited from the Dragon Master's shortcomings. But should I be held responsible whenever he cannot remember where he has left something?"

The prince is sitting beside his father, and he struggles not to laugh. "Is the Dragon Master suggesting that *our* castle kitchen staff does Ki-Yaga's bidding?" he asks.

Sensei shakes his head, amazed. "Next the Dragon Master will be suggesting the kitchen is full of ninja."

"Ridiculous," the Emperor agrees. "My staff is loyal to me. They are not criminals for hire."

"I can prove it was the kitchen boy. I didn't see his

face, as I was concentrating on an extremely difficult exercise. The foolish culprit was in such a hurry that he left something behind in the scroll's room." The Dragon Master places a slipper on the table. "Call the boy who served me last night and we'll see if the slipper fits."

My heart drops onto my foot so hard I want to hop in pain. I recognize the slipper. It belongs to Ako. He can run like wind across rice, but he'll never outrace the Dragon Master's revenge.

The Emperor reaches for his bell.

Fear spreads like ice through my stomach, but in my memory the ghost's red eyes burn lava-hot. Remembering its words, relief thaws me. *I need only one slipper.* Sensei nods, and the White Crane winks back.

"It is not necessary to find the boy," Sensei says. "I have a confession to make."

"I knew it," the Dragon Master gloats.

"It will be best if Niya explains."

I hop forward. Face flushed, I feel the Dragons breathing hot down my neck. But the White Crane stands still and regal, its one foot firmly anchored in the cool waters of the lake.

"Son of Heaven." I bow. "I must apologize. I am the

one who has caused the Dragon Master to wrongfully accuse your staff and our teacher."

Slowly and respectfully, I bend toward the throne.

"Please continue." Shining like the sun, the Emperor's warm voice gives me even greater courage. What I must say isn't easy for me. Sometimes a samurai kid must use a ninja trick to deceive.

"I was the one who served the Dragon Master's meal. There was no kitchen boy in his rooms, only me. But I didn't go into the room containing the scroll."

The prince smiles encouragingly, but the Dragons have faces like thunder. I close my ears to their rumble.

"I swapped with the kitchen boy because Sensei teaches us that a samurai must be good with a sword on the battlefield and a knife in the kitchen. He is always telling us we need more practice."

"Is this true?" The Emperor knows our master cannot lie to the Son of Heaven.

But Sensei is as clever with words as he is with his sword. He can dodge a question as easily as he ducks under a swinging blade. "Yes. I am always yelling 'More practice.' My students complain about it all the time."

Only the Dragon Master is not convinced. "The Cockroach boy is lying."

"Perhaps someone else entered your room," suggests the Emperor.

"No. I felt only one person enter. I am a Zen master, and I would know if someone else sneaked in. Not even a ninja can creep past me. It is the boy's slipper. Make him try it on. It will prove he was in the scroll's room."

"I would be glad to," I say. "But I cannot. It is for the left foot and I only have a right one. Maybe one of the Dragon students left it there. Perhaps they forget where they leave things, too."

The Dragon Master scowls, and the Dragon kids glare. If looks could kill, I'd be dead many times over by now.

The prince tries not to laugh. But this time he can't help it. Laughter is like a river. It runs from face to face, tickling and teasing. The *ronin*'s voice rumbles. Yoshi roars. Mikko giggles. Even the Emperor smiles.

Slowly, he rises to speak. "I have made my decision."

Kyoko reaches for my hand while Nezume fidgets nervously. Will the Emperor's words silence the drum?

"In battle, when one side loses its scroll of orders, it surrenders. And the other side wins. The theft of a scroll is an ancient and honorable military strategy. And while this does not excuse the culprit from punishment if he is caught, in this case, he is too clever for that."

Inside my head, the drumming finally stops.

But the Dragon is not willing to surrender. He has no respect for tradition or honor.

"Everyone in the castle must try the slipper on," he demands.

Sensei pokes a skinny crow foot forward. "Perhaps it might fit me."

"It is not necessary. The Dragon Master has testified that only the boy who delivered the evening meal was in the room and clearly the slipper is not his," says the Emperor.

"It's another trick," fumes the Dragon. "Ki-Yaga is a black magician. You," he hisses at me, "are just like your master."

There's no greater compliment. "Thank you." I bow.

"War is a game with many rules," Sensei says. "Strategy is always an honorable move. Remember the great warrior who left his opponent waiting while he slept late and ate a leisurely breakfast?"

Our stomachs rumble, remembering the missed meal.

"This young warrior finally arrived, barefoot and half-dressed, carrying only a wooden sword. His enraged opponent slashed wildly, lured into carelessness. The young upstart had won the first of many famous battles."

Everyone knows the story about Mitsuka Manuyoto, but the *ronin* is grinning so wide, it's obvious that Sensei is talking about him. It seems there's more to our big friend's craftiness than simply taking off his trousers. And now we know his name. I was right all along.

The Emperor smiles, welcoming the defender of his youth. But the Dragon Master still doesn't know. He's too angry to listen properly. And he hasn't learned the lesson. His face furrows with fury. "It was a pathetic win. He didn't even kill his opponent. The fool let him escape."

"He wisely chose to let him live," Sensei says. "The greatest victory is always the one with the least bloodshed."

"Is that what you think?" The Dragon Master unsheathes his sword.

The blade flashes only inches from Sensei's long beaked nose.

Behind me I hear the Emperor's guards move, but the Son of Heaven raises his hand to stay them. The war is not over after all, and it is only right for two masters to settle their differences with a blade. Except Sensei hasn't brought his sword with him.

The drumming begins again inside my head. Louder, faster. *THUMP. THUMP. THUMP.*

Sensei doesn't move. He's not in a hurry. Only the slow man needs a head start.

The *ronin*'s strong voice fills the room as he places his huge body between Sensei and the fire-breathing Dragon. "No one insults my teacher. I accept the challenge on his behalf."

"You? I'm not fighting a beggar," the Dragon bellows. There's no glory in slicing the head from a street tramp, but the man who collects Sensei's head will have many stories told about him.

But it's not up to the Dragon Master. Ki-Yaga's voice rings with even greater authority than the gong. "I accept my student's offer."

Our teacher waves us to the back of the room, where

the castle guards are standing, hands on their swords. The Dragon kids move, too, staying as far away from us as possible. Only Sensei, the *ronin,* and the Dragon Master remain in front of the throne.

"Cockroaches smell," the big Dragon boy mutters.

Kyoko pokes out her tongue. "And Dragons stink."

Phew. Mikko and Taji pinch their noses shut.

"Shh," Yoshi says.

"This filthy *ronin* doesn't even have a proper sword," the Dragon Master sneers.

I smile, and Yoshi chuckles softly.

A true samurai doesn't need a sword.

"I have all I need." Grinning, the *ronin* pulls the wooden *bokken* from his belt.

The Dragon's mouth curls in contempt. "It's just a practice sword."

"Not in my hands. And anyway, I am only intending to practice on you. Maybe tomorrow I will find a worthy opponent."

If the Dragon Master really could breathe fire, the room would be filled with smoke and ash. Instead, it is choked with rage and anger.

"I will not fight against street trash." He folds his

gold sleeves across his chest.

"All that glitters is not gold," Nezume whispers.

"Sometimes it is just shiny rubbish." Kyoko giggles.

Sensei is a great teacher, and the *ronin* was his greatest pupil. It's not over yet.

"It appears that the Dragon is too timid to fight me." The *ronin* waits, hands on his hips.

"I'll fight," sneers the Dragon Master. "But you'll regret your words when I chop your sword into firewood."

"As my student is fighting on my behalf, may I provide him with a sword?" Sensei asks the Emperor.

The Son of Heaven nods.

Sensei pulls a cloth bundle from under his cloak, then unwraps the extra sword Onaku gave him.

The *ronin* reaches for it, eyes bright as he recognizes the Sword Master's handiwork. From here I can see that the grip is unusual. It melts into the *ronin*'s hand, and as flesh and sword join together, I hear the blade sing. Everyone can. It drowns out the thump of the drum.

"Onaku knows how to make a proper sword." The *ronin* swings the blade in a wide arc, barely missing the gold buttons on the Dragon Master's jacket. Tucking the sword into his sash, the *ronin* stares into the Dragon's eye.

"I am Mitsuka Manuyoto, son of the House of Manuyoto and former student of the Cockroach Ryu. Humble disciple of the great Ki-Yaga. No one insults my master's name unless he wishes to face my drawn sword." Mitsuka doesn't yell his challenge, but his soft words shout in our ears. "I am a Little Cockroach and a destroyer of Dragons. Sheath your sword and apologize. Or fight me."

Mitsuka is a legendary swordsman, but the Dragon is skilled, too. And a cheat.

Can the Dragon cheat enough to win?

"I don't like this," I mutter through gritted teeth.

Yoshi grins. "I think it will be fun."

"What do you mean?" Kyoko whispers, worriedly twisting a stray strand of white hair.

"The Dragon Master has brought only his sword. Mitsuka has his blade and his brain. Already Mitsuka has made the Dragon so angry that he won't even look him in the face. How can a swordsman read his opponent's eyes if he doesn't even look?"

The Dragon Master raises his sword.

"It's true," Mikko says. "The Dragon is a fool to fight blind. Only Taji can do that and win."

"And I would not be so foolish as to fight Mitsuka Manuyoto," Taji adds.

The Dragon Master raises his sword. Mitsuka watches, waiting until the last moment.

"Stop," the Emperor commands, rising from his throne. "I do not wish to watch anyone die. There will be no fight in this room, just as there will be no war in my mountains." He claps his hands, and an attendant appears. The sound of two hands clapping is loud and powerful when they are the Emperor's hands.

"Place a message in the receptacle at the castle keep gate so a runner can collect it and take my decision to the mountain daimyos. The war drum must cease," the Emperor tells his attendant. "And this foolishness must never happen again. As a measure of their loyalty, the daimyos will send their children to me. And as a measure of my esteem, I will ensure that these children receive the best training my court has to offer. Each of the daimyos has a son, and my own son has no companions. It is a perfect solution."

Yesterday the prince made six new friends and today

promises even more. The Emperor's fingers might be fat and clumsy, but there's nothing pudgy about his brain. The lords will do as they're told while their sons are away. And their sons will be happy here. No one dies, and everyone wins.

Except the Dragon Master. But he hasn't given up yet. One of the Dragon boys bows to excuse himself and leaves.

"I bet two servings of pudding there won't be any message for the runner to find," whispers Mikko.

But we know it doesn't matter. The message has already been received. There are eyes and ears all over the castle, especially in the kitchen. And they all have a ninja runner's legs.

"Instead of a duel, let us now have a friendly display of swordsmanship," the Emperor suggests.

"Two of my students are the best in all the mountains," Sensei says.

Nezume and Mikko step forward. The Dragon kids haven't even moved. Remembering the Games, they don't want to challenge us.

The Emperor is surprised. "How can a great swordfighter have only one arm?" he asks.

"Don't be fooled, Father," the prince says. "I've heard that Mikko can fight with a sword in his teeth. And yesterday he dueled against me for a gold coin without even unsheathing his blade."

"Yes, I remember that lesson well. The true samurai doesn't need a sword," the Emperor says, looking at Ki-Yaga.

Sensei bows. "The Son of Heaven was always a credit to his teacher."

"Perhaps one young Cockroach could fight a Dragon?" the Emperor suggests diplomatically.

"It would be a waste of our skill," the Dragon Master says, bowing to the Emperor but sneering at us. "We do not waste time stomping on bugs."

That's because their clumsy Dragon feet would never catch us.

Placing one hand behind his back, Nezume stares into Mikko's eyes. Cockroaches fight with honor. They wait for Sensei's instruction.

"Draw," he calls.

Two swords flash in the sunlight of the Emperor's approving smile. Long arcs of steel swish. Clash. And move apart again. It's a dance. Lizard scurry. Rat scuffle.

Until Nezume's sword point rests on Mikko's chest.

The prince claps and cheers.

"Looks like I need . . ." Mikko waits for us to finish his sentence.

"More practice!" we yell together.

Next Mitsuka steps forward. Famous for his double swordplay, he swings the *bokken* with one hand and Onaku's sword with the other.

"I am impressed," the Emperor says. "My son is also a keen student of swordplay. Now he will demonstrate the techniques he has learned."

It's a solo display. It wouldn't be appropriate to draw a sword against the prince in front of the Emperor. We're not playing in the garden now.

The prince walks to the middle of the floor and draws his sword in a slow, fluid half circle. He strikes, then flicks it to his other hand.

"Not bad," Mikko murmurs. "There goes my advantage. Maybe I was lucky he didn't fight me."

But the prince hasn't had the benefit of Sensei's teaching. Many of his moves are clumsy and unfinished.

"See how skilled my boy is," the Emperor says, beaming.

"The prince is an excellent swordsman," the Dragon Master says.

"And how would you grade him?" the Emperor asks Sensei.

Sensei is a samurai of the oldest ways. Honor before one's own life. And it's one of those times now.

A sharp sword hangs over Sensei's head.

But our teacher's voice is strong and pure. Like Onaku's steel. "Your son is poorly trained."

Fearful, we wait for the sword to drop and slice the silence.

When the Emperor smiles, we breathe a sigh of relief. There's no sword after all. But we should know better than that. Just because we can't see the blade doesn't mean it's not there.

"In that case, you will stay here and teach him," the Emperor commands.

In our hearts, the sword drops with a clatter.

CHAPTER THIRTEEN

礼

THE SECOND
SCROLL

The Dragon Master laughs. And laughs. There's nothing we can do. Even Sensei can't fight his way out of this one. We wait, hoping he will raise his arms and defiantly shout, *"Banzai!"* Then the room will shake with the power of his *ki,* as it did at the Owl Dojo.

But Sensei respectfully bows his head. "As the Emperor wishes."

The Son of Heaven's smile isn't warm anymore. It burns, and the White Crane cringes.

"Father . . ." the prince starts to speak.

But even a son cannot argue with the Emperor.

"You must say good-bye to your teacher," the Emperor commands us. "Tomorrow morning you will leave with Mitsuka. I am sure Ki-Yaga will agree that you are in good hands."

Sensei nods, holding out his staff to me. I reach into his thoughts, desperate for him to say some words of comfort.

I don't understand, I wail soundlessly.

Sensei smiles. *You must read between the lines.*

But there is nothing there.

He nods, pleased. *Yes. I knew you would understand.*

I understand Nothing. But even Zen can't help me this time.

The room is filled with the loud silence that sometimes falls between cicada songs. No one moves. No one speaks. The White Crane listens hard, but Sensei is not talking anymore. Not even inside my head.

When the Emperor rings his bell, another guard appears. "Take Ki-Yaga to the yellow room and make sure he has everything he requires."

"Is he a prisoner?" the guard asks.

The Emperor shakes his head. "There is no need to secure the door." He knows Sensei's honor is a stronger lock than any piece of metal.

"You may go now." With a dismissive wave, we are separated from our teacher. It hurts. More than the thump of the war drum against my chest. More than the time I was caught in a mudslide and couldn't breathe.

Turning, I catch the look of helplessness on the prince's face. The Dragon Master grins triumphantly. His students smirk, twisting their fingers into half-hidden rude gestures.

"Ha!" the largest Dragon boy mouths at us.

Little Cockroaches have no heart for slaying Dragons now. Even Mikko doesn't retort. Our feet drag, numb like our spirits. The White Crane huddles, curled in a tight ball.

Outside in the corridor, Kyoko bursts into tears.

"What will we do?" Mikko's voice shakes.

"Should we go home?" asks Nezume.

Even Yoshi has no answers. Suddenly, we are all children, looking to Mitsuka for help.

Our *ronin* shrugs, unconcerned. "You do not need me to tell you what to do. I am not the one holding Sensei's staff."

All eyes turn to me.

"But Yoshi is our leader," I protest, pushing the staff into his hands.

"That's true, but"—he waves it away—"you are our teacher now."

I can't be. I know nothing.

Perfect, Sensei whispers.

I reach out, clutching for more advice. But it's one last whisper and he's gone. I've always wanted to be a teacher, but I'm not ready. I am still just me. Niya.

Then I understand. I am the White Crane. Brother of the Tiger, the Golden Bat, the Striped Gecko, the Snow Monkey, the Long-Tailed Rat, and the Great Bear. Friend and ally of the Owls. I am not alone.

"Don't worry. Together we'll work something out," I promise. "But we can't talk here. The castle is full of ears, and I bet the corridor is lined with listeners."

I hop ahead in a hurry. The others rush to keep up.

"He thinks he really is Sensei now," Mikko puffs beside me.

"Chop, chop, Little Cockroaches," I say, teasing.

At the door to our room, Riaze is waiting, morning tea tray in hand. He already knows about Sensei. And he also knows we didn't finish breakfast.

"I've come to help," he offers.

"Thank you." I bow, and Kyoko gives Riaze a big hug.

"Go and check that no one is spying," Yoshi instructs Taji. "Make sure all the doors and windows are slid shut," he tells Nezume and Mikko.

Taji takes the ninja listening cup from under his kimono and places it in turn against each of the four walls. Mikko rushes around checking windows, and Nezume ensures that the door latches are pulled tight.

The Cockroach Ryu is a family. My friends would give me the slippers off their feet. But you can't trust just anyone you meet in the castle — anyone outside of the kitchen, anyway.

Sensei isn't talking inside my head, but that doesn't matter. All the lessons he ever taught us are stored there. "You must find your opponent's weakness," he instructed us when we struggled to ride Uma.

"What is the Emperor's weakness?" I ask my friends.

"Bad judgment?" queries Mikko. "He took Sensei away from us."

"No." Yoshi shakes his head. "Keeping Sensei as his son's teacher is a sign of good judgment."

Kyoko sniffs, wiping her nose on her kimono sleeve. "There must be something."

"Are you crying?" I touch her gently on the shoulder.

"Of course I'm not," she says, her voice shaking as she shoves my hand away. "I'm just as brave as you."

I don't feel brave at all. I'd like to tell her that but it wouldn't help either of us. What we need is an idea.

"Remember how the Emperor cowered when

the candles burned out?" Nezume asks. "He is very superstitious."

"That's it! The prince said the Emperor is terrified of *tengu* most of all," I exclaim.

Jumping and hopping, we slap each other on the back, celebrating our cleverness and Sensei's imminent return.

But Mitsuka stands apart with an amused smile on his face. "All you need to do now is find a *tengu*."

Defeated, Kyoko flops onto the floor. "It's a terrible plan. We'll never get Sensei back."

"Sometimes students must think hard to remember their lessons," counsels Mitsuka, helping Kyoko to her feet.

"It's true. Only a blind kid can see what is right under his nose." Taji shakes his head in exasperation at all of us. "What does Sensei say?"

"You don't have to see something to know it's there," we chorus.

"We just have to make the Emperor think it is," Riaze agrees. "Ninja use tricks like that all the time, and a superstitious man is easy to fool."

But Nezume is still unsure. "Is it right to deceive the Emperor?" he asks.

"It's the only way," I insist. "Sensei gave his word. He'll never leave without the Emperor's permission."

Mikko flaps his arms like wings. "I could make a crow noise. *Croak. Croak.*"

"Terrible," we groan.

"You sound like a frog. This is a crow." Kyoko clears her throat. "*Caw, caw.*"

"We could use black ink to dye an owl feather from Sensei's staff," Yoshi suggests.

"And I could use my new ninja skills to make an exploding egg." Mikko waves his arm excitedly. "We can put the feather inside and *poof!* When the smoke clears, the Emperor will see a *tengu* feather. He'll be scared stiff."

Mitsuka's eyes shine with Sensei's familiar twinkle. "How will that make the Emperor release Ki-Yaga?"

"We'll use blood-colored ink to write Ki-Yaga's name on the feather," I say. A name written in red is a bad sign, even on a lucky day. "The Emperor will want Sensei to go as far away as possible."

We're all thinking the same thing. Soon we'll be safely back at the Cockroach Ryu.

"We need to hurry," Riaze says. "The Son of Heaven will be in the library reading now. It's the perfect opportunity. I'll distract the samurai guards while Kyoko uses her new *shuriken* throwing skills to roll Mikko's egg at the Emperor's feet."

We work quickly to put our plan into action. We can't afford to fail. We're not battling for a trophy like at the Samurai Trainee Games. The prize is much more important than that. But the Cockroach Ryu is a powerful team. And we've got an Owl Ninja and a famous swordsman to help us.

The egg lands in exactly the right place. Kyoko caws loudly. We are creeping away when I hear the *pfflt* of the explosion as the egg breaks open, delivering our message. I can imagine the Emperor's fear: I wish we didn't have to frighten him. But we're desperate to rescue Sensei.

Time crawls as we wait in our room, listening to the

flurry of the castle responding to its Emperor's cries. Soon the gong will sound and the Emperor will call us into his presence to announce Sensei's release.

We wait for the summons. We wait and wait.

Finally, Mitsuka gets to his feet. "I'll go and see what is happening."

We wait again. But this time it's not for long.

Mitsuka appears in the doorway at the same time as Riaze. Both their faces tell the same story — and it's not good news.

"The Emperor is terrified," Riaze says in a rush. "He believes the time of the *tengu* prophecy from his unrepeatable stories has begun. He wants Sensei by his side to help and advise him."

Our plan has backfired. Who would have thought things could get worse? We huddle together miserably.

"I should have considered what the *tengu* might have said to the Emperor," I mumble.

"It's not your fault." Mikko tries to comfort me. "We all agreed on the plan."

"And next we'll try a new plan," Yoshi says. "Niya will think of something else. He always does."

If only it was that easy. I grip Sensei's staff for support, wishing I could ask his advice. "Yoshi is right. We can't give up. How many times did we compete in the Trainee Games before we were successful? It takes more than one spark to start a fire."

Taji smiles. "That sounds like something Sensei would say."

"I made it up myself," I say, beaming.

As I look at my friends' faces, the room is full of bright sparks. Surely not even the Emperor could stand firm against all our spirits working together.

"Do you remember the scroll in my grandfather's tearoom?" I ask.

Riaze recites:

"The rat scuttles, the big cat creeps, the monkey dashes,
The bat glides, the white crane soars, the lizard darts,
And the owl hoots
In the middle of the night."

"How do *you* know?" Taji asks, amazed. "You weren't even there."

"I helped Niya's grandfather with the calligraphy."

It makes sense now. The fireworks. The long disappearances. And falling asleep at the inn. Not an old man's laziness, but a ninja watching through half-closed eyes. My grandfather is an Owl, too. He knew the time would come when I would need to be reminded of the power of friendship.

"Tonight we'll help the White Crane deliver a new message from the *tengu*. This time we'll frighten the Emperor into releasing Sensei," I say.

Taji grins. "That's excellent. He'll think he's seen a ghost."

In my mind, the White Crane raises its wings in the moonlight and the haunting begins.

"We'll need a way to get past the samurai guards," says Yoshi.

A samurai guarding the Emperor would be a skilled and fearsome foe. The sort of warrior we all hope to be one day.

"I can help." Opening his hands, Riaze reveals a pill in each palm. One brown. One cloudy gray. "Do you want the samurai to doze for the night, or will I send them to sleep forever?"

"No." Nezume shakes his head vigorously.

"We're not going to kill anyone," snaps Kyoko.

Mitsuka growls threateningly.

It's not the samurai way.

"All right. But they'll have sore heads in the morning." Riaze's eyes gleam with pleasure.

We might be friends with the Owl Ninja, but Riaze's words remind me that we will always be different. But Sensei was right, too. The ninja and samurai must work together. And tonight his freedom depends on it.

"We need to find out as much as we can about the Emperor's sleeping arrangements," I say.

We know where to find his head. The dead are buried facing north, so a fearful man always places his pillow pointing south. In our *ryu* bedroom, we are not afraid and our mattresses are bare. "You are not soft in the head, so you do not need pillows," Sensei told us.

"I'll find out who is delivering the evening meal to the Emperor's guards and arrange for a sleeping tablet to be slipped into their *sake*," says Riaze.

"I'll work out the best way to climb up to the Emperor's bedroom," Kyoko volunteers.

"The rest of us will listen in the corridors and compounds," Yoshi says.

And I have a task to complete, too. The White Crane

wants its feathers back. It doesn't like to see them on the Dragon Master's helmet. And Sensei's staff needs a new feather, too.

Mitsuka grins. "It is a good plan. A samurai must be well prepared. Otherwise he will have to resort to surprise tactics and take his trousers off."

"Never," protests Mikko. "We want to frighten the Emperor, not make him laugh."

It makes *us* laugh, though. And laughter binds us together, tighter than a sushi roll.

"It's going to rain tonight," Riaze says.

Ninja always know these things. And it's good news. Clouds will ensure that the night is deep and dark. Thunder and lightning will help us scare the Emperor.

Everything is organized. Even the weather.

A moment later I notice that Riaze has gone. Even in broad daylight a ninja can disappear into thin air.

As the night lengthens, rain smashes against the roof. The wind howls like a wolf facing into the storm.

At exactly midnight, Mitsuka rises, tucking both his *bokken* and his sword into his sash. Yoshi slides the door open. He hoots softly, then listens for Riaze's answer. We slink into the dripping shadows, our ninja-blue uniforms lost in the darkness, wind, and rain.

Phlat.

A large shape drops directly in front of Kyoko, and her scream is sucked into the roaring wind.

"Shh," we chorus.

"It's not my fault," she mutters, glaring into Riaze's barely visible eyes. Then she giggles. "But I wasn't half as loud as the shushing. SHHH." When the Snow Monkey mimics, we can't help laughing.

"It is always good to begin with laughter," Mitsuka says approvingly.

We creep and slosh across the compound until we reach the eastern tower.

Kyoko points. "There's the window to the royal sleeping quarters."

This afternoon Taji counted twelve guards between

the tower door and the Emperor's bedroom. And that was when the Son of Heaven wasn't even there. So tonight we're going over the rooftops to drop in from above.

Quickly, we attach our hand and foot claws. The stacked rock wall of the nearby servants' building is notched with easy handholds, but the blustering rain pushes and shoves against us. We climb single file, sheltering behind the body in front. Yoshi goes first, his broad shoulders bearing the brunt of the storm.

Below us, Mitsuka melts into the shadows, standing watch until we return.

Ptt. Pttt.

Suddenly, Mikko loses his footing and his leg swings free, dislodging a shower of stones. Just behind him, I maneuver my shoulder under his foot. We're all leaning on one another tonight. It makes us strong.

"Thanks," whispers Mikko.

"You better hope you didn't rain rocks onto Mitsuka's head," I say.

Nezume laughs beneath me. "I bet he could parry them with a single sword thrust."

I bet he could slice them into quarters as well.

224

On top of the roof, I look west to where the ocean rolls beneath the darkness. The wind crashes like waves onto the shore, and the White Crane yearns to fly above the spray. One day, I promise myself. One day we'll go over the sea.

Riaze unloops a rope from his belt.

"Let me do that," volunteers Kyoko.

Expertly, she tosses the rope across the gap between the two towers. *Clunk.* The hooked end claws into stone. Like throwing *shuriken* stars.

Next, Riaze tugs a harness from his bag. "This will ensure that no one falls. We'll cross, one by one, sending the harness back for the next climber."

I know Riaze won't need it. And neither does Kyoko. She brushes it aside, takes hold of the rope, and deftly climbs across. It's easy for a Snow Monkey.

The White Crane can fly, but my foot likes to feel the ground underneath it. It's a long tumble to the courtyard below. I'm not too proud to tie the harness around my waist and inch my way across. My fingers ache, numb against the slippery rope. Rain slaps me in the face, scolding me for my foolishness.

From the main tower roof, it's a short climb down to

the Emperor's window balcony. At the ledge, I remove my claws and drop noiselessly into the Emperor's room. My friends stay on the balcony. The slumbering samurai don't even stir.

There's only one more barrier between me and the Emperor. The nightingale floor.

Taking the flute from her pocket, Kyoko plays a haunting six-fingered tune to hide the sighs and creaks as I creep across the floorboards to the southern end of the Emperor's mattress. We don't want the nightingale's song to call any more guards. We want them to think that the Emperor is listening to a late-night lullaby.

Groaning and turning, the Emperor, with his huge belly, shakes the bed. Gradually, my presence behind him seeps into his dreams. He wakes in fright.

"Guards!" he shouts to his samurai, but they're lost, deep within their ninja-induced nightmares.

Pfflt. Mikko's smoke egg lands on the nightingale floor, perfectly tossed by Kyoko. The smoke rises like an eerie gray fog rolling across the marsh to wrap the White Crane in mist.

I stand still, arms raised high.

Outside, the storm grows, pounding its fists against the roof. The wind batters and bawls.

"Who's there?" the Emperor cries out into the darkness. "Show yourself. I can't see you." His words command, but his voice shakes. "Who are you?"

Only the flute wails in answer, its eerie notes fading as the storm tires.

Into the silence, the White Crane cries, *"Aye-ee-yah."* Four times. Not loud enough to disturb the guards stationed on other floors but harsh enough to scrape like fingernails down a bamboo bucket.

"I am the White Crane, messenger of the black *tengu.*" My voice echoes around and around, until it is impossible to tell which direction it came from.

I see shadows move on the balcony as my friends join hands to support me. The room fills with the strength of our *ki*. Pulling the covers over his head, the Emperor huddles into his bedclothes.

"What do you want from me?" the Emperor moans.

"Whoo, whoo," Riaze hoots through the window.

Not what, but who.

"Release Ki-Yaga," the White Crane shrieks. "Now is not the time foretold. But if you continue to ignore the *tengu*'s instruction, greater disaster will strike."

I'm even scaring myself.

"But I need his help." Desperation makes the Emperor bold.

"Is your need greater than mine?"

The Emperor's answer is barely a whimper.

Pfflt. Another smoke egg breaks open, and the fog thickens. The flute cries. Hidden by the fog, Yoshi creeps with ninja steps across the nightingale floor, placing four candles at the foot of the Emperor's mattress. Four flames facing north. As soon as Yoshi is back on the balcony, the White Crane screeches again.

"Did you not see the candles the *tengu* blew out this morning? Can you not see the flames that burn at your feet tonight?"

Sitting up now, the Emperor gasps at the four wisps of light curling through the smoke.

"Let Ki-Yaga go free," the White Crane shrieks, even louder than before.

"I w-will," the Emperor stutters.

"Samurai's honor?"

"Samurai's honor," he repeats. It's an oath powerful enough to bind even the Son of Heaven.

I place two white crane feathers and a dyed owl feather on the royal pillow. Tomorrow morning, the Emperor will have a reminder and the Dragon Master's helmet will be bare.

Sensing my movement behind him, the Emperor spins around, peering, frightened, into the fog. Lightning flares, and for an instant, my shadow is caught. The White Crane stands motionless, its wings to the sky.

Pfflt. A third egg rolls into the room.

"Time for us to go," Yoshi calls softly. "Quickly." He reaches to help me out the window.

As I climb through, the moon edges from behind a cloud. This is more dangerous than a stab of lightning; Yoshi and I are about to be caught in a slash of moonlight.

Then, suddenly, a large black shape flies in front of the moon. Perfect timing. Yoshi pulls me to safety so fast that I lose my footing and tumble off the balcony ledge. Luckily, beneath me, Mitsuka steps out of the darkness, arms outstretched. I land with a hammering heart and a soft thump in the Bear's great arms.

Then, suddenly, a large black shape
flies in front of the moon.

We hurry across the compound, then finally pause to catch our breath. Mitsuka's eyes stare beyond me, into the sky. But the shape is gone.

"What was that?" Mikko asks.

"Tengu," I murmur.

Mikko laughs. "Don't be silly. *Tengu* don't exist. We were just pretending."

"Before Hell Valley, you didn't believe in ghosts either," Nezume reminds him.

"Maybe it was an owl," Yoshi suggests. But he doesn't look as if he believes his own words.

"It wasn't an owl," Riaze says. A ninja would know.

"It is not our concern," Mitsuka decides.

But it is mine. And one day I'll know the answer. One day I'll ask Sensei my question.

The White Crane ruffles its feathers, rain dripping in puddles at its feet. The Tiger shakes its soggy fur. We're wet, cold, and bedraggled, but we're proud. And Sensei would be, too.

Before we reach our room, Riaze stops. "It's time for me to leave. Good-bye, Little Cockroaches. You have owl wings now."

"You are a friend truly worthy of Izuru," I say, bowing deep.

"We will never forget you," promises Kyoko.

"Until we meet again," Riaze says, and kisses her hand.

He bows to Mitsuka. Then to all of us. One blink and he's gone, faded into the shadows.

Behind me Taji hoots softly. And all along the castle wall, owls echo the Golden Bat's call.

CHAPTER FOURTEEN

勇

FLIGHT OF
THE CRANE

BONG. BONG.

The castle gong rings loud and insistent. We don't care about our interrupted breakfast this time. We race Mitsuka through the garden and along the corridor to spill, breathless, into the Emperor's presence. This morning there are even more charms and candles in the room.

"I have had a dream," he announces. "I have received a new message from the black *tengu*. Ki-Yaga must leave the castle immediately or a great disaster will befall the Empire."

The gong sounds again.

The Emperor has spoken, and his word is law.

Kyoko throws her arms around Sensei. We all follow, and soon our teacher is lost beneath a pile of arms and legs.

"My students are powerful in spirit," Sensei says, unpeeling our layers. "And strong in their loyalty." He winces as Yoshi squeezes him tight.

The Dragon Master frowns disapprovingly at our affection. He doesn't understand. His students are in awe of their teacher. But there's no respect in their groveling, only fear. Still, I don't feel sorry for them.

"We all get what we deserve," Sensei once said to us as he handed out heaping bowls of honey rice pudding.

Some kids deserve extra dessert, and some deserve the Dragon Master.

I do feel sorry for the prince. He almost had the best teacher in the world.

Sensei bows low to the Emperor. "You are both wise and generous. But now the Grandson of Heaven has no tutor to improve his swordsmanship. Allow me to provide him with one of my students."

My mouth drops open. I don't want to stay here.

But it's not me. Nezume has already moved to stand before the Emperor.

"It's a ridiculous suggestion." Pushing his way forward, the Dragon Master knocks against Nezume. This time, our Long-Tailed Rat doesn't cringe. Staring into the Dragon's eye, he stands firm.

"The boy belongs to me," the Dragon Master exclaims, simmering with barely controlled rage. "His father sent him to the Dragon Ryu. He is not Ki-Yaga's to offer or give away."

"Is this true?" the Emperor asks Nezume.

"In the beginning, I was a Dragon boy," Nezume

admits, "but under my first master's guidance, I committed a great wrong. Yet I was forgiven." He bends toward Mikko. "My honor was reborn when I became a Cockroach. My skill as a swordsman grew from my second master's love and care. Today I am proud to be the Emperor's humble servant."

The Son of Heaven smiles. "It would seem that in the end, the boy belongs to me."

Eyes blazing, the Dragon Master bites his lip to hold in the words.

The Emperor has not finished questioning Nezume. "Why should I let you teach my son when *you* are still a student yourself?"

"I am the fastest sword in the mountains. Even Sensei cannot match me."

"Neither can I," admits Mitsuka.

Still, the Emperor is undecided. "I was impressed with your expertise in the demonstration match, but do you have any teaching experience?"

Nezume's voice rings strong and true, like the blade of his sword. "I have never been a teacher, but I have been taught by the best and the worst. I know what a teacher should not do." He lets his jacket slip from his shoulders, revealing a spiderweb of cruel red scars.

The Emperor glares at the Dragon Master. "It seems some *teachers* should be taught a lesson."

Beside me the Bear growls softly, grinding his teeth. "I'd like to do that."

"My service is much more than my sword skills," Nezume continues. "I offer friendship and honest counsel. As you have trusted Ki-Yaga, your son can trust me."

Sensei nods. "All my students are destined for great things. For Nezume, that journey ends here at the castle. This is the task I have trained him for."

"Rubbish," huffs the Dragon Master. "He is just a boy. I should teach the prince."

"I have seen the result of your lessons. You and I will discuss the Dragon Ryu's training methods later," the Emperor says sharply.

I wouldn't want to be standing in the Dragon Master's slippers then. But I'd like to be a cockroach on the wall, listening in.

The Emperor bows to Nezume. "Welcome to your new home, Teacher."

Sensei has sliced another master sword stroke. Now Nezume is safe from the Dragon Master forever. Our friend will grow powerful, whispering in the ear of the future Emperor.

"How can I compensate you for the loss of a student?" the Son of Heaven asks Sensei with a smile. "I recall that we have an outstanding debt to be settled. Perhaps you would like to keep your head."

Yes! We'd all like that.

But Sensei has other priorities. "I do not value my head," he says. "I have a special request."

The Emperor raises his eyebrows. "Then ask."

"It has been decreed illegal to travel outside of Japan. I request a special exemption from the traveling ban. I wish to take my students on a journey over the ocean."

The White Crane stirs, daring to hope. In my imagination it stretches its wings, ready to take flight.

"So be it." The Emperor claps his hands. "Your head is no longer forfeit *and* you are free to leave these shores."

Smirking, the Dragon Master doesn't bother to hide his pleasure. "Finally, I am rid of you." He scowls at Sensei. "A man your age should be dead by now anyway."

The Emperor's stare would slay a lesser Dragon,

but Sensei nods. "Sometimes the Dragon Master is accidentally wise." He strokes his long white beard. "I am always pleasantly surprised to wake up and find I am still alive."

It's probably a good idea for Sensei and the Dragon Master to have an ocean between them.

"Go now, before I change my mind and decide that my son deserves two teachers," the Emperor says. "I must consult my advisers and make an offering to the *tengu*."

Bowing deep and low, we touch our noses to the floor. Our audience is over. The Emperor waves the rest of us away, but he beckons Mitsuka closer.

Halfway back to our room, Sensei stops. A puzzled look on his face, he holds his traveling staff horizontally across his palms.

"Is something wrong, Sensei?" I ask. "I took great care of it. I even added a crane feather to its neck. One I freed from the Dragon Master's helmet."

"The staff is much stronger now that it holds your spirit with mine." The wizard's blue eyes gaze deep into my soul, searching. The White Crane blinks beneath the stare but doesn't look away.

Sensei raps the ground with his staff, and the moment

is broken. "Come along, Little Cockroaches. We have much to do."

We pack slowly, delaying the time when we have to say good-bye to Nezume. But it comes anyway, rushing toward us like a summer monsoon. Nothing will ever be the same once it has passed through our lives.

Kyoko sniffs. "I'll miss you, Rat Boy."

"Don't cry." Nezume wipes her tears with his sleeve. "When Sensei said one of us would stay, I knew it was me. It felt right. I wish I could describe it better."

I understand and I'm good with words, so I help explain. "It's like when I put my foot in my slipper. It fits perfectly."

"Or your mouth." Mikko laughs. "That's a good fit for your foot, too."

Nezume chuckles, and even Kyoko giggles. Mitsuka slides the door open and steps into a room filled with laughter.

"The Emperor has given me a special task," he announces, obviously pleased.

"And what would that be?" Sensei's eyes dance.

I'll bet my second helping of dessert that he already knows.

"The Son of Heaven would like me to teach the Dragon Master a lesson. In the future he will show more care for the welfare of his students." Mitsuka slaps his hand against his scabbard. "It is a task worthy of Onaku's blade."

I wish I could be there, but the way of the warrior has many paths. Not every road leads directly to the ocean. Nezume and Mitsuka will travel their different ways. The Bear will one day return to his cave by the sea while the Long-Tailed Rat scurries the castle corridors.

"I'll walk with you as far as the castle keep gate," Nezume says.

For once Sensei doesn't stride ahead. He shuffles. This is hard for him, too. We walk in silence because truly important moments don't need words to paint their picture. They hang in the mind forever, like an ancient and treasured scroll.

At the castle keep gate, the guards bow deep to Sensei. To Mitsuka. To Nezume, the prince's swordsmanship tutor. And finally to us.

Samurai kids don't like rules. We whine about the tea ceremony and complain about practice schedules. But now we're glad to hide under the formalities of saying

Sensei takes Nezume's hands in
his own and bows.

good-bye. It helps us pretend to be brave. We're not afraid of ghosts or Dragons, but leaving a friend cuts like a ninja dagger; it sneaks up behind, slashing deep.

Sensei takes Nezume's hands in his own and bows.

"*Chi, jin, yu.*" He bows again. "*Meiyo.*"

Wisdom, benevolence, courage.

And honor.

Sensei is proud, and Nezume grows taller beneath his gaze.

The rest of us form a line, ready to offer our own parting words, carefully chosen from Sensei's teaching.

"A true samurai doesn't need a sword," says Yoshi.

We all knew he would say that. It's the first lesson Sensei taught us, and Yoshi's favorite ever since then.

"The point of a sword is very sharp." Mikko prods Nezume in the ribs to remind him.

Kyoko says nothing. Taking her sword from her sash, she slices a twisted thread of snow-white hair and tucks it into Nezume's kimono sleeve.

Taji goes next. "Just because you can't see something doesn't mean it's not there," he says. "We will always be standing beside you."

Even Mitsuka has something to add. "A samurai should be prepared. Otherwise he might lose his trousers."

The Bear can always make us all laugh and, remembering his big hairy legs, we laugh until it brings tears to our eyes. Now I know exactly what to say, too.

"It is always good to begin with laughter."

"But it's not a beginning." Kyoko's tears of laughter drip into sadness. "Our time with Nezume is ending."

We're the only family Kyoko has ever had, and it's hard for her to let a brother go. Six fingers hold tight.

Help her, Sensei says.

"An ending is just another beginning," I say, placing my arm around Kyoko's shaking shoulders.

"That's true," Taji agrees, undoing her fingers from Nezume's hand. "It's all about how you choose to look at things."

And Taji would know. He's always seen things differently, and now he's helping us to look at Nezume with our hearts, not our eyes. Helping us to hang the memory scrolls, so we never forget.

Raising his arm, Sensei signals good-bye. Then he turns, leaving without another word. There's nothing more to say. We hurry after him, but this time Nezume isn't running with us. He stands still, waving. Over and over I look back, until we round the curve in the road and I can't see him anymore.

We thread our way through the maze of streets toward the outer gate. It's not the same without the Long-Tailed Rat scuffling beside me. The others feel it, too. Kyoko's flute wails softly, and in its song, the wind rips the blossoms from the cherry branch. It's left bare. Empty. Incomplete.

"Do not be sad," Sensei says. "We are like seeds blowing in the wind, but Nezume has found the place to plant his roots."

"Sounds like a gardening lesson," I say grumpily.

"Excellent, Niya." Sensei beams at me. "It is how things grow. I am a great lover of trees. And I am always pleased when my seeds sprout roots."

Sensei grows trees all over the *ryu* grounds. Cherry, plum, and oak. But he's not talking about those. He means us.

"Well, now that Nezume is a tree," I tease, "at least we'll always know where to find him."

"Yes," Sensei says, nodding at Mitsuka. "Friends always know where to find each other when they are needed."

We pass through the outer gate and are once again on the Toyozawa road. But Mitsuka is looking in the opposite direction from us. Our *ronin* is leaving, too.

"Don't go," I plead. "Come with us."

He shakes his head. "I have a Dragon to tame. When you return, I will be waiting on the shore, ready to hear your stories and learn the new knowledge my teacher will bring."

"Why would you want to learn anything more?" asks Mikko, amazed.

"There is always one more lesson to be learned, and a teacher is for life," says Mitsuka.

"Life is a very long time." Sensei's eyes smile. "None of my students are ever rid of me."

And I bet they're all as glad as I am.

Mitsuka bows again. "Teacher," he says. Then he envelops Sensei in a giant bear hug.

"Friend," I hear Sensei whisper in reply.

A big bear can move quickly when it wants to, and in no time, Mitsuka is a long way down the road. As I watch, he turns, waving his wooden sword.

"Your students did well in the test you set them,

Master." His voice booms back to us, his laughter chasing behind.

Surely, it wasn't just another test? But then, Sensei never stops teaching.

One day I want to be a teacher. But today has chosen Mitsuka and Nezume, not me.

The time will come, the wizard says. *You will be a great teacher. But first you must learn great things. And you must swim in the sea.*

"Is it far to the ocean?" Kyoko asks.

"Walking quickly, we will reach Japan's edge at sunset," Sensei says.

"Hurrah." Mikko jumps high, kicking his heels together. "If we're not going back to school, we don't have to study anymore. We're on vacation."

Sensei pokes Mikko with his traveling staff. "A school is just a building, but learning is inside you. It follows you around like a shadow."

"And a teacher is forever." Taji pokes Mikko, too. "You'll never get out of school."

"More practice," Yoshi, Kyoko, and I chorus, our voices mimicking Sensei.

Ki-Yaga grins. "There is twice as much to practice now that you have ninja and samurai skills. But this morning, practice must wait. Chop, chop, Little Cockroaches. We must hurry. Before the Emperor changes his mind."

Sensei strides off down the road.

"Are we running away, Sensei?" I ask, finally catching up to him.

"Certainly not." He smiles. "Cockroaches do not run. They scurry with honor and dignity."

And the White Crane flies. With honor and dignity. Sweeping ahead of me, it opens its wings and soars out across the ocean.

THE SEVEN VIRTUES OF BUSHIDO

義 GI — rectitude

勇 YU — courage

 JIN — benevolence

 REI — respect

真 MĀKOTO — honesty

譽 MEIYO — honor

 CHUSEI — loyalty

USEFUL WORDS

BANZAI   Japanese battle cry of triumph

BOKKEN   a wooden practice sword, usually shaped like a *katana*

BUSHIDO   the samurai code

CHI, JIN, YU   wisdom, benevolence, and courage

EMPEROR   the dynastic ruler of Japan; however, true power was held by the military

KATANA   long curved sword, traditional weapon of the samurai

MEIYO   honor

RONIN   a wandering samurai who serves no master

RYU   school

SENSEI   teacher

SHAKUHACHI   bamboo flute

SHOGUN   military ruler of Japan

WAKIZASHI   short-pointed dagger, a traditional weapon of the samurai

ZAZEN   the practice of Zen meditation while sitting

ACKNOWLEDGMENTS

To my sons—Jackson, who chops out any boring bits, and Cassidy, who is always full of ideas. To my friend and mentor, Di Bates, whose advice is invaluable. To Bill Condon, Vicki Stanton, Mo Johnson, and Sally Hall—word masters and mistresses all. To Bill Stuart, who shared his reference books and expertise. To my editor, Sue Whiting, whose work is magic. To the super supportive team at Walker Books. Thank you.